PUPPY *Love*

LUCY GILMORE

sourcebooks
casablanca

Published by Sourcebooks Casablanca, an imprint of Sourcebooks.
P.O. Box 4410, Naperville, Illinois 60567-4410
(630) 961-3900
sourcebooks.com

Printed and bound in the United States of America.
OPM 10 9 8 7 6 5 4 3 2 1

chapter
1

Now *that* was a dog.

Harrison Parks stood in front of the Great Dane puppy, watching as he stumbled over his feet and struggled with the weight of his oversize head. Already, the animal's sleek gray fur was something to behold, those beautiful eyes like the sky after a rainstorm. It was easy to see what he would someday become—majestic and muscled and massive, more like a trusty steed than a canine.

"He's perfect. Where do I sign?"

A cough sounded at his back. "Um, that's a Great Dane."

Harrison turned to find the slight, well-dressed woman who'd greeted him at the door. She looked apologetic and hesitant and, well, the same way most people looked when they met him for the first time.

In other words, like this was the last place in the world she wanted to be—and he the last man she wanted there with her.

"I thought he might be." He attempted a smile. "What's his name?"

"Rock."

Yes. Rock—durable and solid, the kind of dog a man

could count on. Harrison crouched and put a hand out to the animal, his fingers closed in a fist the way the woman, Sophie Vasquez, had shown him. It seemed like overkill, this careful approach to an animal who hadn't yet reached six months of age, but what did he know? The closest he'd come to having a pet was the raccoon that lived under his back porch.

"I think he likes me."

Sophie coughed again, louder this time. "Rock is great, but he's a stability dog, I'm afraid."

Harrison turned to look up at her, struck again by how out of place she seemed among this room of scurrying puppies. It wasn't just her air of fragility, which made it seem as though a strong wind would topple her over. It wasn't her age either, although her short crop of dark brown hair and her round, sweet face made him suspect she was still in the youthful flush of her twenties.

No, it was the ruffled dress she wore, which seemed better suited for a tea party than a dog kennel.

He did his best to smile again. He was trying *not* to scare her away within the first ten minutes. It wouldn't be the first time he'd done that to a woman. Or a man. Or, if he was being honest, any living creature with a heart in its chest and eyes in its head. He wasn't saying he was a *bad*-looking man—a bit rough around the edges, maybe—but he did have a tendency to come across more forcefully than he intended. His friends blamed it on what they called his "resting brick face." *Like you're going to throw the next man who crosses you into a brick wall*, they laughed.

Which was all well and good after a long day of work, but it wasn't the least bit helpful here.

Just smile and relax, they said. *Be yourself. And for God's sake, lower your guard an inch or two to let in some air.*

Well, he'd tried. The smile—both of them—had already fallen flat, and the idea of relaxing under that woman's wide-eyed stare was impossible. No one had warned him that the puppy trainer was going to be a delicate, fragile wisp of feminine perfection. One of those things he *might* have been able to handle, but all of them?

Yeah, his guard was going to stay right where it was. It gave him someplace to hide.

"What's a stability dog?" he managed to ask.

"Well," she began, "some of our clients need dogs that can provide physical support."

When he didn't do more than nod encouragingly, she added, "As he grows up, Rock will be great at leading someone with vision issues or providing a safe landing for someone prone to seizures. You know—for stability."

"Oh." Harrison blinked. "I don't need that."

"Not really, no."

"Well, what about that one, then? He looks like he knows his way around a back alley or two."

He nodded toward the bulldog in the next slot over. Like Rock the Great Dane, this one was prancing about in one of a dozen half-walled pens built in an extension off the back of Sophie's house. Unlike other dog kennels, Puppy Promise kept none of their animals fully caged in. They had room to climb and jump and pop their heads up to say a friendly hello to their neighbors. And they did too, wet noses being pressed and kissed from one animal to another. When added to the bright-blue walls and not-unpleasant smell of organic cleaning solutions and puppy breath, the result was strangely inviting.

"Rusty?" Sophie asked as the wriggling, wrinkly puppy came bounding forward. His expression held a belligerence that appealed to Harrison on a visceral level. This dog might not be as physically intimidating as a Great Dane, but he sensed a kindred spirit. *Grump and grumpier.* "No, you don't want him. He'll be a nice emotional support dog someday, but he can't smell worth anything."

Harrison bit back his disappointment and allowed his gaze to skim over the other options. He immediately bypassed a tall white poodle that looked as if it had been recently permed and a tiny, yappy thing with eyes like raisins. A soft golden retriever with a mournful expression peeped up at him from the corner. "How about—"

Sophie coughed once more, cutting him short. When he turned to see what the problem was this time, he found her standing a few paces back, holding her hands out in front of her as if warding him off. His gaze was immediately drawn to those hands—so smooth and soft, her nails carefully polished to match her outfit. His own hands were like burned leather, cracked and callused all over. That was what happened when you spent half of your life battling wildfires. What the elements didn't scorch, the flames did.

"What is it?" he asked, his heart sinking at the sight of those hands. They were *nice* hands, obviously, but he knew what that gesture meant. *Harrison Parks has done it again.* Ten minutes in this woman's company and she'd already seen through his sorry exterior to the even sorrier contents of his soul.

"The truth is, Mr. Parks, we only have one dog right now that matches your specific needs."

"Okay." He swallowed. "Which one is he?"

"He's a female, actually. And she's really sweet."

"Female? Sweet?" Harrison could work with that. In fact, he quite liked both of those things, despite all evidence to the contrary.

"Oh yes. You wouldn't believe the nose she's got on her. I don't think I've ever worked with a more promising puppy. We were lucky to get our hands on her. Most of our animals come from breeders, but this one was rescued from a puppy mill. She's fantastic, even if she is still a little skittish."

Skittish could have applied to several people in his life right now, including the woman standing opposite him. Ever since *the episode* last week, everyone—from his boss at the Department of Natural Resources to his doctors to his very own father—was acting as though he, like Sophie Vasquez, was one strong wind away from toppling over.

But he was *fine*. It was one small coma. He'd get a dog, and it wouldn't happen again.

"She may need some extra work because of it, but I promise she'll be worth it in the end." Sophie broke into a smile—her first since he'd walked in. It struck him forcibly that it was a good thing she'd been too wary to pull it out before now. A smile like that, so warm and real, was a transformative thing. It made him almost happy to be here.

Almost.

"The best things in life usually are, don't you think?" Without waiting for an answer, she added, "Come on. I'll introduce you. She's been eyeing you since we walked in. I think she knows you're going to become good friends."

Harrison didn't have time to fully absorb that remark before a tiny bark assailed his ears. A *very* tiny bark. One might even call it a yap.

"The great thing about this dog is that she's highly portable. You can carry her everywhere."

Portable? Carry her?

He stopped and tried to dig his feet into the concrete, suddenly seeing the oncoming disaster with perfect clarity. Unfortunately, there were some things he couldn't resist, no matter how hard he tried.

One was the power of a beautiful woman's smile.

Another was the force of a 100,000-acre forest fire devouring everything in its path.

And a third, apparently, was a pair of raisin eyes lifted to his in trusting supplication.

"You've got to be kidding me," he said as the miniature ball of fluff twirled and stuck a small pink tongue out the side of her mouth.

This couldn't be right. He was a man who spent literal *weeks* in the wilderness, fighting fatigue and flames. He walked for days with an ax over one shoulder and a team of men at his back. He needed a trusted companion, a sturdy beast he could count on to keep him alive.

Not…

"This is a joke, right? Someone put you up to it?"

"No joke, Mr. Parks," Sophie said. "Please allow me to introduce you to your new diabetic service dog, Bubbles."

🐾 🐾 🐾

It was a truth universally acknowledged that a large, gruff man in search of a puppy would always choose the largest, gruffest one he could find.

Sophie didn't know how or why it happened, but every time a man entered the kennel, he was drawn inexorably toward the animal most like him in appearance. It was as though they walked up to each pen and, instead of seeing the puppy for its strengths and talents, they saw a mirror instead. Like getting dressed in the morning or buying a car, they wanted a puppy that exactly reflected the image they presented to the world.

Which was why she'd known, the second Harrison Parks walked in the door, that she was doomed.

"Now, I know what you're thinking," she said, watching the expression that crossed his face as his gaze shifted from Bubbles to the Great Dane and back again. *Disappointment* was a disappointingly inadequate word for it.

"No, you don't."

"And I know she's probably not what you had in mind when you signed up for this, but she's very suitable for your needs."

"No, she's not."

"Small dogs require a lot of care, which means you'll be forced to slow down a little when you're working. That's a good thing, right? To be reminded to take more breaks, to put your needs first?"

"No, that's a terrible thing."

"Plus, Pomeranians are much better suited for this type of job than you'd think. They have exceptional noses."

"No."

That was all he offered this time—just that one syllable, that one deeply rumbling sound, a death knell meant to end any and all discussion on a project that she'd thrown her whole self into prepping for. She wasn't sure which part of it caused her to crack, but she suspected it was that last one.

Well, either that or the fact that he looked so unfairly good while he did it. From the top of his disheveled brown locks to the tips of his heavy work boots, Harrison Parks was exactly what she'd imagined when she'd heard about his case. The man was a wildland firefighter, a hero. Every year, when flames swept across the dry lands of the Pacific Northwest's interior, he headed out with his hose and his determination until every last spark was gone. He was tall and muscular, his expression weary with the devastation he'd seen.

A bit on the crusty side, Oscar had described him, *but totally harmless*.

What he hadn't said was that Harrison was also a half-buttoned flannel shirt away from being the quintessential lumbersexual—rugged and outdoorsy and built like a tank.

In other words, he was a Great Dane. A bulldog.

And he wasn't giving either Bubbles or her a fair shot.

"Listen, Mr. Parks." The sharp rap of her voice startled even herself. "I appreciate that Bubbles isn't what you had in mind, but you need to at least consider what she has to offer."

His gaze—that hard, disappointed one—snapped in her direction, and Sophie instinctively froze. Now that she'd uttered her reproach, she wasn't sure what came next. Her sister Lila would probably segue into an articulate and professional speech about the Pomeranian's finer points. Her other sister, Dawn, would try a coy smile and a low purr to get her way.

Sophie didn't have any such methods for handling recalcitrant clients. No one had let her *have* a recalcitrant client before.

"She's not nearly as bad as you think," she said, soldiering on. "In fact, I think you'll like her. You just have to take a deep breath and give her a try."

He held her stare, his eyes a stony gray that made her think of battlements and cavernous quarries, but at least he complied. Even breathing, he seemed to be exercising every muscle in his body, the swell of his massive chest like an ocean rising.

It worked though. Already, he looked much less like he wanted to storm out the door and report her to the authorities—or, worse, to her sisters.

"Okay," he said. "I'm breathing. What's next?"

Sophie blinked. Breathing had seemed like the most logical first step, but she had no idea what came after that.

Yes, she did. *Cuddles*. No one could resist puppy cuddles—it was almost as universally acknowledged as the fact that Harrison had chosen the Great Dane as his first pick. Maybe she wouldn't be so bad at this after all.

"That all depends on you," she said. "Would you rather climb into the kennel with Bubbles for your introductory session or take her outside?"

For the second time in as many minutes, his gaze sharpened as though he couldn't believe what he was hearing. He didn't blink or move, just stood there staring at her as though he were looking through a ghost.

People did that quite a lot actually—looked through her as though she were nothing—but not like this.

He didn't seem dismissive of her or more interested in the greener pastures that lay beyond. He seemed, well, scared.

"You want *me*"—he pointed at himself—"to climb in *there*? Do you have any idea how far the human body can feasibly bend?"

Sophie had to tamp down a laugh. Now that he'd pointed it out, the idea of that six-foot bear of a man climbing into a pen and snuggling with a baby Pomeranian did seem a little preposterous.

"Outside it is, then," she said. "Just scoop her on up. Don't worry—she won't be afraid of you. She likes to be carried."

He didn't, as she'd hoped, follow her orders. Instead, he glanced down at the little puppy, his brow growing heavier the longer he stood there. It was the same glower that had made him seem so fierce when he'd first walked in.

It didn't seem nearly as intimidating when he shook his head and said, "No, thank you."

She laughed again, unable to stop it from fully releasing this time. All of her tension seemed to be seeping out the more she realized this man was nowhere near as hard as his gruff expression indicated. *All bark and no bite*. "Well, at least you're being more polite about it. I promise she won't bite, and she won't pee all over you. She's a very good girl. Aren't you, Bubbles? Aren't you the most precious little ball o' fluff?"

Harrison took a wide step back from the pen and clasped his hands behind his back. If Sophie didn't know better, she'd think he was afraid of touching the puppy for fear she would infect him with her adorableness.

"No way. I'm not calling her that."

"What? Bubbles?" Laughter welled up in her throat. He was *totally* afraid of her adorableness. "Or precious little ball o' fluff?"

His only answer was a snort. Well, that and another one of those wary looks at the puppy.

"What's wrong?" Sophie asked. "She's just a honey-bunny banana muffin."

"*What?*"

"The fluffiest lady in fluffy town."

"Now see here," he commanded. "You might be able to force this animal on me, but you can't make me say any of that."

No, she couldn't. Sophie couldn't make anybody do anything. She couldn't even get rid of those pushy satellite TV salesmen who still tried door-to-door tactics. The last time someone had asked her to switch cable companies, she'd ended up serving him lemonade and buying 230 sports channels that she and her sisters never watched.

None of that seemed to matter to this man. He was a good head taller than her, outweighed her by the size of the Great Dane puppy, and wore a scowl that could have stripped paint from the walls. But as she took a step closer, he only shook his head in a frantic effort to keep her at bay. It made her feel unexpectedly powerful. Unexpectedly *good*.

"Don't say any more," he warned. "I can't be held responsible for my actions if you do."

"It's all right," she said, feeding off that sense of power, feeling herself coming alive under it. "I can take it."

And then he smiled—for real this time.

Her heart suddenly felt three sizes too big for her chest. She'd known smiles to change a man's appearance before, but not like this. This wasn't a charming smile or a kind smile or even a dashing smile. It was *devastating*, plain and simple. All those lines and creases, the well-worn care that was etched so deeply into his skin—they disappeared only to be replaced by an expression so startlingly warm and inviting that Sophie had no choice but to fall right in.

"Sweet, soft snookums," she said somewhat breathlessly. She could have stopped there, but the urge to babble overcame her. In all honesty, it was a wonder that she was able to speak at all. "Plush princess paddywinkle. Beautiful bitty baby Bubbles."

That last one broke him. The smile vanished, but only because it lifted into a laugh.

"Oh, hell no," he said. His voice was no less gravelly than it had been before, that deep sound rumbling throughout the kennel, but Sophie detected something new—something *alive*—underscoring it. "If you think I'm going to stand here and let you make a fool out of me, you're sorely mistaken. I'm taking that goddamn Great Dane home with me, and nothing you do or say will stop me." It was said like a dare—almost as if he wanted her to try. Were they...flirting?

Unfortunately, there was no time to find out. Just as she was about to gamely rise to his bait, a voice spoke up from behind them.

"I beg your pardon?" Her sister Lila's voice, normally so polished, acted like a shock of cold water over the proceedings. Sophie turned to find her standing at the top of the steps leading from the kennel to the house they shared. "Is there a problem out here?"

Sophie did her best to put on her usual bright smile, but Lila wasn't looking at her. Her oldest sister—a tall, statuesque beauty who could command the attention of an entire room simply by walking into it—was staring at Harrison with a look that would have done their mother proud. It told Harrison that if he said one more word, goddamned or otherwise, he'd risk the full weight of her wrath.

Of course, when she spoke, her words were nothing but professional.

"I'm terribly sorry if there's been a misunderstanding," she said, and moved elegantly down the steps. Each click of her heels on the cement carried its own warning. "Perhaps I can be of assistance."

"Assistance?" Harrison echoed. All signs of laughter and friendliness had been wiped from his face, replaced once again by the hard wall that he had carried in here.

Lila inclined her head in slight acknowledgment. "Yes. Did I hear you correctly when you stated your preference for the Great Dane over Sophie's selection?"

"You mean Rock?"

Lila nodded.

"Rock. Yes. Rock." Harrison swallowed heavily, glancing back and forth between the sisters. "That's the one I want. The one that's too big to squish."

Lila smiled, but it didn't touch her eyes. She tsked softly. "You have good taste, but I'm afraid he's not available. He's already been assigned to another case. I'm sure Sophie explained that to you already."

"Actually, I—" Sophie caught Lila's eye and clamped

her mouth shut. *Of course.* It hadn't even occurred to her to try a discreet lie. When a client wanted what they couldn't have, you were supposed to redirect them, not antagonize them. *Why didn't I think of that?* "Um, no. I hadn't gotten around to it yet."

"So it would seem. Mr. Parks, why don't you come inside with me and we'll work it out? There's no need to upset the puppies with all this arguing."

"He wasn't arguing." Sophie tried to explain but was once again quelled by a look from Lila. What else could she do? Technically, he *had* been arguing—and she'd been egging him on. She'd been *loving it.*

What is wrong with me?

"This is all my boss's fault," Harrison said. His words were abrupt, his movements even more so. "I didn't even want a dog in the first place."

"It's a tricky business, matching people and puppies," Lila said, trying to soothe. "Every temperament is different—even we don't always get it right on the first try. Do we, Soph?"

Sophie knew that her sister was only trying to make up for this intrusion, including her in the conversation so she wouldn't lose *all* her professional footing in front of the client, but she couldn't help but feel miserable. What Lila really meant—and what Lila would never say—was that *Sophie* didn't always get it right on the first try.

She managed a weak smile. "No, it's not always easy."

"There. You see?" Lila extended her hand toward Harrison. "Come inside. We'll be more comfortable having this conversation in the kitchen."

"*No.*" He jerked back as though Lila had shot a

lightning bolt from her fingertips. "I mean, no thank you. I'm leaving. That puppy can't... There's no way I..."

He paused and took one of Sophie's deep breaths, a thing she might have appreciated if not for the look of painful reproach he shot her as he did it.

"This was a mistake," he said curtly.

And that was all. Turning on his heel, he made for the back door to the kennel.

Sophie wanted to say something to stop him—apologize maybe, or beg him to give her another chance—but he was already swinging through the door by the time she found her tongue.

"Well." Lila was the first to break the silence that followed Harrison's sudden departure. "Oscar wasn't exaggerating about him, was he?"

When Sophie didn't respond, her eyes still fixed on the gentle sway of the door as if waiting for Harrison to reappear, Lila softened her voice. "That was a pretty nasty scene I walked into. You okay, Soph?"

It was exactly like her sister to ask that question. Given the way things had turned out, Lila could have dumped any number of reproaches on Sophie's head, including the fact that she hadn't wanted Sophie to take on this case in the first place, but of course, she didn't. She never would.

Money meant nothing when compared to Sophie's happiness. Work was secondary to making sure Sophie was taken care of.

Which was why Sophie shook her head. She wasn't okay, not by a long shot. She felt humiliated and ashamed and, well, *small*—but more than that, she felt a strong compulsion to meet Harrison Parks on neutral territory once again. At first, he'd looked at her the way everyone always did, but then, when she'd pushed back, there'd been a spark in his eyes she desperately wanted to see again.

"I'm a little rattled, to be honest," Sophie said. "He's not like anyone I've ever met before."

"No," Lila agreed. "Some men are just like that, I'm afraid."

It was on the tip of Sophie's tongue to ask what Lila meant, but she stopped herself just in time. She already knew what Lila was thinking, because it was the same thing she'd thought when Harrison Parks had first knocked on the door.

This is a man who doesn't like to be told what to do. This is a man to be wary of.

But Lila hadn't seen that smile. Lila hadn't been there when he'd quaked at the mere thought of touching such a precious, golden-haired lump as Bubbles. Lila hadn't felt the surge of exhilaration that had come from confronting him…and *winning*.

"And he wasn't necessarily wrong," Lila added. Her hand touched Sophie's shoulder. "I did warn you that Bubbles might not make a good service dog, sweetie. Not every puppy is cut out for this kind of work."

Sophie glanced down at the animal under consideration, a pang of mingled frustration and disappointment filling her gut. Okay, so Bubbles wasn't the most impressive puppy to come under their care—she was small and soft and had lingering issues from the trauma of the puppy mill—but that didn't make her *useless*.

"Don't worry about it," Lila continued softly. "There

will be other cases. One unhappy customer won't make or break us. I'll call Oscar and get everything straightened out."

"No, don't." Sophie spoke sharply, using the same tone that had snapped out when Harrison had initially refused Bubbles. At her sister's raised brow, she hastily amended it with, "I'll talk to him. It's my responsibility. I'm the one who mishandled the situation."

Lila's brow didn't come down, but she accepted Sophie's decree with a nod. "Sure thing, Soph. Take the rest of the day off. Go see Oscar. He always makes you feel better."

Sophie offered her a tight smile but didn't say anything. Oscar *did* always make her feel better, but that wasn't what she meant. She didn't want a day off. She didn't want someone to hug her and placate her and tell her everything would be all right.

What she wanted—no, what she *needed*—was to get her client back.

Glancing down at the Pomeranian, who was staring at the back door as if she too expected Harrison to come waltzing back through it at any moment, Sophie decided that was exactly what she'd do too.

Even if it was only so she could feel that sudden spark of battle coming alive inside her again.

chapter 2

"You said he was going to be tricky."

Sophie walked through Oscar's door at the Deer Park Department of Natural Resources without knocking. His office was a small, one-room affair used mostly for administrative purposes, but he could be found there almost around the clock during the wildfire off-season. The May weather was still damp enough to stave off most forest fires, so she knew he'd be in.

"Did I?" Oscar didn't bother to look up from the stack of papers he was sorting on his desk. "I must have been in a good mood."

"You said he had a tendency toward stubbornness."

"From your tone, I'm guessing you disagree."

"You said I should tread warily."

"Actually, I believe my exact words were, *you should wear a hazmat suit underneath a flak jacket*, but you've always had more tact than I do."

She clamped her lips and crossed her arms, stopping short of tapping her foot on the floor. It took a full twenty seconds for Oscar to give in and glance at her, but Sophie was nothing if not patient. It was the one virtue all good dog trainers needed.

When he did finally look up, it was with a wry twist to his smile. The heavy lines of the older man's face were both familiar and friendly, but she knew better than to take the wire-rimmed glasses perched on the end of his nose and the bushy gray mustache as signs of a jolly, grandfatherly type. Oscar was as tough as they came.

He sighed and pulled the glasses off. "Oh dear. What did he do?"

Sophie lowered herself into the lone chair that was squeezed in the room with him. The DNR, as it was more affectionately known, was at least accommodating enough to give him one extra seat.

She could be accommodating where this man was concerned too. After all, she owed him her life.

"Let's just say he decided to dispense with our services," she said.

Oscar sighed again, this time with world-weary resignation, and pinched the bridge of his nose. "He stormed out the second he saw the dog, didn't he?"

"Um."

"Sophie?"

"Not exactly?" She frowned and picked at a hangnail. "I mean, he wasn't *happy* about Bubbles, but that wasn't what ruined things. I, um, may have spoken to him in baby talk for a large portion of the time."

Oscar's entire body stilled. "I'm sorry?"

"It made sense at the time, I swear. He liked it."

"He liked it? Harrison Parks—*my* Harrison Parks— let you whisper sweet nothings to him?"

"They *weren't* sweet nothings," she protested, hoping she didn't sound nearly as foolish as she felt. "I was only trying to get him to relax a little. And I did too—he was smiling and everything. But then Lila came in and misunderstood, and, well…" She let her voice trail off.

Oscar was familiar enough with her sister to fill in the blanks. Sophie was afraid that he'd do that thing where he pinched his nose in dismay again, but all he did was fall into a crack of laughter. Well, that and reach into his desk drawer to extract a bottle of Wild Turkey and two mismatched glasses. He poured out a finger for each of them and pushed one across the crowded desktop.

She stared at it. "I don't understand. What's this for?"

"Because, my dear, you've earned it."

She lifted the glass but didn't sip. "I have? But I told you—he left. *Without* a puppy."

"You also told me that he smiled. That's half the battle right there. Drink up."

Sophie wasn't much of a day drinker, but the memory of Harrison's smile seemed deserving of a good toast. Following Oscar's lead, she clinked her glass against his and took a generous sip. It burned and not in a good way, but she managed to swallow.

"Now." Oscar leaned back in his chair, which creaked as his full weight sank in. "Why don't you tell me exactly what happened? I should have been clearer about how difficult Harrison can be to work with. He's a hell of a firefighter, but he's not what you'd call a people person."

"Oh, don't worry—you were plenty up-front about that. What I don't understand is why you didn't tell me how nervous he is."

Oscar sat up. "Nervous?"

She nodded and took another sip of the bourbon. It burned just as much as the first time, but it gave her the courage she needed to keep going. "I think he was afraid that he'd, um, *squish* Bubbles. That was the impression I got anyway. He wanted the biggest, baddest dog we had, and when I told him that wasn't an option, he sort of got this panicked look in his eye."

"You saw all that?"

Sophie shrugged. It sounded ridiculous, she knew, but how else could she explain it? "From the way he reacted, it was like I'd asked him to carry around a cracked egg for the rest of his life."

"No, he wouldn't like that." Oscar chuckled. "He wouldn't like that at all."

"That was where the baby talk came in. Just some cute names I have for Bubbles, you know? I was trying to get him to say a few of them, which was when he started yelling. It wasn't *real* yelling, but Lila walked in right in the middle of it and couldn't tell the difference. Do you know no one has ever yelled at me before?"

Oscar tugged one end of his mustache. "Is that so?"

"Not once. Not even a little." She sighed, remembering. "It was nice."

"*Nice?*"

"I think you should yell at me for screwing everything up. It might help. Go ahead. I don't mind."

Oscar only shook his head, which just went to show how right she was. In the entirety of her childhood and adult memories, she couldn't even remember anyone sitting her down and giving her a stern talking-to.

"Anyway, that's why I'd like to try again," she said. "If you can convince him to work with me, that is. I'm, um, not sure he'll want to."

For the first time since she'd walked into this office,

Oscar allowed a frown to appear. "Oh, he'll work with you, all right. I don't care what tactics you have to resort to—baby talk, speaking in tongues, making him carry a dozen cracked eggs. After what happened last week…"

Sophie didn't say anything, content to let Oscar lapse into thought for as long as he needed. From the report she'd read, it sounded as though Harrison Parks was lucky to be alive. He'd slipped into a diabetic coma after his continuous glucose monitor malfunctioned during a routine wildfire training exercise. Had he been out on a call somewhere remote or inaccessible by road—both common during the height of the wildfire season—they may not have been able to get him to a hospital in time.

As if following the exact thread of her thoughts, Oscar's mouth firmed in a hard line. "If he wants to see any action on the ground this summer, he'll do it. And he'll *like* it, by God. I'm not putting him through that again without some kind of protection in place."

"No, of course not," Sophie said meekly.

"A puppy's the only recourse I have left, short of putting him behind a desk."

"He doesn't seem like the sort to appreciate that," Sophie agreed.

Oscar sighed and scrubbed a hand over his mouth. His glance, when it met hers, was pointed. "He won't make this easy on you, Sophie, not for one minute. I've never known anyone so wrapped up in barbed wire. Are you sure you're up for it?"

"Absolutely," she said the word automatically.

It wasn't automatic enough.

"You're saving my skin to take his case at the last minute like this, but I won't hold it against you if you pass.

Especially now that you've met him. And Lila wasn't sure if this dog of yours would be up to the task, so…"

At the mention of her sister's name, Sophie's chin lifted a good inch. "I know what you're thinking, but it's not like that. Bubbles had a rocky start in life, yes, but she can do the job. I know she can." She hesitated before bringing her chin up even more. "And so can I."

His expression softened. "Of course you can, kiddo. Lila's just looking out for you, that's all. We both are."

Any desire she might have had to abandon this project died at once. It was the *kiddo* that did it, the reminder that the history she and Oscar shared was forged in blood a long time ago.

Literally. Once upon a time, this man had leeched the marrow from his bones for her. Once upon a time, he'd undergone extreme pain and hospitalization so she could have another chance at life. It had been eleven years since the bone marrow transplant took successfully and her leukemia went into remission, but that didn't mean Sophie had forgotten.

She'd *never* forget. She couldn't. No one in her life—family, friend, or foe—would let her.

"Bubbles is a lot tougher than she looks," she said as she raised her eyes to Oscar's. "Please let me do this for you, Oscar. For you and for Harrison."

And, she didn't need to add, *for me*.

"I don't know…" Oscar began.

"I'll find a way to make it work," she said. "That's a promise. Even if I have to beg him to come back on my knees. Even if I have to make him yell at me every day for six weeks to do it."

Oscar rolled his shoulders in a gesture of capitulation.

With that one small move, Sophie knew she was getting another chance.

Her life was filled with second chances. She sometimes wondered what she'd done to deserve so much.

"He's rough, but he's not that rough. I doubt he'll yell at you for the whole six weeks." Oscar grinned and added, "Four at the very most."

chapter
3

*O*scar must have worked fast.

Sophie arrived home from Deer Park to find a house full of people. In addition to her two sisters, who were holding court over a pot of tea in the kitchen, Harrison sat hulking in one corner, looking like a man undergoing extreme torture.

"You know it's going to be a good date when the guy leads with something like that." Dawn winked at Sophie as she stepped into the room. "We broke at least three laws that night. Four if you count some of the really prudish ones in Kentucky. Speaking of, look who's finally returned to the fold. Hello, Soph. You have a visitor."

At the mention of her name, Harrison sprang to his feet, almost knocking over the wooden chair in the process. He was surprisingly swift for a man of his size, but that might have been because she'd never seen anyone look so delighted to see her.

"Oh, thank God," he said. "I've been here for forty-five minutes already."

Right. That wasn't delight so much as it was a deep, profound relief. And who could blame him? Dawn and

Lila together in one room were a lot for any man to handle, let alone one who clearly didn't enjoy the social niceties.

"Forty-five minutes?" Sophie asked with a quick check at the clock. "Oscar couldn't have possibly had time to call you. I was still with him at that point."

"What the hell does this have to do with Oscar?" Harrison demanded. Then, as if aware that he was addressing a room of three women rather than a firing squad, he took a deep breath and added, "I, uh, came to apologize. For earlier. About the puppy."

Sophie hadn't had a chance to apprise Dawn of the day's events, but one look at her sister's face and it was obvious she was up to speed. With that kind of giddy glee lighting her from within, Dawn obviously thought this whole thing was hilarious. Lila mostly looked worried.

Neither of those reactions was surprising. Lila had always carried herself with a serene grace that matched her status as the eldest in the family. It also matched her tailored clothes and the topknot she wound her almost waist-length hair into. Dawn wore her own dark locks—a gift, along with the sisters' deep-brown eyes and light-brown skin, from the Vasquez side of their family—in a tousled bob that made the most of her natural waves. Her wide, sunny face was sprinkled with freckles and a smile to match. Lila's demeanor was one men could admire; Dawn's one they couldn't help but be charmed by.

It was only Sophie who lagged behind. She'd done the best she could to distinguish herself from her sisters, her short, boyish figure offset by a pixie cut that made the most of her delicate features, but it was no use. When the three of them stood side by side, she inevitably faded into the background.

Or, rather, she *used* to fade into the background. From the way Harrison was looking at her, like she was his walking savior, she couldn't help but feel a warm glow start to take over.

"There's nothing to apologize for," she said with what she hoped was breezy unconcern. "It was a slight misunderstanding, that's all. I should have warned you ahead of time that your animal had already been selected for you."

"About that…" Lila began, but Sophie turned to her with an imploring look. Lila might technically be the one in charge of Puppy Promise, the service-dog training organization that provided the Vasquez sisters with their life's purpose, but Sophie needed this. *Bubbles* needed this.

Lila had been uncomfortable with the idea of using a puppy mill dog from the start, since the poor thing had obviously been subjected to more than one cruelty in her short life, but Sophie had no doubts on that score. Five minutes in that animal's company had been more than enough to convince her that she was worth taking on.

With some animals—some people—you just *knew*.

"I realize Bubbles isn't much to look at, but she's smart and eager to learn. All she needs is a chance to prove herself."

Harrison didn't say anything. He kept watching her in that intense, panicked way, as if he couldn't make up his mind whether to sit down again or run screaming from the room.

Please don't run screaming from the room, she wanted to beg him. *Please don't run screaming from* me.

"What do you say we make ourselves scarce, Lil?" Dawn asked, a deep dimple appearing in her right cheek.

"Scott has that new litter of blue heelers he wanted us to come take a look at."

"But we don't need any—"

"They're very promising. I bet they'll get snatched up quickly. We'll need to act fast if we want to make an offer."

"But—"

Dawn took one glance at Sophie's face and put on her sternest expression. "*Now*, Lila."

It took Lila a good ten seconds to pick up on the subtext and agree to give Sophie and Harrison some space. Harrison was much quicker on the uptake.

"A blue heeler?" he asked. "Are they good at—what did you call it—scent detection?"

"Yes, they are," Sophie said. In fact, given Harrison's obvious preference for dogs with size to recommend them, a blue heeler would be a perfect fit. Their noses were more than adequate to pick up on the subtle changes in human saliva that occurred when blood sugars rose or fell, and the larger dog would be able to keep up with him as he plunged through forest undergrowth.

In any other situation, she'd have allowed the client's preferences to outweigh her own. In this situation, however, she was taking a stand.

Bubbles could *do* this. Sophie had done her research, looked into other fire workers with needs similar to Harrison's, and hand selected an animal based on a careful study of his medical and professional records. This wasn't some idea she'd come up with on the fly.

"I've already talked to Oscar about this, and he agrees with me." She crossed her arms and did her best imitation of a woman who inspired awe and confidence in others. "It's Bubbles, or you don't go back to the field."

As it turned out, admitting to a man that she'd run tattling to his boss wasn't an ideal way to win him over. Instead of submitting to her autocratic decree, Harrison's stance became even more rigid.

Sophie's natural inclination was to turn to her sisters for help, but she pushed the urge down as far as it would go. To admit defeat now would only foster Lila's belief that they should have passed on this case. Sophie'd be back on basic training, once again spending her days teaching puppies how to sit and where to pee.

All things that needed to be done, of course, but those were the easy tasks, the *safe* ones. The kinds of things a fluffy, skittish ball of fur might be expected to tackle.

"If you're willing to try again, I'll bring Bubbles out to the side yard so you two can get to know one another. But you have to promise not to reject her this time. She didn't like it." Almost as an afterthought, she added, "And neither did I."

"Well done, Soph!" Dawn cheered from the doorway. Before Lila could say anything to undermine Sophie's swell of confidence, Dawn bustled them both out of the kitchen.

It was a strange location for an impasse. The house Sophie shared with her sisters was as dainty and feminine as Harrison was rough and masculine. Everywhere the eye landed were massive doilies and vintage finds, with dried flowers next to the sink and artfully arranged silver teaspoons hanging on the wall. Only the kennel through the back door gave any indication that this was as much a place of business as it was a home. Harrison wasn't so tall that his head brushed the ceiling or anything, but he did have a way of filling the space in a way that felt both unfamiliar and unsettling.

It's not just his size, Sophie thought. *It's him*. Whatever else might be said about this man, he was certainly a presence. Being in the same room with him seemed to kindle an awareness in every part of her—a *tingling* awareness that started in her toes and worked upward from there. It was almost as though her limbs were awakening from a long, numbing sleep, and she wasn't sure they were ready to support her weight just yet.

"So you really *do* know Oscar," Harrison said by way of breaking their strange stalemate.

"Oh. Um." Sophie blinked. She'd assumed, when Oscar had asked them to take on this case, that he would have told Harrison all about their personal history. That he hadn't—and most likely wouldn't unless Sophie gave him permission to—said a lot about him. "Yes, actually. He and I go a long way back. He asked me to take your case as a kind of favor."

A look of strange relief swept over Harrison's face. His shoulders actually sagged a little. "Then *that* explains why you put up with me for as long as you did. What did he say about me?"

"Um."

"You don't have to hold back on my account. He won't have said anything I haven't heard a hundred times already, believe me."

As if the sudden turn of conversation wasn't strange enough, Harrison paused and pulled out a chair for her. It was *her* chair, obviously, and he was offering it in *her* house, but the gallantry of the gesture was still forefront in her mind.

She didn't sit though. She was already so dwarfed by this man.

"Please," he said, his voice rough. "One of the things Oscar should have told you first is that my bark is a lot worse than my bite."

With that, Sophie relented. She didn't know if it was the reference to canines that did it, or the fact that he sounded so forlorn, but she took the proffered seat and watched as he lowered himself into the opposite chair. Even in a seated position, he still dwarfed her. Those powerful thighs, the broad shoulders hunched as if ready to pounce—there was no other way she *could* feel in his presence.

Before she could think of a tactful way to disclose her earlier conversation with Oscar, Harrison lifted one massive hand and started ticking off fingers instead.

"I don't take orders well. I don't know how to interact with others in a way that doesn't make them uncomfortable. I'd rather cut off my own foot than admit to a weakness." He paused and considered the matter before turning a look of inquiry her way. "Let's see…which one am I missing?"

Heat rose to the surface of her skin. Sophie didn't believe any of those things, not when he'd made such a generous and obviously painful effort to return here and apologize of his own volition, but she could see how someone meeting him for the first time might get that impression. Those deep lines, that unsmiling expression… He just looked so *hard*.

Harrison took one look at her flaming face and swore. "Dammit. He didn't sugarcoat it, did he? Did he tell you how half the volunteer firefighters I train end up quitting after less than a week or that some of them take one look at me and don't even last the day?"

Sophie had no idea how to answer that question, so she didn't try. Dawn would have been able to turn it to a joke, but her sister wasn't here. She'd scurried off so Sophie could have at least one opportunity to prove herself.

"The week," Harrison repeated carefully, "or the day?"

She began tracing the outline of a red wine ring on the table. "Do people really quit after one day?"

"Your sister took my measure this morning after knowing me for thirty seconds," he said. "What do you think?"

Yes, people probably did quit that fast. But people also took one look at her and assumed she had no more courage than a mouse, so what did they know?

"I'm not going to quit, Mr. Parks," she said. "Oscar asked me to help you, and that's exactly what I intend to do. You're not the only one with flaws, you know."

When he didn't say anything, she held up her hand and started ticking off her own fingers.

"I'm the baby of the family, and it shows. I'm dependent on my sisters for almost everything. I've never gone anywhere or done anything on my own." She paused. This next one was going to be the toughest to get out.

As if sensing that, Harrison cleared his throat. "Anything else?"

She shifted in her seat. "I'm a little intimidated by you, to be honest." She met his gaze and was surprised to find that he was regarding her with alarm. "But it won't get in the way of the job, I promise. Bubbles is an amazing puppy, and I've got a whole training plan worked out for the next six weeks. I realize that neither one of us is what you were expecting when you signed on for a service dog, but I want to do this."

I can do this.

"Please, Mr. Parks?" she asked, her voice wavering. Whatever bravery his confession had conjured in her was quickly waning under his continued scrutiny. "You might not think much of me yet, but I have a tendency to grow on people, I swear. I'm like a friendly goiter."

"Harrison," he said.

"What?"

He sat up, no longer hunched as if ready to pounce. "If we're going to be working together, I insist you call me Harrison."

Her first feeling was one of relief—she'd actually done it. She'd gotten through to him. He was going through with the plan and without Oscar being the one pulling the strings.

Her second feeling was more difficult to pin down. This small victory was just the start of the process. If even one-tenth of the things Oscar had said about Harrison were true, there were countless skirmishes ahead.

Strangely enough, she wasn't scared by the prospect. She'd already engaged him in one battle and come out victorious. The idea of waging another campaign—a *lengthy* one this time—made her chest swell.

She'd waited twenty-six years for an opportunity like this.

She stuck her hand out, determined to make their partnership official. It was a good ten seconds before Harrison put her out of her misery, but the end result was worth it. His palm was callused and hard, his skin surprisingly cool for a man of his size. His grip was also

much gentler than she expected. She assumed he'd have
one of those hypermasculine handshakes, the kind that
wrenched her arm out of its socket and nearly crushed
the bones of her fingers, but as his palm lingered against
hers, it felt more like he was holding her hand than striking a deal.

But his next words were all business, gruff and pointed.

"I guess you'd better bring me this damn dog
already," he said.

She was unable to keep the surprise from showing
on her face.

He saw it, of course, and directed a wry, twisted grimace inward. "I warned you. Believe me when I say it's
for the best that we get this thing started. The sooner she
learns how to tolerate me and save my life, the sooner I
can get back to work." He paused a beat and added, "And
the sooner you can get back to a life without me in it."

They both hated him.

Harrison sat on the front lawn of the Vasquez sisters'
home, staring at a puppy that weighed about as much as
a pineapple. Sophie had left the two of them alone with
instructions for him to spend some quality time getting
to know his new best friend.

How he was supposed to do that, she hadn't said.
She'd just unleashed the animal and promised to return
to check on them in ten minutes.

She couldn't get away from me fast enough, he
thought grimly. And he had no one to blame for it but
himself. As usual, he'd let his frustrations get the better
of him, shown his true colors before he could realize the

effect it might have on the innocent woman standing no more than a few feet away from him.

Frustration was, unfortunately, his nemesis. No matter how many times he tried to act like a normal person, he always got buried under his own tongue. He *tried* to control himself, he really did, but the second that mounting feeling of helplessness took over, all bets were off.

And so, it seemed, was Sophie.

"Okay, Bubbles," he said, trying out the dog's name. Those perky syllables felt strange on his tongue, but they were no stranger than the golden-haired puffball eyeing him with a mixture of interest and caution. "I understand you've got a nose like no other. Show me what you can do with it."

Bubbles just blinked at him.

"Okay, I hear you. New experiences can be scary—so can new people." He thumbed a finger back toward the house. "Don't tell anyone, but I'm just as terrified of Sophie as she is of me. Probably more."

He took it as a good sign that Bubbles tilted her head at him in a look of inquiry. Maybe this puppy wasn't such a bad choice after all. There was wisdom behind those raisin eyes.

"Oh, I know it's ridiculous, believe me," he said. "She doesn't seem capable of squishing a gnat. That's the problem. She…"

He frowned. He wasn't sure what Sophie did, except make him feel like a large, ungainly lump. It wasn't a new feeling for him, but this was the first time he *wanted* to be more approachable. Scaring pretty, defenseless women wasn't a thing a man liked to boast of.

"And who can blame her? Have you ever met anyone as bad at this as me?" He rolled onto his stomach and put his head closer to the puppy. The puppy, seeming to agree with him, barked nervously and backed away.

Harrison sighed and propped his chin on his hands. Lolling in the damp grass with a puppy wasn't how he'd pictured his day when he'd woken up this morning, but the truth was, he was grateful to wake up at all. In all his years as a type 1 diabetic, he'd only slipped into a coma one other time, an incident that had occurred during his sleep and led to his initial diagnosis. Even though he'd only been eight years old at the time, it wasn't an experience he recommended. Few things were worse than going to bed only to wake up several days later in a hospital room with no recollection of any of it. A demon you couldn't see coming was a demon you couldn't face in a fair fight.

And there it was again: that feeling of helplessness, the roiling start of frustration taking over.

As if already trained to read his moods, Bubbles quivered.

"It's not you I'm upset with," he said, soothing the puppy. The sight of that tiny body shaking in fear—because of him—plucked at a chord deep in his chest. "She said you were some kind of diabetes wizard, and I have no choice but to believe her. So let's do this thing. There must be a way for us to fast-track our relationship."

Struck with sudden inspiration, Harrison reached into his breast pocket and extracted the granola bar he always carried in the event of blood sugar emergencies. Bubbles heard the crinkle of cellophane and immediately perked.

"You greedy little minx." He laughed. "Is this how

it's going to go? I have to bribe my way into your heart? It's a good thing I always have snacks."

Since he doubted the dog's stomach was much bigger than a golf ball, Harrison crumbled the bar into tiny pieces and began offering them one by one. Wary at first and then gaining interest, Bubbles eventually picked her way over the grass and started accepting the morsels from his fingertips. With each bite of her tiny jaws, her fear seemed to diminish. A quarter of the bar in and she was actually approaching him of her own volition.

"If only it were this easy to gain a person's affection," he said. "I doubt I could hand-feed Sophie and get the same response."

A sharp female voice sounded above his head. "What are you doing?"

He rolled over to find Sophie standing with her hands on her hips and a look of consternation on her face. At first, he was afraid she'd overheard his conversation with the dog. To explain his remarks and admit that he only meant he wanted her to like him—not that he wanted her to sit in his lap and take food from his fingertips—was unthinkable. There was no way he'd get through *that* explanation without making a bungle of it.

After a moment, however, she set him to rights. "You can't give a service dog table scraps." She swooped down to take the granola bar package from him. "She's not a pet. She's your companion."

Bubbles gave a tiny growl and attempted to take the snack back from Sophie with a leap that lifted her an impressive two inches into the air.

"See? You've had her for ten minutes, and she's already acting like a spoiled lapdog." With a stern lowering of her brow, Sophie turned her attention to the puppy. "*No*, Bubbles. You don't get to speak to me like that."

Bubbles reacted instinctively to the command in Sophie's voice. She sat and gulped, looking up at her trainer with a remarkable amount of remorse. Harrison was tempted to do the same.

Since he wasn't an adorable two-pound ball of fur, however, he settled for a gruff, "I'm sorry. It's my fault. I didn't know."

At the sound of his voice, all of the indignation in Sophie's stance melted away. Her eyes widened and a stricken flush colored her cheeks. He could tell he'd done it again—scared her with his inability to react to situations like a normal human being.

"No," she said, flustered. "No, of course you didn't."

He attempted to heal the breach by drawing to his feet, but all that did was highlight the difference in their sizes. At six feet tall, Harrison was hardly a *giant*, but he felt every inch like it was mile, each one carrying him farther away from her.

In an effort to regain some of that lost ground, he said, "Okay, so no table scraps. What other rules should I know about?"

Sophie eyed him with misgiving. "Haven't you ever had a dog before?"

"No. Never."

"Really? Not even as a kid?"

"We weren't a cozy, white-picket-fence-and-puppy sort of family. I never even had a goldfish."

"Well, you can't feed table scraps to goldfish either," she said. "In case it ever comes up."

He was startled into a laugh. She was doing it

again—making jokes. About him, *with* him. "My ignorance doesn't extend that far, thankfully. Can I at least pet her and stuff?"

Sophie shifted from one leg to another, watching him with a wariness he couldn't easily explain. It wasn't a scared wariness; it was more worry, like she was regretting her promise to train both him and Bubbles.

Like she wasn't sure he'd be able to make this work.

But he could. And he would too. He might not be a prince charming, but he wasn't an ogre either. At least, not most of the time.

"You mean I can't pet her?" he asked.

"When she's working, no. You need her to be alert and focused on you, more like an employee than a friend. But during her off time?" She shrugged. "Absolutely. She still needs to be loved, just like everyone else."

"Just like everyone else?" he echoed.

"Yes. That's not going to be a problem, is it?" Sophie's voice took on a sharp edge—the same one that had caught his attention in the kennel that morning. "I know she's not the Great Dane of your dreams, but there's a lot to like about her. Contrary to what you might think, being giant and strong isn't everything."

Harrison found himself rooted to the spot, more intrigued than insulted by the challenge in her voice. People didn't speak to him like that very often. Well, Oscar did, but he hardly counted—he'd practically known the man since birth. He'd only known *this* woman for all of an hour. Although she might claim to be scared of him, something about that puppy brought out the steel in her.

He wished he knew what it was. His own glance down

at that minuscule creature, so helpless and vulnerable, only brought a frown. Bubbles sat exactly where Sophie had told her, awaiting her next command. She was like a stuffed toy soldier, ready to head into battle for no reason other than it was asked of her. The doubts that had assailed him since the start of this preposterous scheme returned anew. He'd been prepared for a big, badass canine companion to head into the flames with him, alert to the changes in his blood sugar that resulted from hard labor and shifts that often lasted more than twenty-four hours. To ask such a sacrifice of a Great Dane or a bull-dog or even that nice golden retriever seemed natural.

To rely on this scrap of a creature, with her oh-so-trusting eyes and tiny beans for toes, was another thing entirely.

"Will it really be so hard?" Sophie asked. "To learn to love her?"

He reared back, unsure if he'd misheard the underlying plea of her words. But one glance at Sophie's gently furrowed brow and he knew his hearing worked just fine. This woman thought so little of him that she was worried he'd mistreat the animal she was giving over to his care—an animal who had already been subjected to cruelties at the hands of a ruthless puppy mill.

"We'll be fine," he said, knowing the response was inadequate but unsure what else he could say. "Just tell me what I need to do, and I'll do it. At this point, I'll try anything."

"Anything?" she asked, one of her brows lifted in a perfect arch.

With any other woman, he'd have taken that arch as an invitation—a flirtation not unlike the one attempted on him by the sister with the wavy hair, Dawn. Not so with Sophie. Not now that he was coming to realize just how much Oscar had betrayed him.

That scurrilous bastard. His longtime supervisor and friend could have easily saddled him with one of dozens of providers who matched people with service dogs and lived to tell the tale. But he hadn't. He'd flipped through his ancient Rolodex and landed on this slip of a woman who made him feel like a bull in the entire goddamn china factory.

In other words, he'd known exactly what he was doing.

"Anything within reason," he amended, one wary eye on Sophie, the other on the puppy. Call him paranoid, but giving the pair of them an open invitation to make demands of him seemed like a bad idea.

Mostly because he had the sinking sensation he'd do it—that all-encompassing, terrifying *anything*.

"Define 'reason,'" she said.

"I know it's all the rage, but I refuse to have anything to do with dog sweaters," he said. "I think they're ridiculous. It's like putting a sock on a potato."

Sophie's lower lip dropped a fraction. He didn't know her well enough to say whether it was surprise or indignation that caused it, but she nodded her agreement anyway. "Noted. No sweaters on dogs, and no socks on potatoes. Is that, um, a thing you've seen before? With the potatoes?"

Not surprise. Not indignation. She was *laughing* again.

"That includes raincoats, hats, and those little boots I've seen dogs wear on TV," he added, reluctantly pleased by way her eyes lit up.

"You hate any type of clothes on dogs and root vegetables. Got it."

"In the spirit of full disclosure, I hate clothes on regular vegetables too."

"I had no idea a man could have such strong opinions on produce. What else is off-limits? Tattoos on fruit? Bread with dentures?"

He opened his mouth to continue his litany of things he refused to have anything to do with—up to and including women who mocked him with their eyes—but decided against it. Some people claimed the things he *didn't* like in this world far outnumbered the things he did like, but one thing was for sure.

He liked Sophie Vasquez.

The thought dropped on him from out of nowhere, all pleasant and squishy and warm. He had no idea what he was supposed to do with that feeling. Ball it up? Shove it deep down? Lay it out on the grass and roll in it?

That last one didn't sound too terrible, actually, which was why it was a good thing Bubbles chose that moment to yap and spin in a circle. Turning as one, he and Sophie shifted their attention to the puppy, the moment of easy friendliness disappearing as quickly as it had come.

"So, what happens next?" he asked, careful to keep any but the blandest of emotions out of his voice. "Training-wise, I mean?"

He was rewarded for his pains with a long, careful look and a plastic bag that looked to contain some sort of brown pellets.

She nodded toward it. "Dog treats."

"Wait. Treats? But when I gave her that granola bar, you—"

"Table scraps and human foods are a big no-no, but

treats during basic training are fine. In fact, you'll find them necessary if you want to get any real results."

"I will?"

"She's a great dog, but she still needs encouragement every now and then. Most of us do." That long, careful look became downright intense, but she moved on before he could come up with a suitable reply. "She's ready to learn scent alerts, and we'll start those within the next few days, but you'll still need to reinforce rudimentary behaviors."

When he still didn't say anything, she added, "Sit. Stay. Heel. Down. Come."

Despite the gentle rap of her words—or maybe because of them—Harrison felt compelled to follow each of those commands as she uttered them. Which was a dangerous thing for a lot of reasons, but mostly because those last few held decidedly sexual undertones.

When he didn't say anything other than to grunt a noncommittal sound, she added, "I've been working with her on those since she arrived, but it'll be better for the rest to come from you."

"But I don't know how—"

"I'll come over to your house every day, of course. It's part of our process. For the first few weeks, Bubbles and I will be on the job from nine to five. Once we move to more intense training, we'll vary the schedule so it includes some nights."

So many parts of that plan blinked red and warning in Harrison's vision. *Every day? Nights? His house?*

The last one caused the biggest flash. His house wasn't a place he'd willingly bring a woman like Sophie. Hell, he could barely stand being there himself.

"Oscar never mentioned anything about that," he said, taking a wide step back. The distance seemed necessary. With any luck, the earth would open up between them and he could fall through to the other side. "Can't we just do it here?"

"Bubbles has to learn in the environment where she'll be spending most of her time," Sophie said. "It's not really optional, I'm afraid. That's kind of the thing that makes Puppy Promise what it is. Each dog is personally selected and trained for the individual."

It was impossible to argue with that. A highly trained and specialized animal was exactly what this was supposed to be all about. He clamped down on his tongue and stretched a tight smile across his face. "Sure. That will be fine."

His attempts at moderation didn't go over as well as he'd hoped. Sophie's expression fell. "Oscar didn't explain this very well, did he?"

Actually, Oscar hadn't explained it at all. As soon as Harrison had checked himself out of the hospital—against the doctor's recommendation—he'd walked out to find Oscar sitting in his sleek black Suburban like a limo driver. "Get in or I'm putting you behind a desk," he'd said. The rest of the conversation had followed much along the same lines.

Take care of yourself or I'm putting you behind a desk.

Get a service dog or I'm putting you behind a desk.

Get a service dog from this place I've already selected and laid out tens of thousands dollars for or I'm putting you behind a desk.

Service dogs didn't come cheap, but Harrison's dignity did.

"Does this mean Bubbles is coming home with me tonight?" he asked warily.

Sophie glanced at the thin silver watch on her wrist and nodded. "It's a little past five now. She's officially off duty. Not," she added in a warning tone, "that this means you can indulge in her every whim. Just get her used to you and your house. Make her comfortable. See if she'll sit for you. There's a box of supplies in the kennel for you to take home as well as a list of directions about her feeding times and quantities. You can grab it on your way out."

It was as good as a dismissal. Harrison would have been relieved to hear it if not for the fact that Bubbles sat at his feet, awaiting events with the air of one resigned to an unpleasant fate.

"She won't hurt you, Mr. Pa—I mean, Harrison." Sophie blushed as she spoke, as if surprised at her own daring. "Just be nice to her, and she'll come around."

Being nice wasn't something Harrison excelled at. In fact, being nice was usually the last quality anyone associated with him.

"What if she doesn't?" he asked.

"I'm still not giving you the Great Dane."

He was startled into another one of those laughs that felt so foreign. "Don't worry. I learned that lesson already. Size and stability aren't for me. Instead, I get..." He glanced down at Bubbles and tried to think of the least offensive way to phrase it.

It was more difficult than he thought.

"You get intelligence and devotion," Sophie supplied for him. The note of steel was back in her voice, daring him to argue. "You get a beautiful little nugget who will risk her life to keep you safe."

"A beautiful little nugget," he echoed doubtfully.

Nuggets *and* raisins.

This was going to be so much worse than he'd thought.

chapter 4

Nothing in the instructions told him how he was supposed to transport Bubbles home.

Bags of food, water dishes, leashes, harnesses, even a minuscule red training vest he side-eyed harder than he'd ever side-eyed anything in his life were there in abundance. But there was no crate or any sort of pad he could set on the floor.

"Are you supposed to ride in the back?" he asked, casting a doubtful glance at the bed of his rusted pickup truck. Even without all the tools and fire equipment back there, he doubted the puppy would be very comfortable. For all he knew, the wind would blow her away like a tumbleweed. "I'll probably get in trouble for this, but I guess you're sitting next to me. Don't tell Sophie, okay? She might yell at me again, and I don't like it when she yells at me."

Bubbles blinked up at him. Harrison took it as agreement.

Throughout his life, he'd heard every kind of insult and every kind of criticism that could be leveled at a man for whom talking to people was a curse. None of it stacked up to Sophie gently questioning his ability to own a dog. Caring for a puppy was something normal people did every day. Puppies provided love, affection, all those things you were supposed to feel when something small and precious wriggled its way into your life.

In other words, all those things that he'd always lacked. Which was fine, in the general way of things. Love and affection had never been his strong points, and he knew it.

But the fact that *Sophie* knew it and on less than a day's acquaintance...

"I'm not going to buckle you in, but you have to promise to sit perfectly still," he commanded. He set Bubbles down on the cracked vinyl seat and slid in next to her. Since it seemed as good a time as any to try out those training commands, he gave her a stern look and said, "Stay."

The puppy's response was to leap nimbly into his lap and stare up at him. Her paws made almost no indentation on his leg, her weight so slight he hardly felt it. She was warm though—a little ball of heat pressed against him.

Since his body temperature usually registered cold due to the lowered amounts of insulin in his blood, he kind of liked it. But, "No, no, no," he said, his voice deep and firm. "That's not how this is supposed to work. You sit *next* to me."

He set her aside once more only to have her leap into his lap again, this time with a nervous shake to her little body. He remembered what Sophie had said, that Bubbles was still skittish, and gave in. *She* might be able to tell this poor, quivering dog to behave herself or else, but Harrison wasn't that strong.

"Only this one time, okay?" he said as Bubbles licked

gratefully at his hand. He stuck the key in the ignition and turned it, pausing to check on the puppy's response as the V6 engine roared to life. "And you have to sit quietly and behave like a lady, or I'll end up driving us both off the highway."

She did neither of those things. Sitting seemed to be beyond her as all the glories of the world passed them by, and no lady he'd ever known would have been lolling her tongue out the open window as though she'd never tasted fresh air before.

The Vasquez domicile was located in the heart of Spokane, which meant that it wasn't *too* bad, having a tiny puppy hanging out his truck window while the speed limits remained well within the thirty mile per hour range. As he hit the highway leading north, however, which provided him with the quick, half-hour commute to Deer Park, the speeds increased dramatically.

Too dramatically.

He cast one anxious glance down at the puppy in his lap and touched the brakes. Veering quickly to the right, he turned onto a side road that demanded all drivers amble along at twenty miles per hour or risk heavy fines.

A car coming the opposite direction honked, startling them both. With a light curse, Harrison dropped his left hand and held Bubbles around the dainty bones of her ankles to keep her in place.

"Don't you dare jump out when I'm not looking," he warned.

The only answer Bubbles gave was a happy twitch of her nose.

"What has that woman been doing to you, anyway?" he muttered. "You don't get any snacks, she never takes

you on fun road trips, you have to put in eight hours of
hard work a day…"

Bubbles turned and licked his face before resuming
her windswept survey of the scenery around her.

Which was why it ended up taking him well over an
hour to pull up the dirt drive that led to his house.

"All right, you minx," he said as he slowed the truck.
There was a light coating of dust over Bubbles's fur,
but it didn't seem to bother her in the slightest. "We're
finally here."

He didn't know whether it was him speaking that
spurred her to realize it, or if the stopping vehicle
tipped her off, but she leaped off his lap. Whatever
else had happened in her short life, she knew what was
coming next.

Home.

Except *home* was hardly the word he would have
chosen to describe the decaying heap of wood and concrete that greeted him as he swung open the truck door.
Sure, the huge, rambling farmhouse had walls and a
roof, and it was filled with childhood memories that no
amount of time would be able to erase. But to Harrison,
it had never been anything more than a place to rest his
head. In fact, he'd have gladly consigned the whole
thing to flames if it weren't for the fact that he spent his
life fighting against that very thing.

Some things are meant to burn.

"Well, Bubbles. This is it. Home sweet home." He
lifted the puppy and gently set her on the ground. It was
still early enough that he didn't fear the raccoon under
the porch coming out to make friends, so he didn't bother
with a leash. Not that it would have mattered anyway.

Bubbles took one look at the unfamiliar surroundings and latched herself onto his leg.

Or his foot, rather. She didn't reach very high.

"You can't stand there, or I'll step on you. Is that what you want? To be crushed underfoot?"

The answer, apparently, was yes. As he moved to the truck bed and hoisted the box of doggie supplies, Bubbles remained stubbornly near his toes. It didn't bode well for their future together. When Harrison was on the job, he barely had time to remember his own name, let alone worry about his service animal running under the stomping feet of several dozen firefighters.

And what would happen if she got caught in a tangle of fiery underbrush or stuck behind a felled tree? It wouldn't take more than a twig to knock the poor creature down.

"I'll bet Sophie didn't even think about *that*," he said, oddly triumphant. "She has no idea what it's like to be out in the trenches."

"Who the hell are you talking to?" an irascible voice called from the front porch. "Have you gone and lost your mind on top of everything else?"

"No, Dad." Harrison scooped Bubbles up and placed her inside the box of supplies. The soothing scent of a twenty-pound bag of puppy chow seemed to bring her commensurate happiness, so she stayed put. "I'm talking to my new dog."

"Eh? You really went through with that?"

Harrison trudged up the steps to find his father standing in the doorway, looking like an extension of the house in faded overalls and a work-worn shirt. As he also had a red-stained apron tied around his waist, it was an interesting picture. "I don't have a choice, unfortunately. Oscar won't let me go back to work unless I play along."

"What'd you get?" His dad leaned to peer around him, a frown crossing his grizzled face when no frisky Great Dane followed in his wake. "Huh. It must not like you. Damn thing ran away already."

"No, she didn't." He turned the box so the puppy's tiny head faced his father. "Dad, meet Bubbles. My new lifeline."

To be fair, his dad's response was about a hundred times better than his own had been. Hearty, chest-heaving laughter might not be the ideal reaction to a service dog, but at least his dad retained the capability of speech.

"That's not a dog," he said between wheezing laughs. "That's a rat in a Halloween costume."

Bubbles, unaware that her appearance was being denigrated in the extreme, panted a friendly hello.

"She's a Pomeranian," Harrison explained. "They're very good at scent detection, apparently. And according to my, uh, handler, she's also very portable."

"What? Are you going to carry her around in your pocket?"

It wasn't a bad idea, actually. Except for the part where she'd fall out the first time he bent over to dig a ditch.

"I haven't worked through the logistics yet."

Harrison moved the rest of the way into the house and set down the box, taking in the strawberry-scented air with a grateful sigh. Today was a good day, then. Those had been few and far between since his dad's retirement three months ago. For Harrison, being forced to take a temporary sabbatical from the Department of Natural Resources had been a blow. For his dad, leaving a forty-year stint as a highway patrol officer over a bad back had been nothing short of a tragedy.

"You've been busy," Harrison added in a voice he hoped was nonchalant. "Preserves?"

His dad grunted. "The damn strawberries are taking over the backyard. I had to do something with them. You hungry?"

Harrison was, but he needed to check his blood sugar levels first, and he had to figure out where he was going to put Bubbles for the night. Instinct told him that no matter what he decided, the puppy would have her own ideas about where she wanted to be.

Small and sweet, she was also manipulative as all hell. He blamed the eyes. Raisins were the cesspit of the food pyramid, the shriveled waste that no one wanted anywhere near their cookies, not the windows to some tiny creature's soul.

"They're not even real food," he muttered.

"What's that?" his dad called.

Since admitting how close he was to losing it wasn't going to do him any favors in his father's eyes, he said, "I was just warning you that the dog isn't allowed to have any table scraps." His father might not have been as susceptible to this puppy's charms as Harrison, but he wasn't going to put anything past the wily creature. "And, um, there's going to be a woman coming by tomorrow. All the tomorrows, actually. Apparently, most of the training has to take place here."

"*Here?*" Although neither Harrison nor his father was what you'd call "house proud," there was something about inviting another human into the dusty, haphazard mess they lived in that caused an automatic recoil.

One look at the living room alone was enough to reveal why. Stacks of books sat next to his father's favorite armchair, most of them cracked along the spine and in various states of disrepair. The bookshelves, conversely, held boxes of broken electronics, most of which would never work again and, if they did, would be at least twenty years out-of-date. Even the furniture was old and mismatched, chosen more for comfort than for looks. On its own, the place suited them just fine. Compared to Sophie's house, however, it was downright deplorable.

Every few months, Harrison tried to fix it up, but his efforts were usually met with resistance at best and outright hostility at worst. To let in light and air would be to let in the possibility of happiness—a thing no respectable Parks man had done for decades.

"Are you sure she can do that?" his dad asked. "How is it legal?"

Harrison had to chuckle. "Because I invited her, Dad. It's part of the process. She comes highly recommended."

Which may not have been true in so many words, but there was no denying that the Oscar seal of approval didn't come cheap. For whatever reason, his boss trusted Sophie. Therefore, Harrison would trust Sophie too.

But not too much.

"And she's going to train the dog?" his dad asked, eyeing the puppy warily.

"So I've been told. Both Bubbles and I need a lot of work."

That, at least, got a crack of laughter. "If there's one thing I've been trying to get through to you for years, it's that. What happens if I step on it?"

"*Her*. And don't."

"What if I can't help myself?"

"Help yourself anyway."

His dad held his stare, long and careful and full of meaning. His father liked the idea of having a dainty puppy around the house almost as much as Harrison did, which was to say not at all. But if there was one thing the two of them had learned, it was that life rarely worked out the way they wanted it to.

"Well, I'm not feeding it."

Harrison didn't bother correcting the pronoun this time. "No one is asking you to."

"And I'm not cleaning up any dog messes."

Harrison refrained from pointing out that he hadn't cleaned messes of *any* kind in the past twenty years. "You'll barely know she's here. I promise."

As if to remind him that she had a will and an agenda of her own, Bubbles let out a yap of protest.

His dad stared at the puppy, hoping—Harrison was sure—to stare her into submissiveness. It didn't work. That stare might work to intimidate neighborhood Girl Scouts and door-to-door Bible salesmen, but it had no effect on a puppy who'd just enjoyed an hour of pure bliss in the front seat of his truck. Bubbles stared back with all the innocence of one who knew herself to be adored.

His dad gave up with a shake of his head. "I hope you know what you're doing, Son."

"Or what?" Harrison couldn't help asking. As far as he could tell, they were both being punished enough already. What else could you call two bad-tempered men living alone in the woods without even the promise of their careers to sustain them? "What will happen if I admit that I don't have a fucking clue?"

He got no answer. Apparently, his father didn't have a fucking clue either.

In other words, they were both screwed.

🐾 🐾 🐾

If Harrison had thought the transportation question was a tricky one, it was nothing compared to the small matter of where Bubbles would sleep.

And, yes. He meant *small* in every sense of the word.

"I already gave you three pillows," he said, staring down at the puppy over the edge of his bed. "There aren't any more. I'm literally sleeping on my sweatshirt."

Bubbles didn't offer a single yap of reproach. She didn't even whimper a protest. She just sat on her throne of pillows and looked at him as though her heart were breaking.

"Do you want a blanket? Are you cold? Is that it?"

The last thing Harrison wanted was to wake up his father or have to answer a series of questions as to why he was up half the night catering to a puppy's wordless demands, so he lifted one of the pillows and shook it out of its case. The floorboards in this house creaked something fierce, so it was in everyone's best interest that he stayed exactly where he was.

"There," he said, arranging the pillowcase so that it wrapped around Bubbles. She looked like a fluffy, brown cherry atop a swirl of ice cream. "Now you can be warm and settle down."

All he got in reply was another one of those mournful blinks.

"Goddammit, Sophie didn't say anything about you sleeping in the bed!"

Since the words had been uttered more forcefully than he intended, he reached down and scooped up the puppy—pillows and makeshift blanket and all. Almost immediately, Bubbles emitted a small, contented sigh and tucked her head in the crook of his arm.

"Ten minutes," he warned as he lay back on the bed. Bubbles stayed exactly where she was, stuck to his armpit like Velcro. "You can be up here for ten minutes, but then it's back to the floor where you belong. I can't have you up here with me all night. If I roll over the wrong way, you'll die."

Apparently, death by his crushing weight held no danger as far as Bubbles was concerned. She'd spent the entire last hour fighting sleep and shivering on the floorboards only to fall asleep within seconds of being cradled against him.

"Goddammit," he said again. This time, it came out more like a whisper. "What am I supposed to do now?"

At least he had his pillows back. Moving carefully so as not to dislodge the sleeping puppy, he arranged things so he was more comfortable. Even then, he only had the flattest pillow of the lot under his head. The other two he set up along the mattress's edge as a kind of barrier. Babies rolled. Did puppies roll? Hell, for all he knew, he wasn't supposed to have pillows in here at all. What if she suffocated?

"I'm going to give that woman a piece of my mind tomorrow," he said, careful to keep his voice low. "In fact, I'm going to start making a list of all the things she forgot to tell me. Does she think we're all born knowing how to take care of dogs? I wasn't kidding about that goldfish thing. You've seen this place—who would willingly bring anything living into it?"

Bubbles gave a twitch of her small body.

Harrison tensed, afraid he'd done something to hurt her, but she only sighed and settled into a deeper sleep. Puppies he might not understand, but the heavy, dreamless sleep of the exhausted was a thing he knew well. Some of the men and women on his wildfire team had been known to literally fall asleep on their feet after a particularly grueling day.

It was what made this whole Pomeranian-service-dog thing so upsetting. It was impossible to explain to anyone who hadn't been on the edge of a forest fire just how close it was to being at the gates of hell. Those flames moved fast—faster than most humans could run, let alone a small animal—and were as unpredictable as the wind.

People died out there. Good people, strong people, people who knew what they were getting into and made the decision to fight anyway.

How could he ask this little nugget—yes, *nugget*—to tackle that with him?

"I'm adding that to the list too," he muttered as he suppressed a yawn. The warm lull of the puppy's body had him sinking lower into the mattress. With a quick, furtive look around the room—which was ridiculous for a lot of reasons, but most especially the fact that no one else had been inside it for years—he planted a soft kiss on top of Bubbles's head.

"Tomorrow, we'll get everything sorted out," he said. "Tomorrow, we'll make her see reason." Tomorrow, he'd say a lot of the things that lodged inside his throat and inside his chest.

It was a thing he could promise with absolute certainty because, tomorrow, he was going to get to see Sophie again.

chapter

5

At first, Sophie wasn't sure she'd gotten the right house. The structure itself was about on par with what she'd expected. A grumpy bachelor who spent most of his time battling the elements *should* live in a huge, ramshackle house in the middle of nowhere. The sense of isolation with each passing mile, the dirt drive leading in, even the weird metal sculpture rusted over and broken at the hinge all seemed to fit Harrison's personality to a tee.

Rough and grizzled. Unwelcoming.

And, with a little work, probably one of the best things she'd ever seen.

But as the tires of her sleek, little Fiat crunched over the gravel, it wasn't a brawny, steely-eyed firefighter who appeared at the door. Instead, there stood an older man, tall but gaunt, slowly lifting a cup of coffee to his lips.

"Hello," Sophie called as she rolled down her window. "I'm looking for where Harrison Parks lives. Do you know if I'm on the right road?"

It took the man a second to absorb her arrival, but he eventually nodded. "You sure are, darling. You found us. Well, most of us, anyway."

Most of us?

She put the car in park and got out, pausing just long enough to grab her canvas work bag. "I'm Sophie Vasquez," she said.

She put a hand out too, but the man only stared at her outstretched palm and took another slow sip of his coffee.

"Um." She jiggled her hand in an effort to bring it to his attention. "Sophie Vasquez? The service dog trainer? Did Harrison tell you I'd be coming?"

"He mentioned something along those lines." The man finally took her hand and shook it. As had been the case with Harrison, it was a surprisingly gentle grip. "You'll find him upstairs. There's been an incident."

"An incident?" Sophie drew a sharp breath. "Is it Bubbles? Is she okay?"

The man gave her a long look. "She'll recover, if that's what you're asking. My son, however…"

"Oh, you're Harrison's dad." That made so much sense. Looking at him, she could see the resemblance. There was a hard wariness to their expressions, a closed-off quality that went deeper than mere grouchiness. "You said upstairs? Do you mind if I head in that direction?"

"Help yourself. But I'd tread warily if I were you."

She paused. "The puppy or the man?"

He laughed his understanding. The swift change of expression wiped decades from his face, made him almost approachable. "Both. I wouldn't care to deal with either one right now."

The house was built in the traditional farmhouse style, which meant a steep staircase rose almost directly from the foyer. Sophie took the stairs two at a time, barely noting the faded wallpaper with brighter patches where pictures once hung. She half expected canine sounds of distress to assail her, but all she heard as she reached the landing was a low, coaxing male voice.

"You have to come out, Bubbles. There are monsters. Big, scary, under-the-bed monsters who will snatch you between their hoary jaws." There was a pause and then, in a more urgent voice, "You're making us look bad. What will Sophie think if she finds you like this?"

Sophie was mostly amused, to be honest. Harrison Parks hadn't struck her as the sort of man who believed in monsters, let alone was scared of them. How could he be? One fierce glare and he'd have the whole lot of them exiled to their dark lairs.

She walked through the closest door on the right to find Harrison's lower half protruding from underneath a ruffled bed skirt. It was a strangely appealing sight, his backside tightly encased in faded jeans, his feet bare. A strip of skin appeared below the line of his T-shirt as he twisted and flexed to reach farther under the bed, showcasing a small plastic box clipped to the back of his jeans. His insulin pump, she was guessing.

"I mean it," he called to the dog. "This isn't what heroes do. You want to be a hero, don't you?"

As much as she appreciated the sight of a large, well-built man wriggling on the floor, she didn't appreciate her poor dog being cornered in a dark, scary place.

"Heroes come in all shapes and sizes, thank you very much," she said.

A loud thump and a howl sounded. From the way the bed shook and the grumble that followed, she guessed Harrison had hit his head on the frame.

He slithered out before she could apologize for taking

him by surprise. His movements were quick and agile, allowing her only a brief glimpse of the undulating muscles of his back before he was standing again.

Standing *and* glowering.

"Your dog refuses to come out," he said, pointing an accusing finger at the bed. "I've tried everything to coax her out—everything *except* table scraps, so don't look at me like that."

"Look at you like what?"

"Like *that*," he repeated. He also didn't elaborate, so she had no idea how she was supposed to interpret his remark. Was she furrowing her brow? Blinking too much?

With a sigh, he added, "She's too damn small. I can't get hold of her."

"Maybe that's because she doesn't want to be held," Sophie said tartly. "What happened to set her off?"

His grim expression turned even grimmer. "Fire."

"What? Where?" She spun, wondering if she'd somehow missed blazing flames. It was only then that she noted the room they were in was distinctly and unmistakably feminine. In addition to the ruffled bed skirt, there was a mirrored vanity in one corner covered with perfume bottles that had long ago been tipped on their sides. The room was also dusty in a way that was normally reserved for haunted houses. Like the faded wallpaper in the hallway, there was something ancient and untouched about it.

"In the living room," Harrison said. "It was cold this morning, so I started a fire in the grate. She took one look at the crackling flames, howled, and ran off."

"Oh. Um." Sophie gulped. "That's not good."

"No," he agreed grimly. "I think we can safely say it's not good. Didn't you test her first or anything?"

Test her? As in, throw a puppy into a flaming pit and see how she'd react? "Of course I didn't," she said. "I mean, I tested her nose, of course, and gauged her reaction to high-stress situations, but I thought we'd introduce her to your actual lifestyle gently. Carefully."

"*Gently?*" he echoed. "Do you have any idea what it is I do for a living?"

A feeling of heat—not unlike the lick of a flame— came over her. It was accompanied by a sinking sensation that stopped in her stomach and decided to take up residence there. When Oscar had first presented her with this case, he'd said that Harrison's main duties involved training new firefighters and playing a supportive role on the front lines. Digging ditches, coordinating teams, making sure supplies got where they needed to go—it had sounded an awful lot like a war zone, but that was okay. Sophie could work with a war zone. Bubbles could too. Dogs were often called on to serve in areas of danger— just look at what they were capable of anytime an earthquake hit or someone went missing in the wilderness.

She'd known from the start that Bubbles was brave and strong and willing to do just about anything. It hadn't even occurred to her that flames would be where the puppy would draw the line.

Partially to avoid having to respond to Harrison and partially because she really *was* worried about Bubbles, she sank to her knees near the bed to peek at the puppy for herself. If the room was grubby, the floor was even more so, with several dust bunnies bigger than Bubbles wafting about underneath. Bubbles hid behind one now, only distinguishable by the dark flash of her wide, terrified eyes.

"Come on, love." She waited until her own eyes adjusted before shifting to her stomach. Now that she was officially on the job, she wore her usual dog-training attire of khaki pants and their official company polo shirt. There was no chance she'd give Harrison a free peep show.

Not that he'd be the least bit interested in one from me anyway.

"We have lots of work to do today," she said, adopting the voice of one settling in for a long, comfortable chat. Her ability to hold long, one-sided conversations was a real boon in this line of work. Most dogs, like most people, just wanted to feel as though they weren't alone. Nothing helped stave off anxiety better than someone chatting away at you as though everything was just fine.

It was a thing she'd learned from personal experience. During her long hospitalizations as a kid, she'd most looked forward to visits from her sisters. With the exception of their parents, they were the only people who didn't tiptoe around her. They'd done what sisters do best: bickered and complained and generally made pests of themselves.

In moments of vulnerability, nothing was more comforting than bickering sisters. It was a proven fact.

"Rock sends his love by the way." She used her forearms, army-crawl style, to pull herself even farther under the bed. Harrison was so large that he hadn't been able to wedge his body very far under here, but she was small enough that she could scoot toward the back where Bubbles stood shivering in a corner. Sophie took one look at that panting, heaving little darling and kept talking. "Actually, I lied. He sends his hate. I'm not sure he'll ever forgive you for going away. Oh, I know he always acted like he couldn't stand you, all growly and mean whenever you wanted to play, but you've never seen anyone so forlorn now that you're gone. What do you think he did once he realized you weren't just out for a walk or getting some training?" She paused a second, as if waiting for Bubbles's response. "He howled. Like, legit howled. He set off a chain reaction through the whole place."

She thought she heard Harrison make a noise from somewhere behind her, but she ignored it. Already Bubbles was reacting to the calm friendliness of her voice, allowing herself to be coaxed out of the corner.

"He keeps peeking into your kennel when he thinks no one is watching. I bet he's hoping you'll show up underneath a blanket or behind the water dish. I didn't have the heart to tell him you've got a big, important job now and won't be coming back. It'll break his poor puppy heart."

Bubbles pulled forward enough for Sophie to get a hand out for her to sniff.

"Yes, I can see that makes you happy. You had poor Rock wrapped around your little paw, didn't you? You left a trail of broken hearts back there, you know. Everyone is rooting for you to succeed. You just can't see it the way we do."

That last bit of encouragement did the trick, drawing the puppy out enough so Sophie could give her a reassuring pat. As soon as she made physical contact, the fight was over. With one swipe of her tiny pink tongue on Sophie's finger, Bubbles lost the last of her fear. Sophie scooped the animal carefully in one hand and crawled out from under the bed.

"Ta-da!" she cried, holding the Pomeranian up like a trophy. "See what I mean? She's not unmanageable. She needs a little extra encouragement, that's all."

Her feeling of triumph lasted all of six seconds. She glanced up at Harrison in hopes of being showered with his gratitude, but he was frowning down at the pair of them like a reluctant executioner whose hand was about to be forced.

Sophie didn't go so far as to quake like Bubbles under the bed, but a definite frisson ran up her spine—not of fear, of course, but of the deep, terrible realization that she'd royally screwed the pooch.

Figuratively speaking, of course.

"This was a mistake." Sophie spoke up before Harrison could say anything. She couldn't bear to hear it from his own lips—that Bubbles wasn't going to be good enough, that Sophie had failed before she even began.

It was going to be awful, crawling back like this, but what else could she do? They were right. All of them— Lila and Dawn and her parents and Oscar. She wasn't equipped to work on a case like this one. She'd failed to properly communicate with the client. She'd been so dead set on Bubbles proving everyone wrong that she'd proven herself wrong in the process.

Poor, little, fluffy Sophie. You aren't meant for the real jobs, but I'm sure someone would love to take you on as a pet.

"I honestly thought Bubbles would be a good fit for you, but I can see that I was wrong," she said. Her lower lip was showing an alarming tendency to quiver, but she forced herself to hold it together. "You obviously have needs that she and I can't meet. I'm sorry to have wasted your time."

With a start, Harrison reached out and plucked the puppy out of Sophie's grasp. She barely had time to notice what had happened before he curled his arms around the animal in a protective cocoon.

"What?" he demanded. "You're taking her away?"

"I thought..." Sophie glanced around, bewildered. Her gaze skimmed over the worn wallpaper and gentle decay of the house before landing back on Harrison. It was such a strange combination, this faded farmhouse and the glorious man contained within it, but somehow it fit. "You were upset. You said she's no good."

"I said the *situation* isn't good. And it's not—I spent half my damn morning crawling around on my hands and knees trying to convince this puppy I'm not out to light her on fire."

Sophie blinked. The harsh words and guttural way he uttered them should have sent her running. He was all those things Oscar had warned her about and more—gruff and rough and uncompromising. In fact, he was the last man on earth to whom she'd willingly hand over something as precious and vulnerable as a baby Pomeranian.

But he hadn't shifted his position. If anything, he'd curled himself even more around the puppy, placing himself between the animal and Sophie.

He was protecting the dog. He was protecting the dog from *her*.

"It might not be possible for her to get over this kind of fear," Sophie said, eyeing him as one might a baited bear. "I can do my best to work with her, obviously, but I can't promise it will be a success."

"Well, you can't just take her away from me."

"Um."

He placed a protective hand on Bubbles's head. "You practically forced me to bring her home in the first place."

Sophie stood still for a moment, watching the pair of them. The idea of anyone believing her capable of causing harm to Bubbles was laughable. The idea of a man like Harrison thinking it was downright ludicrous. Yet that was exactly what he did think—and he was willing to put himself on the line to stop her.

What else might he be willing to do?

Curious, she placed her hands on her hips and put on her sternest expression. "I'm afraid it's my call, Mr. Parks. Until the training certificate is placed in your hands, Bubbles remains under my care. If I feel she's in a dangerous position or is incapable of performing her duties, I'm going to take her back to the kennel and reassign you a new puppy."

"The devil you will."

She almost laughed out loud at the expression that accompanied this oath. In all her life, she'd never seen a more physically imposing man. Harrison obviously hadn't had time to shave that morning, his hard jaw scraped with stubble that gave him a menacing air. His expansive chest swelled with emotion, and his face took on a hard look that could have turned entire villages to stone. He also planted his legs in a subconscious gesture that she assumed was supposed to intimidate her.

And it would have too, if not for the fact that he was

cradling a puppy in his arms with all the reverence one would show a newborn baby.

"Legally, she's still the property of Puppy Promise," Sophie said.

"I don't care."

"You will if I show up here with a court order and the full force of animal control at my back."

He hesitated, casting an anxious glance down at Bubbles. Bubbles, supremely oblivious of the battle currently being waged over her, wagged her tail in response. "You can do that?"

She had no idea. In fact, she was pretty sure Harrison could demand that she leave his property or be charged with trespassing, but she wasn't about to point that out— not when she was finally getting somewhere. She had no idea how or why it was, but Harrison was never quite as accessible as he was when she took a stand against him.

"Your work is too dangerous for her," she said now, testing her theory. "I'm sorry, but that makes you an unfit parent."

"Well, I think you're an unfit dog trainer," he retorted. "Getting a man all attached and then taking his puppy away."

As was the case yesterday, Sophie felt an overwhelming urge to giggle. Harrison Parks was attached. Less than twenty-four hours in, and Bubbles had successfully wooed him—and if the look on his face was anything to go by, wooed him hard.

She took a step closer—not a threatening one, but one of invitation. "What if I promised you could have Rock instead? Big, fierce, oh-so-strong Rock?"

"I wouldn't believe you. You're a liar."

Just as no one had ever yelled at her before, neither had anyone called her a liar. She took another step. She was near enough now that she could feel the power emanating off of him, the heat. She liked it more than was good for her.

"Well, you're a bully," she said. "Scaring a poor, defenseless woman like me. Making me quake in my shoes."

"Bullshit." Despite the severity of the word, there was no force to it. In fact, as Sophie looked up into Harrison's face, she saw the lines lifting, his irresistible smile wiping away every harsh thing he'd ever said or done. "You're not scared of me. You're not even a little bit nervous."

"That shows what you know. I might go hide under the bed."

"Well, I won't come get you."

"I might make Bubbles hide there with me."

"You'll have to pry her out of my cold, dead arms first."

"*What in blazes is going on up here?*"

By this time, Sophie and Harrison had come almost toe-to-toe, his bare feet separated from her tennis shoes by only a fraction of an inch. At the sound of his father's voice, they both jumped back—Sophie, because she was genuinely startled; Harrison, because a flush of guilt replaced his smile.

"Does one of you want to explain why it sounds like there's a presidential debate taking place on the goddamn landing?" his father demanded.

"Jesus, Dad." Harrison's guilty flush didn't abate any. If anything, it grew more pronounced. "You could have just come up here and asked. There's no need to yell."

"Why the hell not? That's what you were doing. Not at this poor scrap of a girl, I hope."

Harrison glanced quickly at her, almost as if assessing whether or not she was about to fall into a maidenly swoon. Since she wasn't—not even close—he took on an almost juvenile defiance. "She started it."

His dad snorted. "I'll bet she did. With a saint like you living under this roof, I've gotten used to nothing but peace and quiet around here." He paused. "Why is your dog covered in dust?"

"We, uh, had a small argument over Bubbles's training," Harrison said. He shot Sophie a look that was equal parts anxiety and warning. "But it's all worked out now. Isn't that right, Sophie? No hard feelings?"

Sophie had a hard time holding back a laugh. Her feelings were anything but hard. These men obviously had no idea how refreshing she found it to be in the middle of an honest, no-holds-barred squabble. She'd spent most of her life behind reverential glass, cherished by her parents, adored by her puppies. Everyone was so afraid she'd collapse at the first sign of struggle that they did everything in their power to protect her.

Well, no one was protecting her right now, and she was doing just fine. In fact, she'd never felt less like collapsing in her entire life.

"Everything's great," Sophie said.

Harrison's dad glanced back and forth between them. "Does this mean we're keeping the damn dog?"

Harrison turned to Sophie for the answer. He was still holding Bubbles, one finger running up and down her spine while she lolled against him. "I know it's not going to be easy to make this work. Her fear of fire, the

hazards of my job, my own goddamn temperament…"
All of the fight drained from him at once. "I get it—
believe me, I *get* it."

Sophie opened her mouth and closed it again. Of all
the things she'd expected him to say, complete and utter
capitulation wasn't it.

But there was more of it coming. Harrison took a deep
breath. "Whatever you decide, I respect your judgment, of
course. But if it's at all possible, I'd like to keep trying."

Sophie was too surprised to do more than goggle at
him. No one, not even her sisters, had ever told her they
respected her…*anything*. She wasn't the type of woman
to inspire that kind of emotion in others. Pity and concern, sure. Love, of course. But never respect.

"Please," he added. "I know it sounds silly considering everything that's happened, but we've reached an
understanding, Bubbles and I."

As if realizing she was the topic of conversation,
Bubbles gave a happy yap. Even though Sophie had
doubts aplenty, and she was questioning her own judgment something fierce, Harrison's confidence caused
something to shift inside of her. It was a new sensation
and a liberating one. She felt strong. She felt capable.

She felt *happy*.

"Where did she sleep last night?" Sophie asked.

Harrison's dad laughed, but a glare from his son cut
the sound short.

"There wasn't anything in the instructions about it,"
Harrison said, his tone defensive.

"I know." Sophie had done that on purpose. Some
families felt the need to crate their animals or put them
in outdoor pens overnight. Which was totally fine when

you were talking about a pet, but not at all ideal for a service dog. Bubbles needed to be able to alert Harrison at all hours of the day and night, which meant she had to be inside and as close as possible.

"It gets cold out here overnight," he said. "And she's so small."

"Hence the fire," Sophie said.

Harrison's eyes narrowed in suspicion. "Hence the fire," he agreed.

Harrison's dad seemed unable to control his delight any longer. "That dog slept curled up on his chest like a goddamned baby. I took a picture, if you want to see it. I'm putting it on my Christmas card this year."

The swift stiffening that took over his son's body seemed not to affect Harrison's dad in the slightest. "You've never sent a Christmas card in your life," Harrison muttered.

"Well, it's a good year to start, isn't it? Now that I have a granddog and all." His father winked at Sophie. "If you've got things in hand here, I'll take myself off. Don't let him scare you. I've got that picture tucked away to use as blackmail the second things get out of hand."

"I won't, Mr. Parks," Sophie said warmly. She liked this man—he reminded her a lot of Oscar. Her own father was a mild-mannered history professor doted on by his wife and daughters. As much as she loved him, she found herself drawn to these gruff, unabashed men. They made her feel almost normal. "And thank you."

Harrison waited until his dad disappeared down the stairs before turning his stiffness on her. "She wouldn't sleep anywhere else," he said, his tone between apology and accusation. "I made her a place on the floor, and gave her all my pillows and then wrapped her in a blanket, but none of it worked. She…"

"Yes?"

He turned a flushed scowl her way. "She looked so lonely, that's all, shaking and shivering and looking at me with those sad raisin eyes. What kind of rig are you running at that kennel, anyway?"

Sophie nearly choked. "She looked at you with what?"

His stiffness became even more pronounced, but he didn't back down from the challenge. "Her eyes." He held the dog out as if for her inspection. "They're like sad, wet raisins."

"You mean grapes."

"What?"

"Wet raisins—those are grapes. You literally just described the fruit that raisins are made from."

He chuffed his annoyance with a swell of his powerful chest. "You're missing the point. Look at her. Take a *good* look at her, and tell me what you see."

Sophie wasn't sure how he expected her to reply, but she took a moment to inspect the animal. To be fair, the puppy's eyes were rather woebegone, but that was because Bubbles was exceptional at luring people in with her innocence and adorable fluff. Harrison was living proof of it—he'd had the dog for one day and was already becoming putty in her paws.

If only it were that easy for me. Innocence and fluff might work well in a puppy's favor, but they weren't the qualities a girl liked to advertise when attracting a partner, especially not one as intense and virile as this one.

Not that she wanted to attract Harrison, of course.

"They look more like obsidian, if you ask me. Like

she was forged in a volcano." She smiled down at the puppy and then up at Harrison. "You did the right thing, by the way. It's better that she sleeps close to you. She needs to be able to smell your breath to distinguish your blood sugar levels while you sleep, and your chest is an ideal place to do that."

He blinked. "It is?"

"Absolutely. And you knew it, didn't you, Bubbles? That's why you were upset when he tried to make you sleep so far away. You weren't being given a chance to prove yourself."

"Then why the hell didn't you tell me all this yesterday?" Harrison ran a hand through his dark-brown locks, casting them into even further disarray. "A warning would have been nice. You could have saved me a lot of time and trouble. Not to mention sleep."

He words were harsh again, but Sophie was no longer fooled. *My bark is a lot worse than my bite*, he'd said yesterday, and she was beginning to realize he hadn't been exaggerating. His bark was loud and fierce, but if there was one thing in this world she knew, it was dogs.

Dogs barked because they were nervous, because they were issuing a warning, because their instinctive urge to protect themselves—and others—was strong. They barked because they felt threatened.

From there, the conclusion was a natural one: Harrison was threatened by her. This big, fierce, firefighting hero of a man had taken one look at little old Sophie and decided *he* was the one at a disadvantage.

This must be what power feels like.

"I could have, but it was more important for you and Bubbles to forge a natural relationship." She smiled gently.

"I'm not going to be here all the time to help you. This is your life we're talking about—yours and hers. You two have to find a way to make it work between you."

Once again, his strong emotion seemed to wash away, rendering him almost boyish. "That sounds fair."

"And it's not going to be easy, getting her over a fear like this one," she added. "If it's even possible in the first place. I'm not going to lie—if Lila were to hear about this, she'd probably pull the plug on the whole project."

He swallowed.

"Hey," she said and laid a light hand on his arm. "It's not as bad as you think. I'll be here to help you every step of the way. Yelling, if I have to. *Pushing*."

A rueful grin touched his lips. "You do seem to do an awful lot of that. Oscar should have warned me how combative you are."

Sophie almost laughed out loud. Before yesterday, *pushy* and *combative* were two words that no one would think to associate with her. Yet here she was, standing tall, asserting herself, getting results.

"You like it," she said.

He grunted a soft assent.

"You like Bubbles too, don't you?"

They both looked down at the puppy, who was staring adoringly up at her new owner. Sophie decided right then and there that nothing—not even the flames of hell—would stop her from making these two happy together. It would be a hard road, convincing a man who loved danger as much as Harrison that a creature as small and vulnerable as this one was worth the effort.

But she was. She *was*.

"Okay," Harrison said. His assent came so suddenly

that Sophie had to ask him to repeat himself. He did with another of those hesitant, almost apologetic smiles.

"It's not going to be easy, you know," he added. "I'm not used to being pushed. I'll fight you every step of the way."

She nodded. "I look forward to the challenge."

"It could get ugly. *I* could get ugly. I usually do." He hesitated, his eyes anxiously watching her own. "Most people give up on me long before we get to this point."

"Yes, well. I'm not most people."

"No, Sophie Vasquez." His voice dropped so low that her name sounded almost like a caress. "I think we can safely agree on that."

She had no time to follow up on this promising turn of events. At that exact moment, Bubbles decided she'd had enough of playing second string to the pair of them. With another of her small, plaintive barks, she demanded that she be pet, made much over, and otherwise coddled as befitted a lady of her stature. And Harrison, proving himself a pushover of the highest order, gave right in.

As much as Sophie appreciated the picture made by a large, attractive man and his tiny canine overlord, there was still quite a bit of work to do if she was going to make a success of this.

Clearing her throat, she cast a look at Harrison's bare feet and officially started the day. "If you want to hand her over, I'll set up the morning training while you get dressed," she said. "Did you two eat?"

He blinked at the sudden shift in the conversation but accepted it with a shrug. "Only half of us. Bubbles has been fed, but I didn't have time, not with the fire situation."

"Then I suggest you do that first."

"Thanks, but I'm fine." His stance indicated that the topic wasn't open to negotiation.

And so it begins.

"I have no doubt that you are, but you need to make sure your blood sugar level is as normal as possible before we get started," she said, her voice clipped. "We have to establish a consistent and stable baseline, or she'll get confused later on."

"But I—" he began before stopping himself with a nod. "Okay. You're the expert. You're in charge."

Sophie was so startled by that—*me, the expert; me, in charge*—that she almost dropped the puppy being placed in her arms. She might have done it too, but Harrison handed over his precious burden with so much trust that she didn't dare let go. Now that she'd accepted the challenge he'd offered, she was beginning to realize the enormity of it.

He hadn't just given her his puppy to hold; he'd given her his entire life. His career, his future, his happiness— all of it now depended on her.

She gulped as she watched him turn on his heel and trot easily down the stairs. He paused just long enough to cast a glance over his shoulder, a slightly mocking lift to one of his heavy brows.

"You coming?" he asked.

She nodded, unwilling—and unable—to commit the folly of speech. She was on her way, all right. She was in this now.

She had to push. She had to fight.

But most important, she had to win.

chapter 6

"I need you to tell me everything you know about driving a man crazy."

Sophie slid into the vinyl booth of her favorite diner, pleased but not surprised to find a generous slice of cherry pie with a scoop of ice cream melting into an ocean around it. If she knew her sisters, they'd already asked the waitress to bring her a Cobb salad afterward. For now, dessert came first.

Childhood habits were hard to break that way. When every day's survival was questionable, eating pie before vegetables was just common sense.

"Why, Sophie, you beautiful little hussy. I thought you'd never ask." Dawn swiped a bite of pie and licked her fork clean. "Step one is all about the wardrobe. What you want to do in the early days is expose just one body part at a time. Pick something that's normally innocent, say, a shoulder—"

"No, no. Not the sexy kind of crazy. The other kind. The annoyed kind."

"Why did you look at me when you said that?" Lila demanded. Unlike Dawn, she would never presume to eat from someone else's plate. Her own dishes were arrayed in front of her in a perfectly square pattern—fruit, vegetable, protein, carbs. "I don't annoy men. Men love me."

Dawn snorted.

"It's true!" Lila protested. "I don't always love them back, that's all. I have high standards."

Neither one of them could argue with that. Nor, Sophie reflected, would they want to. Lila deserved her high standards. Not only was she the best-looking of the sisters, her thirty years worn like a diamond tiara, but she was the smartest too. She had a master's degree in animal behavior—a valuable tool for training dogs… and, Sophie hoped, for training men.

"This is serious, you guys," Sophie said. "Harrison and Bubbles and I had a very productive day. I know how I'm going to make a success of them."

"And the answer isn't hard work and the tried-and-true practices of dog training we've been instilling in you for years?" Lila asked.

"Well, yes, obviously." Sophie squirmed, not quite able to meet her sister's eyes. If she had any idea just how far from the tried-and-true practices Sophie planned on going, she'd yank this entire project out from under her. A puppy-mill puppy was bad enough. A puppy-mill puppy who was afraid of fire and a firefighter who was afraid of his puppy-mill puppy was another thing altogether. Her head whirled to think of it.

"Of course I'll follow all the regular training techniques," Sophie said primly. "But it's going to take a little more than that. You have to admit this case is special, Lila. Not only is Bubbles unlike our usual puppies, but Harrison is unlike our usual clients. Most of the time, they're the ones coming to us, eager to adopt a dog and willing to do whatever it takes to train it. Harrison is only doing this because he has to."

The waitress came by to whisk Sophie's now-empty dessert plate away and replace it with the leafy salad—her usual. The Vasquez sisters had talent to spare when it came to academics and training dogs, but none of them were any good at cooking. If it weren't for the Maple Street Grill across the street from their house, they'd probably all starve.

"So, your grand plan is to annoy him?" Lila asked.

"Yes."

"Every day?"

"If I have to."

"For six weeks?"

"I told you I needed help." Sophie cast her most-pleading look up at Lila's face. The one good thing about having overprotective sisters was that they were highly susceptible to begging. "Please? I know you didn't like Harrison, but he's really quite sweet once you get to know him. And he's already agreed to this alternative approach. In fact, I think he's enjoying it."

Lila's brow came up. "What about the puppy?"

"You should have been there today, Lil." Sophie was unable to keep the enthusiasm out of her voice as she leaned over the table, waving her fork all the while. "I've never seen anything like it. It takes her one time to learn something, two to make it routine. I mean, she could barely keep her eyes open by the end of the day, but she wouldn't even lie down until she'd been given permission."

"If the dog's so obedient, why do you need us?" Lila asked.

"I told you already. Because the man isn't."

Dawn cracked a laugh, her eyes crinkling around the edges. "The ones worth having rarely are. What did he do?"

Sophie paused, stabbing at her lettuce in an attempt to stall. It wasn't that she was *afraid* to tell her sisters about her conversation with Harrison, but it felt...disloyal somehow. He was clearly a man who protected his private life—who protected himself—at all costs. Opening up to her, even that tiny bit, must have been painful for him.

She wouldn't betray that. Not now that she knew he *respected* her.

"Let's just say that he doesn't play well with others," Sophie said. At the shared look of alarm that passed between her sisters, she rushed to add, "Not in a bad way. Just in a closed-off way. It's like he's got this wall up and he refuses to let anyone past it. But if I push him just enough..."

She paused, struggling to find the right words.

"You can sneak past the wall?" Dawn ventured.

"Not sneak past it," Sophie said. "Demolish it entirely. He was super awkward with you guys at the house yesterday, right?"

"He said all of three words to me," Lila said.

"I managed six, but that was only because I was trying really hard," Dawn said. "He *definitely* perked up when you walked in though."

Sophie nodded and did her best not to blush, but Dawn wasn't done putting her on the spot.

"He's not a handsome man," she said, tapping a french fry in ketchup. "Not in the classical sense, anyway. But the second he saw you, I couldn't help but think that he's a hell of an attractive one, if you know what I mean."

Sophie did. She definitely did. Harrison's features might not be regular, and he might grumble and stomp like a giant atop a beanstalk, but he still managed to radiate virility. Even now, miles away, she could feel his magnetism.

"I can't imagine why you'd want to annoy someone who looks at you like that," Dawn added with a swooning sigh.

"That's because you don't know him," Sophie said. "He only likes me *because* I annoy him. I mean, when he saw Bubbles for the first time, it was as if I'd just shown him the moment of his own death. But then I told him to crawl inside the pen and cuddle with her, and he was so outraged at the prospect that everything flipped over. He started laughing and joking, finally willing to give her—to give *me*—a try. The same thing happened today. It's like he can't move forward unless he reaches some kind of breaking point first."

Sophie paused, aware how strange all this must seem to her sisters, but she didn't know how else to explain it. "I know it's weird, but I can't get started on any real work with him until the wall comes down."

"So you're smashing through his walls?" Lila asked. "With what?"

She couldn't help but grin at the disbelief in her sister's voice. Sophie was hardly known for her ability to ride a wrecking ball through other people's lives. "Well, *I* can't smash them, obviously. I doubt I could even pick up a sledgehammer that big. But if I push him far enough, he does it for me."

"Does that mean you pushed him today? Enough to get the wall down, anyway?" Dawn propped her chin in her hand and watched Sophie with a gleam in her eyes. "How?"

Sophie's grin turned into a giggle. "I threatened to take away his puppy."

It was a credit to both her sisters that she didn't have to explain the joke. The idea that Sophie could physically wrest *anything* away from a six-foot tank of a man was preposterous in the extreme. The fact that they were talking about a two-pound Pomeranian puppy only made it that much funnier.

"But I can hardly do that every day. Especially not now that he knows what I'm doing. That's why I'm asking for your input. I don't have enough experience with men like Harrison Parks." Or, if she was being perfectly honest, with men in general. "What else can I do that will send him over the edge?"

Dawn opened her mouth to respond, but Lila forestalled her with a stern look and some advice of her own. "Correct him when he's wrong and don't be modest about it. Tell him to smile more. Talk about religion and politics every chance you get, and always act like you're an expert. Critique his driving. And above all else, never apologize for anything, even—*especially*—if you're the one at fault."

Sophie eyed her oldest sister with a growing sense of wonder. "You didn't even have to stop and think about any of those."

"Of course I didn't." Lila picked the napkin out of her lap and daintily dabbed the corners of her mouth. "Those are all the things that men do to annoy *me*. It'll serve one of them right to have the tables turned for a change. Now if you'll excuse me, I'm going to run to the ladies' room."

Sophie didn't dare look at Dawn until their sister had woven through the tables and disappeared around a corner. And a good thing too, because the moment their eyes met, they fell into a peal of laughter that drew the attention of every patron in the place.

"Well, crap," Sophie said. "How long do you think she's been harboring that particular grudge?"

"Years, at the very least. Poor Lil. She's too good for ninety-nine percent of the men on this planet. Then again, so are you. The only difference is that you haven't realized it yet." The gleam was back in Dawn's eyes. "Are you *sure* you're only interested in driving him the bad kind of crazy? I wasn't kidding about how attractive he is, Soph. Men like that don't come around every day—believe me, I know."

"Um." She bit her lip. "Maybe you'd better go over that exposed-shoulder thing before Lila gets back. Just so I know I understand it."

The irrepressible dimple broke out in Dawn's cheek. "Oh, Sophie. The shoulder is only the beginning. Just wait until we get to the midriff."

chapter 7

"Well, well, well. What do we have here?"

At the sound of Oscar's voice, Harrison glanced up from the kitchen table, a scowl on his face and a sharp pair of scissors in his hand. If it weren't for the puppy napping blissfully on his lap, he might have jumped to his feet and used the scissors as a makeshift shiv.

Relentlessly. And with absolute glee.

"You heartless bastard," he said. "I'm surprised you dare to show your face here after what you've done to me."

"What I've done to you?" Oscar tsked gently and lowered himself into the nearest chair. It spoke volumes about their history together that he'd willingly put himself so close to a potential stabbing. "You mean when I called in a personal favor and laid out a huge chunk of my annual DNR budget to keep your sorry ass alive and on the job? You're right. What was I thinking?"

It was a rhetorical question, so Harrison didn't bother answering. The next question, however, was more pointed.

"Is that the infamous puppy?"

Harrison glanced down at Bubbles, who was showing signs of waking. It was always a production with her, her tiny limbs twitching, her tinier tongue stretching as she yawned. Awake she might be, but she wouldn't move from his lap, that much he knew for sure. It was warm there, and the damn dog wouldn't stop shivering.

And who could blame her? There was a faulty latch on the back door that caused it to swing open at the first sign of a gust of wind, so the blasted thing had been open half the night. The baseboard heaters were older than Harrison was, and the fireplace obviously wasn't an option. He had no other choice.

"Bubbles, meet the man who betrayed me. Judas, meet the ferocious rescue puppy you've saddled me with for the rest of my life."

"Aw, she's a cute little thing, isn't she?" Oscar said, ignoring Harrison's commentary. He turned his attention to the project Harrison had laid out on the table. "Why are you cutting holes in your socks?"

He waved the scissors at Oscar. "If you know what's good for you, you won't ask that question."

Oscar shrugged. "Suit yourself. Is Wallace around?"

"No, he went into town to run a few errands."

"And by that, you mean he's sitting alone at the bar in the bowling alley?"

Harrison glanced at the clock above the stove and snorted. "At eight thirty in the morning? Of course he is. The alternative is to sit around the house all day with me."

Silence descended over the pair of them, broken only by the snuffling sounds of Bubbles coming to full awareness. It wasn't an uncomfortable silence, but it *was* heavy. Long before Oscar had become his boss, he'd been his father's best friend. He knew all of their secrets, all of their problems—including the toll a long period of enforced inactivity was having on a man like Wallace Parks. Without the promise of his job, his dad had nowhere to go, nothing to do, and no one to do it with. And for the first time in his long, miserable life, he was forced to realize it.

It was what made this whole you-can't-come-back-to-work-until-you-get-a-service-dog thing so cruel. Oscar knew what kind of a toll it would have on Harrison too.

"How's he doing, by the way?" Oscar asked. "Enjoying retirement?"

Harrison measured out a length of three inches on the sock and made another cut. "No."

"How are you doing?" was the next question. "Enjoying your leave of absence?"

"No," he said again.

Oscar wasn't put off by monosyllables. "How about Sophie? I hope she's not a disappointment, at least."

Harrison eyed his boss warily. The question might sound casual enough to an outsider, but everywhere he considered stepping was riddled with land mines.

She's great, thanks. She somehow got me to allow her free rein to push and pull and make me generally uncomfortable in my own skin, but that should be fun, right?

I can't stop thinking about her laugh, thanks. Or her smile. Or the fact that those two things have made me reconsider anything and everything I've ever known.

"She's fine," Harrison said, hedging. "Bubbles likes her."

"I'm sure she does. The question is, do *you* like her?"

Of course he did. He had a Pomeranian puppy in his lap and he was doing crafts at his kitchen table before nine o'clock in the morning. If that wasn't a clear sign of how far he'd fallen, he didn't know what was.

When he didn't answer, Oscar cleared his throat in a way that didn't bode well for the conversation to follow. "Harrison?"

"She seems like a very capable dog trainer," he said.

"That's because she *is* a very capable dog trainer. She's also kind and generous and has overcome more pain and suffering than most of us see in a lifetime. I like you, Harrison, I really do, but if you hurt that girl in any way, I'll make sure you regret it for the rest of your miserable life."

Harrison's head snapped up.

"I can, you know." Oscar's voice was calm, but his expression was one Harrison knew from experience meant it was better not to cross him. "I don't like it any more than you do, but it needs to be said. So I'll ask you one more time: How about Sophie?"

For the first time in Harrison's life, he didn't react poorly to being challenged. A few days ago, that question might have boiled every frustrated nerve, sent him off on a tangent that would have Sophie resolutely squaring up to him. Today, he could only find himself in complete agreement. Any asshole who broke that woman down deserved the worst the world had to offer.

Including him.

Especially him.

"I don't think you need to worry about her." Harrison held up his finished product and sighed. "If she wasn't enjoying herself before, I promise she will today. All right, Bubbles. Let's see if this does the trick."

Oscar didn't say a word as Harrison stretched out the

sock and slipped it over the puppy's head. It went easily. There was so much fur on her, she could be decompressed to half her size. Gently guiding her limbs to fit through each of the holes he'd made was more difficult, especially since some of his measurements had been a little off, but the end result was about what he expected.

In other words, Bubbles was wearing a sock. One of his favorites too, the sweat-wicking kind he wore when he was out fighting fires for long stretches at a time.

"What the hell did you just do to that poor creature?" Oscar demanded.

"What do you mean? She loves it." Harrison set Bubbles down on the table. The puppy wriggled once, scratched twice, and decided she'd never been so pleased in all her life. With a toss of her head, she began prancing along the table's edge, just in case they hadn't noticed her the first time. "Look at her—she's preening."

Oscar scratched his chin. "Well, I'll be damned. She does like it."

"Hello, boys." A soft, feminine voice arose from behind them. "Sorry to barge in, but I rang the doorbell three times. No one answered."

Harrison's pulse leapt at the sound of Sophie's arrival. It wasn't a scared leap or an alarmed leap—it wasn't even a wary one, which *should* have been his reaction given how far she'd managed to push him already.

No, this was the most dangerous kind of leap of all—*attraction*.

His heightened pulse didn't lessen when he turned to find her standing in the doorway to the kitchen. He'd been more grateful than words could express when she'd showed up yesterday wearing sensible pants and a shirt with a Puppy Promise logo embroidered on the front. She'd still looked amazing, of course. The playful wisps of her short hair set off her pretty features, and the simplicity of her attire only enhanced her neat figure. But the uniform had helped.

I'm here to do a job, that uniform said. *I'm here because of the dog.*

Today, she'd gone back to wearing her own clothes. He wasn't sure why the sight of her in faded jeans and a loose gray top should be so alarming, but he suspected it had something to do with the gentle curve of neck exposed on one side of her shirt. He'd seen women wear similar clothes before, but there was something about the sight of Sophie's bare clavicle that made it difficult for him to breathe.

He wanted to kiss her there. He wanted to run his fingers up and down that slope of perfect skin until she shivered under his touch.

She shifted slightly, the shirt shifting with her. As if aware he was watching, the material slid even farther, giving him a glimpse of the rounded softness of her shoulder, broken only by a thin pink bra strap.

Shit. What was he doing? He couldn't lust after Sophie. Not when she showed no signs of reciprocation. Harrison might go numb at the sight of her dressed in casual wear, but he doubted his jogging pants and decades-old Pink Floyd T-shirt were doing anything in return. Nor was she likely to lose herself at the sound of his rough grumbling.

"Sorry," he said in a voice that was, unfortunately, both rough *and* grumbling. "The doorbell doesn't work. It hasn't worked in years."

"Nothing around this place has worked in years," Oscar added with a cheerfulness that seemed inappropriate, given how recently he'd been threatening Harrison's life and livelihood. "Except for Harrison and Wallace, of course. Two more dedicated workaholics I've never met in my life—it's the only thing they're good at, if you want the truth."

He wasn't wrong. As much as Harrison would have liked to leap to his own defense, there wasn't much to say. He wasn't a man with varied interests or a whole hell of a lot going on in his personal life. Fighting fires was literally the only thing he was good at—the only thing he'd ever been good at since the summer he'd turned fourteen and made friends with a group of delinquent kids from around town.

His dad had been working around the clock at the time—his default for as long as Harrison could remember—so when he'd caught his son in the middle of a tractor-stealing incident, he'd handed him over to Oscar with plea that he *do something with the blasted boy*.

Oscar had done it, of course, and in the process, created a monster. An irritable, overworked, firefighting monster who had nothing to offer a woman except a newfound talent for making dog sweaters out of socks.

"Speaking of, when can I expect to have him back?" Oscar asked. "I've got a contract to start training a team from Fairchild Air Force Base with his name written all over it."

"Right now." Harrison almost shot out of his chair in his enthusiasm. Work would get him away from this house. Work would distance him from Sophie and her goddamn shoulder. "Pull the crew together, and I can start the training as soon as you want. You know how valuable the air force support can be for the flyovers. We've been after a contract with them for years."

"I do know, which is why I'm going to delay the training until you're free to run it." Oscar turned his attention to Sophie. "What do you anticipate? What's the expected timeline?"

Sophie glanced down at the puppy, considering. Not by so much as a flicker of a long, curled eyelash did she betray that she noticed anything out of the ordinary about Bubbles's appearance.

Harrison couldn't decide whether to be grateful for her tact or outraged at her disinterest. He'd worked really hard on that sock.

"Well, I set aside a total of six weeks, but there's natural chemistry between Harrison and Bubbles, so it might go faster."

"Natural chemistry?" Oscar said.

"Oh yeah. It can take some dogs months to warm up to their new owners and vice versa. But I don't think I could tear this pair apart now even if I wanted to. Isn't that right, Bubbles?"

Bubbles yapped an affirmative.

"See? She agrees with me. She took one look at Harrison and fell hard." Sophie glanced up at Harrison, a challenge in her dark eyes. "It doesn't always happen that way, unfortunately. A lot of times, canine attraction is a one-sided thing."

Harrison might not have been an expert on canine attraction, but he knew enough about the human kind to realize he was on shaky ground.

"She's not bad, as far as puppies go," he said. The

frankness of Sophie's gaze made him more flustered than usual, which was the only reason for what he said next. "Except for the fact that her very existence is going to keep me from properly doing my job. She's scared of fire."

The smile vanished from Sophie's face.

At the sight of that stricken look, Harrison felt as though he'd been sucker punched, all the air leaving his lungs at once. He would have taken it back—said something to smooth over his misstep—but his chest felt too tight to let air in or words out.

Like it usually does.

"I did tell you Bubbles was skittish, Oscar, remember?" Sophie said. There was a plea underscoring her voice, a desperation that hit Harrison on a visceral level. "We're having a few minor issues where she's concerned, but it's not a big deal, I swear. I'm fully confident that we can get through them. Harrison might not ever be able to work the front lines again, but that was going to be the case no matter which dog we chose. All I can promise is that we'll get Bubbles as close as we can."

"Then there you have it," Oscar said with maddening calm. "We'll get Bubbles as close as we can, even if that means Harrison has to stick to training from here on out. His health and safety are too important to risk."

"Like hell they are," Harrison said.

He may as well have not spoken. In fact, his terse defiance had Sophie squaring her shoulders and lifting her head, confidence radiating from every part of her.

"I'll need to see how Bubbles reacts to different stimuli and in different environments," she said. "Including places like the wildfire training grounds and the DNR office. We can work up to those though. It's better to start in more low-key social environments—parks, libraries, bars. Wherever you go for fun."

That last bit was directed at Harrison, who echoed her with a monotone, "For fun?"

"Sure. If you belong to any clubs, play any sports, that sort of thing, I can easily work them into the rotation. It'll be good for Bubbles to get a feel for her routine."

He continued staring at her, more fixated on her mouth than was good for him. He hadn't played a team sport since a brief flirtation with basketball in high school, and he'd never belonged to a club of any sort unless you counted grocery store memberships. As for parks and libraries, she had to be kidding. He was a grown-ass man with a demeanor that scared children. Not exactly who they wanted showing up at story time without an actual kid in tow.

It took Oscar's crack of laughter to snap him out of his daze. "You're out of luck there, Sophie. I can't remember the last time Harrison went anywhere he wasn't required to. His idea of fun is to practice digging ditches in the backyard."

"I can tell," Sophie said. Her eyes moved up and down his body, lingering on his shoulders and torso with something akin to admiration. Then again, she could also be focusing on the fact that he looked like a man whose idea of fun was…well, digging ditches in the backyard.

"It's no different than going to a gym," he said in his defense. In fact, it was substantially better. No man-made machine could emulate the full-body experience of digging in the earth for eight hours straight.

"Except for the part where you have to interact with

other people at a gym," Oscar pointed out. "It's a good thing this dog-training stuff takes so much time. I was starting to worry about how Harrison would fill the days without work, but I can see you have it covered. Speaking of, I think I'll go hunt down Wallace at the bowling alley and say hello."

Harrison had been wishing Oscar to the devil for the past half an hour, but at the hint of departure, a perverse urge to beg him to stay kicked in. Oscar couldn't leave Harrison alone here with Sophie. It wasn't right—not after that lengthy speech about doing her no harm. Couldn't he see that it was only a matter of time before Harrison did something catastrophic?

He might storm. He might rage. He might pitch caution out the window and Sophie into his arms.

"Don't work him too hard, eh?" Oscar added. "Just look at what he did to that poor dog. I think he's cracking under the strain already."

Ha. That showed what Oscar knew. Cracking was an ongoing process, and Harrison was obviously already there.

"Don't say it," he warned as soon as Oscar swung out the back door—*whistling*, of all damn things.

"Say what?" Sophie asked. "I think Bubbles looks nice."

She was the picture of innocence, standing there with her exposed shoulder and a look of disinterest, but Harrison wasn't fooled. She was practically vibrating with suppressed laughter. There was something infectious about it. Already, he could feel the bands around his chest loosening.

"I didn't want to start a fire without your permission," he said.

"That was wise."

"And she wouldn't stop shivering."

"The poor honey. Their coats aren't very thick, despite how soft and fluffy they are."

"And it's not like I have tiny dog sweaters lying around the house."

"We'll start with a knitting circle, I think." Reaching into her canvas bag, Sophie extracted a notepad and started jotting things down. "That way you can expand her wardrobe however you want."

"I'm sorry—what did you just say?"

"Once we have that down, we'll add a trivia night. There's also family dinner and book club, which might be fun. Oh, I know! Beer choir. And definitely dodgeball practice—you'll like that one."

"Those sound like made up things. Why are you listing made up things?"

"For socialization, obviously."

He held up his hands as if warding off something evil—which, in a way, was exactly what he was doing. "I don't need socializing. I don't care what Oscar said— I'm fine the way I am. You'd be surprised how satisfying it is to dig and refill those ditches."

Her laughter rang through the kitchen like a dinner bell. "Not for you, Harrison. For Bubbles."

Ah, yes. The puppy. Puppies needed socialization. He knew that. The only problem was that men—at least *this* man—definitely did not.

He cast a doubtful look at the puppy. "You think Bubbles wants to go to a *knitting circle*?"

"I think Bubbles will do whatever you tell her to. That's the benefit of working with a sweet girl like her."

This was getting out of hand. "No," he said, his voice firm. He crossed his arms and let his power stance do the talking. "Let's do the other thing you said first. About the training grounds. And the office."

His power stance had no effect on Sophie. "You should smile more," she said.

He jolted as if struck. "*What?*"

"I was just thinking that you don't smile enough. You'd be so much prettier if you smiled."

He glanced around the kitchen, half-expecting Oscar or his dad to pop out of a cupboard, laughing their asses off. "Is this a joke?"

"You're not bad-looking, you know. I mean, your wardrobe is a little rustic, and I'm not sure what you have against the sharp edge of a razor, but you'd be surprised how much a smile can transform a man. Go on—try it."

He riveted the kind of stare on Sophie that could— and had—send many a man scurrying for cover. Harsh it might be, but it was a necessary skill set as far as he was concerned. Working as a wildfire firefighter wasn't for anyone who could only commit halfway. Each contract the Department of Natural Resources offered in the summer was for a minimum of two weeks—two weeks of pain and hard work, of exhaustion unlike most people would ever experience. If a recruit couldn't make it through a few hours of Harrison's rigor in the training field, there was no way they'd make it when the harsh realities of Mother Nature's wrath hit.

And, yes, that applied to his personal life too. Harrison was cold. Harrison was callous. Harrison was closed off in ways that prevented intimacy of any kind.

The sooner people learned that about him, the less hurt they'd feel in the end.

And by *people*, he of course meant Sophie.

"Um. I think we can safely call what you're doing right now a frown. Your lips are supposed to go the other way—see? Like this."

Sophie punctuated this statement by demonstrating her own smile. The brilliance of it, the simple and radiant joy, had Harrison's chest growing tight all over again.

"Now you try."

A few days ago, the idea of smiling for no reason other than because a woman demanded it would have sent him running for the hills. Today, he only wished these things came as easily to him as they did to other men.

As if recognizing this, Sophie drew forward, enveloping him all at once in a swirl of sensation. She didn't wear any kind of scent—probably for the sake of the dog training—but he could still smell her as she came near. It would have been impossible not to. Warmth and life radiated off her, the gentle aroma of soap and fabric softener wafting through the air like a cloud.

It wasn't just the smell of her though. He could *feel* her, even though she had yet to reach out and touch him. Her presence was that strong.

"Here. Let me help you."

Even though Harrison knew what was coming, he was powerless to stop her. He could no more have raised a hand to Sophie than he could have to the furry pineapple who'd taken up residence in his home.

"Sophie," he warned as her thumb started to snake its way toward his lips. The closer that thumb came, the less he felt like smiling. All we wanted was to kiss the wide pad of that digit, run his tongue along her skin until she felt the tug inside her gut as strongly as he did. "I can't."

"Sure you can. I've seen it." She paused. "You have a really good smile, Harrison. Probably the best I've ever seen."

"I do not," he protested.

Sophie made the motion of an X over her chest. "I wouldn't lie about something that. You have my word."

"You're just saying all this as part of your plan to push me."

"Maybe. But that doesn't make it any less true."

He had no idea whether or not to believe her. Reason told him not to give in to the lure of her, the promise of a woman who could make him feel so big and so small at the same time. The rest of him, however, wanted nothing more than to give her exactly what she demanded.

"It's just a smile, Harrison," she said, her voice low. "How much damage could it possibly do?"

She has no fucking idea.

Casting aside all scruples and warnings, he took her wrist and loosely circled it with his fingers. It took almost no strength to hold her that way. Every muscle in her body stilled the moment he made contact, her eyes wide and unblinking as she looked up at him. Even now, with him shackling her wrist, his body thrumming with the roiling sensation of frustration, she didn't back down.

She had to realize how dangerous it was to poke him. To taunt him this way.

She didn't.

"We're getting closer, I think," she murmured, gazing up at him the same way Bubbles did. Full of adoration. Full of trust. "All you have to do now is—"

He didn't bother waiting to find out what she had planned. The overwhelming urge to kiss her took over first—and it did so with a vengeance. Not content with sweeping down and crushing his mouth to hers, he began running through a virtual checklist of All the Bad Ideas.

Release his grip on Sophie's wrist.

Move a hand to her neck, her clavicle, that damnable shoulder just begging for his touch.

Clasp his other hand around her waist and yank her close.

Groan at the sensation of all those soft parts pressed against him.

Groan again when, instead of backing away like a normal person, Sophie opened her mouth to let him in.

This wasn't the way things were supposed to work. The rules of Harrison's existence were straightforward and had been for years. When he clammed up and broke down, people backed off. Sometimes, they walked; usually, they ran. The results, however, were always the same.

And by *the same*, he didn't mean this sweet, terrifying scrap of a woman winding her arms around his neck and kissing him back with an intensity that made his head spin. To look at Sophie Vasquez, with her oh-so-deceptive fragility and claims of dependency, you'd think the demands of his tongue would have her cowering in fear. Instead, she was giving back as good as she got, nibbling at his lower lip and arching into his touch. Even when his hand slipped under the loose neckline of her shirt, his rough hand palming the upper swell of her breast, she did no more than sigh into his mouth and press even harder against him.

He proved to be useless against a supplication like that one.

Sophie was still flush against him in a full-body press, so all he had to do to turn her toward the table was move his own body slightly to the right. Using his free hand, he reached down just far enough to graze the side of her thigh. He had every intention of hoisting her up to the table and using the leverage that afforded to start exploring that enticing shoulder with his lips, tongue, and teeth, but he was forestalled by a sharp yap.

Bubbles.

Harrison almost cried out his relief at the interruption. Had anything else happened—an earthquake, a volcano eruption, the sky literally falling down around them—he wasn't sure he'd have been able to stop himself from spiraling out of control.

But at that small sound, Sophie pulled away with a gasp.

"Oh!" she cried. Her color was heightened, and her eyes didn't quite meet his. With a presence of mind he couldn't help but admire, she turned her focus toward the puppy. "You poor little love. Did we forget about you?"

Harrison didn't know about Sophie, but he sure as hell had. If anything should have convinced her that he wasn't fit to have charge of this puppy, it was this. One kiss, one huge loss of control, and he'd pretty much abandoned his charge.

"Here you are, all dressed up in your finery, and no one is paying you any attention."

Bubbles barked again, this time with less outrage and more delight, her tongue lolling to the side.

Harrison could hardly blame her for her enthusiasm.

Having just had Sophie's full attention, he knew how powerful it was—powerful enough to throw common sense and decency aside.

"Yes, Bubbles, I know. You look very nice. Not at all like a potato. And I don't know why your daddy is making that sound. I said you *don't* look like a potato."

There were so many things wrong with that statement, but he settled on one. "I am not that dog's father," he said.

Sophie gasped and put her hands over the puppy's ears. "Harrison, how could you? You're going to make her cry. Just when she was starting to get used to it around here."

He tried to stop himself. He used every ounce of will-power he had left. But just as he'd been unable to keep himself from ruthlessly kissing her, so too was there no way to stop his mouth from quirking into a smile.

It was too ridiculous—the puppy and the sock, the fact that he'd just done his valiant best to cop a feel from a sweet five-foot-two-inch dog trainer who terrified him. If Oscar found out about any of this, not only would Harrison be doing paperwork for the rest of his natural born life, but the man would also probably tear him limb from limb while he was at it.

But still, Harrison smiled. Being in the presence of Sophie demanded nothing less.

"Don't," he warned as he caught Sophie's eye. The gleam of triumph was impossible to ignore. "You already made your point. There's no need to rub it in."

"I wasn't going to say a word."

"Not a single one?" he said. "Not even about the kiss?"

Her color rose again, a spot of pink on either cheek.

She looked adorable like that, flustered and unsure, but her chin came up in a gesture he was coming to recognize.

And fear. In moments when any logical person would retreat, Sophie doubled down.

"What is there to say?" She shrugged and tugged her shirt's neckline back into place. There was still too much shoulder showing for Harrison's peace of mind, but at least she wasn't so...disheveled. "It was nice."

"*Nice?*"

A gurgle of laughter escaped her lips. She slapped a hand over her mouth, but it was too late. The damage was already done. "I meant that it was amazing. Earth-shattering. You totally rocked my world, Harrison Parks."

He didn't want to laugh. There was nothing funny about a man being rejected in his own kitchen by a woman who should, by all rights, never have been there in the first place.

But laugh he did, and there was no denying how good it felt. It shook his frame and his resolve, made him wish he could take her in his arms again and *really* rock her world this time.

"Point taken," he said. "Next time, I'll smile the first time you tell me to. That way we can avoid another situation like this one."

"No, don't." Her hand dashed out and grabbed his sleeve. "I liked the kiss, Harrison. I, um. Well. It's just...I also like you."

His smile wasn't optional this time. It broke out without his permission, refusing to be held back—refusing to let him hold *himself* back. "Me too, Sophie. I don't say that about many people, but you bring out something good in me. Something I haven't felt in a very long time."

She hadn't let go of his sleeve yet, her clutch on the flannel twisting at his words. "So it's okay?" she asked, peering anxiously up at him. "Pushing this way? Playing a little?"

He remembered what she'd said during the introduction with Bubbles, about how even working dogs needed downtime, that everyone needed to play and be loved, and nodded.

He wished he could think of something else to say—put into words the mass of emotions she was churning up inside of him—but his tongue felt too big for his mouth, his heart too big for his chest. Whether she recognized this and knew that there was only one thing in the world that could save him, or because she was much better at this than him, she let go of his sleeve and nodded.

"Well, that's good news. Are we ready to get to work now?"

He latched on like a man grasping at his final meal. "Work." His voice was guttural, terse. "Yes. Work."

"Good, because we've got lots of ground to cover if we're going to stay on schedule. Knitting circle starts up next Thursday, and you don't want to miss any meetings. Those ladies do *not* take well to truancy."

"Wait—that's an actual thing? That we're doing? Together?"

"Absolutely. It's all part of the training." She cocked a playful eyebrow at him. "Unless you have something to say about it?"

He stared at Sophie, hoping to find some loophole, but it was futile.

"Fine," he said, heaving a sigh. He knew when he'd been beat, and he'd been beat the moment this pair walked into his life. "But make a note that I'm only doing it under duress."

She chuffed a soft laugh. "Don't worry. I'm beginning to realize you won't do things any other way."

🐾🐾🐾

"Geez, Dad. Have you been here the whole damn day?"

Harrison dropped to the barstool next to his father, his shoulders heavy with exhaustion. He wasn't the only man to do so; a dark bowling alley bar might seem a strange watering hole to some, but in their town of four thousand, it was the best place to be after a long day of work.

Well, technically it was the *only* place to be, but Harrison wasn't about to quibble over the details. Especially since he, unlike every other blue-collar worker unwinding after a long day, lifted a Pomeranian puppy out from under the flap of his jacket and perched her on his lap.

"Really, Harrison?" his dad asked, shielding his pint glass as if fearing puppy contaminants. "You brought her with you? To a bar?"

"That's how it works," he said. He turned his attention to the bartender, an energetic, outspoken woman who could pass for fifteen or fifty, depending on the lighting. The dingy bar fluorescents softened her to somewhere in the thirties. "And before you say anything, Meg, Bubbles is a service animal, so you can't kick us out. See what her vest says? I need her to save my life."

"Save your life?" she echoed. "From what? A squirrel attack?"

Next to him, his dad guffawed. "Fat chance of that. My money's on the squirrel."

Harrison placed his hand on the puppy's back and glared at his father. Bubbles ruined the gesture's efficacy by turning her head into his caress and licking his thumb. He maintained his pose anyway. At least *one* of them was going to have a little dignity.

"She's very sensitive about her size," he said. "She's also tired after a long day. What do you have that might perk her up a little?"

Meg leaned on the counter and stared at the puppy. Her eyes, heavily lined in black, moved up and down between Bubbles and Harrison, as if she was waiting for the catch.

She could wait forever as far as Harrison was concerned. He *knew* it was ridiculous to saunter around a town like Deer Park with a designer dog wearing a red training vest layered over a sock. He'd grown up here, gone to school here, worked here. Almost everyone knew him as the hard-ass at the Department of Natural Resources who lived like a hermit on the outskirts of town and liked it. The last thing he needed was for any of them to point out that he was more likely to tattoo daisies on his eyelids and take up, well, knitting as a hobby.

"Maybe she'd like some whiskey?" Meg eventually suggested.

It was Harrison's turn to guffaw. He could only imagine Sophie's reaction if she found out he'd even *considered* giving Bubbles hard alcohol. She'd yell again. Either that, or she'd kiss him.

With that woman, it was hard to tell.

"Water will be fine," he said. "For both of us. I mostly just needed to get out of the house."

"That girl still there?" his dad asked with a surprising show of astuteness.

"No," Harrison admitted. She'd left at exactly five o'clock with a promise to return the next day at nine. She was a consummate professional from head to toe—well, except for the part where she made out with him in the kitchen and filled up his calendar with a whirl of social activities that he in no way, shape, or form wanted to take part in. "But she did make a few changes around the place."

"Good for her." Meg set down a glass of water in front of Harrison and a small bowl in front of Bubbles, both of them on coasters—Meg was a consummate professional too. "It's about damn time someone took that place in hand. That gorgeous old farmhouse, just sitting there going to ruin…"

"It is *not* going to ruin," his father said. "It took me years to get it exactly the way I like it. You'd better tell her not to touch anything without my permission."

"You can tell her yourself. I'm not that brave." He balanced the water dish on his lap so Bubbles could reach it, which the puppy did gratefully. She was exhausted, poor thing. It had been a long day of sitting and smelling and trying not to be distracted by Sophie.

Well, that last one had been mostly him.

"What'd she do?" his dad demanded.

"Candles."

"Candles?" Those two syllables were all it took to voice his outrage and alarm.

"They're everywhere," Harrison said. "She put unscented ones in jars in the living room and those long, skinny ones that people use at holidays in the kitchen. And there are a few bigger ones in the fireplace instead of logs, but we aren't supposed to light them yet. I have a schedule for you."

"You have a candle schedule? Are you *trying* to ruin my life?"

Harrison dug in his pocket and extracted the notes Sophie had handed him as she'd placed the candles around the house. She'd also pointed out several hazards that he might want to take care of, including the precarious stacks of books in the living room and a hallway floorboard that had a jagged hole just big enough for a puppy leg to fall through.

She seemed to excel at highlighting flaws—and it hurt. He *knew* that floorboard was bad. He'd been meaning to fix it for years.

"It's to get Bubbles used to small flames," he said. "We're supposed to light them and then ignore them in hopes that she'll do the same. *Normalizing the situation*, she calls it. There's even one in your room."

"No."

Harrison had to laugh at the expression of disgust on his father's face—an expression that would only get worse once he realized it was lavender-scented one. "It's known to have soporific effects," she'd said. "Bubbles won't be in here very much, so she won't be distracted by it during scent training. And who knows? He might end up liking it."

There was a much better chance it would end up chucked out the window and broken on the front lawn, but Harrison hadn't said so. He'd have plenty of opportunities to crush Sophie's enthusiasm for reforming the Parks household. No need to go all-in before they barely got started.

"What sort of plague have you brought down on our house?" his father demanded. "This is how it always goes. The candles are just the beginning. Before you realize it…"

"What?" Harrison asked, genuinely interested in the answer. It seemed wise to be prepared for whatever she had planned next. *Never go in unprepared.* That was good advice for battling wildfires and petite, beguiling women.

"Tablecloths." His dad set his jaw and stared mulishly at him. "Fresh flowers. Piles of fruit arranged on a bowl on the table, but woe to the man who actually picks one up and eats it."

Meg fell into laughter. "If that's your idea of a plague, Wallace, I'm beginning to realize why you're such a miserable bastard all the time."

Harrison could have easily enlightened Meg as to the true source of his dad's misery. He'd never been a happy man—not the kind who laughed and played and enjoyed long walks on the beach—but Harrison could remember a time when he hadn't been quite so hard.

Once upon a time, their house had been a home—well cared for and full of light, the sort of place most people only dreamed of growing up in. But that light had gone out the day his mother left. Even though Harrison had *tried* to get that flicker going again, his father quashed any and all attempts at illumination.

Better not to see the cracks. Better not to know what lurks in the corners.

"When I see an apple, I'm going to eat an apple," his dad said. "And no one—not God and certainly not your dog trainer—is going to tell me otherwise."

"I'm sure Sophie won't start putting fruit out," Harrison said, though he couldn't be at all sure. That woman made him do things. She made him *feel* things.

"Besides, I thought you liked her. You promised to send her a Christmas card and everything."

"That was *before* she brought candles into my house," his dad muttered.

Meg laughed again. "She doesn't sound so bad, if you ask me."

"Good thing no one asked you, then."

Meg could have easily taken offense at his dad's harsh words, but she was far too used to him to bother. Instead, she shrugged and took herself off to tend to customers at the window leading to the bowling alley side of the bar.

"I meant what I said about the tablecloths, Harrison," his dad warned. "It always starts with tablecloths."

Harrison pictured their kitchen table, the rough-hewn planks and serviceable build, and nodded his understanding. That table had been there for a decade, built by his dad's own two hands. It might have been ugly, but it was functional. To cover it with something soft and floral would only make a mockery of it.

You can't hide a table's true nature.

He caught a glimpse of himself in the mirrored wall behind the bar, his expression grim and so much like his father's it was uncanny. He might be younger and not quite so hard, but there was no denying they were cast from the same rough mold.

It was only a matter of time before he was just as old and miserable as his dad.

Guess you can't hide a man's true nature either.

chapter
8

"You're sure you don't mind keeping an eye on Bubbles while we go for a run?" Sophie turned her sunniest smile on Harrison's dad. "Considering what good shape Harrison is in, we'll probably have to do five miles before we start to see his blood sugar dip enough to register. We may have to go even farther."

Harrison fully expected his father to refuse—a thing as natural to him as breathing—but the man took one look at Sophie's bright expression and blinked.

"She might not like it, since we're training her to avoid separation from Harrison at all costs, but you should be able to distract her with this."

The *this* in question was a squeaky toy in the shape of miniature rubber chicken. Sophie squeezed it once, the long whine of it causing Bubbles to leap out of Harrison's arms and station herself at Sophie's feet.

"What am I supposed to do with it?" Harrison's dad asked doubtfully.

"Throw it. Squeak it. Hide it." She beamed up at him. "It doesn't really matter. Just play with her."

His dad blinked again. "What if I just put her in a box and close the flap?"

"I imagine she'd have something to say about that."
Sophie laughed and handed over the toy. "Thank you,
Wallace."

Wallace? Since when were Sophie and his father on
a first-name basis? Come to think of it, when had his
father done anything remotely resembling play? Unless
you counted their annual Alone for Thanksgiving Poker
Tournament, where they sat and played cards for eight
hours, smoking cigars and eating cold lunch meat, he
couldn't remember the last time his father had willingly
participated in a game.

"By the way," Sophie added, "did you have a chance
to burn the candle in your room? It's nice, right? My
sister Dawn makes them, so there's plenty more where
that came from."

Harrison braced himself for the inevitable outburst.

"It was all right," his dad said with a soft grunt.
"Little flowery for my taste."

She nodded as if that made perfect sense. "I was
afraid it might be. How'd the puppy do with it?"

"Little flowery for her too," his dad said.

Harrison could only stare at his father. *He'd* been
satisfied with how little attention Bubbles had paid to
the lit candles as long as they were on tabletops and well
out of reach, but to his knowledge, his father refused to
have anything to do with the candle schedule. In fact,
he'd taken one look at it posted on the refrigerator and
muttered his intention to invite the raccoon inside to put
an end to this whole sorry mess.

"Maybe you should bring me a bacon one," his dad
added.

Sophie laughed. "Dawn doesn't make those,

unfortunately. But I'll bring you a cedar-and-bergamot scented one tomorrow—it's just as calming, but the fragrance is a lot more understated. Well, Harrison, are we ready?"

Wait—that was it? He paused, waiting for those promises of telling Sophie off, of taking a stand against encroaching tablecloths, but his dad wouldn't even meet his eyes.

The coward. All that talk at the bar had been nothing but braggadocio. His father could no more stand up to Sophie Vasquez than Harrison could.

Not that he could blame his father. She'd shown up this morning with her shoulders fully covered by a long-sleeved athletic shirt—a thing he'd noted with profound relief. Unfortunately, she'd paired it with a pair of running pants with inexplicable bands of sheer material wrapped around her thighs. How was that even a thing? Her legs were technically covered against the biting spring wind, but those fabric windows offered glimpses of skin and muscle that no one should have to face this early in the morning.

At least, not without a cold shower first. An arctic one, in fact. A painful, plunging descent into numbness.

"Are we sure this is such a good idea?" Harrison asked, casting a careful look at first Bubbles and then his father. Bubbles was still too intrigued by the rubber chicken to notice she was about to be abandoned, but the realization would come soon enough—and so would the howls of betrayal. "He was only halfway kidding about that box thing. She's going to cry."

Sophie tilted her head and stared at them. "Of course she is. You just have to think of it like dropping a kid off at daycare."

"Daycare?" his dad echoed.

"Yeah—you know. While the parents are watching, the kid acts like the world is going to end. Then, the second Mom and Dad finally tear themselves away in their guilt and despair, the kid shrugs it off and has a perfectly good time. Didn't you ever have to leave Harrison with someone?"

Harrison could count the number of times his dad had willingly spoken of his childhood on one and a half hands. There weren't many rules in their household, but two of them stood out loud and clear: Parks men didn't discuss the past, and Parks men didn't discuss the future. Theirs were lives lived in the moment. The past contained too many memories, and the future too many dreams—neither of which had any place in their terse, stoic existence.

In their experience, memories only caused pain. So did dreams.

"My sister used to help out a lot," his dad said after only a brief struggle with himself. "When Harrison was little and I had to go work, I mean."

Sophie had no idea the ground she'd just shattered, so she was perfectly serene as she asked, "And did he cry when you left?"

"Well, no." His dad laughed. "He saved that for when I came back."

"I did no such thing," Harrison said through his teeth. If his dad was going to finally take a trip down memory lane, he could at least turn on the right road.

"What are you talking about?" his dad asked. "You wailed every time I walked in the door. The second I stepped in, you ran and clung to your aunt's leg like I was going to feed you to a pack of wolves."

"I wasn't upset because you were home. I was upset because Aunt Caroline was leaving."

"How is that different?" his dad demanded.

Harrison could have given him a thousand answers. His dad's only sister was a Parks through and through. She was brusque and hardworking. She had a temper like a berserker on a bender. And she'd taken none of the attitude thrown her way by an eight-year-old boy who'd just been diagnosed with diabetes and was learning to live in a world without cookies.

But she'd also kissed him. Hugged him. Loved him, in her own bristly way.

In other words, she was the closest thing he'd had to a mom after his own had left. *She*'d packed up and gone without once visiting the hospital bed where Harrison had woken up from the coma that led to his diagnosis.

His aunt, however, had stationed herself firmly at his bedside and held his hand until that first—and only— bout of tears finally ended.

Forgive him for growing attached.

"She smelled better than you," Harrison eventually said.

His dad laughed. "If that's how you measure a person's worth, then Sophie over here must be your goddamn queen."

He tried not to look at her—he really did. Nothing good would come of turning his gaze in that direction and letting her see just how true that statement was. Sophie smelled amazing. She tasted even better.

He looked anyway. As if fully aware of what he was thinking—and how hard he was fighting it—her lips twitched even more. There was only one good way he could wipe that smirk off her face, and it involved making her mouth so exhausted she could do nothing more than moan his name. Repeatedly.

Which was why he did the one thing necessary to keep himself in check. He didn't bother fumbling for the right words, and he didn't sweep her into his arms.

Instead, he ran.

🐾 🐾 🐾

Sophie watched Harrison go, trying not to look as disheartened by his rapid departure as she felt.

He'd taken off down his drive at a brisk clip, his long legs eating up the distance as though it were nothing. One look at him in his track bottoms and tight-fitting shirt had been enough to set every feminine feeling she had fluttering. He was powerful without being aware of it, his movements graceful and easy.

In other words, he was as hard on the outside as he was on the inside.

His speed only confirmed it. As he loped away from the house, it was obvious he couldn't get away fast enough—from Bubbles, from his father, from *her*.

Which, okay, wasn't exactly the outcome she'd been looking for, but no one had said this was going to be easy. That was how walls worked, right? Every time they came down, he had to rebuild them. Except he used stronger materials, better techniques.

He was learning. Like artificial intelligence gone rogue, he was becoming more powerful with each passing day.

With a sigh, Sophie took off after him. Although she'd hoped he might be a *little* more approachable after that kiss in the kitchen, it seemed she was out of luck. A hard, painful run it would have to be.

To be fair, it wasn't the worst possible way to approach this task. For Bubbles to learn what Harrison's low blood sugar smelled like, he had to *have* low blood sugar. And since his was so often caused by physical exertion, a long and carefully supervised jog was the best way to do it. They'd gotten his doctor's approval and calibrated his continuous glucose monitor, which meant all that was left was the actual task of running.

But if he thought he was going to outpace her, he had no idea what was coming. For years, Sophie's primary job had been puppy care. She fed the animals, cleaned up after them, taught them the basics. She also took them for runs—long, tiresome, rambling runs to build up their stamina and reveal their personalities under stress.

There was no better way to get to know someone—human or canine—than to gently push them to the brink of exhaustion and see how they reacted. Sophie already knew that Bubbles would keep going, even though her short legs and less-than-impressive physique weren't built for long distances.

She was mightily curious how Harrison, with those formidable thighs and a body like a tree trunk, would handle it.

"I don't want us to go too far from the house, since your safety is the most important thing," she said as she pulled up alongside him. "So I mapped out a loop that goes through that patch of forest over there and down the field behind the house. It's about a mile, so we'll just put it on repeat as many times as necessary to get

your levels down. We'll keep an eye on your monitor, of
course, but you'll let me know if you start to feel faint?"

"I won't feel faint."

"That'll certainly make things easier," she replied
without any loss of cheer. "You're lucky to have such a
nice place to do this. Normally, we'd have to take you
to a track or a treadmill to get enough distance. But it's
so much prettier out here in the open air."

"It's all right."

"That's just because you're used to it. Bubbles will
like living out here. There's so much space for her to
roam." She paused only long enough for them to turn
out of view of the house. "I didn't know you have an
aunt. Is she your dad's sister?"

"Yes."

The monosyllabic responses might, on any other day,
have shut her own flow of chatter off. But she hadn't
been kidding when she'd said it was beautiful out here.
The mountain views were pretty in the city, but out
here, they were a breathtaking spectacle of hazy, blue
rockiness everywhere she turned. It was impossible to
be surrounded by all this and feel anything but grateful,
anything but *alive*.

"You can go faster, by the way," she said. "It makes
the most sense for you to set whatever pace you're comfortable with. Don't worry. I can keep up."

He hesitated at first, an innate sense of chivalry holding him in check. But the challenge, once issued, was
impossible for him to ignore. After about thirty seconds
of loping along, he began to jog faster.

"I have six aunts, but I'm not really close to any of
them," Sophie said as they whizzed down a steep turn

and entered the outskirts of the forest. "We're a pretty scattered family, so we didn't see a lot of them growing up. One of them is pretty cool though. She's a bassist in a rock band."

She'd thought for sure the rock band would pique Harrison's interest, but he continued to hold out.

"My sisters, now, that's a different story," she said. "We're about as close as three people can be without being physically attached to one another. I couldn't shake them even if I wanted to."

That finally got him. "Do you want to?"

The question surprised her—not just because Harrison was finally talking to her, but because it was the one thing no one else would think to ask. Her sisters were vibrant and fun and intelligent, and they would drop everything to help her if she needed it. They'd done that exact thing more times than Sophie could count. No one with any common sense would willingly give up such a great support system.

But... "Yeah, actually," Sophie said. "I do."

"Because you're dependent on them for everything?"

She slowed, alarmed that he could have seen so much of her in such a short period of time. He noticed, of course, letting out a breath that could have been a laugh. "That first day, when we were sharing flaws— remember?" he said. "You told me you were the baby of the family and that they took care of you."

Heat rushed to the surface of her skin. That Harrison had not only listened to what she'd said, but actually remembered spoke volumes. What he was saying, she didn't know. But at least they were communicating for a change.

"I didn't mean I'm *literally* dependent on them," she protested. "I'm a grown woman. I can feed and dress myself. I have a stable source of income."

"As part of their business?"

"As part of *our* business, yes, but it's not like I'm contractually obligated to live at the kennel. There's no reason why I couldn't move out and be on my own."

"So why don't you?"

For some reason, his questions—and the way he kept asking them—stirred something hot inside her. Lila and Dawn had spent the bulk of their adolescence in hospital waiting rooms, enjoying only a fraction of the parental attention they were entitled to. And they'd done it without a single complaint because Sophie was their sister and they loved her. It was impossible to just cast that kind of devotion aside.

At least, it was impossible for *her* to throw it aside. She wasn't putting anything past this grump.

"I don't know," she countered. "Why do you still live with your dad?"

He laughed—actually laughed, the raspy sound doing strange things to her already-rapid heart rate. "Fair enough."

"Is that what you're going to say instead of giving me an answer?"

For the longest time, she was afraid he was going to stop there. His steady breathing and the slap of their feet on the trail beneath them were the only sounds that reached her ears. But he eventually spoke, his voice surprisingly even.

"I can't move out," he said. "It wouldn't be fair to leave him all alone in that house."

And that was all there was to it. No explanation of why his dad was so attached to the farmhouse, no soul-bearing confession of the family ties that bound the two of them. Harrison couldn't leave his father alone in that house, so he wouldn't.

Sophie didn't need to know more—she'd seen the rest for herself. In the few short days she'd known Harrison Parks, she'd had plenty of time to take his measure. He was the kind of man who would protect a puppy he'd known for twelve hours because the animal had been given over to his care, and that was that. The kind who would fight forest fires with everything he had, even if it meant he was putting his own health at risk every time he did it, because the job needed to be done. The kind who would stay with his dad even when it was clear he'd rather be anywhere else.

In other words, he was a good man. A *really* good man.

And the best part—or the worst part, depending on perspective—was that he had no idea.

"If you could leave, where would you go?" Sophie asked.

"I don't know," he said with something like a shrug. "I've never really thought about it. What about you?"

"France. Spain. Egypt. Peru. Thailand. New Zealand. Mongolia."

"So just a few places, then."

"I'd like to go everywhere. Or nowhere. I don't think the destination matters so much as getting there on my own terms."

They'd almost completed the first mile by now and were approaching a barnlike structure near the back of the field. She cast a sideways glance at Harrison to see how he was holding up. His face was hard and his expression flat, but not because of weariness. Oh, no. Never that. It'd take a lot more than a single mile to wear him out.

Unless she was very much mistaken, it was also going to take a lot more than a single conversation to demolish today's walls.

She ran through a mental checklist of Lila's suggestions, casting each one aside as it popped up. Religion and politics were way too serious on a gorgeous morning like this one, and she could hardly critique Harrison's running style—the man's form was impeccable and, frankly, a sight to behold.

Which left only Dawn and her shoulders.

From a purely technical standpoint, Sophie knew how flirtation worked. It wasn't that difficult. A laugh and a smile, the brush of her hand on his—most men were primed to read the signs and react accordingly.

Not so with Harrison. He might have agreed to let her play with this thing between them, to lean on their mutual attraction as a way to break through his barriers, but *saying* it and *doing* it were two very different things. Especially since it appeared that she was going to have to do most of the heavy lifting.

Show off a body part like a sex goddess—just a flash, nothing more—and then start using it the way God and nature intended, Dawn had said at the diner. *Men hate it when you go all functional on them.*

It had sounded like strange advice at the time, but Dawn was something of an expert on the subject. Her sister was also a strong advocate of striking while the iron was hot.

The iron might not be feeling the burn, but Sophie certainly was.

The barn's entrance was approaching, so Sophie slowed her steps. Feigning a hitch in her side, she bent at the waist. "Oh, dear," she said. "I don't think I stretched very well. My muscles are starting to feel really tight."

Harrison immediately slowed his pace to match hers. "Do you want to head back? There's a footpath right over there—"

"No, no. You need to keep moving. You don't want to lose your progress. I'll just go through a quick series of stretches and catch up."

He didn't, as she'd halfway feared, take advantage of his freedom to take off in a mad dash away from her. He started jogging in place instead, following her orders to keep moving to a nicety.

"Where does it hurt?" he asked.

"Um. My hamstring?"

Sophie, never adept at lying—or anatomy—twisted and began a series of leg stretches that had more to do with showing off her body than physical exertion. With one hip jutting to the side, she lifted her arms above her head and stretched as far in the opposite direction as she could go.

Harrison watched her—not as a man being wooed by a sex goddess, but as a highly skilled firefighter trained in first aid.

"Uh, I hate to break it to you, but that's not going to help your hamstring."

Sophie dropped her arms, disappointment rendering her movements jerkier than usual. Practical advice was *not* the response she was going for here. "Maybe it was my deltoids?"

He released a sound halfway between a grunt and a laugh. "They're not anywhere near your legs. Why don't you just point to where it's feeling tight?"

It was too late to back out now, so she turned to the side and ran a hand along the outer edge of her right thigh. Not only was it the location of the largest sheer panel on her running tights, but it was one of her favorite body parts. She might not have Lila's tiny waist or Dawn's great rack, but the one thing her smaller, boyish figure had going for it was a good butt.

Harrison noticed.

"Maybe we should just head back—" he began before he stopped jogging altogether.

Emboldened by his inactivity and the fact that his eyes hadn't moved from her backside, she said, "But we're making such good progress, Harrison. I hate to abandon everything now."

He blinked and took a wide step back, suddenly recognizing her tactics for what they were.

"Oh no you don't. Not now. Not like this. That's cheating."

A laugh bubbled to the surface. Sophie had no idea how a man could manage to look both outraged and intrigued, but that was the only way to explain Harrison's expression right now. "How is it cheating?"

He pointed in the general direction of her ass. "Because you're wearing.... Because you look..."

She nodded, hoping to encourage him along these promising lines. "You never said there were rules about what I could wear or how I could look. Maybe we'd better write some of them down."

"Like hell I will. I'm not committing any of this to paper."

Her laughter sprang free. "Are you changing your mind about this whole thing? All you have to do is say the word, Harrison, and we can get back to running. Word of a Vasquez."

He didn't take her up on the offer. He pointed a finger at her instead, his voice showing signs of strain. "I know what you're trying to do. I can see right through you."

Yes, well. That was the whole point of these pants, wasn't it?

"And what's that?" she asked. Her own voice was coming out none too strong. If he didn't stop looking at her like that—like she was his tormentor, like she was his *everything*—she wouldn't be able to speak at all. "What am I doing?"

He watched the movement of her tongue with agonizing intensity. "Tablecloths," he said.

"Um."

"Flowers."

"What?"

"Bowls of goddamned fruit."

"Are you sure you're feeling okay?" she asked.

"No, Sophie," he said, his voice tight. "I'm not feeling okay. I haven't felt okay since I woke up in that hospital bed and found my entire life turned upside down. *Again*."

It was the first time he'd willingly referred to the coma that had kick-started this entire puppy project. In fact, it was the first time he'd willingly admitted that he was in anything but perfect fighting condition—that he, like everyone else on this planet, needed a little help from time to time.

It just about broke her heart.

Sophie knew better than anyone how it felt to wake up to an uncertain world, to feel like the one thing everyone took for granted—their health—was so far out of reach it might as well be the moon. She also knew the surefire way to combat it. After all, she'd learned from the best.

What this man needed more than anything else was a pair of bickering sisters. Companionship. *Laughter*.

"You know, now that I think about it, you're a lot like Sleeping Beauty," she said, the words popping out before she could stop them.

He blinked, the movement so careful and deliberate it was like watching a video in slow motion. "What did you just say?"

"You're like Sleeping Beauty," she repeated. "Gorgeous and grumpy, awakening after a long, deep sleep to find everything overtaken by thorns."

Considering the decay of the barn behind them, it seemed an apt metaphor. The red paint had long since faded to a burnt pink, the roof sunken in several places. The scent of animals and hay had given way to a more general earthiness.

Just like the house, just like the man, it was a kingdom in ruins.

"That would make me the prince, you know," she said. When he didn't answer right away, only stared at her like she'd been taken over by body snatchers, she added, "Because I kissed you."

That got him to snap to attention. "The devil you did. I was the one doing the kissing."

She did her best to ignore the force of Harrison's words — and how forcefully they set off a reaction in her body, setting her pulse thumping in ways that no amount of running could match — but it was no use. There was something so liberating about the way he handled her. Not carefully or delicately, or even like a thing to be cherished, but as a woman of courage.

As a woman of *strength*.

"They say the Sleeping Beauty story is a metaphor for sexual awakening," she said, emboldened by this realization. "I wasn't sure I bought into it at first, but it grew on me after a while. I mean, on top of that whole waking-up-from-a-kiss nonsense, she pricks her finger on a spindle. Have you ever seen a spindle? Like, a real one?"

"Where would I have seen a spindle?" he demanded. "Do you think my dad weaves textiles in his spare time?"

She giggled, unable to picture her second-favorite Parks man going anywhere near a textile. "Well, I'll save you the trouble. It's basically ye olde phallus."

His lips quivered as he fought a smile — the reluctant one, the devastating one, the one she was beginning to realize had the power to change her whole life. "Okay, now you're just making things up."

"I'm not!" she protested. "I'm just calling it like I see it. You're the beauty, I'm the prince, and the spindle is a literary device meant to shame women into chastity."

"You are no prince, Sophie Vasquez."

"How dare you? I could totally be the prince."

"In this story?" He laughed and shook his head. "I don't think so. Not when you're so clearly the dragon."

Her eyes widened in surprise, the laughter in her throat replaced by a sudden swelling of elation. No man—no person, actually—had ever looked at her and seen anything but a petite approximation of her sisters. She was a little less bright, a little less exciting, a little less strong. She didn't have their confidence or their drive and had long since reconciled herself to a life lived in their shadows.

Until now. Until she squared off against this magnificent, quarrelsome man who looked at her and unhesitatingly drew his sword.

Because I'm so clearly the dragon.

Unable to hold herself back any longer, she launched her whole body at Harrison. She caught him off guard, a fact borne out by his heavy grunt as she hit him with the full force of her weight. He didn't budge though. He was too much like a rock, too much like a wall. Everywhere her body touched his was hard. He was warmer than he normally was, exertion giving him a heat that almost felt like a glow.

Which was why she didn't pull away from it. So much of what Harrison said and did was meant to keep her at a distance, but the way his arms came up to catch her worked a number on her senses. For what felt like the first time, he was letting her in.

In was suddenly the only place she wanted to be. Before his reserve could come back up, she cast aside all of her scruples and fears and did the unthinkable.

She kissed him.

She caught him off guard with that too, her lips reaching his while they were still partly open. It was a good thing, because she might not have gone through with the rest of the kiss otherwise. There was something hugely intimidating about attacking a bear of a man with one's tongue, even if he did look and taste like this one. Besides, he was so much softer than she'd expected.

Oh, his body remained like stone, of course, and his arms were more like a pair of manacles than anything else. Those things were good—those things were *great*, actually—but nothing could have prepared her for the press of his lips against hers. His mouth was gentle, his tongue, when it slid past hers, like a silken embrace.

It made her yearn to discover the other hidden parts of him, those places where he hadn't yet turned off against the world. They were all her favorite parts of a man. Not—contrary to popular opinion—the rock-hard abs and rigid cock, but the places where pleasure could be found unexpectedly. The dip of an upper lip, right where the skin began to grow soft. The smooth curve of a well-formed buttock. Any spot where he might let his guard down long enough to admit to being ticklish.

Any part that would cause him to smile.

"Sophie, you devil." When Harrison pulled away, the smile was fixed in place. Even though it was accompanied by a rueful laugh and a shake of his head, nothing could dim its power. "What are you doing? I thought we were supposed to be getting my heart rate up and my blood sugar down, not cavorting in the wilderness."

"Who says we can't do both?" she retorted. "They say sex burns just as many calories as a thirty-minute jog. That's three miles we could lop off our final tally."

He stared at her with a look so staggered she almost feared she'd gone too far. Pushing Harrison a little bit outside his comfort zone was fine—in fact, it was the only way she was going to get through to him—but she didn't want to push him *away*.

Then he dropped his mouth to hers, and she realized that he wasn't going anywhere. There was no time to revel in that searing heat of his or the way his body felt against hers. There was no time to do anything, really, besides accept the demands he made, one after another.

One hand was in her hair, his fingers tugging at the short strands. His other hand wound toward her lower back, pulling her flush against him. His lips bypassed the playful nuzzling stage and pressed her own open, allowing him to sweep his tongue into her mouth until her head swam with possibilities.

In other words, he *kissed* her—not just a sample or a nibble, but a hot, throbbing, full-body demand that left her weak in the knees. It was also tender in ways she hadn't been expecting.

She would have had difficulty pinpointing exactly how that tenderness was taking shape. It was the way he cradled her in his arms, his body making a nest for her to burrow into, her limbs coiling into the warmth of him. It was the way his kiss moved away from her lips and along her jawline, soft pecks and light nibbles giving over to what she could have sworn was an actual bite on the curve of her neck. That was what *really* gave the show away.

He was tasting her, sampling her, devouring her.

Sophie had been kissed plenty of times before. In fact, she'd started young. The teenage cancer ward was a breeding ground of exploratory vice, so many of the kids unsure how much time they had left that they weren't leaving anything—including sex—up to chance.

But this? *Wow*. She wasn't sure she'd ever been devoured before.

"Holy crap, you're good at this," she said, and turned her head to give him better access to her neck. She also buried her hands in his hair, holding his head in place in case he got any funny ideas about stopping before things got really interesting. "Amazing, actually. Do you practice on your pillow at night or something?"

It was a good thing she'd had the foresight to hold on to him, because he tried lifting his head at that. "Yes. I routinely make out with my pillow. That's what we Sleeping Beauties do."

She moaned, letting him know she wasn't about to let him put a wall up against what had to be one of the hottest make-out sessions she'd had in a long time—or, you know, ever. She also pressed her hips against his, doing a lot more than moan when the hard line of his groin hit her right in the sweet spot. Would it be awful if she gyrated against him a few times? Just a little?

"Lucky pillow," she said, and this time, she was the one doing the kissing. She had to hitch a leg around the back of his thigh and tug on his hair to reach his lips, but it was well worth the effort when his mouth opened to let her in.

Harrison's hand naturally found its way to her leg, his wide palm searing her skin through the see-through panel. The sensation of tingling, liquid heat didn't abate any as his hand began moving in a determinedly upward direction, skimming along the rounded curve of her thigh until he was almost in derriere territory.

"Why, Harrison Parks," she chided—as much as a woman could chide when she was climbing a man like a tree. "Do you also feel your pillow up like that?"

"Every chance I get. Fortunately, it's not made of memory foam."

Oh dear. Harrison had just made a joke. He'd made a joke while his body burned against hers. She wasn't sure she could take this much novelty at once. The only solution, she decided, was to make a mad grab for the bottom of his T-shirt. As long as she was being shocked with revelations, she might as well get a glimpse of his abs too.

But he stopped her just as she managed to snake a hand against the flat, muscular plane of his abdomen. She caught a glimpse of the patch on his stomach where his pump attached, but that was all before his free hand pressed over the top of hers.

"I'm not some sad, solitary charity case, Sophie."

She knew, in a second, that she'd pushed too far. Instinct told her to say something playful and light, anything to get him back to the serious business of kissing her, but she took a deep breath and met his gaze instead. His eyes were still steely, still gray, but they weren't nearly as hard.

Swallowing heavily, she said, "Of course you're not."

His fingers tightened around hers, their hands near enough his waistband that there was no mistaking how much sexual urgency pulsated between them. "I'm serious. I know I'm not good at people, and I can come across all wrong sometimes, but I don't want you to think I'm…" He frowned, struggling to find the right word.

"Desperate?" she ventured.

He halted. "I'm not desperate."

"Alone?"

"I *am* alone most of the time, but I've always been that way."

"Human, then," she said, refusing to let him close back up. "Human and fallible and in need of a little comfort from time to time. Just like the rest of us."

It took him a long time to answer. *Too* long, making her fear that she'd made yet another misstep, forcing him to withdraw once more into his hard shell. But he drew a deep, shuddering breath and said the words she'd been waiting her whole life to hear.

Well, almost.

"No one is like you, Sophie," he said. "Thank God for us all."

Instead of backing away, he lifted his wide palm to her cheek. She readied herself for another kiss. Half of her hoped it would be one of those hard, fierce ones. The other half yearned for something tender and slow. But as they stood there together, Sophie's head cradled in Harrison's hand, all she got was a long, lingering stare.

Strangely enough, it was as powerful as the feel of Harrison's tongue sliding along hers. There was magnetism in those stony eyes of his, the lure of a powerful man drawing her in.

"How's the heart rate now?" she asked.

The question was mostly an excuse to place her hand against the hard swell of his chest, but it also served as a reminder that she had an actual job to do out here. As much fun as it would have been to have Harrison lift her against the rough side of this barn and ravish her until both of them were shaking and weak, she doubted even Dawn would approve of that methodology.

He remained silent.

"We should probably get running again," she continued with real reluctance. His heart was steady and strong, just like the rest of him, but it wouldn't remain that way indefinitely. Nothing could. "If we don't pop out of the forest soon, your dad's going to wonder what happened to us."

"I'm pretty sure he already knows," Harrison said, but he released his grip on her and stepped back. The physical separation was disquieting, like someone yanked a pile of warm blankets away. "He's the one who warned me in the first place."

"Warned you?" Sophie echoed. "About what?"

Harrison shook his head and turned to take off running once again. "I told you already. *Tablecloths*."

chapter
9

"Wool is going to be your warmest option, obviously, and it's good for beginners because it's so forgiving." Sophie took a few steps forward and started jabbing her finger at the colorful bundles lining the wall.

The *whole* wall. As in, a hundred feet of storefront, all of it lined with shelves and so tightly packed with yarn you could probably knit a scarf from here to the moon. Harrison couldn't decide if he was impressed or alarmed.

"Acrylic is lighter, so you might want to consider it for summer wear or if you plan to make Bubbles something purely decorative. It's also easier to work with if you're a beginner. If you care about sustainability, of course, you could always go for something organic and cotton. Now, me? I'm obsessed with this alpaca stuff right here. It can smell a little funny when you get it damp, but you get used to it after a while. It reminds me of wet dog—which, to be honest, is my standard eau du cologne." She turned to him with an expectant look on her face, eyes wide and her lips slightly parted. "Well? What'll it be? The pink wool? I feel like you've been eyeing the pink wool."

Harrison sighed. As far as he could tell, there were

twelve identical pink wools, each one looking more like bubblegum than yarn. "You're loving this, aren't you?"

"The yarn store? Um, yes. This is my happy place."

He paused, waiting for the rest of whatever Sophie had to throw at him, but she just kept watching him with that same earnest expectation. And joy—that's what that was on her face, what made her look so much like an angel atop a Christmas tree.

She wasn't kidding. She really loved yarn that much.

Since Sophie had decided that knitting was the only way—short of regularly making out in front of his barn—of breaking down his barriers and integrating Bubbles into his life, he turned his attention to the task at hand.

What other choice did he have? Yarn was a *much* safer activity than kissing.

"It's all the same to me, to be honest," he said. "Maybe I should let Bubbles pick, since she's the one who's going to have to wear it."

He didn't wait for an answer or look at Sophie, since he could guess how she looked right now.

Smiling. At him.

Laughing. At him.

"As much as you love your sock, Bubbles, Sophie said you don't look up to snuff. She thinks you need to be dressed up in handmade finery." He ignored the choking sound of Sophie's laughter behind him and picked up the puppy, who had been sitting patiently at his feet. Holding her up to the wall of yarn, he asked, "Which one do you like?"

Bubbles gave a Pomeranian squirm—a movement he was rapidly coming to realize was her standard

expression of joy. Since he had no other way to interpret her mysterious canine desires, he decided to go with
it, passing her over the wall and seeing which wooly
bundle caused her to wriggle the most.

"White?" he asked as she worked her way toward
a pearly, bridal-looking thing in one corner. "Are you
kidding? After Labor Day?" That was a thing, right? He
vaguely remembered that being a thing.

The choking sound became strangled.

"Pick something more practical, please," he admon-
ished the puppy. "Black is what I recommend. The color
of soot and ashes. You have no idea how hard those
are to get out of clothes after a few weeks of nonstop
exposure."

"Maybe fire engine red? That seems appropriate."
Sophie stepped forward to stand next to him. As he
expected, her voice and her shoulders were shaking with
laughter. "A lady always looks striking in red. They say
women who wear it are more attractive to members of
the opposite sex."

As Sophie had chosen to wear a deeply vibrant pair
of red pants that day, Harrison could only assume she
was pushing him again. The pants themselves weren't
overwhelming—other than the color, which drew the
eye inevitably toward the rounded curves of her ass, they
were like any other pair of pants. Except, for some godforsaken reason, they stopped just above Sophie's ankles.
Capri pants, he'd heard them called. In no way, shape,
or form an item of clothing to be sexualized—especially
since she'd paired them with a simple black T-shirt.

But damn. Every time she walked into his line of
vision, his gaze was drawn inexorably down to where

the flash of her ankles peeked above a pair of shiny, black heels. Like the rest of her body parts, those ankles looked sleek and delicate, and he wanted to explore them at his leisure.

Ankles of all fucking things. A few more weeks in this woman's company, and he was going to have to start asking people to cover their piano legs like some scandalized Victorian maiden.

"It's biological," Sophie added, continuing the conversation as though Harrison were taking part in it instead of growing hard while staring at a wall of yarn. He was beginning to realize what she saw in this place. "I read this study once that said women who are ovulating wear red without even realizing it. It's like an advertisement for fertility."

"I am *not* putting Bubbles in a walking fertility advertisement."

She giggled. "Dogs are mostly color-blind, so I think she'll be safe from all those unwanted male advances."

He turned on her with a glare. "Then what the devil are we doing in a yarn store picking out colors? You're telling me she can't tell the difference between any of these?"

"I mean, she might like the texture of some better than others. This one is awfully soft. It's like running your fingers through cotton candy. Here. Feel it."

Sophie grabbed his free hand and pulled it toward a bundle of yarn the exact same color as her pants. He knew she was doing it on purpose—this slow brush of her palm against his, this fingering of textiles that made his heart pound—but it didn't seem to matter. Whether playing or pushing, the results were always the same.

"See?" she said, casting a shy look up at him. Her

fingers slipped through his. "Who wouldn't want that against their bare skin?"

Harrison wanted to snatch his hand away, but he was stuck, transfixed by desire and his inability to withstand the power she had over him. He also wanted to tell her exactly what he was thinking: that cotton candy wasn't his vice. *Pulled taffy*—that was his poison, and that was exactly what Sophie felt like. Taut muscles and soft skin, the endless tugging and straining that happened whenever she drew near.

Naturally, he could say no such thing. Even if he *were* a master of oratory prowess, he had no way of knowing what that kind of reaction a declaration like that would elicit. Wide-eyed shock seemed a likely possibility. Revulsion was definitely a contender. Or Sophie might, as she was doing much more often these days, laugh.

Which was why the only thing that eventually left his lips was something gruff and inadequate to capture his feelings.

"Is all that why *you're* wearing red today?" he asked with a whirl of his finger in the direction of her legs.

Her hand twitched in his and her cheeks broke out in twin pink circles, but she didn't let go. It was as good a metaphor for this woman as anything. *Tenacious*, that was what she was. She had to be, to have stuck this thing out with him for this long.

"It was Dawn's idea," she said. "Which, since you've met her, I'm sure you can understand."

He didn't. Sophie's sisters hadn't seemed to be overly fond of red to him. In fact, the only thing he'd been able to glean during that painful session in their kitchen was that they were terrifying. "She seemed okay," he said, hedging.

Her mouth fell open in a slight part. "*Okay?* Dawn? The one with the wavy hair and killer smile?"

He nodded.

She stared at him for a moment, her eyes narrowing in disbelief. "That was your takeaway? After forty-five minutes in her company? That she's okay?"

He shrugged uncomfortably. "Why? Isn't she?"

The stare only intensified. "She's more than okay, Harrison. She's gorgeous and she's fun and everyone loves her. I mean that literally. *Everyone*. Wait—what did you think of Lila?"

"If I say she's okay, are you going to go off on me again?"

A light giggle escaped her lips. "I'm sorry. I'm just not used to anyone—any man, that is—meeting Dawn and not instantly falling in love with her. Lila too. She's the most beautiful person I know, both inside and out."

Harrison could have easily corrected her on this score. The Vasquezes were a well-formed lot, it was true, but he didn't see how anyone who'd spent five minutes in Sophie's company could prefer her sisters. Sophie's beauty was more subtle and delicate, yes, but it was all the more powerful because of it. Her feelings weren't a maze or a puzzle that a man had to figure out—they were right there on the surface, easy to interpret and free for anyone who cared to pick them up.

Most important, she was *kind*. To him and to animals, to his father and to everyone who crossed her path. Maybe that was a commonplace thing where she came from, but to him, it was like reaching an oasis after twenty years of dry, desert living.

"I hate to disillusion you when we're making such good headway, but this isn't my normal way of progressing through life," Sophie said. She tugged her lower lip between her teeth and fixed her gaze out the storefront window. "With *you*, I don't seem to have a problem asserting myself. With them, however... I don't know. It's like I'm powerless. Poor little Sophie Vasquez, always last choice, always third place."

Of all the harsh things Sophie had said to him in the course of this puppy training, none of them caused his insides to roil quite like that one. He'd willingly withstood everything she had to throw at him in the name of progress—Pomeranians and candles and bare fucking ankles—but this was where he drew the line.

"Sophie, I—" he began, but the words were difficult to get out. His tongue stuck to the roof of his mouth, all moisture sucked dry.

By the time he managed to figure out what came next—*Sophie, I want you; Sophie, I need you*—she'd dropped his hand and gasped at the sight of a flash moving across the street.

"Is that your dad?" she asked.

"What? Where?" His thoughts successfully diverted, Harrison craned his neck to get a better look. "That guy crossing the street? But he's..."

"Yeah, I know. Wearing normal human clothes."

The figure, who wore a checked shirt that looked freshly ironed, paused and turned. Only a fraction of a second passed before he turned again and trotted the rest of the way across the street, but it was enough for Harrison to confirm that it was, in fact, his father. Not only was his shirt ironed, but he had a clean pair of

Dickies on and his hair had been combed back with what looked like a whole can of styling product.

"I think he looks nice," Sophie said. "Maybe he has a date."

Harrison stared at her. Sophie was, without question, one of the most starry-eyed and optimistic souls he'd ever met, but even *she* couldn't take things that far. "Are you kidding? My father hasn't had a date since the eighties. He's a confirmed misogynist."

"No, he's not. He's just a little crusty. You both are. But believe me when I say it doesn't make either one of you unattractive." A shy gaze flicked up and down his body. "If anything, it only adds to your appeal."

His heart gave a stutter. "You think my dad is attractive?"

"Well, no. But that's only because I have my sights set on someone else."

He didn't ask. He couldn't. To hear those words out loud would only mean he'd have to face the reality of them and admit the truth.

He didn't just like Sophie anymore. He liked her *a lot*.

It was, without question, the worst thing that could have happened. This game of theirs—the push and pull, the breaking of barriers—was just that. A game. *Playing*, she'd called it. *Pushing this way. Playing a little*. Nowhere in that was there any hint of permanence. Nowhere in there did she promise anything more.

Fortunately, there were other issues he could focus on. None of them were more pressing than the desire that was taking over both his body and his reason, but he could pretend.

He had to.

"He told me he was going to the bar this morning," Harrison said.

"He goes to bars before noon?"

"Morning, noon, and night." He nodded. "I warned you that Parks men are no good. But he wasn't wearing that when he left this morning. In fact…"

He'd thought it was odd at the time, but his father had left the house wearing the exact same pair of overalls he'd had on yesterday. The man might dress like a farmer left out too long in the sun, but he was pretty fastidious about cleanliness. All those years in police uniform would do that to a man.

"What is it?" Sophie asked.

Harrison shook his head, hoping to corral his thoughts into order. Bubbles, Sophie, his dad, red pants—it was a lot to take in.

"Nothing. I just…" He frowned. "He *has* been going to the bar a lot lately. More than usual. But not even he can nurse a drink for ten hours every day, and what's he even doing in Spokane? He never leaves Deer Park unless he has no other choice."

A sound almost like a squeak left Sophie's mouth. "It *is* a date! A secret date he doesn't want you to know about."

He grunted to indicate how ridiculous he considered that idea.

She ignored it, latching on to the theme with an enthusiasm not even Bubbles could rival. "Do you think he met her online? Do you think they're Facebook friends? Ooh, do you think he Tinders?"

"Sophie Vasquez, if you know what's good for you, you will never refer to my dad and Tinder in the same sentence again."

She giggled. "What? Everyone has needs."

"Yes, and my father suppresses them the way all iso-lated, bad-tempered men do."

"Is that what you do?" she asked.

He didn't know how to answer her. It was the sort of question that would, a few weeks ago, have caused him to break down and turn off, storming away from the conversation. *Now*, however…

"Let's just get the stupid red cotton-candy yarn," he muttered.

That wasn't even close to what he wanted to say, but it was the only thing he could think of in the heat of the moment. Sophie said knitting would help relax him, so he'd knit. He'd knit until his fingers bled. He'd knit until he forgot how good it felt just to stand next to this woman in a yarn store, discussing his private life as though it were the most natural thing in the world.

He yanked the yarn from the shelf, almost bringing an entire rainbow column descending upon them both. It made him irrationally angry, to be felled by so much tantalizing softness, so he turned on Sophie with a glare. "But I want it stated for the record that if Bubbles turns into a wanton harlot after this, I'm holding you person-ally responsible."

"Got it." She held up her fingers in a mock Girl Scout salute. "As a wanton harlot myself, I promise to wel-come her to the ranks with open arms."

"Goddammit, Sophie! That isn't what I meant."

Her sparkling laughter caused several heads to turn their way. So much public scrutiny would normally have Harrison ducking into the back of the store, but all Sophie did was reach up on tiptoe and plant a kiss on his cheek. The soft press of her lips was quick and light, but it still had the power to ignite the desire that he no longer knew how to control.

He *would* control it though. He had to.

"I know it wasn't," she said, smiling up at him. "But I had to say something to do justice to Dawn's pants. You don't know her very well yet, but believe me when I tell you she'd be proud."

chapter

10

I *did* loop that piece around my finger, see? It fell off before I could hook it on the other thingy. Why do they make these needles so slippery?"

The woman sitting next to Harrison, who was guiding his large, rough hands under her own, clucked her tongue as he tossed the ruined knitting aside. "They have to be slippery, dear. Otherwise, they'd slow you down once you get the hang of it."

"*If* I ever get the hang of it," he said. "My hands are too damn big to do it right."

He cast an accusing look at Sophie, but she sent him an apologetic shrug in reply. Retaliation wasn't an option when her sister Dawn was sitting next to her, watching every interaction like it was a soap opera written especially for her. Dawn wasn't much of a knitter, but when Sophie told her that Harrison had not only agreed to come to the circle, but had chosen his own yarn for the occasion, she'd insisted on witnessing the event for herself.

Naturally, nothing Sophie could do or say would stop her.

"Nonsense," the woman said. "You're just not used

to it yet, that's all. Now try that bit again, and this time do it without all the damn profanity, if you please."

Harrison's rare smile lit his face. "Yes, ma'am. Sorry, ma'am. I'll do my best, ma'am."

He said something more, but Sophie was unable to distinguish it from where she sat on the other side of the church basement. The room where they'd gathered was large and damp and lit with an ancient fluorescent light that buzzed in and out like it had a dozen angry bees trapped inside. The lack of ambiance and stale scent of coffee didn't stop the half dozen women from meeting here every week to ply their needles making hats, scarves, and socks to be shipped off to those in need.

"Oh, wow," Dawn said in a low voice that bubbled over with laughter. "You were right about his smile, Soph. That's a hell of a thing for one man to wield."

Yes, Sophie was well aware of that fact. On Harrison, a smile wasn't just an expression of joy—it was a transformation. It was a momentary glimpse at a man who existed somewhere just beyond her reach.

"You'll notice that he didn't actually direct it at me," Sophie pointed out.

"Well, the smolder isn't bad either, so that's no real loss," Dawn said. "I finished this one. Hand me another, will you?"

Sophie paused knitting long enough to hand Dawn a tangled skein of yarn to unfurl and roll into a ball. Although Sophie had been knitting for years—a hobby developed during one of her many long stays in bed— her sister didn't have the patience to sit still for extended periods of time.

"How's the little darling doing, by the way?" Dawn asked.

For a moment, Sophie thought the little darling in question was Harrison, and she wasn't sure how to answer. As a client, Harrison was almost too good to be true. Oh, he grumbled, of course, but that was more from habit than a desire to prevent her from doing her job. Ever since that day in the yarn store, he'd done everything she'd asked with efficiency and a resolution that could only be described as *dogged*.

It was almost as though he was afraid of what would happen if he fought back again—of what he might do if he let Sophie push him into tearing down the wall one more time. He was subdued and compliant, determined not to let anything push him too far. Not even a shirt that opened at the back to reveal a strappy, crisscross patterned bra had been able to move him.

"She seems to be settling in well," Dawn continued. "Even Lila's starting to come around. She's no longer looking for families who might want to adopt her if everything fails."

Oh. Yes, Bubbles was the little darling. Because she was little. And a darling.

"Um." Sophie willed the blood away from her cheeks and said the first thing that popped into her mind. "She's doing great, just great. No problems, no worries."

"None at all?" Dawn asked without looking up from her pile of yarn.

"Well…"

Sophie bit her lip and pretended to work through a particularly complicated cable stitch. She'd never been a great liar, especially where her sisters were concerned, but she wasn't sure how to respond in a way that was truthful and wouldn't undermine her progress.

"To be honest, she's still wary of a few things," she said and superstitiously crossed her knitting needles since her fingers were busy.

"What kind of things?"

Oh, you know. Fire. Flames. The catastrophic infernos Harrison had dedicated his life to subduing.

"Um. She didn't react very well to a fire Harrison started in his fireplace one morning. She seems to be doing okay with your candles though."

"My candles? When has she been anywhere near my candles?"

"Didn't I tell you?" Sophie looked up at her sister with her most innocent expression. From the way Dawn was watching her, her eyes narrowed and her nose wrinkled at the tip, Sophie knew she was nearing trouble. "I took a few over as a...gift. To win over Harrison's dad. He likes the bergamot one. He says it helps him sleep."

"That's not a surprise, Soph. But they're awfully strong, and you know it's not a good idea to confuse the puppy's sense of smell this early on. Not while—"

"Of course I know that!" she protested. The moralizing note in Dawn's voice was veering far too close to Lila's for Sophie's peace of mind. "The ones in the rest of the house and Harrison's room are unscented. I'm not an idiot."

"Why do there need to be candles in Harrison's room at all?" The question was asked with heavy suspicion, but Dawn's imagination soon took over. "Ooh, don't tell me—I can make several guesses, and all of them are rated Not for Church Basements. You made it to the crop top already, didn't you?"

Sophie winced. Unfortunately, there was nothing sexy or fun about Harrison's bedroom candles. She had him lighting three of them at a time in there now. Bubbles seemed to tolerate them without too much fuss, but there was no denying she wasn't a fan. She had a tendency to turn her head away and burrow into Harrison's chest, pretending the flickering lights weren't there. She was like a child closing her eyes and willing the monster under the bed away.

In other words, the puppy was still scared, still a liability, still a failure on paper.

But paper only told part of the story. A person was more than the sum total of their awards and accolades, had more to offer than the sad, sorry tale told by their medical records. And so was a puppy.

All she needed was a few more weeks with Harrison and Bubbles, a few more weeks without a pair of well-meaning sisters peering over her shoulder. The trouble was convincing *them* of it.

"Dawn, I—"

A loud, impatient siren interrupted her before she could come up with a story that wouldn't perjure her soul.

Because the basement was isolated from the rest of the church, the red blaring lights and screaming whir hit as if from out of nowhere. However, not one of the ladies in attendance showed signs of distress. An introductory cooking class was held in the upstairs kitchen the same night as the knitting circle. Half the time, they got to sample an array of cookies and pancakes as they left for the evening. The other half of the time, someone burned the cookies and pancakes, and everyone had to immediately evacuate the building.

As the acrid scent of charred carbohydrates wasn't too far behind the whirring alarm, it seemed tonight was going to be one of the latter instances.

Ladies stabbed knitting needles into balls of yarn as they got to their feet, stretching and yawning and grumbling about which of the unfortunate pupils had done the damage this time. Sophie rose to join them only to glance over at Harrison and realize her mistake.

Or, to put it more accurately, she glanced over at *Bubbles* and realized her mistake. The puppy, already showing signs of distress at the loud noises and sudden commotion, had also noticed the shifting scent in the air. All the fur on her little body stood on end, and even Sophie had to admit that her eyes looked an awful lot like sad raisins.

"Sad, *wet* raisins," she said with a groan.

"What are you talking about?" Dawn asked, but there was no time to answer her. The moment everyone started shuffling for the stairs, the puppy decided she wasn't about to be abandoned to the fire and left for dead. Harrison reached for her, his arms swooping down to rescue her from the terrors all around, but it was no use.

With one last scared yip of protest, Bubbles tore away.

Sophie was closest to the stairs, so she jumped up to try and head Bubbles off. All she managed to do was run into the nice woman who'd been teaching Harrison how to knit, almost knocking her over in the process. The skitter of puppy nails on wood stairs indicated that Sophie was going to have to move faster if she planned on catching Bubbles before the animal escaped somewhere with *real* hazards.

She was halfway up the stairs before she realized she wasn't alone in her pursuit. Harrison's tread was surprisingly light for a man his size, and he reached the door at the top of the stairs the same time she did.

"You'd better let me." His hands came down on either side of her waist and lifted her neatly out of the way. The ease with which he was able to physically set her aside, his palms almost spanning her waist, was impressive. "I'll be able to catch her faster on my own. She won't want a search party after her."

"Now isn't the time to play hero, Harrison." She clutched at his forearm. "The *street*."

He caught her meaning in an instant. The church was located on a fairly busy street off the freeway, which meant cars zipped by much faster than they would have on an ordinary city road. With everyone filing in and out of the building, it would be all too easy for Bubbles to head outside and straight into traffic.

"She won't—" he began, his face pale.

"She might."

Without another word, they both pushed through the doorway, heedless of the way their bodies pressed together, fitting so perfectly they might have been built to squeeze and slide as one.

"I'll take the north exit," Harrison said, his voice clipped. "You go through the back hallway and take the south. She won't go in the direction of the kitchen—not while there's smoke. Two long whistles if you find her. Three if she makes it outdoors. I'll do the same."

He turned on his heel and moved off in the direction

he'd indicated, not checking over his shoulder to make sure Sophie was following his instructions. There was no need. Harrison's abrupt manner might not have made him the easiest man to get to know, but there was no denying its power. Sophie had been attending knitting circle in this church for two years and couldn't have mapped all the exits if she wanted to. He had appraised the building at a glance.

It was impossible not to feel reassured by his commands, empowered by his confidence. Whatever else one could say about the man, he knew his fire safety.

Sophie pushed past several people evacuating in the opposite direction, determined to do justice to Harrison's faith in her ability to rescue his puppy. The back hallway was long, but it was empty, which made searching it easy. There was nowhere for Bubbles to cower and hide, nowhere she could take cover during a mad dash to safety. The door at the end of the hallway was still closed, and the emergency exit alarm untriggered.

"Bubbles!" Sophie called, not expecting an answer but determined to do something anyway. "Come on out, love. The fire's all gone now. You're safe."

No yapping response or puppy whimper met her ears. She spun on her heel, holding her breath as she waited for any kind of whistle from Harrison, but all she could hear was the clamoring fire alarm in the distance.

"Think, Sophie," she commanded herself. "You're tiny, you're terrified, and you're in a strange place. Where do you go?"

The answer to that question was more difficult to come up with than she would have thought. Tiny and terrified were two things she'd felt more times than she cared to admit, and it hadn't been uncommon for her to fall asleep in one hospital only to wake up in another halfway across the state.

But she'd never really been alone when it happened. If her sisters or parents hadn't been hovering anxiously nearby, there had been scores of friendly nurses and doctors, every one armed with a smile and a promise that they'd take care of her, and would she like a warm blanket to help her feel better?

But Bubbles hadn't had that. She spent her first few months of life isolated and ignored, curled up in a wire cage that offered no protection or comfort. She craved small, dark spaces and warmth. She wanted to feel less alone, if only for a few minutes.

"The ruffled bedroom," Sophie said aloud. She might not have known all the fire exits in this church, but she did recall once seeing a nursery. A cursory peek inside had revealed several cribs, toy boxes, and play structures to keep the little ones entertained during the service.

It also had a ruffled toddler bed for anyone who needed an impromptu nap. She wasn't sure what it was about those swaying bits of fabric that appealed to the puppy, but they did. If that was the first place she went in Harrison's house, there was a good chance she'd do the same thing here.

Sophie found the nursery behind the third door she checked. It was slightly ajar, which made her think she was on the right track—a feeling that intensified at the sound of a light snuffling. As was the case the last time she'd found Bubbles in this situation, she dropped to her stomach and scooted under the bed, lulling the puppy with a conversation that was mostly nonsense.

"There you are, my precious," she said, wincing at the pitiful image of the Pomeranian curled in on herself in the corner. "You're pretty fast for such a small thing — has anyone ever told you that? You knew there was danger the second you smelled smoke, and you reacted without even thinking about it. That's what makes you such a good alert dog, you know. You see a thing that needs to be done, and you do it. No questions, no doubts. I envy that about you."

"Uh, Soph?" Dawn's voice came from behind her.

Sophie stuck a hand out from under the bed and waved her sister away. "That's my sister you hear out there, Bubbles. If she knows what's good for her, she'll stand exactly where she is and be quiet, so you don't get even more scared."

Dawn took the hint. Sophie proceeded to spout more nonsense, mostly about knitting and dog sweaters and some people's inability to follow the simplest of recipes without burning a church down. Bubbles relaxed a little, but she didn't show a desire to leave her safe haven.

That didn't happen until a gruff voice sounded overhead, causing them both to perk up.

"Goddammit, Sophie. What part of two whistles didn't you understand?"

Strong hands clamped around her ankles and pulled her out from under the bed. She barely had time to register what was happening before Harrison let go.

He didn't, as expected, drop to his knees next to her to grab Bubbles for himself. Instead, he planted his booted feet firmly on the ground and said, his low voice rumbling. "Be quiet, Bubbles. And get out from under there."

"You can't—" Sophie began, but the dog's gentle whimpering stopped almost immediately.

"*Out*, Bubbles. I've had just about enough of your antics for one day."

The soft skitter of nails over linoleum sounded from under the bed skirt. Seconds later, the puppy's small, twitching nose peeked out into the open.

"Come," he said. "Sit."

Sophie watched from her perch on the floor as the commands she'd been working so hard to instill in both man and beast worked to perfection. Harrison might sound gruff and rough, but Bubbles knew that voice, took comfort in that voice.

She came. She sat. And she waited, looking expectantly at her owner as though he contained the answers to all the world's problems.

He paused just long enough to murmur a commendatory *good girl* before sweeping the puppy into his arms and turning his anxiety on Sophie instead. He'd all but forgotten about Dawn standing in the doorway watching the pair of them, a look of intense curiosity rendering her more silent than usual.

"Is this what we're training her to do?" Harrison demanded. Fear made his expression harsher than usual, lines of worry pulling his mouth down at the corners. "To run away from me at the first sign of danger?"

Sophie hated to see him like this. Not the bluster, which was only to be expected from a man like this one, but the worry. The *pain*. Bubbles had obviously wormed her little way much deeper into his heart than she'd ever thought possible.

"She's not hurt, Harrison," she said, her voice gentle.

"That's the most important thing. A little shaken, yes, but none the worse for her adventure."

"*Adventure?*" he echoed. "Is that what you'd call this?"

"Yes, actually. I would. At least she came out from under the bed willingly this time." Sophie got to her feet with a brush of her knees and a squaring of her shoulders. Already, Harrison was looking less like a man who'd been pulled back from the edge of a cliff. "And she didn't try to escape, which is a plus. She follows a pattern when she's scared. Patterns are good. Patterns are predictable. I can work with patterns."

"Abject fear is not a pattern. It's a problem."

."Not paying taxes is a problem. Yelling at your very expensive and highly professional dog trainer is a problem."

His lips began their telltale quiver. "I wasn't going to yell."

"Yes, you were. You've been wanting to do it all day. Think about how much you hate knitting. Think about all those eensy-weensy loops and tangles in your big man hands."

"Nice try, Sophie, but you can't break me with yarn."

She thought she heard a chuckle from her sister's direction, but she didn't dare pull her gaze from Harrison's. This wasn't at all how she'd choose to break down Harrison's walls, but there was no denying that they were crashing down around them.

"I, on the other hand, am an amazing knitter," Sophie continued. "I could make you and Bubbles matching rainbow glitter sweaters by tomorrow."

"I wish you would. I love rainbows."

"Hats too," she warned. "And I can make you wear

them as part of your training. If I tell Oscar it's necessary for bonding purposes, you know he'll back me up. Matching hats and sweaters for every day of the week."

"I know what you're trying to do, and it's not going to work."

"Are you sure about that? It sounds an awful lot like it's working."

And it did. The more they stood there talking, the more Harrison's smile widened, his eyes lighting with laughter. If they had time, she would have turned around and demanded that Dawn take a good look at those eyes. Her sister might think Harrison's smile was dangerous, but Sophie found that lurking twinkle to be much more powerful.

He could be happy, if only he'd let himself. If only he'd let me in.

He squared his stance to meet hers, Bubbles held under one of his arms like a football. With his broad shoulders and menacing air, he might have been preparing to tackle any number of oversize defensive linemen.

But he wasn't. He was preparing to tackle *her*.

And if the look on his face was anything to go by, he knew he was up against a formidable foe.

"You, Sophie Vasquez, are nothing more than a tyrant." He took a step forward, drawing so close their toes bumped. His were encased in steel-toed boots and big enough to give Sasquatch a run for his money; hers were daintily shod in ballet flats with vibrant teal bottoms.

"A tyrant?" she echoed. "Me?"

"Yes, you. You're a tyrant and a deceptively innocent tormentor who delights in making me dance at her bidding."

"Getting better." She tilted her head up to his. "Keep going. What else am I?"

"A devil. A fiend. A hellhound in puppy's clothing." Each word was quieter than the one before, as though he was wooing her with sweet nothings. They felt like that too, his gruff voice causing a ripple of delight to shiver up and down her spine. "In other words, you're my worst nightmare."

She swallowed heavily, unable to look away from the intensity of his gaze. She'd thought his kisses by the barn had devoured her, but they had nothing on this total engulfing of her soul. In all her life, she'd never felt this powerful, this beautiful.

This strong.

"Anything else?" Her voice was hoarse.

"It'll never work." For the first time since this whole conversation had turned, he didn't sound playful. Nor was he his usual rough and grumble self. In fact, he'd never sounded more earnest. "That's the one thing I can guarantee. No matter how hard you fight or how many times you try, I'll never be anything but *this*. The sooner you realize it, the better it will be for both of us."

A gasp from the doorway caught her attention before she could process anything Harrison had just said. She turned, prepared to scold Dawn for what had to be the worst timing known to womankind, only to find that two of the ladies from the knitting circle had joined her. Her sister appeared to be doing her best to usher them out of the room, but it would take someone much more determined than Dawn to get rid of a busybody like Paulette.

"Well, I never," Paulette said, a hand clutched to her throat. She wasn't wearing a pearl necklace—she was more of a New Age, healing-crystal sort—but the idea was the same. "Sophie, honey, we came to ask if you needed any help with that puppy. I can see we're not a moment too soon."

Sophie bit back a groan. "I'm fine, Paulette. Hey, Hilda. As you can see, we found Bubbles safe and sound. Is the kitchen fire all cleared?"

She'd hoped the change of subject would encourage the women to move on, but Paulette pushed past Dawn and planted herself in the center of the room. She wasn't a large woman, but she was a formidable one. It was the result of forty years working as the charge nurse on the pediatric cancer ward. She mothered and bullied in equal proportions.

Sophie had known her for just about forever. In fact, Paulette was the one who taught her how to knit in the first place. *You can either knit or sit around this hospital room feeling sorry for yourself, Ducky. And I, for one, am getting sick of all the moping.*

"I don't think I care for the way this young man was talking to you," Paulette said. "Why don't you come with me, and I'll see both you and your sister safely home?"

"There's really no need—" Sophie began, but Paulette cut her short.

"I'm sure it's what your mother would want me to do. We won't take no for an answer, will we, Hilda?"

Sophie cast a silent plea in Dawn's direction, but all her sister could do was mouth an apology and shrug. Sophie was just as powerless in this situation. If there was a way to oust a well-meaning family friend who had held and rocked her during her worst moments, then it was a way Sophie had yet to discover.

She was hemmed in on all sides and had been for as long as she could remember. Had there been a villain in her story, a malicious being she could stand up to once and for all, she would have banished him years ago.

But she didn't have a bad guy. She had good guys. Dozens of them. She had people like Paulette and Hilda, Lila and Dawn, her parents, even, to some extent, Oscar. Each and every one of them would put their life on the line to keep her safe, and they had no qualms about making sure everyone knew it.

What they couldn't understand, however, was that Sophie didn't want to be safe.

She wanted to be *set alight*.

"She's right," Harrison said, his voice quiet but determined. "It's not a good idea to leave you here with me."

Sophie whirled on him. The overwhelming solicitude from family and friends she could bear—she didn't like it, but she could bear it.

But not from Harrison. *Never* Harrison. That was what made him so incredible. He didn't look at her and see a hundred-and-ten-pound weakling who needed to be shielded from the world. He saw a strong, confident woman who had the power to seduce him. He saw someone to fear, to fight, and maybe even to fuck.

And, oh, how she wanted to *be* that strong, confident woman bringing him to his knees. She wanted it more than she'd ever wanted anything in her life.

"Don't," she said, her voice dangerous.

He didn't flinch. "Go with your friends and family. We've done enough work here for one day."

"So help me, if you take their side in this—"

"You'll what, Sophie?" he asked. This time, his voice

carried only kindness, his eyes touched with a smile. "Tell Oscar on me? Take my puppy away again?"

It was impossible not to answer that smile with one of her own. "Don't think I won't," she warned. There were a dozen other things she longed to say—a dozen other things that needed to be addressed between them—but this was neither the time nor the place. And Harrison, for all his self-professed inability to understand people, knew it.

That's because he does *understand me.*

"You and Bubbles should take a long weekend," she eventually said. "Relax. Unwind. Have fun. We'll pick up where we left off on Monday."

Paulette's *harrumph* signaled her displeasure with this plan, but Sophie wasn't moved.

"I *will* be there," she said, just in case he thought this was the last of the conversation. "And we *will* figure out what to do next about all this."

To the bystanders in the room, *all this* could have easily meant Bubbles and the fire, the fact that Sophie was training a dog for a job that it appeared to have no qualifications to hold. To Harrison, however, her meaning was clear. She knew it the moment he caught her eye and nodded his consent.

"Sure thing, Soph," he said. "We'll take care of it first thing on Monday."

chapter
11

"Surprise, my darling!" Sophie's mom stood on the front porch, her arms flung out and a beaming smile on her face. Those two signs were ominous enough on their own, but they were accompanied by a stack of suitcases more suitable to a lengthy cruise than a brief visit. Her next words confirmed it. "I've come to batten myself on you and the girls for a few weeks. I hope you don't mind."

"Mom!" Sophie cried, and then, because it was the only thing she *could* say, "Of course I don't mind. But I don't understand. I thought you were going with Dad on his sabbatical to Greece."

Her mom engulfed her in a warm hug, the lavish scent of her floral perfume blanketing them both. "I know, and I was so looking forward to it, but I've had this dratted tickle in the back of my throat I can't seem to shake. You know how hard your father goes when he's out in the field. My immune system would never be able to catch up."

While it was true that Victor Vasquez had a tendency to lose himself in his antiquity studies whenever he slipped off the collegiate leash, her mother had never looked in better health. Not even the fake cough she remembered to emit a few seconds later was enough to convince Sophie that this was anything but a ploy.

"Lila called you, didn't she?" Sophie asked.

"I don't know what you're talking about. Lila never tells me anything. That girl is an oyster."

"Dawn." Sophie clenched her hands. "The sneak. What did she say?"

Her mother adopted her loftiest pose. "Dawn doesn't tell me anything either. None of my daughters do. I might as well be in my grave for all they care about involving me in their lives."

She added a disdainful sniff for good measure. It was a good look on her—like her daughters, Alice Vasquez was a beautiful woman. Her hair was a light brown that her hairstylist kept from fading into gray, and strategic makeup applications and good lighting held her crow's feet at bay. Her figure was still the envy of many, if a little more on the buxom side than in her youth, and she dressed with the ease of one who'd had a lifetime to learn what suited her best.

In other words, her mother was an impressive woman—confident and elegant and controlled in all the ways Sophie would never be.

"I don't understand. If neither one of them ratted me out, who called you?"

"If you must know, I had a chat with Paulette late last night."

"I should have guessed," Sophie groaned, but she pushed the door open to let her mom in anyway. If there was one thing she'd learned from long experience, it was that her mother wouldn't be shaken off easily. If Sophie wanted to put her on a plane bound for the

Mediterranean—and she wanted nothing more—it would take a concentrated effort on her part.

"It wasn't me." Dawn sprang from the couch the moment Sophie and her mom struggled into the living room under the weight of all the luggage. "I have an alibi. Three of them."

"Honestly, you're both acting as though I'm not welcome." Alice pulled a genuine frown. "I know I'm only your fusty old parent, but I thought it would be nice to spend some time together. Just the four of us girls, you know? Shopping, a spa day or two, maybe a weekend trip to Seattle. We haven't done anything like that in ages."

Sophie instantly felt guilt-ridden. Even though her parents only lived twenty minutes away, she didn't spend nearly as much time with them as she should have—especially since her mom's entire life revolved around her daughters. Or *daughter*, rather. While she was an affectionate parent to all of her offspring, there was no denying that the bulk of her maternal worries had been tied up in Sophie for so many years that it was impossible for her to shake the habit. She'd even given up her career as nonprofit executive to take care of Sophie, which meant that now, at fifty-eight, she had little to occupy her time.

Other than, you know, stopping by for unannounced visits that lasted weeks at a time.

"What did Paulette tell you?" Sophie motioned for Dawn to resume her seat on the couch. Her mom didn't follow suit. Instead of sitting in her favorite floral armchair, she elected to stand there among her suitcases, looking like the picture of staged rejection.

"That daughter of hers just had twins. Did she show you

the pictures? She's up to eight grandchildren now. It must be so wonderful, being surrounded by all those babies…"

"Mom."

"What? It's not unusual, you know, for a woman of my age to fantasize about grandchildren. You'd have thought, with three daughters of a marriageable age…"

"*Mom*." Dawn was the one who spoke up this time.

"Oh, I know. The marriage part isn't required in this day and age, but it would be so nice to see at least one of you settled down. Lila would be such a responsible parent. And you, Dawn, have so many men to choose from."

"Gee, thanks," Sophie said dryly. She studiously avoided her sister's eye for fear that tacit commiseration would cause them both to break out into laughter. That or tears. "Does this mean I'm the one who's been chosen to grow into lonely spinsterhood and take care of you and Dad in your old age?"

Her mother's cluck was neither an assent nor a denial. It lay somewhere in between, a confirmation that whatever else Sophie was—or wasn't—she'd never be like her sisters. Her life had never been one of independence and adventure. And if her relatives had their way, it never would be.

Even though no one in this room had said the word *cancer*—or even alluded to it—it was still everywhere around them. In the extra wrinkles around her mom's mouth, where frowns had outpaced smiles for seven long years. In the way Dawn sat with her body angled on the edge of the couch, ready to jump to Sophie's aid should Alice's care get too officious. The room itself was a testament to everything this family had sacrificed for her. Her sisters would have happily gone off to live in separate apartments, but no one had felt comfortable with the idea of Sophie being on her own, so their parents had put a down payment on a lovely house with a kennel out back.

Oh, how she loved these people. And, oh, how she resented them.

"I don't care what you do as long as you're happy," her mom said. Then, in direct contradiction to this, she added, "I also talked to Oscar this morning."

Sophie passed a hand over her eyes. This was so much worse than she'd feared.

"You know I like to check in with him every few weeks to see how he's doing," her mom said, fully on the defensive. "I worry about him, living all alone as he does."

It was true. Poor Oscar had no idea what he'd gotten into the day he'd agreed to meet the girl whose life he'd saved. Not everyone agreed to the patient-donor meetings, since they could come with quite a bit of awkwardness, but her mother had been determined to thank Sophie's savior in person. That had been ten years ago, and thanking him had been the least of it. Oscar was now invited to every holiday gathering, sent homemade baked goods at least every other week, and received regular phone calls from the family matriarch to ensure he didn't want for anything.

The Vasquez family didn't do things by halves. They were like a gang that way. Once you were in, it was a lifetime deal.

"He told me he has you helping him with a little project," Alice continued.

Dawn snorted. "*Little* isn't the word I'd use to describe him."

Sophie shot her sister a warning look, but the damage was already done.

"Oh?" their mother asked, her intense gaze shifting to Dawn. "So you *had* met the man before yesterday?"

"Of course. He stopped by that first day to apologize after Sophie yelled at him."

"Sophie Josephine! You yelled at a client?" Her mother's surprise lasted all of two seconds before it took a sharp turn. "Why? What did he do?"

"I didn't yell at him," Sophie protested, her cheeks flushed at the memory. "It was more like a strongly worded conversation. Harrison is…difficult."

"Difficult?" her mom echoed. She gave Dawn a questioning look. "What does that mean?"

"Don't ask me. I'm not the one working with him. But he didn't check off any of my serial killer boxes, so I'm sure Sophie will come out of this with all her skin intact."

"I'm not sure I trust your serial killer checklist, my love. I've met some of the men you've dated."

"It means exactly what you already wrangled out of Oscar and Paulette, Mom," Sophie said with what she considered admirable patience. "He's a large man, yes, and it takes him a while to warm up to people. But it's not a big deal, I promise. I can handle him."

Her mother clucked in a way that could denote either sympathy or disbelief but was most likely a combination of the two. "Maybe you should hand this off to one of your sisters, sweetie. I know you mean well, but you don't have Dawn's experience when it comes to this sort of thing. Or Lila's firm hand."

"He's not a problem," Sophie said, this time through her teeth. She *knew* she wasn't as competent as her sisters. She *knew* she never would be. But she still deserved a life of her own, no matter how small.

Ironically enough, Harrison would have been the first to back her up on that. He was so used to seeing her assert herself, watching as her self-confidence unfurled, that he probably wouldn't recognize the woman she was when her family was around. He might not even *like* her when her family was around.

To be perfectly honest, she wasn't sure she liked herself that way.

"You know what?" Sophie said, feeling a sudden urge to push back. "I like him. He works hard and he's good with the puppy. He's also a really good kisser, in case you were wondering."

This time, her mother's clucking sound was closer to a growl. Sophie recognized that growl—knew it down to her bones. It was the sound of a mama bear awakening from hibernation. In a few seconds, the bear would be fully awake, prepared to throw herself on anyone who dared to even *look* at her precious cub the wrong way.

Which was why Sophie decided to take matters into her own hands. Too many people—herself included—had been suffocated by that bear. All she wanted was a chance to *breathe*.

Throwing caution and common sense to the wind, she added, "Besides, it doesn't matter if he'd be better off with Dawn or Lila. It's too late. We've already started the more specialized training. To back off now would only compromise the relationship between Harrison and Bubbles, which the puppy's fear of fire has already strained."

"But—" her mother began.

She was on a roll now and doubted whether she could stop even if she wanted to. "In fact, we've decided the best thing to do to help Bubbles get over it is for me to live in for the duration of the training."

Both women swiveled to stare at her.

"Live in?" her sister echoed.

"You can't!" her mother cried.

Sophie held up a hand to stop them both. She was proud to note that it didn't waver in the slightest. "*Stop*, you guys. Lila did it last year with that nervous bichon, and no one said anything. You know it's our standard operating procedure. If the puppy or the owner has difficulty adjusting, the trainer should be there as much as possible, even if that means around the clock."

Both women opened their mouths to protest, but Sophie didn't let them speak. She *couldn't*. She knew exactly what would happen if she did. They'd talk her back from the ledge, pull her into their arms, and stuff her with cookies and rainbows and promises that everything would be okay.

She liked cookies, and rainbows were pretty, but things weren't always okay. Life was hard and messy and, where Harrison was concerned, a bit of a battleground.

And that, to be perfectly honest, was just fine with her.

"Well, I'm finally going to admit it," she announced. "This puppy has difficulties. A lot of them, actually, and I'm still not a hundred percent sure she's going to work out. If Bubbles is going to battle forest fires someday, she'll need lots of extra attention and lots of extra time. And I'll have to do a few nights for the scent training anyway. It makes sense for me to stay there."

"But he's practically a stranger," her mom said. "And

Paulette said she'd never heard such language before."
She looked to Dawn for support. "Honey, she can't do
this. Tell her."

Dawn appeared to struggle with herself. She was by
far the most forgiving and fun-loving of all Sophie's
family members, but old habits died hard. She looked
back and forth between them for a few seconds before
shrugging and giving in. "How bad can he be? I mean,
he's a friend of Oscar's."

"Yes, and Lord knows there isn't anything I wouldn't
do for that man, but this is taking things too far. Sophie's
not like you. She's not—"

Help came from an unexpected source, stopping their
mother before she made the mistake of finishing that
statement—not that Sophie needed to hear the rest. She
already knew all the things she wasn't: self-sufficient,
significant, *strong*.

"It's not our decision to make though, is it?" Lila
stood in the doorway to the kitchen, an apron over her
clothes and a dishrag in her hands. Her sister must have
been in there the entire time, listening in. "Soph, I'm
assuming you already cleared it with the client?"

Sophie, who had done no such thing, nodded a solemn
lie. She was too surprised by Lila's championship to
do more. In personal and familial situations, there was
nothing her sister wouldn't have done to support her.
Professional situations, however, were another story.
Lila was a stickler for doing things by the book. She
loved rules the way most people loved cupcakes—or,
you know, puppies.

"If it's in the best interest of the placement, then it's
the right call." Lila took one look at their mother's face

and laughed. "Relax, Mom. She's twenty-six years old. She'll be fine."

"Yes, but her health. If something should happen—"

"The client has been diabetic nearly his entire life. I'm pretty sure he knows how to call an ambulance."

Sophie had never felt so lifted up—or so close to being crushed. Lila and Dawn providing their support without once questioning her professional judgment was everything she'd ever wanted out of Puppy Promise. No one was reprimanding her for her handling of the case; no one was doubting her ability to make it work. It would have been her idea of heaven, if not for the fact that she *didn't* need to live out at Harrison's house.

Nor, she suspected, would she be particularly welcome.

"Don't worry, Mom," Dawn added. "You can still stay here with me and Lila, and we'll do all the spa days you want. Look at her face—have you ever seen anyone who needs it more? There were three new wrinkles around her eyes this morning. I counted."

Lila, who had the smooth, unruffled beauty of a woman ten years her junior, gave a grimace. She also tossed the dish towel at Dawn's head. "Just for that, I'm not finishing the dishes. You can eat off dirty plates for the rest of the day."

But Dawn tossed the towel to their mother, passing it on like a game of Hot Potato. "What good is having Mom come to stay unless we make her earn her keep? Don't worry, Sophie—we'll have her regretting her decision before the weekend's up."

Alice laughed obligingly, but there was no mistaking her worried expression. She'd come all this way to rescue her beloved daughter, and she rarely backed down from a mission until she'd seen it all the way through.

"You didn't really kiss that man, did you, Sophie?" she asked. "That was just a joke?"

Sophie paused, unsure how to tackle this rocky territory. She wanted to spare her mother's feelings, of course, but not at the cost of her freedom. It was too powerful, too alluring, too *new*.

In the end, she decided to trample forward. After all, it was exactly what she would have done to Harrison in this situation.

"Oh, I kissed him, all right," she said. "And if I have my way, I fully intend to do it again."

chapter 12

"Sit. Stay. Blink. Breathe."

Bubbles followed each of Harrison's commands in succession, though he doubted he had much to do with those last two.

"Good girl," he said and gave his finger a twirl. "*Now* you may show me your outfit."

It was the moment Bubbles had been waiting for. The woman who'd been teaching him how to knit had gifted him a minuscule yellow sweater that the puppy had been dying to try on. Personally, he thought the sweater made her look like a piece of dryer lint, but Bubbles had never been so happy. He could almost swear she knew the difference between wearing a sock and sauntering about in doggy couture.

She spun three times in succession before stopping with a wag of her tail. Lifting her head, she waited for the inevitable praise—and treat.

He bestowed both with a lavish hand.

"Yes, yes. I know. You're beautiful and charming, and you won over every woman in that knitting circle with one friendly smile." He sighed and tried to

discreetly tug the box of supplies closer to them. "You
and Sophie have that in common."

The trust Bubbles had in him was so absolute that she
didn't question the cardboard box sneaking closer to his
side. He almost wanted to warn the poor creature—*I'm
not to be trusted; I'm going to betray everything*—but he
kept his lips sealed.

"Now, I know it's cruel to give a gift with strings
attached, but I'm going to do it anyway," he warned
the puppy.

Bubbles cocked her head.

"And you're not going to like these strings, but there's
nothing I can do about that. Life is hard sometimes. It's
just a thing we have to get used to."

A loud snort sounded behind them. "I see you're
imparting all your life wisdom to your offspring now,"
his dad said. He stood in the doorway to the living room,
leaning a little *too* casually on the frame for it to be a
natural pose. "Don't be surprised if she chucks it all in
your face. That's what children do."

"Noted, Dad. Thanks."

"What are you doing, anyway? It looks like you're
going to light a fire in the grate."

Harrison sighed again. "That's because I *am* going
to light a fire in the grate." For some reason, putting the
action into words felt like just as much of a betrayal as
the actual task. Bubbles knew it too—her head cocked
in alarm.

His dad paused for an ominously long moment.
"Sophie know what you're doing?"

And there it is. "Nope."

"Don't you think you should check with her first?"

"Nope."

"I think you should check with her first."

Harrison gave an involuntary chuckle. It wasn't just the knitting circle ladies who would have gladly laid their lives on the line for Sophie's sake. Or Oscar. Or, Harrison was forced to admit, himself. His dad had clearly fallen under the same spell as the rest of them.

Not that he'd ever tell her as much out loud. He'd seen that look on her face yesterday when those two ladies had rushed to her rescue. No woman had ever wanted to be rescued less.

No woman had ever *needed* to be rescued less too.

"I know, but I want to surprise her," Harrison said.

He'd hoped that would be the end of the conversation, but his dad pushed off the doorframe and drew closer to examine the box's contents. "That's not going to make much of a blaze," he said.

Yes, well, that was the whole point of this exercise. A small fire. A small step. A small gift.

It wasn't much, but Harrison had racked his brain trying to come up with a way to show his appreciation for everything Sophie was doing for him. Gift-giving had never been his forte, but even he knew that the standard offerings—money, a thank-you card, jewelry, hand-knit yellow dog sweaters—wouldn't suffice. Not when the thing she was giving him was so huge.

And he didn't mean the stupid weekend off. That was more punishment than gift: Friday, Saturday, Sunday. Three whole days of boring, quiet, *empty* living without her in it. It had only been one night, and he was already feeling the burden of it. He and Bubbles had enjoyed a long heart-to-heart last night about the merits of square-shaped versus circular kibble. This morning, their talk centered mostly on the crossword puzzle on the back of the cereal box.

In other words, Harrison was just as pathetic a man now as he'd been a month ago. The only difference was he knew it now.

So he'd use his three days, dammit. He'd use them hard. Since the day he'd walked into her kennel, Sophie had pushed him and encouraged him, supported him and yelled at him.

But more than that, she *believed* in him.

No one had ever believed in him before, and he wasn't sure how to repay her. All he had to offer her was this one small thing, this one small success. He'd give it to her too. He'd give it to her if he had to sit here in front of the fireplace every day for the rest of his life, encouraging Bubbles to draw just a little bit closer to the flames.

They might burn you, little one, but that's the cost of being warm. That's the cost of being alive.

"Well, I'll leave you to it," his dad said with a shake of his head. "But don't say I didn't warn you. You're fighting a losing battle."

"Believe me, Dad, I know," he replied. "But I'm going to fight it anyway."

❖ ❖ ❖

"What do you mean, you're not coming?" Derek Williams, a man Harrison would normally be glad to see standing on his front porch with a giant cooler and a fishing tackle box, frowned and set his burdens down. "It's our annual trip. If we don't go before the fire season starts, we won't have another chance."

"I'm sorry." Harrison could hear the skittering of tiny claws over the hardwood floors and angled the door more closely shut behind him. "I wish I could, but I have a thing."

"A thing?" Derek lifted one of his brows and tried peering around the door. "What kind of thing?"

"A personal thing."

"False. You've never had a personal thing a day in your life. You're the least sociable man I've ever known. What are you hiding back there?"

"Nothing," Harrison insisted—a lie that was quickly followed by a small thump as Bubbles made it to the door. *Damn.* She must have gotten through his kitchen barricade. That was the problem with rodent-size dogs: they could worm their way through the unlikeliest places.

"It doesn't sound like nothing." Derek put a hand on the door and gave it a nudge. Fortunately, Harrison was expecting it. He was also a good forty pounds heavier than the other man, which meant his hold on the doorknob remained fast.

Like most of his friends, Derek was part of the wildland fire crew, composed of equal parts muscle and nerve. Also like most of his friends, Derek was a persistent bastard. The two men had traveled through the fiery gates of hell together so many times it was impossible to maintain anything resembling emotional distance.

A small whimper, almost humanlike, emitted from the tiny open crack.

Derek's eyes lit up. "Harrison, you wily bastard—that's not nothing. That's a woman. You're hiding a woman on the other side of that door."

Aware that he could do nothing but give in, Harrison

heaved a sigh. "You're only half-correct. She's female, but she's no woman."

"What the—?" Derek began, but he didn't have a chance to finish. The moment Harrison nudged the door open an extra inch, Bubbles shoved her way through, her tongue lolling with pleasure at having vanquished all the obstacles in her path and made it to her master.

"What the hell is that?" Derek asked, blinking down at the Bubbles.

Harrison scooped the puppy up and held her out for inspection. "This is my service dog."

"Why is it dressed in a Barbie sweater?"

Harrison pulled Bubbles closer to his body. *He* might think the puppy looked ridiculous, but he wasn't about to stand here and listen to Derek denigrate her appearance— not when the yellow sweater made her happy.

"She gets cold," he said, scratching Bubbles under her chin. "And we've had some problems with alternate heating options, so we're making do with what we've got."

"Is this some kind of joke?" Derek made a big show of looking around the front porch. "Is your dad going to pop out with a camera and make me a YouTube star?"

Harrison couldn't help but smile. *This* was exactly what he'd been afraid of happening, what he'd tried to warn Sophie about to no avail. If his best and oldest friend found the idea of this little dog impossible to swallow, then Harrison had no idea how the rest of the guys were going to take it.

Wrong. He did know. That was the problem.

"My dad feels the same way about this puppy as you," he said. "But I'm stuck with her, I'm afraid. Oscar's orders."

Derek opened his mouth to say more, but the crunch of tires on gravel drew their attention. Harrison almost groaned aloud to see Sophie's tiny green Fiat pull up the drive. A few hours ago, nothing would have made him happier than to see her ignoring her own orders to take the weekend off, especially since the small fire he'd made in the grate hadn't caused a complete and utter reversal of Bubbles's training.

A few hours ago, however, he hadn't been staring at Derek's sorry mug. Introducing him to Bubbles was one thing. Introducing him to Sophie was an entirely different beast.

"Well, well. You're quite the social butterfly these days, aren't you?" Derek asked, his lips lifted in a mocking smile. Then Sophie swung her bare legs out of the car, and that smile turned downright evil. "And don't try telling me this one isn't a woman. I can see that for myself."

Harrison could see it too. Sophie made it impossible to do otherwise, what with the short, tennis-style dress she'd opted to wear today. It rivaled the one she'd worn the day he met her and seemed all the more ominous because of it. He didn't know what he'd done in a past life to deserve a dog trainer who looked as tempting as this one, but it must have been something terrible.

Or, he thought, taking in the sight of her unloading a box of supplies from her car, her legs leading up to the gently swishing skirt that skimmed over the rounded curve of her ass, something wonderful.

"Be nice," he growled to Derek. Then, seeing that his friend's eyes were riveted on the increasingly exposed expanse of skin near the tops of Sophie's thighs, he added, "But not too nice."

"Good morning!" Sophie called cheerfully as she made her way up the stairs. She didn't even blink when she saw Derek standing there, nor did she explain what she was doing at Harrison's house a mere twelve hours after giving him the weekend off. She shifted her box to one hip and extended a hand in Derek's direction. "I'm Sophie, the dog trainer."

"I'm Derek, the best friend," he replied easily. He also made a motion to grab the box. "Let me take that for you. It looks heavy."

"It's not," she said, but she handed it over anyway, sealing Harrison's fate in the process. Now Derek had an excuse to linger—and linger he would. He too was more like a friendly goiter than anything else.

Before she could get far, however, Sophie noticed the cooler and fishing gear. Her eyes widened, and she sent an alarmed look Harrison's way. "Uh-oh. I didn't realize. Are you going somewhere for the weekend?"

"Of course not," he said, just as Derek perked up.

"Hell yeah he is. He's supposed to be going on a fishing trip. We head over to Farragut State Park around this time every year."

"You do?" Sophie's alarmed look didn't lessen. "Why didn't you say something?"

Harrison hunched a shoulder. "To be honest, I forgot about it until Derek showed up. But it's fine. They can go without me. Bubbles is more important right now."

"Bubbles?" Derek guffawed. He looked like he wanted to say more, but Harrison turned on him with a fierce glare.

"Bubbles," he echoed, daring his friend to argue.

Derek didn't argue—at least, not about the name. Turning to Sophie, he put on his most wheedling smile and said, "There's no reason why the dog can't go too, is there?"

"Well, no," she said, blinking at the sheer force of that smile. "Not really."

"Except for the fact that she's supposed to be in training. And that we need *you* to help with it." Harrison wasn't sure why the idea of going camping with Bubbles had him reacting so strongly, but that wasn't anything new. Toss him out of his comfort zone, and this was what happened. The calm acceptance on both Derek's and Sophie's faces proved it. They would have been more surprised had he *not* growled a protest. "Besides, what about the c-a-m-p-f-i-r-e?"

"First of all, Bubbles is a dog, so you don't need to spell it out," Sophie said with a giggle. "Second, it might be good for her. The candles obviously haven't been enough. We need to step up her exposure if we're going to beat this thing."

Harrison didn't mention the small success he'd had in the grate that morning. It would kill him to get her hopes up only to dash them back down again. "But what about our regular training?"

She shrugged. "We can continue it there. A service dog isn't supposed to change your lifestyle, Harrison; she's supposed to fit into it. If camping is something you do every year, then you should absolutely keep doing it. Bubbles will adjust. She might even like it."

Harrison barely heard any of what Sophie said beyond that ominous *we can continue it there. We* implied more than one of them. *We* included herself.

"All right!" Derek cried. "It's a plan. You'll like it out there, Sophie. Some of the wives and girlfriends come, so it's not like you'll be the only one."

He caught the swift look of embarrassment that colored Sophie's face and amended his words. "Not that you're a girlfriend, of course, but you know what I mean. You'll have company out there. More than this sorry bastard, anyway."

This sorry bastard didn't much care for the plan either way. He wasn't ready to share Bubbles with the world. He wasn't ready to share *Sophie*.

"We can't ask Sophie to change her plans at the drop of a hat," he said. "I'm sure she has other appointments, other places to be. We weren't even supposed to work this weekend."

"I'm in." Sophie's response was so quick it made Harrison's head spin.

"But—"

"Are you leaving today?" She directed the question at Derek, bypassing Harrison entirely. "I'll need about an hour to pack and make arrangements, but I don't foresee any problems. In fact, it's fortuitous timing. My mom came for an unannounced visit this morning. A *prolonged* unannounced visit. You'd be doing me a favor by letting me come along."

Derek, who Harrison knew visited his mother almost every day for no other reason than his pure delight in her company, shuddered. "Oh, shit. It doesn't get much worse than that. Is she a gorgon?"

"No." Sophie sighed. "She's the nicest woman in the world."

Derek laughed. "I wouldn't want to subject anyone to

such horrors. By all means, let's get you packed up and out of the way."

"Yes, please."

As if suddenly realizing that her plans hinged on Harrison's acceptance, she turned to him and smiled prettily. It was the same look Bubbles had given him when he'd wrangled her into the goddamn sweater. "That is, if you don't mind my coming along," she added. "My reasons for wanting to go are selfish, I won't lie, but I do think it'll be good for you—and for the puppy. Give her a taste of what it's really like out there."

Harrison glanced doubtfully at said puppy and then back at Sophie. Both of them stared at him expectantly, like all their hopes and dreams hung on his willingness to play along. He couldn't decide if it made him want to laugh or howl. It wasn't as if he had any say in the matter.

"Fine. We can all go on the stupid camping trip. But," he added before the bright light in Sophie's eyes toppled him over, "you have to help me figure out what to pack for this creature. I have no idea what a skittish, traumatized service puppy is going to need for a three-day stay in the wilderness. There are cougars out there, you know. And coyotes."

Sophie nodded solemnly, but it was impossible to miss the gleam in her eyes or the way her suppressed excitement made her whole body come alight. This was not a woman who got out much, that was for sure. *No one* should be this excited at the prospect of a weekend in a tent with the wildfire crew. He sure as hell wasn't.

Well. Maybe he was a little now.

"It's a deal." She extended her hand and held it there. If it wasn't for Derek standing there, watching the interaction with unholy glee lighting his face, Harrison might have been able to avoid taking her hand. As it was, he was forced to slip his palm against hers, once again feeling that sharp juxtaposition of his own rough skin and her soft, supple touch. "You and Bubbles won't regret this."

Which showed just how little this woman knew. He was regretting it already.

chapter
13

"She's okay like this, isn't she?" Harrison asked with a worried look at his lap, where Bubbles stood at full attention, her tongue lolling and her ears perked. "She doesn't need to be in a...car seat or anything?"

Sophie barely managed to tamp down an unseemly giggle. For such a self-sufficient man, Harrison sure lacked confidence when it came to his puppy. "Do you feel comfortable with her on your lap?"

He cast a doubtful glance at the animal. "I don't have any choice in the matter. She refuses to sit anywhere else."

Sophie could have pointed out that, as a two-hundred-pound human being with opposable thumbs and a stare that could bring down a forest, he had the power to make Bubbles do anything he wanted—up to and including riding in a crate on the floor.

But Sophie didn't. She *liked* that he was so much at the puppy's mercy. It was sweet. It also made her feel as though she too might have a shot at worming her way into his heart.

"Then I guess that's where she sits," she said cheerfully. "If it makes you nervous, though, they do make doggy seat-belt harnesses that work just like ones for humans. I bet if you put one of those in, she'd wear it with pride."

Harrison's only response was a grunt, but Sophie didn't let it bother her. Why would she? Grunting was one of his primary methods of communication. He could lose the capability of speech altogether, and she'd still be thrilled to sit next to him as his truck rumbled in the opposite direction of home.

This was what freedom felt like. Sweet, rebellious freedom—the kind that most people enjoyed in their teens, sure, but she wasn't in a position to cavil the opportunity. She might be a decade too old for this kind of behavior, but that didn't mean she regretted it. In fact, she was enjoying herself. Derek had driven off in his own car while she made arrangements with her family, leaving her to Harrison's sole care. She'd left behind a worried mother, an oddly supportive Lila, and a winking Dawn—all of whom she loved to pieces and didn't want to look at for another minute.

"No offense, Mom," she'd said, "but I'm sick to death of you acting like I need to be taken care of all the time. Lila could decide to move to an off-grid remote island, and all you'd do is remind her to take sunscreen. Dawn once dated that cult leader, and you invited him to Christmas the next year. But not me. I sneeze one time, and all of a sudden it's like someone ordered my headstone."

"For the last time, he was *not* a cult leader—" Dawn protested, but Sophie had cut her off.

"I'm a fully functioning adult human being whose bill of health has been clear for years," she'd stated, simply and with a stern look that would have made Harrison quake. "Unless you'd like to hold me hostage in the basement, you have no choice but to bid me a cheerful farewell."

And it had worked.

Well, mostly. Her mom hadn't been *cheerful* about her goodbye, but that went without saying.

"We're going to have so much fun this weekend, aren't we, Bubbles?" she asked the puppy now, her enthusiasm overflowing to the animal seated next to her. "All those tents and fishing poles and marshmallows…"

Harrison grunted again. "Can you name one other thing associated with camping?"

"Um." She scanned her vast childhood reading list for any and all mentions of the great outdoors. Most of what she'd read involved children hiding in train boxcars and rafts barreling down the Mississippi, so there wasn't much to go on. "Cans of beans?"

This time, his grunt was closer to a laugh. "You weren't kidding when you said you don't get out much, were you?"

"Alas, no." She heaved a mock sigh. "My life has been much smaller than you realize. Although, to be fair, I did go to Disneyland once with my parents and sisters."

She didn't add that it had been part of the Make-A-Wish program, and that the trip had been overshadowed by the deep but unspoken fear that it might be Sophie's only chance to see the Magic Kingdom. There was something altogether depressing about riding through the Haunted Mansion when you had more in common with the ghosts than the passengers.

"You've got one over me, then," Harrison said. "I've never been to a theme park of any kind. My dad wasn't big on family vacations."

"But you camped?" she asked, a determined note of optimism in her voice. "Together, I mean? You had no pets and you had no trips to Disney, but you did that much, right?"

He cast her a sideways glance. "Yes, we camped. It's one of the only things I can remember doing with my dad. One of the only *good* things at least."

That was one of the saddest things Sophie had ever heard, but she knew Harrison well enough to realize that showing him pity would only shut him down. "Well, now you have a pet—kind of—so that's something. I know you think I'm being silly, insisting on this trip when Bubbles is still so new, but if you spend half your life outside, she needs to get used to it. The tents, the people, the atmosphere—all of it. And the timing is perfect. We can introduce the pouch."

The truck lurched as Harrison touched the brakes. "What did you just say?"

"We can introduce the pouch." She reached into the bag at her feet. Fortunately, Derek had said there were more than enough camping supplies to go around, so she hadn't had to pack much more than her clothes, toiletries, and her newest stage of the Harrison-Bubbles training routine. "I know you've been worried about how you're going to carry her around on the job, but I wasn't kidding when I said her size is more of an asset than a drawback. I have a plan."

"You have a plan?" he echoed.

"Of course. And it should be easy once you get used to wearing it. I found it online. I think you're going to like it. It's not bad, as far as pouches go."

The truck lurched even more, this time grinding to a

halt on the side of the highway. Sophie barely had time to lift a hand and brace herself on the glove box, but Harrison was on top of things, his arm shooting out to prevent Bubbles from cascading to the floor.

He didn't even realize he was doing it either. Like a mom protecting her kids from an oncoming accident, he was all instinct. And his instinct was to keep that sweet little dog safe at all costs.

Sophie's heart swelled in her chest. It was impossible to feel anything but admiration for someone so un-self-consciously, heroically *good*. Protecting Bubbles came as naturally to him as breathing. She felt, down to the tingle in her toes, that those protective urges extended to all the living creatures lucky enough to cross his path.

Of course, getting him to admit that...

"Say that word one more time," he said.

"What?" she asked. "Pouch?"

She wasn't able to stifle her giggle in time. Yes, Harrison's thunderous look was dark, but he'd scooped up Bubbles and was holding her against his chest. It was impossible to be scared of a man clutching a Pomeranian puppy like a shield.

Poor Harrison. Bubbles was a great dog, but she wasn't a miracle worker. Even she couldn't save him from himself.

"If you think for one minute I'm going to wear this dog like a kangaroo bouncing through the outback—" he began.

"You'll do what? Turn this truck around?"

"For starters, yes. And don't think that sweet, innocent smile is going to save you. I've had just about enough of you two wriggling and squirming and licking me until I can't think straight."

Sophie raised her eyebrows. "Is there something you need to tell me about what you and Bubbles get up to after hours?"

"That is *not* what I meant, and you know it."

"I mean, I don't like to judge, but there are better ways to work out some of those downstairs feelings. If you want, I could show you—"

He turned to her, his eyes sparking with the laugh she knew so well. "Sophie Vasquez, I swear on my life, if you finish that sentence, I'm getting out of this truck and throwing my keys in a ditch."

"Go ahead. I've got nowhere to be and no one to answer to for seventy-two blissful hours. Nothing you do can bring me down."

"You're a strange woman, you know that?"

She nodded happily. Being called strange might not sound like a compliment to most women, but most women weren't being called strange by a man like this one. The way the words formed on his lips made it sound like both a curse and a term of endearment. In fact, she doubted whether he knew which it was. That was what made it so delicious.

He was just being himself—Harrison Parks. Raw and honest, volatile and real.

"The pouch is a lot less ridiculous than it sounds, I promise." She gave his arm a squeeze, holding the pressure until his gaze melted into hers. "And you won't be the only person using one. There are quite a few first responders who carry diabetic service dogs this way. It keeps the dogs close enough to be effective, but out of the way of any potential danger."

Harrison didn't look as though he was fully convinced,

but he glanced down at Bubbles, who watched him intently, awaiting further cues. Seeing the love for that animal shining so clearly in his eyes, Sophie released his arm. That love was half the battle right there.

"Besides, that's what Bubbles wants most when she's scared, remember? I finally figured it out. Hiding under a ruffled bed, nestling against your chest—that's her pattern, that's what she's been telling us she needs. Won't you feel better out there knowing you're carrying her close?"

He didn't answer right away. At first, she was afraid her sentimentality had pushed him too far, but all Harrison did was sigh and scrub his free hand over his mouth.

"If you say so," he said, his voice heavy with resignation. "But you'd better let me see this stupid pouch so I can try it out. If we're going to unveil it in front of my friends, the least we can do is get some practice in first."

🐾🐾🐾

"I can't believe you're making me do this." Harrison swung himself down from the truck, his movements restricted by the squirming ball of fur affixed to his chest with what could best be described as a baby blanket made of canvas.

At least, that's what it looked like to him. Sophie had assured him, in her typically beguiling way, that it was nothing less than a specialized fire-retardant material to protect Bubbles from the elements. It twisted over one shoulder and wrapped around his upper torso, allowing him full freedom of movement in his arms and legs.

Or so she kept telling him. She had obviously never tried to walk around with a Pomeranian strapped to her chest.

"It's so beautiful here," Sophie said as she hopped down from the truck. With the exception of helping him figure out the logistics of the pouch and checking to make sure Bubbles was comfortable, she'd taken no more notice of the puppy. He wasn't sure how she did it, but she had a way of making the most ludicrous plans seem perfectly rational.

Harrison, I'm going to make you run like a pack mule until your blood sugar drops. And if you stop, I'll make you kiss me instead.

Harrison, you're going to wear a baby sling with a puppy in it—and you're going to do it with a smile.

Harrison, you're taking me camping for a whole weekend, where the only escape from my soft skin and bewitching smile is jumping off the nearest cliff.

Except now, even the nearest cliff was off the table—unless he wanted to plunge Bubbles into a watery grave with him. Which, as Sophie was fully aware, he'd never do. Not when he was coming to value the little creature more than his own skin, and she damn well knew it.

He never should have put the damn sock on the puppy. It was the sock that had given him away.

"It's a lot greener than I expected, but that's probably because of the time of year, isn't it?" She didn't wait for an answer, opting instead to reach into the truck to hoist the one small bag she'd brought with her.

That was another thing—how she intended to survive the weekend out here with a single knapsack was beyond him. The bag he'd stuffed with sweaters for Bubbles was bigger than that. Either she was the greatest outdoorswoman the world had ever seen, or she had no idea what she'd gotten herself into.

Call him pessimistic, but he guessed it was the latter.

"Do you need any help carrying things? It might feel strange at first, trying to go through your regular motions with Bubbles in the way, but you'll be surprised how fast you get used to it. Women have been carrying babies like that for all of human existence, and they've made it work just fine." She paused long enough to take a breath and look around before adding, "Where are your friends, by the way? I see cars, but there aren't any people."

"We don't camp in this spot. We hike in. Three miles in, actually."

If he expected that piece of news to slow down the indomitable Sophie Vasquez, he was bound for disappointment. At the thought of an hour-long walk through rugged terrain with only him for company, her face lit with a beaming smile. "Do we? How fun. We'll be so remote, even cell phone reception won't be able to reach us. My mother may never recover."

The power of her smile nearly made him stagger. He'd never met a woman so full of joy for no reason other than because she *felt* like it. He'd grunted like a caveman, resisted every opportunity to grow, and kissed her like someone who hadn't touched a woman in years, and she'd responded to each with unadulterated pleasure.

He had no idea what to do with so much happiness within his reach.

Actually, he did have a few ideas. That was the whole problem. More than anything else, he wanted that same happiness for himself. Unfortunately, he couldn't see any way of getting it that wouldn't involve stealing it out of Sophie's grasp.

"Yeah, well. Don't get too excited. Where cell phone reception can't reach, neither can indoor plumbing."

Her nose wrinkled at that, but it didn't stop her. "You're just trying to scare me."

"Is it working?"

"No. I've suffered worse discomforts in my life than peeing in the woods."

He laughed and handed her a pack containing most of his food and medical supplies. It wasn't as heavy as the one with the rest of his camping gear, but she still staggered under the weight. He would have gladly carried it himself—that and everything else he'd brought for the weekend—but he knew her well enough by now to realize that his chivalrous urges wouldn't impress her. In fact, she'd buck against them with everything she had.

He had no idea what was wrong with Sophie's family, but they obviously had blinders on when it came to her capabilities. He'd yet to find one goddamn thing this woman couldn't do, and the way she set her face and hoisted the thirty-pound pack onto her back confirmed it. Especially when she turned to him with her beaming smile and said, "I'm ready when you are."

It took Harrison a few minutes to get everything bundled on his own person. Every movement of his arms seemed like it would send Bubbles tumbling out of the sling, so he took things slow.

Up and down. Left and right. Twist and turn.

Huh. It seemed to be working. Not once did Bubbles protest or give any indication that she was uncomfortable. In fact, she seemed to be loving it. All it took was one glance at her head, held high as she took in the sights from her exalted perch, and Harrison knew. He could strap that damn dog to the top of the Empire State Building, and she'd eat it up.

Since he knew Sophie would be able to tell if he slowed his pace for her benefit, he finished strapping on his pack and headed toward the trailhead with his usual long stride. He also asked the question that had lingered on the tip of his tongue for the past ten minutes.

"What discomforts?"

"Huh?" Sophie's voice came from right behind him, her presence so palpable the air between them seemed to crackle with electricity. "What are you talking about?"

"You said you've suffered worse discomforts in your life than peeing in the woods." He did his best to ignore that *thing*, that sensation that pulsed in all the places their bodies didn't touch. From the way his voice almost broke at the end, however, he wasn't sure he managed it. "I'm wondering what those could possibly be. I mean, I've met your sisters. I doubt they duct-taped you to walls and made you eat bugs when you were a kid."

"Ew. Of course they didn't. Who eats bugs on purpose?"

He had to laugh. "You will, by the time this weekend is over. I should have warned you that we hold an annual cooking contest for our first meal—but the trick is, you can only use food that you find or catch. Most of us try for fish or small game, but it usually dwindles down to twigs and bugs by the time the deadline's near."

"Really?" Once again, Sophie defied all reason and logic by squealing in excitement. He even caught a flash of movement out of the corner of his eye that he could have sworn was a victory leap. "That sounds so cool.

Does anyone oversee the process to determine what's safe to eat?"

"Nope. The risk is half the fun."

"Camping is weird," she said happily.

"So are my friends." Harrison hesitated, unsure whether he should forge ahead. The logical part of his brain issued a warning to back off, to avoid the personal disclosures that would inevitably bring them closer together.

But he couldn't help it. His urge to get to know this woman, to talk about her feelings, was even stronger than the urge explore every inch of her body.

"So if it wasn't torture at the hands of your siblings, what was it?" he asked. "Corporate icebreakers? Blow-up furniture? A clown living in your sewer?"

"Um."

"I can keep listing uncomfortable things." He paused. "Oh! I know. It's those little wooden spoons that come with the cups of ice cream. You know, the ones that feel like tongue depressors? God, I hate those things. There's something unnatural about putting a stick of wood in your mouth."

She laughed, the sound tinkling like bells through the wilderness. "You have bizarre dislikes."

"You only say that because you've never tried sitting on an inflatable couch."

He thought that would be the end of it, and they'd keep marching along the trail to the tune of their playful banter, but Sophie's feet crunched to a halt. He stopped, more out of instinct than anything else, and looked back at her.

His breath caught. She looked so much like she had the day they met, when he'd come to the kennel to find a wary, worried young woman who'd been told, in no uncertain terms, that she was about to face a monster.

He'd thought she'd seen past that—realized Harrison was coming to cherish her happiness more than his own—but now he wasn't so sure.

"What is it?" he asked, his throat tight with suppressed frustration. *It's happening again. It's happening with her.* "What did I say? Sophie, please—you know I'm not good with words."

She didn't flinch at the emotion in his voice. Instead, she tilted her head and examined him in her usual inquisitive manner. "Didn't you ever wonder how I know Oscar?" she asked. "Or why I agreed to help him out with your case?"

The question took him by surprise—mostly because he *didn't* know, and it had never occurred to him to ask. He'd been so wrapped up in his own affairs that he hadn't wondered what Oscar had done to coerce this kindhearted woman into doing his bidding.

"No, but I'm wondering now. Was your…? Did you…?" He paused and forced a deep breath. Before Oscar worked the desk at the Department of Natural Resources, he'd been a more-than-adequate firefighter of his own. He always joked that he planned to stay behind that desk until Harrison finally decided he was too old to dig ditches and take his place. The number of lives he'd saved in the line of duty probably numbered in the thousands. "Did he save you from a fire?"

"Not a fire, no." Sophie's voice became remote, a part of her drawn inward. "But he did save me."

Harrison waited, aware that she was struggling with something he couldn't fathom. The location was perfect for it, the winding dirt path silent save for the rustling of the breeze through the trees and the occasional call of a friendly bird. Sophie was perfect too, her features taking on a firm resolve that transformed her from a pretty woman to a beautiful one.

Nothing was more heart-stoppingly stunning than Sophie Vasquez in a state of determination. It was what made her so good at breaking him down. When that determination zeroed in on him, he didn't stand a chance.

"He donated his bone marrow to me," she eventually said, for once without her usual smile. "I, um…well…I had leukemia for a really long time. For most of my adolescence, in fact."

"Wait. *You're* the miracle girl?"

She winced.

"I'm sorry—that's what he used to call her. The girl. You, I mean. That must have been…" He covered his flustered response by doing some rapid calculations in his head. He'd been working with Oscar a few years by that time, no longer a volunteer or summer contract worker, but part of the year-round team. He'd been a bit of a cocky shit too, but most of the people who joined the crew were. Plunging into blazing infernos required a certain level of brazenness. "What—ten, twelve years ago?"

"Eleven, give or take a few months." She shifted from one foot to another, still looking unaccountably distressed about the whole thing. "It's why my family is so overprotective of me. I was sick for so long they got into the habit of taking care of me and never learned how to stop."

He wasn't sure why she looked so uncomfortable—of the two of them, he was obviously the biggest ass. Here he was, joking about the deprivations in store for her on a fully funded state parkland when she'd gone through so much worse. Hell, even his two diabetic comas seemed paltry in comparison.

Foot, meet mouth. Harrison Parks, meet speaking before you think. It was a tale as old as time.

"Shit, Sophie," he said. "I'm sorry."

She transformed almost before his eyes. How a woman as small as she was could suddenly seem larger-than-life was beyond him, but that was what she did. Her eyes flashed a dangerous warning and she vibrated with some unknown energy.

"Don't you dare say that to me," she warned, that energy sparking out her eyes. "Not ever again, not if you want to keep standing."

He didn't laugh. The idea of this five-foot-two pixie forcing him to the ground was ludicrous in the extreme, but he didn't doubt that she could do it. She'd already flattened him so many times—and in so many different ways.

"I'm sorr—" he began before her grunt of exasperation stopped him short.

"Don't pity me," she said. "I only told you because I wanted you to understand. Why I'm here, why I'm determined to see this thing through no matter what."

Pity had been the last thing on his mind, but her meaning hit him like a punch to the gut, preventing him from defending himself the way he wanted to.

"You're here because Oscar asked you to be," he said, his voice flat.

"Yes."

"Because you'd do anything for him."

"Yes."

"Because he saved your life."

"Yes."

He didn't say the next one out loud. He didn't need to. *Because the only reason anyone would be willing to dedicate that much time and energy to someone like me is to pay off a debt.*

All the pieces suddenly clicked into place—why Sophie pushed so hard, why she was willing to give so much of herself to him, why she was so determinedly, irrationally cheerful about it all.

It wasn't for *his* benefit. It was for Oscar's.

And the worst part was he couldn't even be upset about it. Since the moment Sophie had walked into his life, he'd known he didn't deserve her. He wasn't warm. He wasn't welcoming. He wasn't even all that amusing.

In truth, he was just a job. A fun job, maybe, and an occasionally pleasurable one, but still just a job.

Finally—*finally*—things were starting to make sense.

"Okay," he said.

She looked at him through narrowed eyes. "What do you mean, okay?"

"I mean, okay. Thank you for the piece of backstory. It explains a lot about this situation. But we should probably keep going if we want to get to the campground sometime today."

Her gaze didn't grow any less suspicious. "That's all you have to say? That you want to keep walking?"

Yes, if only because he didn't trust what would come out of his mouth if he opened it again. With a tight nod, he turned and continued down the path.

Their sunny walk through the wilderness suddenly felt like a death march. Nothing lasted forever. Nothing stayed the same. Harrison had known it for almost as long as he'd known his own name. Even his Aunt Caroline had left by the time he'd turned twelve.

Now, history was repeating itself with a vengeance. Sophie was only on loan to him for as long as it took to complete the puppy training, and then she too would walk away without a backward glance. It should have made him happy to be back on this oh-so-familiar ground, to see the end before it blindsided him, but it didn't.

Just once, it would have been nice to see what happened if someone stayed.

Just once, it would have been nice to know he was worth sticking around for.

chapter
14

"Fish are, of course, the best way to win the contest, but you have to actually be able to catch them. Can you catch them?"

"Me?" Sophie glanced around, even though it had only been her and a fearfully capable woman named Jessica standing at the river's edge for the past few minutes. "Um. I don't know. Is it hard to do?"

Jessica grinned. She'd been doing a lot of that since she was paired with Sophie for the infamous cooking challenge. Sophie wasn't sure she cared for it—her outdoor capabilities weren't *that* bad—but at least the other woman didn't seem to hold her lack of skills against her. "It can be. Did you happen to bring your own rod and tackle?"

Sophie sighed. "I'm assuming that's not a fun euphemism for a date, is it?"

Jessica shook her head. "Unfortunately, no. And even if you didn't bring *that* kind of rod and tackle, there are plenty of extras to go around. I don't know if you've noticed, but this is something of a boy's trip."

Oh, she'd noticed all right. Derek hadn't been lying when he'd said that a few of the men brought their significant others on this trip, but the ratio skewed decidedly male. And not just the ordinary kind of male—these guys were intensely masculine, flannel-clad outdoorsmen.

She didn't mean that in a bad way. Harrison was an attractive man, there was no doubt about that, but the amount of scratchy-bearded overgrowth and well-sculpted swagger out here was nothing short of miraculous.

Dawn would have loved it.

Unfortunately, Sophie was less prepared. She could appreciate Harrison hoisting firewood with the best of them, but as for the rest... Well. She was both unequipped in terms of outdoor gear *and* severely underdressed for adventure. Jessica had been introduced to her as one of the summer volunteer firefighters, a fact that was not only evident in the ease with which she pitched tents and carried a backpack the size of a large child, but also in her clothes. The curly-haired redhead could have been a walking advertisement for an outdoor catalog. Cargo pants that were mostly pockets, a vest that she'd been informed doubled as a floatation device, and a pair of rugged hiking boots were just the start of what she had to offer.

Sophie, by comparison, wore a pair of worn jeans and one of her dad's old dress shirts tied in a knot at the waist. Her Converse shoes, which had seemed like a good idea at the time, were already muddy up to the ankles and making her feet ache.

"Sorry," she said, looking down at those shoes with an apology. "What you see is pretty much what you get. This isn't my usual scene."

"Oh, don't worry," Jessica said. "It's not mine either."

Sophie swept a doubtful look over her new friend, what with her dangling compass and water pouch strapped to her waist. "What *is* your usual scene?" she asked. "Foraging on Mars?"

Jessica shook her head, her curls bouncing playfully. "I'm a kindergarten teacher. You can usually find me knee deep in finger paint and parent-teacher conferences."

"Really?" In Sophie's experience, kindergarten teachers were much more likely to wear chunky sweaters and velvet jumpers. "Then what are you doing out here?"

"There are quite a few teachers on the volunteer crew, actually." Jessica started rummaging around her pockets until she extracted a spool of clear fishing line. She handed it to Sophie, who could only hold it awkwardly and wonder what else Jessica was hiding in those pants. "We have summers off, which makes it easy for us to drop everything and come running when there's a forest fire."

"Oh," Sophie said. Her response felt inadequate, but then, so did she. It wasn't a new sensation for her, since the majority of her life had been spent trying to catch up to the rest of the world, but she still resented it.

She'd done her time, paid her dues. What would it take for her to finally feel like a competent member of the human race?

"Don't worry so much." Jessica bumped Sophie with her hip. "I was just as out of place as you once upon a time. You get used to it. I never would have discovered this stuff on my own, but my ex-boyfriend roped me into volunteering one year, and I've never looked back."

"Your ex-boyfriend?" Sophie thought of the friendly greeting between Jessica and Harrison and had to ask. "Was it…?"

"Harrison?" Jessica fell into a hearty burst of laughter. "No way. He's scary."

A flush that was equal parts relief and indignation rose to the surface of Sophie's skin. "He's not bad—not really. All those grizzled, gruff bits are mostly for show."

Jessica just blinked at her.

"It's true," Sophie insisted. "He's really very sweet."

"Sweet? Are we sure we're talking about the same man?"

Sophie's hand clenched so firmly around the spool of fishing line, it started cutting into her palm. Okay, so he took a little while to warm up, but he was a sight better than most of the people she knew. At least he was up-front about who he was, honest about what he had to offer. Even his response to her health history was on par with what she expected of him. Grunting silence and a steady emotional retreat were his favorite states of being.

She didn't get a chance to voice her indignation, however, because Jessica stopped her with a strange look.

"Didn't you notice how no one said anything about the fact that there's a puppy strapped to Harrison's chest like a baby?"

"Well, yes." Sophie shifted from one foot to the other, unsure if she cared for the intensity of Jessica's gaze. "But it's not as if he has any other choice. He has to get her used to it—the puppy, that is. Bubbles will be heading out with him during the fire season for hours at a time, so they both have to be comfortable with the pouch. It's good practice."

"So…it was your idea?"

"Yeah. I read a few case studies. It's the best way for

someone as active as Harrison." And a puppy as skittish as Bubbles, but she didn't say that part out loud.

"You just handed him a baby sling, and he put it on?"

"I mean, he wasn't *excited* about it, but I hardly expected him to be." Sophie smiled, remembering his expression. "He came around in the end. I knew he would. He'll do anything for that puppy."

Jessica release a long, low whistle and shook her head. "You're a stronger woman than I, that's for sure. I doubt I'd have made it through Harrison's training if my ex hadn't been so determined that we do this together. I cried three times the first day."

"He made you cry?" Sophie asked, incredulous. This woman looked like she drank tears for breakfast.

"He makes *everyone* cry." Jessica heaved a sigh. "Well, he didn't make my ex cry, but I learned that was only because the jerk doesn't have a heart. We broke up not too much later, but Harrison fought to make sure I got the wildfire crew in the split, so it wasn't all bad. He saved me in a way. Volunteering was one of the only things that got me through that mess. You'll like it—you pick stuff up much quicker than you realize."

Sophie raised her hands and took a step back. "Oh, I'm not part of the team. I'm just here to—"

She bumped into a warm male body. Two hands dropped to her waist to steady her, lingering long enough for her heart to leap in her chest. She turned, trying to temper her reaction to one that was more appropriate to the time and place, but there was no need. It wasn't Harrison coming to see how she was faring; it was Derek.

Like Jessica, Harrison, and pretty much everyone besides Sophie, he looked fearfully capable of handling any and all feats of outdoor athleticism. His shorn head and fatigue-style camouflage spoke to a military past, but his wide smile made him highly approachable.

"I came to see how you were holding up," he said. "She's terrifying, right?"

"Oh, no, Jessica's been lovely—" Sophie began, but Derek laughed and turned his attention to the other woman.

"I haven't asked her yet how she managed to get Harrison to wear a puppy, but I like to think it involved blackmail or witchcraft. Possibly both."

"Witchcraft is my guess," Jessica said with a warm, crooked smile that robbed her words of any cruelty. "Sophie doesn't seem like the blackmail type, but I could totally see her chanting curses over a lock of Harrison's hair."

"I'm really not..." she tried again, but there was no point. These two had obviously already made their own highly inaccurate assessment of her relationship with Harrison. If Sophie could get him to bend with a few muttered hexes, she'd have done so long before now.

"Oh, she's done a lot more than curse him," Derek said. "I was inside Harrison's house this morning. He *baby proofed* it, Jessica. There was a gate in one doorway and those plastic doohickeys in all the electrical outlets."

It wasn't *that* strange. "Puppies are naturally inquisitive creatures," Sophie protested. "Even the well-trained ones. And to be fair, I thought the toilet locks might end up being the deal breaker. Even his dad was a tough sell."

Both Jessica and Derek turned to stare at her.

"You've tackled Wallace too?" Derek asked. "Damn, honey. I underestimated you—you're nothing short of a sorceress."

"I have high hopes of winning the cooking contest now," Jessica said. Was it Sophie's imagination, or was that woman looking at her with something akin to awe? "What's the game plan, oh wise one? Do we attempt to fish this part of the river, or would you rather set traps in hopes of getting something with a little red meat on its bones?"

"Um."

"Red meat," Derek said with a nod. "It's the only way to take home the prize. That or something with wings."

"Don't you have a partner of your own?" Jessica angled her body in a possessive stance in front of Sophie. "I already called dibs on Sophie. Besides, I thought you and Harrison always teamed up."

"We do, but he's in a mood to sour Mother Mary's breast milk." He rubbed his hands together, a wide smile lighting his face. "I'd much rather help you ladies. Shall we do one of each? By air, by land, and by sea?"

"I want sea," Jessica said, finding nothing strange in this plan.

"Then I call land," Derek decided. "I saw a family of ground squirrels over by the camp that looked mighty lazy. I can probably catch one with my bare hands."

Their expectant gazes turned Sophie's way once more. Their misplaced confidence in her was touching, but she had never purposefully killed anything that didn't belong to the arachnid family—and even then, she always felt a twinge of conscience. "Um, I'll take air?"

Jessica started clapping, while Derek slapped a meaty palm on her back. "That's our girl. Between the three of us, I'm sure we'll end up with something. Right, sorceress?"

Sophie looked down at the spool of fishing line in her hand and sighed. She could no more trap a bird than she could trap a man, but short of turning tail and asking Harrison to take her home to her mother, she didn't see what choice she had.

"Why not? I'm sure I'll bring down a hawk in no time."

Derek laughed at the doubt in her voice. "Don't worry so much, Sophie. From the way Harrison was glowering at everyone who so much as *looked* at either you or his puppy the wrong way, you've already brought down much worse than that."

❧ ❧ ❧

"It's called a bolas." Derek lifted his arm overhead and started whipping the long rope in an arc. As the rope was weighted on both ends with a rock the size of Bubbles, Sophie felt it was prudent to duck out of the way.

Way out of the way. Behind the nearest tree, in fact.

"Hey, where are you going?" Derek called. "I'm just getting to the good part."

"I can see everything better from over here," Sophie called back. Then, because he'd spent quite a bit of time handcrafting his weapon and it seemed rude to go into hiding, she added, "So, what happens now? You throw it and hope it murders something midair?"

"First of all, it's not murder." Derek's chest puffed up as he continued his maniacal rotations. Honestly, it was a good thing most of these people were first-aid experts of some sort. It would be a wonder if any of them got out of here alive. "It's a time-honored gaucho practice that you're lucky to witness firsthand. And secondly—well, yes, but I've never actually brought something down this way."

Sophie laughed. Apparently, the *by land, by sea, and by air* idea was more of an excuse to play with ropes than to catch anything. It was a good thing Jessica had the foresight to hand Sophie a pouch and point out which roots were edible, so she could gather a backup plan while she watched Derek at work.

"Am I supposed to scare up some birds or something?" Sophie asked after a few minutes of Derek whirling his bolas in a fruitless effort. "By like…running through the bushes and making lots of noise?"

"If you're smart, you'll tell him you saw something over by the trailhead." A crunch of leaves underfoot and the sound of Harrison's deep voice caused her to turn.

She tried not to swoon at the sight of him carrying a fishing rod and wearing a puppy strapped to his chest, but it was difficult. A ruggedly handsome man in outdoor gear and a baby sling was a more powerful sight than most people could stand, she was sure—especially as he looked completely at ease while he did it. His wide shoulders and casual stance spoke of a level of confidence Sophie could only dream of.

And dream of it—of *him*—she did.

"*Is* there something by the trailhead?" she asked. She was pleased to find that her speaking abilities remained intact, even if her reason wasn't.

"No. That's why it's your best bet. The only person he'll maim over there is himself." Without waiting for Sophie to decide whether she wanted to be alone with Harrison, he called out to his friend. "Yo, Derek. Make yourself useful and clear out, would you?"

Derek looked over with a grin. "Why? So you can have Sophie all to yourself? No way. I was just about to impress her with my mad throwing skills. Ladies love mad throwing skills."

Harrison didn't say a word, but before Sophie could do more than blink, Derek had dropped his throwing arm and was grumbling good-naturedly about his defeat. "Fine. I'll go, and I'll take your stupid puppy for a walk too. You win this round, Parks, but I don't give up that easily."

Sophie looked back and forth between the men, wondering what had passed between them in that brief moment. From what she could tell, Harrison looked much the same as he always did—a little more relaxed than usual, in fact—but he had still managed to convey to the other man that his stake had been claimed.

She, for one, didn't mind being that stake. No one had ever tried to claim her before. She kind of liked it.

"Keep Bubbles away from fire, and don't give her any table scraps," Harrison ordered. "I'm not kidding, Derek."

Derek nodded once. "Aye, aye, captain."

"I mean it. Put her on a leash and hold it like your life depends on it."

"*Does* my life depend on it?" he asked with a playful air.

Harrison's only response was a gruff "Yes."

As was the case when Harrison had told her to sweep the back hallway at the church, Sophie knew that Derek would follow those orders to the letter. Some things in this world were too powerful to deny, and Harrison Parks issuing commands in his rumbling, authoritative voice was one of them.

Of course, her awe at Harrison's authority didn't last long. She did her best to hold on to it as he began the task of unbuckling Bubbles from her pouch. She tried even harder when he told Bubbles that her look of utter despair wouldn't move him from his intentions.

She gave up altogether when he handed the puppy to Derek as one handing over the Holy Grail.

"It's like taking a kid to daycare," he said, careful not to meet Sophie's eye. "She'll cry for the first few minutes, but it's all for show. I know it looks and sounds like it, but her heart won't actually break in two."

"How's she doing so far?" she asked as soon as her giggles subsided and Derek disappeared from view, Bubbles tucked firmly under one arm. Although she knew there had to be a dozen or so men and women wandering around, they appeared to be alone. "I heard you give the order not to light any fires until dusk."

"I'm not taking any chances," he said in a voice of grim determination.

"That was smart. We can make sure you two are good and snuggled before it gets going."

Harrison showed a marked tendency to twitch at the prospect of being *good and snuggled*, so she quickly changed the subject.

"You brought your own rod and tackle, I see," she said.

"What?"

She nodded down at his hand. "Your rod and tackle— for fishing. Not, according to Jessica, a euphemism for something fun."

Suddenly, she could understand how Derek could have interpreted a brief Harrison expression as an order to turn tail and run as fast as his legs would take him. That cloudy look signaled an incoming storm of the cataclysmic variety.

Fortunately for her, she didn't mind getting a little wet. Or, you know, *a lot* wet.

"You don't have to look at me like that," she said. "I said it *wasn't* a euphemism for something fun, if you know what I mean."

"I know damn well what you mean," he said. "Just promise me you will never refer to a man's junk as his rod and tackle again."

She laughed, more pleased than she could say that he was still willing to fight her. Telling him about her history with Oscar had carried a risk; there was a good chance that he, like everyone else in her life, would start treating her like she was breakable, delicate.

But he hadn't. Even with all of Harrison's flaws, the one thing he'd never done was handle her delicately. He'd never treated her as anything other than a hot-blooded woman capable of standing up for herself.

Which, for the first time in her life, was exactly what she felt like.

"His frank and beans then," she suggested.

His lips began their telltale twitch. "No."

"Pillar and stones?"

"You stole that from George R. R. Martin."

"Prince Harry and the twins?"

"Stop it."

"I'm running out of options. How about the lieutenant and his rearguard?"

The smile on his face was now unmistakable. "That's not even a real one."

"Fine." She heaved a fake sigh. "Lay it on me. What do you call them?"

Despite the devastating grin that lightened her soul,

his stare remained molten fire. She felt it burn all the way down to her toes, sparking awareness in every part of her body. Strangely enough, it was a slow burn. She'd have thought, with a man like Harrison Parks, that once he started kindling, he'd set fire to everything he touched with passionate, unchecked fury.

She was wrong. Instead, heat flooded to the surface of her skin, warming her from the outside in, making her feel as though his entire body was pressed on top of hers. She shivered despite the heat. Having his body pressed on top of hers was suddenly the only thing she wanted.

Well, besides the lieutenant and his rearguard. But that went without saying.

"Do you mean me specifically, or options I'd find acceptable in the general sense?"

"Oh dear." She clucked her tongue. "I never realized you'd made such an in-depth study of the scepter and family jewels."

"I didn't have to let you come on this trip, you know. I could have left you at home to deal with your mom and sisters."

"Okay, fine. You win. What are my options?"

He crossed his arms and did his best not to look like a man about to break into laughter. "Penis. Testicles. Cock. Balls. Dick. You can't go wrong with the classics."

"Bo-ring," she teased. "Maybe I should go find Derek and ask him what he thinks. I bet he has lots of exciting names for his parts."

"Derek's idea of excitement is throwing rocks at birds. You really want his opinion?"

She giggled. "Okay, then. What if we compromised? Big D and the gang seems like it might suit you."

There was no helping it after that. She found herself glancing down to where Harrison's male parts were contained. Dressed in ragged jeans that clung to his powerful thighs and a puffy vest layered over worn flannel, he was a most appealing sight. The fact that she could clearly detect his package underneath it all was an added bonus. Rugged and standoffish, he was the itch she longed to scratch—long and deep and hard.

"There's no way I'm falling for that."

"Falling for what?" she asked innocently.

"The second I tell you anything about my manhood, you're going to use it against me. I *know* you, Sophie. You're ruthless."

"Your manhood?" That was almost too much. "Is that what you call it? Manhood and marbles? Manhood and the motley crew?"

He stepped closer. "If you know what's good for you, you'll stop there. I'm *trying* to keep a distance here. Or hadn't you noticed?"

Getting him to willingly come closer was a step in the right direction, so she counted that as a win.

"Come on, be a good sport," she cooed. "If you tell me what you call them, I'll let you know how I refer to my lady lumps."

He stopped midstep and paled, the smile wiped from his lips. "You named your tits?"

Even though Sophie considered herself an open-minded sort of woman when it came to sex, the way he said *tits*—all harsh and guttural—caused her to blush. She couldn't help it. There weren't many men in the world who looked at her and found themselves reduced to their baser urges.

"Yes," she said. Her cheeks were aflame, but she kept her eyes locked on his. "And I refuse to disclose that information until you give me something to work with in return."

"Jesus, Sophie." His curse was more like a caress. "Do you always have to be so—"

"Yes, I do," she said, perfectly serious. "How am I supposed to get you to kiss me otherwise?"

His eyes flashed. "You could always ask."

A simple answer from a simple man. She liked it.

With more bravado than she'd ever thought it possible for her to muster, she said, "Harrison Parks, you are one strapping beast of a man, and I can't stop thinking about you. Would you please kiss me already?"

There was no need for her to finish the question. By the time she got past that *strapping beast* part, he'd already closed the distance between them, already grabbed her around the waist and pulled her flush against him. She'd barely gotten the last word out when his mouth pressed down on hers hungrily, his lips tasting and testing to see how much she would give.

The answer, as he would soon come to learn, was *everything*.

She'd never wanted anything as much as she wanted Harrison Parks exactly like this—powerful and insistent yet still the same sweet man who could fall head-over-heels in love with a puppy overnight.

Each touch of his mouth against hers demanded that she return his kiss, but the way his hand cupped her face and the way he held her body against his spoke of a hesitant affection. It was as if he knew he was holding something precious but not breakable, someone willing but not compliant.

Determined not to let him go this time, Sophie wrapped her arms around his waist. She took a moment to slide her hands underneath the back of his vest, bypassing the insulin pump hitched to his belt to skim her touch between warm flannel and even warmer skin. Although she would have gladly stood there and let him keep nibbling at her lips with the urgency of one who could never be sated, she pulled away enough to catch her breath and speak.

"If asking for a kiss gets me exactly what I want, what happens if I make other requests?" she asked. "Do you have to do everything I ask, like a genie granting wishes? Is that how it works?"

His lips curved in a smile—that deep, enticing one that set her...well, everything quivering. Not only was he kissing her and making jokes, but he was playing along. He was playing, period.

"Why the hell not? I'll give you exactly three wishes." His smile dropped. "And no, you can't wish for more wishes."

"I wasn't going to!" she protested. "I only play honorably."

"No, you don't. That's what got us into this mess in the first place." His laugh was more like a groan. "So...bearing in mind that it's sixty degrees and Derek is nearby with a heavy projectile, what do you want from me?"

What she wanted was for it to be dark and the pair of them to be sharing a tent, but not even Harrison had the power to move time. However, that wasn't going to stop her from trying.

"I want to feel you on top of me," she said.

He blinked, as if waiting for more. When she didn't do anything except stare expectantly up at him, awaiting his response, he laughed. "Fine. Never let it be said I didn't hold up my end of the bargain."

Without another word, he swooped down and lifted her in his arms. Sophie could feel the sheer strength of him, the way every muscle was taut and vibrating with energy. She could also tell that lifting her caused almost no strain on his physique.

Nor did it seem to tax his strength any as he lowered her to the ground right then and there. It was a patch of rock and dirt, no sign of any mossy embankment or field of flowers where she could rest her head, and she could have kissed him for it. There was nothing romantic about the pebbles pressing through her jeans; nothing comfortable about the way he stretched her body out, her shoulder narrowly missing the sharp edge of a boulder. She commanded, and he gave. That was all.

He did, however, shrug out of his vest and fold it into a pillow for her head. As he quickly followed it by pressing the entire length of his body on top of hers, she couldn't find it in her to complain. He was gloriously heavy, his limbs and pelvis pinning her into place.

It was like bedding down with a rock, assuming the rock was made of lava and had designs on her maidenly virtue. Harrison's chest was broad and his arms strong, locking her in place so he could once again crush her mouth under his. There was nothing to do but open up and let him in, so that was exactly what she did. He smelled like pine and tasted like the sky—two things she'd never thought could be intoxicating together, but she was wrong.

Because this was *right*.

Whatever else was happening in the world at this exact moment—wars, crime, a dozen rugged outdoorsman close enough to march by at any moment—didn't matter. All she cared about was the fact that Harrison's lips wouldn't stop moving over hers and that the press of his body wasn't softening in the slightest. In fact, if she wasn't mistaken, there was zero softening going on anywhere.

But there was definitely some hardening. Oh, yes. That was a *cock*, no playful names about it.

It was too cold to do much in the way of disrobing, but Harrison managed to unfailingly find all the exposed patches of her skin. His fingertips moved along the arched slope of her neck, tracing the delicate line of her clavicle as one memorizing a masterpiece. They slipped along the bare skin above her waistline. They even, for one glorious minute, gave in to the urge to travel northward, skimming over her stomach and making a tantalizing approach near her breasts.

She arched in an attempt to get him to reach the urgently tingling tips of her nipples, but Harrison pulled himself away before he got close. He released a sound halfway between a groan and a growl, his large palm not lifting from where it rested against her rib cage. His rough skin attested to all those years of fighting fires, and she could feel the scrape of his calluses against her skin.

It was impossible not to make the leap from there, to imagine the hot, work-hardened fingers slipping into her softest parts, rubbing her body in ways that would scandalize the birds and the bees.

She might have even whimpered. It wasn't her most elegant moment.

"Well?" Harrison lifted himself away just enough to speak, his words a breath against her lips. "That makes one. What's your next command?"

Gone were all thoughts of bugs crawling into her jeans or rocks working their way into unseemly places. Sophie could think of only one thing she wanted, the rest of the world be damned.

She wanted him.

"Your hands," she managed, her words escaping on a gasp. "I want to feel your hands on my bare skin."

Technically, he was already doing that, but it wasn't enough. She wanted more.

"What part of your bare skin?" he asked with a small tsk. "Don't you know that you have to be specific when making wishes? Otherwise, the genie is going to trick you. He's not to be trusted."

On the contrary, she trusted *this* genie with both her life and her body. She blushed at the thought of giving voice to exactly what she wanted him to do with the latter—that she wanted him to move his hand upward until he was cupping her breasts, or even to forgo a gentle exploration of her torso and slide his hand between her bare thighs. Sophie wasn't squeamish about sex, but there was a difference between enjoying an act and making that request under the stark, open sky.

"Well?" he prodded. He knew how hard this was on her, the jerk, and was making it more difficult on purpose. With Harrison, she had the feeling every victory was going to have to be earned.

Challenge. Accepted.

She'd never felt so ready—so excited—at the prospect of battle.

"Lady," she said, and arched her back against his hand's taunting withdrawal. "And Tramp. I want you to touch Lady and the Tramp."

His entire body stilled. For a brief moment, it was as though he'd turned to stone, pinning her to earth for all of eternity. It wasn't as daunting a fate as it seemed, but she couldn't help being relieved when he released a tortured groan.

"Please tell me those aren't the names of your—"

"Tits?" she interrupted, pleased and surprised at how easily the syllable rolled off her tongue. "Yes, they are. Would you like to meet them? I warn you—Lady can be a bit shy. You may have to coax her out a little."

The last of her inhibition fled as Harrison muttered something about the folly of falling into such an obvious honey trap. The idea intrigued her. She'd never been anything close to a honey trap before. But for this man, she was willing to try.

"Touch me, Harrison," she said. "Anywhere and everywhere you want."

"You're going to be the death of me. You know that, right?"

His question was rhetorical. Without waiting for her to agree or argue, he dropped his lips to hers for another searing kiss. This one was accompanied by his hand sweeping past the soft swell of her stomach and heading straight for Lady. He had no way of knowing which breast was which, but it didn't matter because he obviously planned on giving them both the same thorough treatment.

Her bra was an expensive one, unsuited for support and comfort while out in the elements, but ideal for man exploring the softly molded cups. His fingers slipped over the top and caressed her skin, teasing the edge of her nipples until she moaned into his mouth. She tried arching again, but his weight had become so settled that it was all she could do to lay there and let him explore her the way he saw fit.

As that included the graze of his rough fingers over the tips of her breasts and the grinding of his hips against hers, she was fine with whatever he planned to do to her. Her nipples grew tight and hot under his touch, her belly taut with anticipation. She could practically feel the blood coursing through her veins and down between her thighs, her body throbbing with the ache of emptiness.

"How can one person be so fucking soft?" he asked.

"I don't know. How can one person be so fucking hard?" She groaned as the ridge of his erection pressed against her. "I'm ready for my third wish, by the way."

His voice was hoarse. "I don't have much more to give, Sophie. You have to realize that by now."

"Oh, there's a lot more you can give. What I really want—what I've wanted since the moment I met you—is to feel you inside of me."

"*Fuck*." He swore with a vehemence that was difficult to interpret. Was he agreeing with her and announcing his intentions to perform said deed? Or had she pushed him too far, and he was refusing to comply?

God, she hoped it was the first one. She wasn't sure how much more of this agony she could take.

A discreet cough sounded from above them, "Uh, Harrison?"

"Fuck," Harrison said again, pulling himself away from her.

Understanding dawned—and with it, the realization that she was writhing on the ground with a man's hand firmly up her shirt. Jessica had the decency to be looking off somewhere in the distance, her gaze fixed on a rolling green bluff, but Sophie was pretty sure she must have seen—and heard—plenty already.

"I'm sorry," Jessica said. "But there's been an accident."

Harrison shot the rest of the way up, leaving Sophie with her stomach bared to the elements. She might have been insulted if not for the wholly honorable way his thoughts went to his puppy. "Is Bubbles—?"

"Fine, she's fine. Great, in fact. The problem is with, uh, Derek. His bolas…"

Harrison groaned and closed his eyes. All of the anxiety that the idea of Bubbles in danger had brought out in him was reduced to a guttural, "That debauched troglodyte. Whose idea was it to let him anywhere near a weapon?"

Sophie couldn't help but giggle. It was hard to believe that this man once looked at that puppy with anything but love and adoration. She'd never seen anyone fall so hard for an animal before—and she'd seen her fair share of happy placements.

He reached a hand down to help Sophie to her feet, pausing just long enough to meet her eye with a look of mingled pleasure and embarrassment. She could tell he wanted to say something that would rob the moment of awkwardness, but there was no opportunity.

Sophie found she didn't mind too much. This...*conversation* would hold.

"I guess you'd better take me to him," Harrison said, giving in with a sigh. "But I swear to everything that man holds dear, if he's not bleeding out somewhere at the bottom of a ravine, I'm going to truss him up and toss him in the back of my truck for the rest of this trip. And you'll be back there with him, Sophie, if you don't stop laughing."

"I'm sorry," she said, not sorry at all—not even when Jessica relaxed enough to laugh with her.

"I'd say it's just a muscle contusion, but you're our best medic," Jessica said. "I really am sorry. It looks like you were—"

"There's no need to finish that sentence," Harrison said, but it was too late. Any and all fear Jessica may have felt at interrupting her superior in the middle of frolicking in the wilderness had all but disappeared.

I should probably feel guilty for ruining his reputation, Sophie thought. But she didn't. Not when her body was still thrumming with the memory of his touch.

Not when she had high hopes that, this time, the wall was so far gone she could get him to touch her again.

chapter
15

"Your card is a four of hearts," Sophie said, her face lit by firelight and a shy smile. "Either that or the queen of spades, but I think Marcus has that one."

"Goddammit, she's right again!" Derek thumped his good foot on the hard-packed earth. His other not-so-good one was elevated and had an ice pack pressed against the calf.

A muscle contusion, just as Jessica had suspected. A muscle contusion that Harrison could only consider the best—and worst—timed injury known to mankind. Five minutes later, and he had no doubts that he would have fulfilled Sophie's wishes right then and there.

On the ground. In the cold. Unaware of anything except the suppleness of her every goddamn curve.

"I thought for sure I had you that time." With the flick of his wrist, Derek consigned his card to the campfire, offering only a glimpse of four hearts before it flared and disappeared from view. "You tricked me."

Marcus, a somewhat gangly youth who'd only finished his first summer with them last year, turned his card. It showed a stony-faced monarch clad all in black. "It *is* the queen of spades," he admitted. He also handed his card back to Sophie, though what good it would do when Derek had already burned up half the deck was beyond any of them. "How did you do that?"

"A good magician never reveals her tricks," Sophie said with a mysterious air. She promptly ruined it with, "It's mostly done by counting the cards. I can show you, if you want."

"Would you really?" Marcus's eagerness was matched only by his crestfallen expression when he glanced over at Harrison and changed his mind. "Uh, maybe some other time. It's more fun if you don't know how the sausage is made, you know?"

Harrison attempted to arrange his features in a more conciliatory pattern of parts. He wasn't supposed to scare everyone away from the campfire before the ghost stories even started. Besides, Marcus could hardly be blamed for Harrison's current state of mind.

And body.

Harrison might be emotionally conflicted when it came to his relationship with Sophie, but his body had no qualms about asserting what it wanted.

It wanted to feel her writhing on the ground underneath him again. It wanted to explore the swells and dips of skin that felt like ribbon-wrapped satin. It wanted to enter her so slowly she came screaming before he made it all the way inside.

"I, for one, love sausage and all its incumbent parts." Derek winked and grinned at Harrison from across the fire. "Tell us, Sophie. Tell us about the meat."

There was nothing Harrison could do to recoup his position after that. He'd lost his edge. He'd lost his edge, and everyone—with the exception of Marcus, who was still young and new enough to regard him with awe—knew it.

It helped to glance down and check on Bubbles, who was strapped to his chest in what he could only describe as a state of sleepy euphoria. The campfire had been going for a full hour now, with various pots of food-like items bubbling away on top. Other than one scrambling attempt to free herself from the pouch when they first approached, the puppy was doing well. Mostly because her head was burrowed against his chest and she refused to roll her eyes in that direction. As long as she could pretend there were no flames and that her whole world was the steady beat of his heart next to her, she was perfectly fine.

It seemed that Sophie had been right about the pouch all along. Not only had it been easy for him to set up camp with the puppy safely strapped to his chest, but Sophie had known, with her usual insight, exactly what Bubbles needed to feel safe. To be cradled like a baby. To be held somewhere tight and warm.

In fact, if it weren't for the fact that everyone was watching him with a wariness that made him feel like the village freak, this pouch would have been the ideal solution to all his problems.

"Where'd you learn all that stuff anyway?" Jessica asked. She paused to stir the bowl of roots and dirt that was the only thing she and Sophie had managed to catch after a full afternoon's harvest.

That, at least, made him feel somewhat better. Sophie could worm her way under his skin, charm his father into lighting aromatherapy candles, and mystify his friends with magic tricks, but her hunting-and-gathering skills could definitely use some work. It was the most primeval

of triumphs, to gloat over a woman who couldn't trap
and maim animals, but what he could he do?

He was man. Hear him roar.

Sophie's gaze shifted to Harrison's, a somewhat wary
light glinting in the reflection of the fire. He immediately regretted his triumph. *What an ass I am.* Of course
Sophie was less than proficient at wilderness survival.
He didn't know all the details of her illness—Oscar
wasn't the kind to just tell someone else's life story—
but he had enough imagination to picture it.

*She's overcome more pain and suffering than most of
us see in a lifetime*, Oscar had said.

*I've never gone anywhere or done anything on my
own* had been the confession from Sophie's own lips.

The familiar burn of frustration started to mount in
Harrison's gut, but for the first time in his life, it wasn't
directed inward. Diabetes was challenging, yes, and it was
something he'd always have to account for, but it was nothing like what Sophie must have gone through—still went
through, if her family situation was all that she said it was.

"Um, I spent a lot of time lying in bed when I was
a kid," Sophie admitted, continuing to look at him. He
nodded once, hoping to convey even a fraction of the
admiration he felt for her. It must have worked, because
she quirked her lips in a smile and added, "I'm also
weirdly good at crossword puzzles and soap opera trivia."

Marcus opened his mouth to ask why, but he was
stopped when he caught Harrison's eye.

The silent warning worked in keeping the younger
man from badgering Sophie, but Bubbles decided she
didn't much care for it. She snuffled against his chest,
whimpering despite the protective wrap holding her close.

As something from one of the pots sizzled and jumped into the campfire, sending crackling flames in all directions, Harrison assumed it was the sudden flare that scared her, so he murmured something low and soothing.

In a louder voice, he asked, "How much longer until we have to eat this monstrosity?"

Jessica dipped a ladle in the pot and tasted its contents, barely managing to hide her grimace in time. "Twenty minutes should do it. I'll just, ah, add some more salt."

"Don't worry. I have beef jerky and granola bars in my pack." The woman seated next to Jessica, the wife of firefighter named Burke, patted the backpack at her side.

"And we caught enough fish for a feast," promised another man, Burke's younger brother and an aspiring firefighter. "We've got this competition in the bag. Or, er, the net, I guess I should say."

"You caught one—one fish, and he looked diseased. His fin was practically falling off."

"That just means the filet will be tender."

Under normal circumstances, Harrison would have been more than happy to join in the smack talk, comparing culinary disasters and planning a pizza run for later. It had been a long, wearying day with an even longer night beckoning. Jessica had offered to share her tent with Sophie—and had been accepted—but moving a sleeping bag was no difficult task. If Sophie kept peeking at him through those long lashes, there was a good chance neither one of them would be doing any sleeping of any kind.

So much for preparing myself for the inevitable.

Sophie might have one foot out the door, but her other foot was well within his reach.

The fire crackled again, causing Bubbles to whimper louder. Her legs wriggled against his chest, her head moving frantically as she struggled to free herself from her binding.

"It's just a fire," he said, keeping his voice low and calm. When he'd had the small fire in the grate that morning, the sound of him talking—however inane the words—had seemed to soothe her. "A chemical reaction between the oxygen in the air and the wood in the pit. Chemistry can explain a lot of things that seem scary at first."

Attraction, for example. Lust. *Desire*.

It didn't work. Instead of having a pacifying effect on the dog this time, his voice only served to increase her anxiety. He rose to his feet in a swift movement, determined to put distance between the dog and the fire.

And between him and Sophie, but that was an effort in futility. No matter where he went, she followed.

Literally. He'd made it no farther than a few hundred feet away from the campfire before he realized Sophie was standing at his back.

"It's not getting better," he said, his voice more frantic than he cared to admit. Since his version of frantic sounded more like anger, the words came out as an accusation. "I thought the extra training I was doing with her would help, and that the pouch was making a difference too, but look at her. She's bound tight and still hates the flames."

He paused, waiting for Sophie to wince or back away, but she didn't. She stepped closer, drawing so near he could smell her, feel the residual heat from the fire rising up off her tight-fitting jacket. That small action, that step forward—toward him, *to* him—almost broke him. Nothing he seemed to say or do caused this woman to back away.

"Extra training?" she asked.

"It was nothing. Just some things she and I were trying together. I wanted to, uh... It sounds dumb now that I'm saying it, but..." He shrugged helplessly. "I wanted to make this work for you."

There wasn't much light this far from the campfire, but Sophie's eyes opened so widely that they captured the full luminosity of the moon and flung it right at him.

He wasn't sure what to make of that look—that *shock*—so he cleared his throat and kept going.

"Maybe you were wrong after all," he said. "Maybe she *can't* do this. I want her to succeed, I really do, but that was just one little crackle, one little flare. Do you have any idea how much worse it can get out there?"

"Harrison, stop."

"You can't make things happen just because you want them to," he said. Now that the verbal floodgates had been opened, he didn't seem to know how to close them again. All the anxiety of the past month, all the worries and agonies and inadequacies, seemed to be tumbling out of him at once. "I know it makes me an asshole to say it, but one of us has to. She's not fit for the job, and no number of candles and camping trips are going to change that. Working around fires will end up hurting her. *I* will end up hurting her."

"Harrison, *listen*."

"I can't, Sophie," he said—*pleaded*, really. How could he reasonably be expected to drag the poor puppy out into the wild like this? What kind of a man would he have to be to subject her to this kind of whimpering agony day after day? "I'd like to keep her if I can, maybe as a pet, but—"

"For the love of all things stubborn, will you stop talking for five seconds and *look* at her?"

Harrison glanced down. Even though they were a good distance from the fire now, the Pomeranian hadn't stopped her shifting, whining movements. He'd assumed she was trying to get free, and that she wouldn't be happy until she'd put as much distance between herself and the flames as possible, but something about Sophie's crossed arms gave him pause.

So did her question. "When was the last time you did a finger stick? Or, for that matter, the last time you ate something?"

His eyes flew open as he appraised the tiny dog. She'd managed to free herself from the sling just enough to bring her face to his, her little head nudging his chin with an urgency that couldn't be denied. Now that he was paying attention, he recognized that nudging as the action they'd been working on for the past few weeks.

It was what she did whenever she was brought the swab containing the smell she was trained to alert him to. It was what she did whenever she was brought the swab containing the smell that meant danger.

"You mean she's—?"

Sophie's face broke out in a grin. Even in the deepening twilight, the stars and nearly full moon providing the sole illumination, that grin was breathtaking. It lit up every part of her. "She's not letting you down, Harrison. She's not scared of the fire. She's doing exactly what she's been trained to do."

He stared in wonder down at the puppy. He knew, from Sophie's careful explanation, that this was exactly what he should expect from having a service dog. He could relax some of his own vigilance, slow down to assess Bubbles's needs and his own at the same time, trust in the puppy to know what he needed before his continuous glucose monitor registered the changes in his blood sugar.

It made sense, from an intellectual standpoint, that Bubbles could handle all this, especially given how well she'd handled training back at the house. To see it in action, however, to know that this tiny, quivering ball of heat was saving his goddamn life right now, was almost more than he could take.

"Come on." Sophie held out a hand. "Let's go get you checked. I assume your things are in your tent?"

His first impulse on hearing the words *your tent* was to dig his feet into the dirt and refuse to allow Sophie anywhere near it. Nothing good could come of having her inside those ten square feet of nylon with him.

But that was ridiculous. She wasn't going to attack him. She wasn't going to ravish him.

At least, not without asking first.

"What a good little nugget you are," she cooed. "So smart. So brave."

Harrison knew she was complimenting the puppy for a job well done, but he couldn't help a feeling of pride from swelling up in his chest. Smart and brave were right—and that was *his* service animal they were talking about.

The raccoon under the porch had nothing on Bubbles.

It was asking too much for Sophie to politely keep

her distance while he ducked into his tent to pull out his testing gear. That damnable woman wasn't happy unless she was pushing him—physically, mentally, emotionally. Before he could suggest she take the puppy back to the campfire, she'd followed him in and promptly arranged herself on top of his sleeping bag. She even grabbed his pillow and held it in her lap like it was a stuffed animal.

He bit back a groan. He'd never get the smell of her out of it now. He'd end up being exactly like the Sleeping Beauty she'd mocked him as—snuggling up with that puff of down and fabric in order to feel close to her once again.

"You could give me a little privacy, you know," he pointed out, his voice gruff.

"I know."

"You could also take that comment as the hint it is."

"I know." She peeped up at him through her lashes. "But you wouldn't deny me this moment of triumph, would you? I'm just as curious to see if Bubbles is right as you are."

She had him there. He was, after all, her project— her job. This puppy and this woman might be rapidly becoming Harrison's whole world, but she had other things at stake.

He unhooked the sling and let Bubbles down. The puppy still showed signs of distress, but Sophie made no attempt to soothe her. She simply let the dog whimper and snuffle about, watching her with a fond, detached smile.

"I know you want me to pick her up, but you're going to have to get used to the idea that she has to be uncomfortable sometimes." Sophie spoke in a calm voice that could have been designed to set his teeth on edge. "It's literally what we're training her to do. You *want* her to be emotionally invested in your health."

"Easy for you to say," he muttered as he rummaged around in his bag. He zipped open his kit and pulled out a testing strip. "You're a cold-blooded monster."

Sophie's soft peal of laughter filled the tent. "Do you know no one has ever insulted me as well as you before? Or ever?" She settled more comfortably in her seat, pushing out the sides of the tent as she did. "Tell me what else you think about me, please."

"You have some serious problems."

"That doesn't count. Everyone has problems. Will it help if I go first?"

He glanced up from the prick of blood pooling on his forefinger. "What?"

"You're right. I should go first." She tapped one smooth finger in the center of her chin. "Let's see… you're a softhearted baby."

"Excuse me?"

His protest did nothing to deter her. "A marshmallow, really. Soft and squishy and so in love with this little puppy I doubt you'll ever be able to look at a Great Dane again."

"You have no idea what you're talking about. I'm uncommunicative and stubborn, remember? A difficult bastard. Lots of bark and plenty of bite."

She ignored him, the smile on her lips so serene he might as well have been speaking in a foreign language. "You even like wearing Bubbles in that pouch, though you won't admit it. You like having her close, knowing she's safe." The smile spread. "You're a protector—that's what you are. You'd give your life for this little dog. You'd give your life for anyone who needed it."

The beep that sounded indicated that his blood sugar was, in fact, low. It was a moment of triumph—for Bubbles and for Sophie and for him—but he needed to focus his attention on regulating his equipment. He also reached for his glucose tablets and popped three of them under his tongue, pausing to commend Bubbles for a job well done and settle her on her favorite blanket in the corner of the tent.

"You don't know what you're talking about," he countered. "You've known me for all of four weeks. That doesn't make you an expert on all things Harrison."

"The problem, of course, is that you can't turn it off." Sophie was still rattling off his apparent flaws in that same cheerful matter, but the smile had dropped from her face.

The moment of seriousness didn't make her any less attractive. If anything, it only made her *more* attractive. Fun, cheerful, friendly Sophie was easy to fall for and hopefully just as easy to leave behind. Serious, earnest Sophie was a different matter entirely. Once she got under your skin, she was likely to remain there permanently.

"That's why you're so closed up, why you hide behind such thick walls." Her voice softened. "Why you have such a difficult time letting people past them."

Something in his chest gave a painful, lurching clench.

"It's hard, isn't it?" she asked. "To care so much, to protect everyone from everything that's terrible in the world? It's easier to keep them as far away from your heart as possible."

"No," he whispered.

"Yes," she replied, her gaze so full of sadness and understanding that he wasn't sure he could take another second of it. "It doesn't hurt so much then, does it?"

Something inside him roared and broke free. Flying across the tent, he chucked that stupid pillow aside and took Sophie into his arms. She was soft and warm, but his words were anything but.

"You want to know what I think about you?" he demanded. Without waiting for an answer, he said, "You're a pushing, interfering nuisance I wish I'd never met."

"Oh dear," she murmured, undaunted. "Was it something I said?"

"Goddammit, Sophie. It's not fair. It was never fair." He spoke into her hairline, down along the side of her nape, into her neckline. She smelled like campfire and the clean, simple soap that would forever haunt his dreams. "How many times can I say it before you finally realize I'm not worth the effort?"

"I don't know," she said. "But you might be a lot more effective if you weren't kissing my neck at the time."

Incongruous laughter shook him. Nothing about this situation warranted joy, but being with Sophie demanded nothing less. Joy, happiness, pleasure—she was offering them for the taking. A smarter man would have pulled away while he still had the chance, but no one had ever accused Harrison of possessing an excess of intelligence.

"Your neck isn't the part of you I'd like to be kissing, but I'm not going any further unless you ask me to. The least I can do is give you one more chance to make the right decision."

"Screw the right decisions." Sophie tilted her head, giving him better access to the soft slope of her clavicle. "Kiss me wherever you want, Harrison. Bite me, if that's what it takes. I promise I won't break."

"No," he muttered. "But I might."

He had no way of knowing whether or not Sophie heard him. Before he could gain hold of his sanity and leave the warm safety of the tent, she twined her arms around his neck and pulled him close, not stopping until his mouth was inches from her own. Every move was calculated to cause him anguish, the sweet curve of her mouth too tempting to ignore.

"I'm not such a bad person once you get to know me, I swear," she said. "I smell like dogs and I'm not much good at this wilderness stuff, but I can make up for it with other things. Want to know how? Most of them involve my legs."

Harrison groaned. "Are you trying to kill me?"

"No," she said and lifted her mouth to his. "I'm *trying* to kiss you. And I'm going to do it too."

He would have liked to have resisted the pull of her kiss, especially while so much between them remained up in the air, but he wasn't that strong.

No mortal man was. All he needed was the sound of his name on her lips, a laugh issuing from between them, and he was done for.

"I like kissing you, Harrison," she said the moment she pulled away, proving his point to perfection. That *Harrison* almost slayed him. "And I think you like kissing me too, but you're a chicken."

He stiffened. "I'm not a chicken."

"Yes, you are, but only where I'm concerned. You

think I'm sexy and you think I'm scary, but you refuse to admit that you like those two things together. You like them a lot."

It was true. He did appreciate the combination of those two things, especially where Sophie was concerned. She was quite literally the most desirable woman he'd ever laid eyes on, and the fact that he cared less about that than he did for the fact that he'd fallen hard for her scared the shit out of him.

But he liked it. He liked it a lot.

"I'm never going to be a good boyfriend, Sophie," he said, groaning again. It was much less effective this time, since her lips pressed against his, capturing most of his words. "I'm never going to be cheerful or pleasant or even all that likable."

"I know." Her mouth brushed his—softly at first at, then with increasing urgency. As was always the case when this woman started pushing, he let her in.

"And there's a good chance I'll say something wrong—maybe even make you cry."

"I know," she said again, her lips moving down his neck. She ran her palms flat against his stomach and lifted his jacket, exposing his abdomen as well as the two ports—one attached to the insulin pump via a small cord, the other attached only digitally. He wasn't squeamish about very many things and had no problems testing his blood sugar in front of others, but he'd always made it a point to remove the pump and put on a patch before things got too far with a woman.

Whirring mechanical devices weren't exactly sexy, but he needed to keep them on while his body regulated itself. Which meant they'd have to slow down. They'd have to wait. He'd have to sit here with a cock so hard it could crack ice…

Sophie, however, didn't so much as blink. Nor did she stop what she was doing.

He barely had a chance to get over the shock of it, of Sophie tugging off his clothes with an urgency that bordered on the frantic, before she started working her way inexorably down his body. No part of him was left untouched, her lips pressing against his pecs and his abs and—oh God—farther still, until she reached the line where his jeans hung low his hips.

"Sophie, stop. Wait." It was an agony to stop her as her hands reached for his belt buckle, but he had to do it. "My pump… I can't …"

She peeked up at him, a playful dance in her eyes as she continued her assault on his senses. Before he knew what was happening, she had his fly undone and was greedily tugging at his jeans.

"You think you're the first guy I've been with who's hooked up to medical equipment?" she said. "For that matter, you think I've never gotten down and dirty with my own IV in? Oh, Harrison, you sweet innocent. I came of age in a hospital, remember?"

He stilled again, but this time out of incredulity. "Wait, what? Are you talking about your leukemia?"

"Of course. What else would I be talking about?"

"But you were a kid." The words came out as an accusation—mostly because they were. "You were sick. What the devil were they doing to you there?"

There was so much laughter in her eyes it was like looking into another world. "They weren't doing any-thing to me. Well, not unless the *they* in question were the other kids on the ward. Oh, man. There was this boy with Hodgkin's who could do the most amazing things with his—"

Harrison held up a hand, his whole body rigid. "I don't want to hear it. I thought hospitals were supposed to be a place of healing, of convalescence. Not dens of juvenile vice."

Sophie tilted her head and blinked up at him, looking the picture of virtue. "That shows how little you know about the real world, doesn't it? You wouldn't believe some of the parties we used to have. It'd be all fun and games and Methotrexate, but the second the nurses turned their backs…"

"You wicked little monster. Don't say it."

"…orgy time."

His whole body shook with laughter. There was nothing funny about the things she was telling him. The idea of a young, fragile Sophie lying in a bed somewhere, struggling to make it through each day, was a thing that made his chest grow tight. She'd suffered and suffered heavily, and no amount of making out with other kids behind closed doors could make that okay.

But he laughed anyway. Whatever trials she'd gone through, she'd managed to come out intact. Intact and, well, happy.

He wished he knew how.

"All those tangled IVs and anti-nausea drugs…" She heaved a mock sigh. "It wasn't always pretty, but we did the best we could. You don't know sexual resourcefulness until you sit down with a group of teenagers who don't dare let their heart rate monitors get high enough to set off alarms. The trick is to switch them when the doctors aren't looking."

"Okay, now you're just making things up."

"I guess you'll never know, will you?" she asked, a coy lift to her brow. "The misdeeds of my youth aren't a story for someone as uptight and proper as you."

"Uptight?" he said.

"I mean, you are the one freaking out over a tiny pump while there's a hot and willing honey trap on your sleeping bag."

Hot? Willing? This woman had no idea what she was doing to him over here.

...or maybe she did. The coy lift to her brow turned downright taunting. "Or is it Bubbles watching us that you object to? I gotta warn you, Harrison, you can't kick her to the curb every time you bring a woman to your bed. I guess, if you're one of those guys who just gets in there and bam-bam, crank-crank, finishes the job, it won't matter so much. But I was sort of hoping you'd be the kind who takes his time—"

"Sophie Vasquez, if you don't stop right now, I'm going to..." He trailed off, struggling to think of a punishment that would vindicate a fraction of the things she was making him feel right now.

"What will you do to me?" she purred. She shifted onto her knees and drew so close they were practically kissing. Her breath was warm against his mouth, her lips a smile against his. "You'll bam-bam, crank-crank, finish the job? Don't worry—I'm ready. I promise to come the moment you enter me."

There was nothing for it then but to give up. Give up, give in, give this woman everything she demanded and more. He could go to his grave knowing that he'd fought his valiant best—and that his valiant best wasn't even close to enough to defeat a woman like Sophie.

He acknowledged his helplessness by touching his mouth to hers and kissing her until both of them were breathless. He didn't know if it was the close air of the tent or if kissing Sophie would always leave him with a whirling head and no sense of his surroundings, but he was forced to push her to the ground so they both had somewhere to rest.

There wasn't so much space in the tent that they had much in the way of room to navigate, but it didn't seem to matter. She accepted the full weight of him as if he were nothing, bore the press of his body as a delight rather than a burden.

Harrison paused to unzip her jacket, his fingers shaking like he was some goddamned teenager who'd never felt up a woman before. Sophie didn't help matters any by moaning and arching her back, the warm jut of her breasts—Lady and the Tramp—tempting him into skipping his slow, sultry plan of disrobing her piece by piece. As much as he would have liked to take his time with each button, exposing her soft skin in inches, he didn't have the willpower.

So he yanked. Her oversize white shirt popped open with a satisfying scatter of buttons around the tent. The delicate band of a pink, lacy bra peeped up at him, encouraging him to explore with fingers, lips, tongue, *teeth*.

"This is not the kind of bra you're supposed to wear camping," he said in the absence of more appropriate commentary. A better, more sophisticated man might whisper sweet nothings or compare the dips and valleys of her body to the majestic mountains all around them, but no one had ever accused Harrison of being sophisticated.

"Yes, but it *is* the kind of bra you wear when you're trying to tempt a man into fucking you."

His mouth grew dry at the harsh yet sweet resonance of that word on her lips. *Fucking*. Not rolling in the hay. Not tumbling in the sheets. Not even making love. This sweet, beautiful woman was revealing more than just a tempting pair of breasts swelling out of a lace bra. And Harrison—God help him—loved it.

He groaned and ran his fingers down the midline of her stomach, her skin warm and impossibly soft. That feeling of heat and silk only increased the farther south he went, skimming past her navel and down the gentle swell of her belly. By the time he managed to reach the top lace of her underwear, she was scorching.

Although he was scorching too, he forced himself to take a deep breath and slow down. Sophie might think she could taunt him into making a botched, rushed job of this, but no matter how animalistic his urges tended to be, he was still capable of *some* restraint.

"I'm a man of honor, goddammit," he said as he moved back up her body. He intended to make that same journey, over her bra and down to her panties, but this time, he was going to do it with his mouth. "I want to taste you. I want to savor each limb."

Sophie's body shook with laughter, all those soft, rounded parts quivering against him. Burying her hands in his hair, she stroked and teased her nails against his scalp. "Oh, dear. I had no idea you were capable of so much eloquence. All that reserve was just part of your plan to lure me in, wasn't it?"

He yanked himself out of her grasp and tugged her jeans down her hips. Without bothering to remove her pants all the way, he laid his hand flat against the soft upper swell of her mons, eliciting a gasp. "I am *not* eloquent."

"No?" she asked and tipped her head back against the ground, grinding her hips upward until his hand was forced to move lower. Even through the thin satin of her panties, he could feel how wet she was, how ready. "Darn. I was looking forward to it. I guess you'd better spread my legs and fill me with your mighty oak instead. I don't know how much more of this I can take."

He was in the middle of doing just that when he stopped. "*What* did you just call it?"

"Your thundering maple," she replied, her head tipped back in ecstasy as his hand lay heavy against the wet heat of her. "Your turgid member, your one-eyed snake, the purple menace. I need it hard, Harrison, and I need it now."

"Purple menace?" he echoed.

"Well, I can't see it from here, obviously, but I've pictured it plenty of times. Would you mind if I make a more detailed survey later? I need you."

He proved powerless against a supplication like that one. "Your wish is my command—as long as you return the favor."

"Oh? And what do you wish?" The gentle mockery in her tone indicated she had no intention of doing anything she damn well didn't want to.

"You. Naked. In the sleeping bag. It's going to be a tight fit to squeeze both of us in there, but I've never known a tight fit to be unpleasant where sex is concerned."

"Oh, you sweet talker, you," she teased.

Her movements as she removed her clothing were not designed to entice a man. She didn't coyly expose her skin one inch at a time, and she didn't shimmy or shake as she pulled her jeans over her hips to showcase the rounded curves of her ass. Her movements were neat and efficient and even more seductive because of it.

All those parts of her that had been brought to his attention over the past few weeks—her naked shoulder and her bared neck, the sweet curve of her back and her strong, capable legs—hit him at once with their perfection. Not because *they* were perfect, but because *she* was.

"Don't gawk," she chided, but with enough stiffness in her voice that he knew she was feeling shy. "You're not the only one who feels awkward sometimes."

"That's not what you'll be feeling in a minute," he said, and swiftly unplugged his port before swabbing it down and putting it away. He paused long enough to grab a condom from his insulin kit—those zippered pouches proved handy from time to time—before stripping his own clothes.

"There is no way you're going to fit inside," Sophie said as he approached. As she was only halfway sitting up at the time, she was exactly on eye level with his erection—a thing his body interpreted with literal enjoyment.

"That's what they all say, but you'd be surprised how much nature allows for—"

She squeaked. "That isn't what I meant, and you know it! Although, um, congratulations? And it's not nearly as purple as I'd thought."

She followed this bit of insight with a giggle.

Harrison wasn't a vain man, but hearing a woman giggle while he was naked and about to fuck her wasn't his customary response.

It was *Sophie*'s response though, and he shouldn't have expected anything less.

"Scoot over, you provoking brat. I'm coming in there to make you regret your insolence."

"Ooh, I like the sound of that. Make me regret it. Make me regret it so hard."

She'd been correct in assuming that the two of them in a single sleeping bag would be a tight mishmash of body parts, requiring plenty of shifting and tugging and laughter. What she hadn't realized, however, was that once he was in and the length of her naked body was pressed against his in a perfect fit, nothing else mattered. She was impossibly soft, her limbs sliding up and down his in a way that made him ache to be inside her. And he would too, but not before he took her face in his hands and kissed her—long and slow, savoring the way she squirmed and moaned with each slide of his tongue along hers.

She was a body in constant motion, a woman full of vitality and joy. And he wasn't going to lie—the wet, searing heat of her as she wrapped first one and then the other leg around him was more temptation than any flesh-and-blood man could bear.

Before he penetrated her, however, he halted his wandering inspection of all her soft and slippery parts to cup her face. The two of them were perfectly immobile inside the sleeping bag, the only movement the rapid beat of her heart against his chest and her quick, panting breaths.

"I like you, Sophie," he said. It was both everything

and nothing and somehow the only thing he could think of to say.

A smile curved her lips, almost as though she could read his thoughts and see what he really meant. She proved it by her next words. "I know you do. It was inevitable. I warned you, remember? I'm like a goiter. A heaving, podgy pustule that grows out of your—"

Which was why he was laughing when he finally entered her. There wasn't much in the way of room to navigate the mechanics of bam-bam, crank-crank, but some things didn't require a ton of finesse.

Sex with Sophie was one of them. She was so inviting, so warm, that he felt at home the moment he slid into the wet heat of her. She angled her body to receive him, murmuring only once about how proud she was of nature for making it possible for even so big and wicked a man as him to fit.

"Now you're just being mean," he said, but he was still laughing.

"I won't ever be mean to you," she promised and, with an angelic look he knew was calculated to drive him crazy, added, "At least, not unless you deserve it."

There was nothing for it after that but to give her exactly what *she* deserved, which was as good an excuse as any to flip the sleeping bag so she was lying pinned underneath him. The friction and undulations of her hips against his did most of the work, and with his body on top of hers, gravity took care of the rest.

As was the case with most things where Sophie was concerned, she made all the noise she damn well pleased as her body rocked, an orgasm shaking her. Since Bubbles might take it into her head that those sounds required investigation—and because the majority of his friends were seated only a few hundred feet away—he silenced her with a deep, penetrating kiss that echoed the slide of his cock inside her. He didn't fully capture her scream that way, but it still felt amazing, that combination of sound and sensation entering his body at the same moment he released into hers.

He would have liked to stay that way forever, snuggled inside a sleeping bag—snuggled inside her—but the snuffling sounds from the corner picked up with an urgent whimper Harrison recognized. He might not be great at knowing when Bubbles was trying to alert him to a health hazard yet, but he'd spent enough time cleaning up puppy messes to realize that now was a good time to take a quick walk.

"Your timing is worse than a postcoital confessional," he grumbled to the animal as he reluctantly unzipped the sleeping bag enough to slip out. At Sophie's laugh, he turned to her with an accusing finger. "You should put that on the brochure, by the way."

"What? That puppies have to be potty trained even when you'd rather be fucking the trainer?"

There was that word again—*fucking*—so incongruously hot on those sweet lips of hers. Even though his body was still reeling from his orgasm, he could feel the stirring of interest taking over again.

Especially when she laughed and added, "Sure thing, Harrison. I'll ask Lila to put that in the next one."

"If you know what's good for you, you'll be sound asleep by the time I come back," he said, making quick work of discarding the condom and putting enough clothes on so he wouldn't lose any limbs to the cold. "I can't be held accountable for my actions if you aren't."

She sighed with mock heaviness and pulled the sleeping bag up to her chin like a child hiding from a monster under her bed. "With threats like that, I'm not sure I'll ever sleep again. I guess I'll just have to pay for my sins, won't I?"

Harrison's response was a long, hard look that had no power to move her. As he was rapidly coming to learn, he had no power over her at all.

And to be perfectly honest, he didn't care one bit. Pain was inevitable, loss a way of life. For now, he just wanted to enjoy Sophie for as long as he could manage to hold on.

chapter
16

As was the case with most things in life, all good things had to come to an end.

"Um, you know how I mentioned that thing about my mom?" Sophie asked as she, Harrison, and Bubbles pulled up the road to the Parks farmhouse. All three of them smelled like stale smoke and looked like dried meat, but that seemed about right. Camping was serious business. "About how she's staying at my house right now?"

Harrison grunted a noncommittal response. To be fair, his attention was taken up with his truck's sharp turn into the drive, but he could have at least provided a yes or a no answer. She wasn't such a fool that she assumed a few hot sexual interludes in the wilderness would cure Harrison of his taciturnity forever, but she'd hoped they'd at least have reached the monosyllabic stage.

Alas, not even the lure of her mighty vagina was that strong. Her determination to prove the rest of her *was* that strong, however, compelled her to keep going.

"According to this series of increasingly outraged texts from Dawn, it seems she has no intention of leaving anytime soon," she said. "She's even talking about installing one of those beds that pulls down from the wall and making her stay a prolonged one."

The truck came crunching to a halt, and Harrison cranked the parking brake. "Because she's being overprotective?"

"Well, yes."

She shifted in her seat, grateful for the need to get Bubbles comfortably out of the cab. Nothing provided a distraction quite like a puppy. They were a lot like babies that way. Slinging her bag over one shoulder and her purse over the other, she scooped the dog up and opened the door. To her surprise, Harrison was waiting on the other side. Wordlessly, he placed his hands on either side of her waist and helped her down.

His truck was tall—taller than her Fiat, certainly—but she could have easily made it down on her own. In fact, this kind of assistance, this careful solicitude, was the exact thing she resented from anyone related to her by blood. She was no small, precious thing that needed to be guarded from the world.

But as Harrison's hands lingered and his fingers crept down toward her ass, she felt nothing but a delightfully girlish thrill. To be cherished and protected because she was perceived as weak was a thing she loathed. To be cherished and protected because Harrison couldn't keep his hands off her was something she could get used to.

Way too used to, if the sudden throb between her legs was any indication.

He set her on the ground with his hands still in place. Sophie had to look up to meet his gaze, which she did with easy frankness. Just as frankly—but not as easily—she said, "The reason my mom is being like this is because of you. She heard about our, um, altercation at knitting circle and decided you were out to destroy her precious darling."

A frown touched the corners of Harrison's mouth. "I was afraid of that."

"I'm sure this weekend has given her time to cool off, but—"

"You should stay here," he said, the offer fairly tripping off his tongue.

Those words were exactly what Sophie had been angling for, but she'd expected to have to put forth a lot more effort first. This weird, old house was Harrison's castle, his home. Considering how strongly he'd reacted when she'd brought out the candles, she'd been prepared to plead her case—and plead it hard.

With sad, raisin eyes if she had to.

"Only if it's what you want, I mean," he added. His hands on her waist tightened, gripping her almost urgently. "I can't promise my dad will like having a houseguest, and it's hardly the Ritz around here, but you did say there would be some night training, didn't you?"

"Well, yes. But—"

"Then there you go," he said. "We might as well start now."

"You're sure you don't mind?" Her gaze searched his, but she was having a hard time reading him. The offer sounded sincere enough, but there was something shifty in the way he made it. It was almost as if he had an ulterior motive in asking her to stay.

What that motive might be, however, she had no idea.

"I'm sorry." He dropped his hands from her waist and

stepped back. "I didn't mean to be pushy. If you don't want to—"

"No! No, I do." Sophie put Bubbles into his hands, once again grateful that the puppy gave her something concrete to do. Her fingers brushed against Harrison's as they made the exchange, both of them weirdly fumbling.

Huh. Arguing with this man was easy. Sleeping with him a delight. But for some reason, this attempt at honest conversation was seriously tripping her up. The fact that he seemed just as awkward as she did helped her to add, "I do have one stipulation though."

"Why do you sound so cautious?"

"Because I don't think you'll like it."

His breath came out as a laugh. "When has that ever stopped you from doing things your own way before?"

A relieved grin spread across her face. *Here*, at least, she knew what she was doing. "Good point. I appreciate the offer to stay here, and I'm going to shamelessly take you up on it, but I think I should be in my own bed—my own room."

The expression on his face fell with such speed it might have been a bowling ball dropped from the top of the Space Needle. She leaped forward to reassure him, to tell him that it wasn't a personal choice so much as a professional one, but his dad sauntered out of the front door before she could get the words out.

"Harrison, I only meant—"

"There you are." Instead of his usual overalls, Wallace was dressed in thick black canvas pants and a checked shirt that fit him tighter than his usual garb. "I've been sitting around this house all damn day, waiting for you kids to get back."

Harrison swiveled to stare at his dad. "When have you ever cared about my whereabouts?"

Wallace's laugh was a cackle. "Never—and I still don't, so you can get down off your holy steed. I was talking to Sophie. Do you have a few minutes before you head home?"

"Actually, I—" she began.

"Dad, I invited Sophie to stay with us for a little while." Harrison's voice was equal parts defiance and trepidation. "I told you early on that she might need to stay overnight for some of the training, remember?"

Wallace's face lifted, and he snapped his fingers. "That's perfect! She can stay in the bedroom at the top of the stairs. It's probably dusty as all hell, but I'm sure the pair of you can set it to rights in no time."

Sophie felt more relief than she cared to admit at that invitation. As much as she would have loved to stay in Harrison's room—and in his arms—to do so would push the bounds of what she could reasonably sell to her family. What happened at the campground on her weekend off stayed at the campground on her weekend off, but she was technically earning a salary during the week. Having her own room would make it impossible for her family to storm the Parks lands in hopes of retrieving their lost damsel.

"Thank you, Wallace. That would be perfect. Since it's across from Harrison's room, we won't disturb you for the puppy's night training."

"Then it's done." Wallace clapped. "The room is yours."

"Wait—what?" Harrison glanced back and forth between them. Sophie had thought he'd be pleased to find his father such a willing convert to their cause, but he looked more hurt than anything else. "Are you serious? You're giving her your old room? *Mom's* old room? Just like that?"

A sinking feeling took over Sophie's gut. She'd known that bedroom was weirdly shrine-like, untouched by cleaning products or time, but she'd assumed it had occasionally been used by the beloved Aunt Caroline.

Not a mother and father. Not a husband and wife.

"It doesn't have to be that one," she said quickly, eager to keep the peace. "I'll be just as happy on the couch, I promise. Besides, it'll only be for a few nights, so it doesn't really matter where I stay."

She might as well have not been there for all the attention the two Parks men paid her.

"Why not?" Wallace asked as he crossed his arms and squared to meet his son. "It's been sitting there empty for twenty goddamn years."

"Twenty-*two* goddamn years, you mean," Harrison replied. "But who's counting?"

"You, apparently."

"Oh, right. Because I'm the weird one here. I'm the one who forbade anyone to touch anything in that room after she left."

"I never said that."

"Yes, you did. You said it all the time." Harrison lifted the puppy in a protective curl against his chest. He didn't even seem to notice that Bubbles took an equally protective pose, her eyes appraising Wallace as if trying to decide whether or not he was about to disturb her beloved master. "You said it on birthdays. You said it on holidays. You said it when I graduated. In fact, you said it anytime I showed the least desire to move on with my life."

"I don't remember—"

"*Leave it*, you said. *Leave it all. I like it this way*."

The older man looked uncomfortably away. "Well, you should have known better than to listen to me."

"I was a kid! Listening to you wasn't really optional."

It seemed prudent for Sophie to intervene. Whatever her family's problems, they paled in comparison to the emotion pulsing between these two hard, stubborn men. "I didn't mean to start anything, you two. Honestly. Why don't I head home, and we'll revisit this plan later? You guys can probably use the space."

"You're staying here," Harrison said, turning his attention to her. His eyes were hard, but they softened as they landed on her. "You can't abandon me yet, Sophie. Please."

"Yeah, you're staying here." Wallace sounded just as determined, though without the intensity that was exuding off Harrison in waves. "It's my house, and I'll invite whoever I damn well please to stay in it."

Sophie looked back and forth between them, a smile playing at her lips despite the gravity of the conversation. They were literally fighting for the same thing, and neither one of them seemed to notice the irony of it.

"With such polite offers from you both, how can I refuse?" she said sweetly. "I'll call my sisters and have one of them bring me a bag. But I'll be staying on the couch until you can work something better out between you. I'm not about to sleep in a room that hasn't been touched in over two decades. I didn't want to have to admit it to two such robust outdoorsmen as yourselves, but I'm scared of ghosts."

"The devil you are," Harrison said, watching her. "You aren't scared of anything."

"Of *this* kind of ghost?" she asked. Of the past, of the woman who somehow broke these two glorious, hard-headed men? "Are you kidding? I'm terrified."

🐾🐾🐾

Despite her most earnest protestations, Sophie ended up in Harrison's bedroom. The weird embargo on the room that had belonged to his mother stayed in place, but instead of letting her crash on the couch like she wanted, he insisted she take the privacy and comfort of his room instead.

"That couch is too damn lumpy," he'd said as though it were the clincher in the argument.

It had been another one of those moments that could have easily riled her temper—she was just as capable of sleeping on lumps as the next girl, thank you very much—but Harrison's motives had been nothing but chivalrous. Well, mostly.

It's the least I can do after subjecting you to all that.

I mean it—there could be things living in that couch that no human should have to cohabitate with.

Goddammit, Sophie, would you stop being difficult and just do as I ask for once?

With such obvious displays of affection on the table, she had no choice but to relent. Besides, there was something so deliciously forbidden about being invited into the place where Harrison Parks slept. Unlike the rest of the house, it was cozy and neat and incredibly like him. The wallpaper was a more masculine blue pinstripe than the faded florals in the hallway, and the floors had been meticulously sanded and redone sometime in the past decade. She'd almost expected him to go for sleek metallics and modern fixtures, but all the pieces had the worn look of well-loved furniture—antiques, probably, and as old as the house itself.

It was, she realized, a glimpse at what this house *could* be, if only it were allowed to recover from whatever blight had placed it in a time warp oh so many years ago. Twenty-two so many years ago, most likely.

A knock sounded at the door before she could make the mistake—or delight—of snooping through Harrison's drawers. Assuming it was one of her sisters with a suitcase full of clothes and toiletries, she sprang from the bed to answer it. With any luck, it would be Dawn. Lila was a gem of a sister, and Sophie wouldn't trade her for the world, but she'd probably pack things like full-length flannel nightgowns to ward off chills and the retainer Sophie hadn't worn since she was eighteen. Dawn could be trusted to throw in something with straps or lace. Possibly both.

"I know what you're thinking," she said as she pulled on the handle only to stop and find herself facing the tall, sparse frame of Wallace Parks.

"Doubt it" came his prompt reply. He peered around the door as if to ensure she was alone. Finding that she was, he added, "I came to ask you a favor."

"Of course."

She gestured for him to follow her inside. From the surprised way he took in the sight of his son's room, it was obvious he hadn't been in there in some time—if ever. It seemed strange to her, this disinterest so intense it bordered on the perverse, but there was obviously a lot about this family she didn't understand.

Wallace was careful to close the door behind him, sealing the two of them alone in the quiet of the room. He looked distinctly uncomfortable, casting furtive glances to each of the corners as if expecting a hiding shadow to pounce, so Sophie did her best to put him at ease.

"I can't thank you enough for letting me stay here for a bit," she said with what she hoped was calm friendliness. She sat on the bed, the soft mattress sinking under her weight. "I know it's not always pleasant, having a virtual stranger drop in and tell you all the work that needs to be done on your home—"

"Work?" Wallace's voice was sharp with suspicion. "What do you mean, work? You already put all those damn plastic things in the outlets and made it impossible to pee in the middle of the night. What else is there to do?"

She'd never be able to say what prompted her to reply the way she did, but she repressed a smile and said, "I'd like to put tablecloths out, if you don't mind. They really improve the appearance of a room, don't you think?"

Wallace's only response was to harrumph, which told her everything she needed to know.

"Oh my," she said. "You totally like Bubbles now, don't you?"

He didn't meet her eye. "She's all right."

"With that adorable little face…"

"I still think she looks like a rat."

"And those tiny clacking paws…"

"Keeps me up all night."

"And the way Harrison has fallen completely and totally in love with her…"

Wallace blinked, and just like that, he relaxed. He didn't go so far as to sit in the leather club chair in the corner, but his shoulders came down and some of the heavy lines of his face sagged. "She's been good for him, hasn't she?"

"I think so, yes."

"You both have." Wallace spoke with the certainty of a man who was accustomed to having his word accepted as law—a fact borne out when he didn't give Sophie time to do more than blush and struggle to come up with an appropriate reply. "You're good at people, right? At women people?"

Her embarrassment quickly gave way to laughter, but she was careful to suppress it. As delightful as it was to laugh at Harrison, she doubted that approach would prove as effective with his father.

"I'm pretty good at women people, yes. My whole family is." Almost as an apology, she added, "In addition to one very opinionated mother, I have two very opinionated sisters. My poor dad has been dominated by femininity for as long as I can remember."

Wallace nodded as though this made perfect sense. He didn't, however, speak.

"Um. Is there a woman in your life?" she prodded. "One you're…seeing?"

He cast her a sharp-eyed glance. "What do you know about it?"

To tell him that she and Harrison had witnessed him gallivanting through Spokane dressed to impress would only fluster the poor man, so she said the only other thing that made sense—the truth.

"You seem happy."

His face folded in a smile, the deep lines around his eyes crinkling in the process. "I am happy." The smile disappeared as easily as it had come. "I should say I *could* be happy. I'm not so sure I deserve it."

Her heartstrings gave a strong tug. "What's her name?"

"Minerva."

"Oh, that's a lovely name." Sophie patted the mattress next to her. "Where did you meet? Online? A dating app?"

He didn't take her invitation—or her bait. "How we met isn't important. And I don't need your advice on any of that other stuff…the love stuff. The thing is, I want to buy her something big, something nice. But not jewelry."

"No, that's much too cliché," she agreed gravely.

"And not flowers."

"They never last."

He shifted from one foot to the other. "I was thinking a puppy might make a nice present, but I don't know what kind to get. You know women *and* puppies. What do you think?"

Sophie thought quite a few things, not the least of which was that a dog made a terrible gift unless you knew with absolute certainty it would be welcomed. Dropping an animal with a bow around its neck on a person was akin to leaving a baby in a basket on their front doorstep.

"I don't know, Wallace, a pet is an awfully big commitment."

Instead of taking offense at her words, Wallace perked. "Yes, that's it. A commitment."

"I mean, are you sure she even *wants* a pet?"

That one got to him. "Well, of course I do," he said. "I'm not a born idiot."

"Yes but wanting a pet and being able to take care of one are two different things."

"Now see here, young lady!" Wallace puffed up his chest and lowered his brow, looking so much like Harrison, Sophie was hard put not to laugh. "I asked for your *advice*, not your opinion. If you must know, Minerva and I are going to move in together. I'll be the one doing most of the cleaning and feeding, so all I wanted to know is what kind of creature she might like that won't keep me up all goddamn night with its howls and clackety claws."

Sophie choked. "Something more along the lines of a Great Dane, perhaps?"

Wallace relaxed. "Now you're talking."

As much fun as it would have been to provide Wallace with a list of puppy options, there was a part of his speech that left her unsettled.

"Um, when you say you're going to move in together, do you mean…" She cast a careful look around Harrison's room.

"This old dump?" Wallace laughed, though there was a caginess to his gaze that made her feel he had more fondness for this house than he let on. Which, to be fair, seemed about on par for a Parks man. God forbid one of them admit to such a normal thing as emotional attachment to an old family home. "No. Too many bad memories. We want a fresh start."

Her next question wasn't any easier. "Does Harrison know?"

"No!" Wallace's head jerked up with a start. "And

you're not to go telling him, understand? Nothing is finalized yet. Not but what he'll be glad to see the back of me… We don't get on. We never have."

On the contrary, Sophie had a suspicion that they were as tied to each other as two people possibly could be. Oh, they were grumpy and antagonistic, and both obviously liked to have things their own way, but they were all each other had. With the exception of Aunt Caroline and the occasional helping hand from Oscar, neither one had mentioned another friend or relative who'd stepped up to help a struggling single father raise his diabetic son.

In fact, they'd been alone together for so long, she doubted they were aware just how weirdly codependent they'd become.

No one knew that kind of relationship better than Sophie. When sacrifices were made—when one life was put on hold for the sake of another—it was impossible to just pack up and move on. No matter how much you might want to.

"I think he has a right to know," Sophie said gently. "It's as much his life as yours."

Wallace pointed a gnarled finger at her. "If you say so much as a word to him, young lady…"

"You'll what?" Her voice took on a hint of the steel that had been appearing so much in Parks company lately. "Let me remind you that I don't work for you, or even for your son. I work for Oscar."

Wallace's internal struggle was visible on every line of his face. His lips twitched and twisted and finally turned flat. "Please," he said. "I'm asking as a personal favor. I'll tell him the moment my plans are finalized, I promise."

Had he turned surly or made more of those gruff demands, Sophie might have been able to stand her ground. That bleak look, however, and that plea in his voice...

She sighed. "The *moment* they're finalized," she warned.

"Word of a Parks," he promised. Before she had time to wonder just what she'd gotten herself into, he added, "Well?"

"Um. Well, what?"

He released an exasperated sigh. "What kind of dog should I get for Minerva? Something friendly but not too friendly. Clean and low-maintenance. And none of that messy shedding everywhere, yeah?"

She splayed her hands helplessly. Although she might be comfortable selecting service animals for clients with very specialized health and professional needs, she had no idea what to tell him. What she wanted to say—that he couldn't move out without at least *talking* to his son first—was clearly off the table.

"A cat," she finally said.

"Eh?"

"What you're describing isn't a dog—it's a cat. And not a kitten either. You want one of those gnarly old ones from the animal shelter that everyone else over- looks because it has one eye and mangy fur and hates children."

"I do?"

"Yes. Those cats need good homes more than kittens, and they're almost always well-trained. They practically take care of themselves."

She'd half expected Wallace to be up in arms at her

suggestion, but he nodded and scratched his grizzled chin. "A cat. Yes, a cat. With one eye and a terrible personality. She'll love that."

Sophie wasn't sure whether that was a point for or against Minerva's taste, but she merely echoed, "She'll love that."

With a cackle and a wink, Wallace turned to leave. "Of course. After all, she chose me, didn't she?"

chapter
17

W hat the hell did Sophie do to your father?"
Harrison turned at the sound of Oscar's voice.
The older man strode across the wildfire training
grounds. It was impossible—and ill-advised—to set fire
to actual trees, so most of their training included mock
scenarios played out over this huge expanse of land
attached to the Department of Natural Resources offices.

Oscar halted when he reached Harrison, who was
holding a clipboard in one hand and a pen in the other.
He also had Bubbles strapped to his chest, which was,
of course, what Oscar zeroed in on first.

"Never mind. The real question is, what the hell did
Sophie do to you?"

Harrison felt none of the irritation he expected from
such of a question. Strange though it seemed, he was
starting to feel more uncomfortable *without* the puppy
than he did with her. He supposed that was the inevitable outcome of spending almost twenty-four hours a
day with someone. You grew attached.

He glanced over to where Sophie had seated herself
on a folding chair near the edge of the field and smiled.

You grew *very* attached.

One week of this woman living under his roof and he'd come to depend on her in ways that were both alluring and terrifying. Yes, she'd dragged him to a dodgeball practice or two. And, yes, he'd sat through the infamous beer choir, which turned out to be a group of about twenty drunk millennials discussing craft brews and signing show tunes.

The promised social whirlwind hadn't been nearly as unpleasant as he'd feared, especially since it had the benefit of distracting him from Sophie's constant proximity—a proximity she refused to consider anything but work related.

While we're together under this roof, she'd said, *consider me officially on the clock*. As was the case with Bubbles, he wasn't allowed to pet her during training hours, had to treat her more like a coworker than a friend.

Which, as it turned out, was a thing he was weirdly okay with. The agony of not having her naked and underneath him was offset by the simple joy he felt when she stood humming in the kitchen as she made coffee. Or how she littered the bathroom sink with lotions and potions he'd rather not examine too closely. Her presence in that house was so natural, so comfortable, it made his chest grow tight to think that he'd somehow lived for so many decades without her in it.

Or that he might somehow have to do it again.

"Go ahead," he said to Oscar, forcing himself to focus on the man standing in front of him. Sophie might only be on loan to him, but Oscar was the sort of fixture that never left. "Light something on fire. Anything on fire."

Oscar made the motion of patting himself down and

shrugged. "I seem to have forgotten my arson kit at home. Is she comfortable like that? She doesn't look very comfortable."

"I'm serious. I'm sure you have a lighter or something. Here—ignite this stick."

Oscar eyed him warily but complied with the request, extracting a Zippo from one of his vest pockets. "Will this do? And aren't we supposed to be training people to be *more* careful with their outdoor fires?"

"Just do it."

It took a few tries for Oscar to get a flame going on the slightly damp stick Harrison had handed him, but if there was one thing his boss knew, it was how blazes worked. He brandished the smoldering flame like a torch, wafting it back and forth in front of the puppy. Bubbles twitched, but she didn't seem overly distressed. In fact, her nose twitched in recognition of the familiar smoke scent—and then she dismissed it as something unworthy of her attention.

"Well, shit." Oscar waved the stick a little closer. "She barely seems to notice it."

Harrison nodded, his heart swelling with pride at everything Bubbles had overcome. He found it hard to believe he'd once thought he needed a big, ferocious dog to do the job. A big dog didn't have to work to be strong. A big dog didn't have to fight to earn respect. This tiny, scrappy thing had been required to put in five times the effort right from the get-go, and she'd done it even when she quaked in fear.

She was a badass, this little one. And she was *his*.

"It's not a perfect system yet," Harrison admitted. "And we won't know how she reacts in the middle of a real forest fire until she's in one, but I'm beginning to think we may have reached a compromise."

"Is that a hint for me to clear you for duty?" Oscar asked.

Harrison laughed. "Well, it *wasn't*, but if you want to take it that way..."

He didn't actually expect it to work. He'd spent enough time under Oscar's leadership to know that nothing would move that man—he was like a rock that way. But there was a softening in Oscar's expression, a small crack in his armor.

Finally.

Or so he thought. Oscar scratched his chin and cast a glance over Harrison's shoulder, quelling his optimism with "I'm leaving that up to Sophie. As soon as she thinks you two are ready, I'll schedule a date to bring the air force team in. That'll be a good test for you both."

Harrison didn't bother to stop his groan. If Oscar was an unmovable rock, then Sophie was a whole fucking mountain. Like Bubbles, her small stature and air of fragility were deceptive. He'd battle a dozen rabid Great Danes before he'd willingly tackle her.

"Well, Sophie?" Oscar asked, all geniality. Harrison didn't have to turn to know Sophie was walking up behind him. He could practically feel the air vibrating around her. "What's the word on our boy here? Is he ready to get working again?"

"I don't know about the boy, but the puppy seems A-OK for duty."

"Wait—really?" He spun, unable to keep the joy from his face.

She shrugged. "Sure. I told you the pair of you have

natural chemistry, and you've both worked really hard these past few weeks. Starting Monday, I don't see why you can't step up the fire exposure. You just have to promise you'll slow down and step away if she starts to show signs of distress. You can undo months of hard work that way."

As delighted as he was to hear that he wasn't going to have to fight a dozen rabid Great Danes to get what he wanted, Harrison frowned. "I'm not a monster. Of course I'm not going to push her too hard if she's upset."

Sophie laughed and held up her hands. "Don't shoot. I forgot how much you love that little dog."

She was mocking him again. "I never said I loved her."

"You started knitting her a sweater, Harrison. If that's not love, I don't know what is."

"So far, all I've managed is half of a crooked scarf."

"You let her choose the color."

"Of course I did. I don't know what looks good on a goddamned dog."

Sophie's eyes twinkled. "He and Bubbles get the all-clear from me, Oscar. Let them loose to do their thing."

Harrison had been under the impression that he and Sophie had doing a pretty good job of keeping their relationship from showing, but Oscar watched their interaction with narrowing suspicion in his eyes. Sleeping with Sophie probably ranked up there with hurting Sophie in terms of Oscar's ultimatum, so Harrison decided to change the subject.

"What were you saying about my dad?" he asked.

"Eh?"

"Earlier, when you walked up, you asked me what

Sophie had done to my dad." Harrison paused. "If it's about the candles, you're asking the wrong guy. She's turned him into some kind of essential oil convert. I have no idea how."

"It wasn't difficult," Sophie said primly. "You should never overlook the healing properties of aromatherapy."

Oscar chuckled, but he shook his head. "No, that's not it. I asked him out for a drink last night, but he turned me down. He said he had plans. I can't remember the last time he had plans."

"Maybe he had a date," Sophie suggested.

Harrison snorted, recalling her ridiculous Tinder suspicions from earlier, but Oscar turned to her with interest. "You think? I was wondering the same thing."

"Wait—what?" Harrison asked.

"Um." Sophie was careful not to meet Harrison's eye. "It wouldn't be too weird, would it? I mean, he's not *that* old."

"Old, no. A miserable old bastard, yes."

"He has been looking awfully...sunny lately," Oscar admitted. "And when I went to visit him at the bar a few weeks back—you know, Harrison, when you said he'd gone out early in the morning—he wasn't there. Meg says she's been seeing a lot less of him these days."

"Aw. Maybe he *feels* sunny," Sophie suggested.

Both Oscar and Harrison laughed at that.

"Sorry, Sophie, but Wallace Parks hasn't been anything but doom and gloom since VHS tapes stopped being a thing. Come to think of it, Harrison, neither have you."

There was Oscar's look of suspicion again, all narrowed eyes and furrowed brow.

"He's not wrong," Harrison said with a grunt designed

to allay suspicion. "Digital streaming is just another way for the government to keep tabs on your movements."

"I don't see what the big deal is either way. He's a grown man. If he wants to date someone and be happy, I think he should do exactly that." Sophie reached for Harrison's shoulders in a move he misinterpreted as a gesture of affection. He stiffened, but she only reached for the buckle of his sling strap to unhook the dog.

The effect of this exchange, however, seemed to work wonders on Oscar's suspicions. Harrison and Sophie laughing together might put up all his red flags, but Harrison awkwardly shying away from any and all physical contact was right on par with what the man expected from him.

He stood still and let Sophie finish extracting the dog, careful to look as unpleasant and annoyed as possible.

"What are you doing with her?" he asked with a quick glance at his watch. "It's nearing five o'clock—quitting time. Unless you wanted to run through those training exercises one more time, we should be done for the week."

"Oh, I know," she said with her usual cheerful calm— that same cheerful calm that disregarded everything he said and did. "But I'd like her to explore the training grounds once or twice while *not* attached to you. You don't mind, do you, Oscar?"

He waved her off with a fond smile, thus confirming Harrison's belief that Oscar too was incapable of telling that woman no. Whether it made him feel better or worse, however, he wasn't prepared to say. While it was nice to know he was no anomaly, it would have been nice to have at least *one* person out there who could be trusted not to fall under her spell.

"Monday morning, Harrison," Oscar said to him, all signs of that indulgent softness gone from sight. "Nine o'clock. Don't make me regret this."

"No, sir."

Oscar looked as though he had more to say—or perhaps he was reluctant to leave Harrison and Sophie alone—but he eventually took off, heading through the field to where his Suburban was parked in the lot.

Harrison waited until the car had pulled away before turning to Sophie. "Are we really going to walk Bubbles around out here, or was that a ruse to get rid of Oscar?"

"Um. A ruse, obviously. The second Bubbles is off the clock, that means I am too."

"Why does that matter—" he began, but there was no need to finish. One look at Sophie supplied all the answer he needed. She licked her lips in what had to be deliberate leisure, making it impossible for him to look away from the soft, gently parted plumpness.

He took a wide step back. "Oh no you don't."

"What?" she asked. "I didn't say a word."

"Oscar knows there's something between us. He can tell."

"Can he? I wonder how."

"You know very well how. Ever since you started staying at the house, you've been exuding sex at me."

Those oh-so-plump lips parted in a laugh. "I've been exuding sex?"

"At *me*," he added, lest she forget the most important part of that accusation. Sex appeal in a woman who looked like her was no mystery, but the fact that it was unfurling his direction was. It was as though tendrils of ivy were wrapping around him, drawing him closer and closer until he had no chance of escape.

A gorgeous plant, ivy, but destructive as all hell.

She did it now with a firm step in his direction, careful of the puppy who lay obediently at their feet. The tugging started in his gut, a churning of desire that worked up to his throat and choked him from the inside. From there, it moved lower, drawing him inexorably forward.

"No one has ever accused me of exuding sex before," she said, her voice a low purr. "How am I doing it?"

"We can start with this ridiculous thing you're wearing," he said, since it seemed as good a place to start as any. It also seemed as good a place to *touch* as any, so he slipped a hand out to grab her about the waist—which, as any man with eyes in his head and blood in his veins would notice, was stark bare. "Where is the rest of your shirt, young lady?"

She giggled and arched into his touch, allowing his palm to slide down the gently sloping softness of her back. He stopped just above the line of her jeans. "It's called a crop top, Harrison. All the kids are wearing them these days."

He highly doubted it. Whatever seductress of a designer had come up with this shirt obviously had a woman built like Sophie in mind. There wasn't a whole lot of skin showing between the high waist of her jeans and the tightly fitting black shirt, but what was there was bound by two straps that crossed over her belly button and drew in the narrowest part of her waist.

He fingered one of those straps now, over and under the fabric, pulling it out just far enough to snap it back into place. Sophie gasped, but she followed this up by tugging his lower lip between her teeth and giving back as good as he gave.

"If Oscar knew what kinds of things I want to do to you, he'd have me killed," Harrison muttered.

"Such a scaredy-cat," she teased.

There was no use denying it. He was scared of Oscar. He was scared of Sophie. Hell, he was scared of himself—particularly of how quickly he was casting aside every scruple he'd ever had for a chance at feeling this woman in his arms again.

"What are some of the things you want to do, by the way?" she asked as she coiled her arms around his neck and pulled him closer. "You should tell me. In explicit detail."

He gave up on trying to keep his hands above her waist and tugged the front of her jeans until her pelvis lined up with his. The sweet agony of sensation rocketing through his groin caused him to groan.

"Nice try," he said. "The only thing I'm going to do to you is put you in my truck and take you home."

She jolted back. "Home?" Her voice was small and her frown intense. "What for? I thought it was going well—the training, the cohabitating."

He realized his mistake almost immediately. To him, *home* meant only one place—the same place it had always been, whether for good or bad or, as was more often the case, terrible. Since Sophie had been staying there, however, he'd found himself seeing it with a more optimistic eye. It was rundown as all hell, yes, and there was no mistaking that it contained memories that should have been exorcised a long time ago, but she could make even a backwoods cave feel like the only place he wanted to be.

To her, however, home meant Spokane. It meant her mother and sisters. It meant those people who loved her and underestimated her in equal proportions.

Although how they could go twenty-six years of living with this woman and not see how superior she was to every other goddamn person on the planet, he had no idea.

"Home," he repeated more firmly this time. He moved his hands around to her backside, forcing their hips into more perfect alignment. The rounded softness of her ass filled his hands, and he realized that he probably wasn't going to make it the entire twenty-minute drive home. "But you wanted to show Bubbles around here first, didn't you?"

He released her, causing her to blink up at him in some perplexity, but he took her by the hand before she could misunderstand. "I think she should see inside the DNR building, don't you? Especially my office."

"Your office? But—"

"But isn't the building empty?" he asked. "Yes, it is. I, however, have a key. We'll be all alone in there."

"Oh," she said and, with dawning understanding, "*oh*."

"If you don't like it, you have nothing to blame but that shirt," he added. "Why can't you wear sweatpants like a normal person? Have you ever noticed that no matter what you have on, there's always at least one part of your body on display?"

She giggled and allowed herself to be pulled across the field, Bubbles trailing happily in their wake. "Do I? How strange."

"Not strange," he grunted. "Torture."

The Department of Natural Resources didn't employ

very many full-time employees. It was something he'd often lamented in the past, especially when trying to get any kind of equipment budget passed, but he could only be grateful for it today. Everyone had already gone home for the evening and, given the time of year, weren't likely to return until morning.

"I didn't know you had an office here," Sophie said as he let them in the front door and flicked on the reception lights. "Poor Oscar only has a tiny room, so I figured space was at a premium."

"I should probably warn you that my office is more like a dark hole I've claimed as my own," he said. He still had her hand firmly in his—and had no intention of letting go anytime soon. At her look of surprise, he released a gruff laugh, "I'm the guy they send out to the front lines, Sophie, not some goddamn executive. Between July and October, I'm lucky to sleep in my own bed for more than a week at a time. And the season can last through the end of the year if they loan me out to California, which they almost always do."

"I know, but you said—"

"I lied."

"Well, that wasn't very nice of you. I was hoping for a quickie on your desk. You implied there would be a quickie on your desk."

He'd just lied. He'd just admitted that for six months out of the year, he was practically nonexistent. And Sophie's only disappointment was that she wasn't going to get tossed over his desk?

"Oh, there's not going to be anything quick about what's about to happen to you," he promised, and hoisted her over his shoulder.

Bubbles took instant exception to this action with a bark of protest, but Harrison wasn't about to unload such a delightful burden. Sophie's upper half hung over his back, her ass in the air and right on level with his head. She kicked ineffectively at him, laughing and protesting to be put down, but Harrison only tightened his hold.

"I'm getting really tired of the two of you telling me what to do," he said. He tried to keep his voice authoritative and stern, but it was impossible. He'd never felt less authoritative or stern in his life. He lowered himself—and Sophie—just enough to scoop Bubbles into his arms and carried the pair of them to the far end of the hall. "For the next hour, you're both going to do exactly as I say."

"Yes, sir," she said with a laugh that made it impossible for him to buy her obedience. She proved it two seconds later when he set her down and tugged at a cord dangling from the ceiling. A pair of seldom-used stairs floated down, beckoning the pair of them into an open panel above their heads. "Wait—are you about to lure me into an unused attic where no one can hear me scream? I should probably warn you...I've read that horror story. I know how it ends."

"It *is* pretty dark up there," he admitted, suddenly feeling unsure. "And dusty. And not...glamorous."

"Hey." Her hand touched his arm. "You don't have to do that. What is it? Some kind of storage?"

He nodded, more grateful than he could say that she was making this easy on him. She *always* did that— pushed when he needed it, stopped pushing when he needed it more. "It's where they keep a lot of the out-of-date equipment that the state refuses to get rid of."

She smiled. "That sounds promising. Hefty hoses and fire poles and all that."

"It's not that kind of equipment. It's mostly filing cabinets."

The mention of filing cabinets and dust should have had Sophie running for the hills—and taking Bubbles with her—but she seemed to sense that there was more to that upstairs hole than he was letting on. "I'd like to see it. May I?"

He nodded and watched as she swung a leg onto the bottom step and fearlessly made her way up the rickety contraption. It creaked and groaned a protest, but that didn't seem to stop her. Harrison had a nice view of her ass as she neared the top, and then a quick glimpse of her ankles before she disappeared altogether.

She didn't appear to be making any sounds of disgust, so he grabbed Bubbles and followed her up the steps. They creaked in even *greater* protest to his weight, but he'd been coming here for close on sixteen years now. They'd always held him before.

He paused on the landing to allow his eyes a moment to adjust. A skylight provided a beam of sunshine in one corner, highlighting dusty motes that danced in the air, but other than that, there was no lighting up here. No electricity, no running water, no real walls, even. Bare studs and rough floorboards were all that had been done to make this space usable.

"You have a bed up here," Sophie said without looking over at him.

He grunted. It wasn't a bed so much as an old mattress laid in one corner and heaped with blankets, but he'd slept in it enough for it to count.

She drew closer to the sunlit corner, her head tilted at a curious angle as she took in the rest. "You have books. And a flashlight. And snacks."

He grunted again, but it was more of a chuckle this time. Sophie didn't sound the least appalled at how pathetic that list sounded for a grown-ass man of thirty. She cast a look back at him over her shoulder. "Why, Harrison Parks. Is this your secret clubhouse?"

He set Bubbles on the ground and gave her permission to sniff out the area. "I know. It's pretty sad, right?"

Her eyes widened. "Are you kidding me? I *always* wanted a secret clubhouse. My dad built a playhouse one year and put it up in the backyard, but there was nothing secret about it. Either Lila or Dawn or, most of the time, one of Dawn's boyfriends, was holed up inside. God, they used to smoke so much pot in there."

Harrison's chuckle was impossible to subdue that time. "Sounds a lot more exciting than this place."

She returned her attention to the small bookcase that contained most of his reading materials. "What is it, exactly?"

Even though she couldn't see him, he shrugged. There was something comforting in making that gesture, as if he was robbing this place of its significance. "At first? A place to crash. I started working here when I was really young, just fourteen, so having a bed that *wasn't* under my dad's roof was everything to me. I'd sleep here whenever we had a fight. Which, to be honest, was pretty much every day."

As usual, Sophie cut straight to the heart of the matter. "Do you still use it?"

He shrugged again, but it was less comforting this

time. "Yeah. It's stupid, but I like it. There aren't…"
He paused. As usual, finding the right words to express
himself was a challenge. This is where he'd usually give
up and close off, finding it easier to retreat than to keep
struggling. It still *would* be easier, but he wanted to try.
Sophie deserved nothing less. "I don't have many places
that are just mine."

She nodded her understanding. Now that she'd lived
inside his house, she *knew*. For decades, it had been
a cold place, a dead place, a place no rational person
would choose to be.

Until you walked through the door.

"Oscar gave me this place as a kind of present,"
Harrison said, his voice thick. "He knew I needed to get
away and clear my head sometimes, so he gave me a
key to the building and made sure everyone knows this
place is off-limits."

She whirled, her lips parted in surprise. "You mean to
tell me that no one else has been up here in sixteen years?"

He nodded.

"Yet you brought me?"

He nodded again.

"But…" Her eyes remained wide, a question burning inside them. It would have been easy to wave that
question away—to pull her into his arms and distract
her with how comfortable and warm that mattress could
be—but she needed to hear this. She needed to know.

"You've been trying to push past my walls since the
day you met me," he said and extended his arms wide.
"Well, this is what I've been hiding. It's a little stark and
a lot underwhelming, but it's all I've got."

Sophie didn't say a word. Disappointment began to

take shape in the back of his throat, but she took a step forward and placed a hand on his cheek. "Thank you," she said.

And that was all.

It was exactly what he needed to hear. Not pity and not enthusiasm—not even an awkward change of subject. Just gratitude.

His own gratitude took the form of a kiss. Given the imposed chastity of the past week, it would have been so easy for that kiss to become frantic and desperate, for his need to have this woman in his arms pushing aside all other considerations.

But he didn't feel frantic. He didn't feel desperate. He just felt whole.

She responded to the kiss by melting into him. Her body was pliable and warm, her mouth a soft place for him to land. He didn't know what to do with such a gift—with the offering she gave him every time she opened up and let him in—but *she* did.

"And here I thought you were just bringing me up here to ravish me," she said, smiling up at him. The upturn of her lips filled his heart, the happiness in her eyes impossible to ignore.

Laughter. That was the one thing this place needed, what it had been missing all those years.

It was what had been missing from his heart too.

"I guess that's what I get for jumping to conclusions," she added. "Your way is a lot better."

He answered her laugh with one of his own. Almost immediately, the attic began to feel airier, lighter. *More like home.* "Ravishing you can still be on the menu, if you want," he said. "In fact, there's nothing I'd like to do more."

"Yes, please."

It was all the invitation he needed. The moment was right to put the mattress to good use, but Bubbles had taken up a patient perch right in the middle. Harrison didn't have the heart to move her, nor did it seem all that important—not when Sophie was standing right in front of him.

He sank to his knees and grabbed her by the hips. Sophie's surprised gasp lasted only a second before it transformed into an enthusiastic murmur of appreciation.

"I'm going to need you to remove these jeans," he said, his voice rough with desire. "Ravishing requires nothing less."

She eyed him with a kind of laughing disbelief, but she obeyed him all the same. "I thought it was the shirt you took exception to," she said as she unbuttoned her jeans and began sliding them down over her hips. Her underwear had taken a drastic turn for the scandalous since their camping trip, today's offering some kind of red lace contraption it looked like he could tear with his teeth.

He decided, right then and there, to do just that—especially once Sophie took her time unzipping her little black ankle boots and tossing them to the floor.

"I hope you aren't too attached to these panties," he warned.

"Well, actually, I—"

The rest of her sentence was lost in her squeal of delight as he pulled her forward using both his hands and his teeth—his hands cupping the sweet curves of her ass, his teeth caught on the upper band of the lace panties.

Then he tugged. Hard.

The sound of his teeth ripping through delicate fabric

was oddly satisfying, especially when it was followed by Sophie's low moan. Her hands dropped to his head, those perfect fingernails scraping against his scalp as she threaded her fingers through the strands. A tingling sensation worked down his spine, not stopping until the rest of his body quivered alongside it.

"This is Chantilly lace, I'll have you know," she said as he managed a particularly good tear. One more tug, and he'd have reached the gusset—not to mention the hot apex of her thighs. "From La Perla."

"I don't know what any of those words mean, and I sure as hell don't care right now."

Sophie laughed and tightened her hold on his hair. "You silver-tongued devil, you."

He tugged one last time. "You have no idea."

He made quick work of the tattered remnants of her panties, sliding them down her naked thighs and tossing them to the ground below. Sophie was a glory to behold from any angle, but there was something about this one that set him over the edge. Her legs were long and impossibly smooth. They met in a perfect V of dark curls, already damp with desire, which was where he focused his attention now.

His tongue might not be silver tipped when it came to talking about his feelings, but he didn't need it to be. Not when he was about to taste her.

Running his hands up either side of her right leg, he began his siege there. A soft kiss on the skin above her knee elicited a gasp—a sound that intensified as he worked his way up, pressing tongue and teeth against the suppleness of her upper thigh. She showed a tendency to wriggle, a thing he had to combat by holding her more firmly in place and parting her legs to give himself better access.

"Cold," she said with a gasp as he opened her legs and held her there, blowing a long, slow breath against her damp heat. "I can feel everything when you do that."

Yes. She needed to feel everything—not just in a physical sense, but in every other possible meaning of the word. *Feel me on my knees before you. Feel me tasting every part of you. Feel me begging you to extend this moment into infinity*.

"Good," he said and lifted her leg even more. With one swift movement, he had her thigh hitched over his shoulder. Most of her weight shifted over to him, a feeling he gloried in much more than he probably should have. "Now hold still, will you? I want to do this right."

"You can't possibly hold me—" she began, but he *could* and he *did*.

With one hand pressed flat against her bare belly, he anchored her in place. He also anchored himself to her with a kiss pressed at the juncture of her thighs. One taste, one lick, one swirl of his tongue against her clit, and all arguments came to an end.

She whimpered and arched her back, causing her legs to open wider and allow him better access to the sweet heat of her.

"Oh, dear," she moaned as his kisses intensified, his tongue seeking purchase everywhere it landed. "Harrison, I think I changed my mind about that ravishing thing. I don't know how much more of this I can take."

He paused long enough to give her a moment to back out, a moment to give up on him, but she didn't. She only kept clinging to his hair like a woman about to fall off a precipice, her eyes glazed with desire and something more.

"You took me at my worst, Sophie," he said, though he didn't know how much of it she heard. "You can take anything."

Her moans gave way to whimpers, which soon transformed to an increasingly low humming sound as she neared orgasm. That was the part of her he wanted to taste most, so he pressed one last kiss against her clit, holding the pressure there until she came. She shook and cried out, her grip on his hair so strong he couldn't have pulled away even if he wanted to.

He didn't want to though. He wanted to stay there, on his knees before this woman, buried in the sweet, glorious heat of her forever.

Forever.

That word rattled him almost as much as Sophie's body quivering against his lips. He wanted her with him for everything—not just while puppy training lasted, and not for a few hot weeks while his life settled back into a semblance of normal.

He didn't just like Sophie Vasquez.

He fucking loved her.

That thought shook him even more than the feel of her orgasm crashing tight and hot against his lips. It was the worst possible moment for such a life-altering realization. He should have been reveling in her body, tossing her to the mattress and making love to her until neither of them could stand anymore.

Not clutching her legs like he'd never touch her again. Not feeling—for some inexplicable reason—like all he wanted to do was cry.

"Hey," she said and released her hold on his hair. "What's wrong? Harrison—are you okay? You look like you've just seen a ghost. Or, um, tasted one."

A light laugh shook him. Even now, she was giving him a gift. Even now, she was lifting him up simply by being herself.

It was on the tip of his tongue to tell her what he felt, to admit that he was so far from being okay, that his life's happiness was now entirely in her hands, but he didn't. That was one of her gifts too. With a smile that stitched the last piece of his heart into place, she took his hand and helped him up.

"Come on. We can scoot Bubbles over and snuggle in your secret clubhouse bed. I think I spied some Neruda on your bookshelf. I had no idea you were such a romantic."

"He's okay," Harrison admitted with a blush.

Sophie lifted his hand to her mouth and placed a soft kiss in the palm of his hand. "You're okay too, Harrison."

He blushed deeper. He wasn't willing to go *that* far just yet. But the one thing he did know for sure was that if Sophie was willing to stay in his life for good, he *could* be.

chapter
18

"That's weird. Are you expecting one of your sisters?" Harrison turned his truck into his drive, not bothering to lift his hand from where it sat on Sophie's leg.

She liked the way it lay there—naturally and heavily, an extension of the man himself. He often held Bubbles that way, with that one hand curled possessively over the puppy's fluffy coat. Sophie had always considered it more of Harrison's way to comfort himself than to protect the animal, and she liked that hand on her thigh for the very same reason.

He could have stroked it too, if he'd wanted. In fact, she kind of hoped he would. She was ruined for all other normal human interactions. She wasn't thinking about work or dinner or even the blue sedan parked in the drive that looked an awful lot like the one her mom drove. All she wanted was to go back to that quiet, perfect attic space where Harrison had *finally* let her in.

And she hadn't been forced to push even once. He'd just opened the door and followed her up those stairs.

Harrison, however, had other things on his mind. "I thought you said you expressly forbade them from contacting you for anything less than a major medical emergency," he said.

"I did, but that's not going to stop either of them stopping by anytime they darn well please. They might even be compelled to bring my mom."

She stole a look at Harrison's profile, but he didn't appear unduly worried by that declaration. Then again, he did have a hand curled around her upper thigh, so maybe he was preoccupied with other thoughts.

But when he spoke, it was with nothing but a relaxed, calm air. "Would they? Huh. I've been wondering what she's like."

"She's intrusive and overbearing, but in such a nice, likable way that it's impossible to complain. Once you open the door and let her in, you'll never get rid of her again."

"She's like you, then."

She smacked him on the arm. "Excuse you. I'm a freaking delight."

He leaned down and pressed a kiss onto her hand, which lingered on the swell of his bicep. "Yes," he said, his voice grave. "You are."

Those simple words, simply uttered, sent a thrill through her. Harrison Parks wasn't a man who gave compliments very often—or very effusively—but that was what made this one so powerful.

He liked her. He took delight in her. And more to the point, he wasn't scared of the possibility of meeting her mother.

They pulled up next to the car, which Sophie quickly realized didn't belong to her mom. Alice Vasquez's car was a mess of her husband's academic papers and books, with half a dozen stuffed puppies of various breeds crammed below the back window. Dawn had given them to her for Christmas one year, joking that dogs were all the grandchildren she'd ever get. The toys were faded and lopsided now, but she'd never remove them. They'd been there so long they'd become a family totem.

"That's not my mom," Sophie said as the truck came to a halt. "Her car isn't nearly that clean, and she'd never dangle a crystal from the rearview mirror like that. She read an article once about how many people crack their windshields that way."

"Then who—?" Harrison asked before cutting himself off.

Sophie didn't have to say what she was thinking.

"No," he said. "I don't believe it. You and Oscar can conjecture all you want, but he's not seeing someone. My father doesn't even like regularly seeing the dentist."

"Would it be so bad?" she asked, wishing Wallace hadn't sworn her to secrecy about his moving-out plans. "If he did find love?"

"No." Harrison turned the key and sat back against the seat, his rugged face relaxed into a semblance of calm. Then he grinned, his smile so devastating and warm she almost feared her heart would stop. "If it had happened a month ago, I might have called the FBI and warned them about a case of body snatchers in the area, but not now."

She couldn't resist. "But not now?"

One of his fingers came up and brushed her cheek. His hands were always a little rough, a little callused, and now was no exception. She loved that about him, actually, the gruff exterior that hid the soft, melty marshmallow inside. "No, Sophie. Not now."

It wasn't the declaration of love and affection she was aching to hear, but it was enough to give her a feeling of buoyancy as she and Harrison followed Bubbles into the house. She was also propelled by rampant curiosity. She had no idea what kind of woman could capture the heart of a man like Harrison's father, but she had to be something special.

And hardcore.

"Knock, knock!" Sophie called loudly. As much as she wanted to meet Wallace's mystery woman, she didn't want to meet her in a state of undress. "We're back."

A grunt from the direction of the kitchen proved that her warning had been a wise decision. It didn't *sound* like a mid-coital noise, but there was that gorgeous, work-worn table in there that seemed ideal for being bent over...

"What the hell are you doing home?" Wallace appeared in the kitchen doorway before either she or Harrison could walk through. Despite his lean build, he acted as a great barrier, his arms crossed and his brow furrowed. "I thought you two were going to a movie in town tonight."

"We are," Harrison said, his voice low with suspicion. "We just needed to grab a few things for Bubbles first. Speaking of, where did she go?"

"Uh-oh." Sophie made a darting grab for the puppy, but she too had noticed a visitor in the kitchen. Her tiny size made it easy for her to slip past Wallace's firmly planted feet to investigate.

"Well, hello there, little doggy," a low-pitched female voice cooed. It was a pleasant voice, confident and warm. "Aren't you just the sweetest thing? Wallace, you never told me you had a puppy. You hate animals."

"It's not mine—" Wallace began in a scrambling, almost desperate way, but he didn't manage to finish the sentence. Harrison had stepped forward, his whole body stiff.

"Mom?" he asked. His voice was strangely hollow, sounding as though it was coming from the end of a long tunnel. "Mom, is that you?"

A face materialized next to Wallace's. At one glance, Sophie recognized the woman as Harrison's mother. It would have been impossible not to. Harrison's rough-and-gruff exterior might have come directly down Wallace's bloodline, but his size and those hard, gray eyes had obviously come from her.

So had the smile.

That was the thing that struck Sophie the most. The woman's first response at seeing Harrison standing in front of her was one of unadulterated joy. Her eyes flew open in shock, but the lines of her face spread in the same devastating smile that had so much power over Sophie.

Not a beautiful woman, Harrison's mother, but with a smile like that, she was magnificent.

Like most magnificent things, however, her smile didn't last long.

"*No.*"

The moment that oh-so-familiar syllable left Harrison's lips, his mom's face fell. Sophie's did too, but she stepped forward to place a restraining hand on Harrison's arm.

"Oh dear," she said, but he didn't register her touch. "Harrison, why don't we—"

"No."

"Harry, my love," his mother said. She hadn't

regained the smile yet, but she wasn't put off by the stony-faced front he presented. "It's so good to see you. And your friend too."

When no one said anything, she added a tentative, "Girlfriend? Wife? Wallace, why didn't you say anything?"

"No."

That final no was Harrison's last attempt at gaining some semblance of control over himself, but it didn't work—especially when his dad's sole contribution was to cough heavily and say, "She's the dog trainer, actually. The one I was telling you about."

Sophie winced. To be so reduced in this moment, with tensions so high they were thrumming like a too-tight guitar wire, was hardly the way she'd have chosen to go about things. Apparently, Harrison felt the same way. He turned on his father with a snarl that reminded her of a dog who'd been pushed into a corner and betrayed by the person he loved most.

In other words, it broke her heart.

"How long?" Harrison asked.

Instead of being intimidated by the fury in Harrison's voice, Wallace squared his stance to meet his son's. "Not long."

"How long?" he echoed, his voice growing dangerous.

"A few weeks, that's all. A nurse called her when you were in the coma. She's still listed as next of kin at that hospital, and—"

Harrison had yet to even look at his mother, but he did so now. Sophie wasn't able to get a full reading of his mood, but from the way he held himself, like a bomb that would explode at the slightest touch, she realized it was a dangerous one.

"And you came to take care of me, is that it? You came to sit up by my bedside night after night, watching to make sure I'm still breathing? You came to sing me to sleep and kiss away my troubles and do all those things that moms are supposed to do when their children are suddenly knocking on death's door?"

"Harrison, I—"

"No. I'm not going to listen to this. I don't know what you're doing here or why you're doing it, but I'd like you to leave. *Now*."

Sophie had no idea what to do in the face of such strong emotion. She'd always known that Harrison's history with his parents was a strange one—as different from her own as possible. Her parents had reacted to her illness with an overzealous desire to protect her from anything and everything this world had to throw at her. From the sound of it, his had done the exact opposite. This woman, who looked so ordinary and kind, had packed her bags and run away—leaving not just her husband, but her son too. And she'd left them both broken.

A part of Sophie hated her.

Looking at Harrison's face right now, she felt kind of sorry for his mother too. By leaving when she had, this woman had missed out on twenty-two years of this man's love and respect, twenty-two years of his hardships and his joys.

And the worst part was, she had no idea what a loss that was.

"You will not talk to your mother that way, young man." Wallace stepped forward, his expression mulish. "She's here because I asked her to be. If you can't be

respectful, then maybe Sophie should take you somewhere to cool off."

Sophie felt as though Harrison had every right to his
anger, and she was about to say as much, but Wallace
made that impossible.

"Minerva and I are taking a few boxes over to the
apartment, Sophie," he said. "If you could explain to
him, help him understand…"

All of Harrison's emotion—all of it justified, all of it
simmering under his parents' watchful stares—should
have exploded at once. In all honesty, Sophie wanted it
to. She'd worked so hard to get him to open up, spent
so much time helping him realize that it was okay to
wear your feelings on the outside, rather than bury them
deep inside.

For him to close off, to rebuild those walls, to isolate
himself in a cocoon of razor wire and loneliness… She'd
do anything to stop that from happening again.

But it was too late. He turned to Sophie with a look
so full of icy, disdainful cold that the chill permeated to
her soul.

"You knew?"

"Yes, but it's not what you think," she explained.

"You knew." Flatter this time. *Broken.*

"I wanted to tell you, Harrison. I—"

He turned away from her, and that was when she knew
she was lost. She was no longer talking to Harrison, the
myth, the hero, the man. She was talking to the little boy
who'd been left all alone at what must have been the
scariest moment in his life.

"Where's my goddamned dog?" He pushed past his
parents to the kitchen, remaining only long enough to

scoop up Bubbles and curl her against his chest. "I don't care what you do with your life, Dad. I don't care what you do with yours either, *Minerva*. The only thing I want is for everyone to leave me the fuck out of it. I've been fine on my own for years, and I'll be fine long after the entire lot of you leave."

Sophie didn't know if that last bit was meant to keep her away as well as his parents, but Harrison had to know it would never work. Like the goiter she'd always been and always would be, he was stuck with her.

With only one meaningful look at Wallace—full of equal parts sympathy for his position and annoyance at him for putting her there next to him—she followed Harrison and Bubbles out the door.

"Goddammit, Sophie. Can't you leave me alone for five minutes?"

She took a page from his book and kept doggedly following his tracks with one hard syllable. "No."

"It's the least you can do after stabbing me in the back like that."

"No."

He kept moving toward the direction of the barn, his steps long and furious. Sophie had to pick up to a jog to keep up, but she didn't mind. As she'd already shown, she could more than keep up with this man.

Harrison knew it, of course. He came to a stop at the barn door and waited for her to catch the rest of the way up.

"Thank you," she said, her voice prim. "I was starting to get a hitch in my side."

He snorted on a laugh. "Bullshit. You could have followed me for hours. Over mountains and through lakes—into a fucking volcano, if that's where I was heading."

She tilted her head and watched him, careful to give nothing of her feelings away. Her heart ached for this man—for the little boy—and the only thing she wanted to do was pull him into her arms and tell him that everything was going to be okay. But that wasn't what Harrison needed right now.

"I'd probably make it over a mountain just fine, and I *might* be able to survive a fall into a volcano, but I'd definitely die in the lake. I can't swim."

Her distraction worked, his attention caught. "What are you talking about? Everyone can swim. You just wiggle your arms and legs."

"First of all, I think it's slightly more complicated than that, and secondly, of course not everyone can swim. Especially not people who spent most of their girlhood in the hospital. By the time they were done with me, I barely knew how to take a shower on my own. I'm great at sponge baths though, in case you're wondering."

He fought the smile rising to his lips. "I'm not going to feel sorry for you."

"No one is asking you to."

"I'm not going to let this go either. How long have you known?"

That one was easy. "I didn't know she was your mom. He told me right after the camping trip that he was seeing someone, but only that her name was Minerva."

The rest was hard. She didn't know what to do, what to say—or even if there *was* anything to do or say in a situation like this one.

"Oscar knew." Harrison's mouth was a grim line. He was still clutching Bubbles, but he set the animal down now.

Like the obedient, well-trained puppy that she was, Bubbles took her release in stride and settled herself comfortably at Harrison's feet. Sophie's chest tightened at the sight of it. He'd accepted that animal into his life so easily—fell in love with her after a few hours. In a short time, their lives had become so intertwined it was hard to imagine the two of them existing separately from one another.

Naturally, human relationships were a little more complicated than that, but that didn't stop her from feeling jealous.

"Yeah, he probably did know," Sophie agreed. "You can hardly blame him for not telling you though. Your dad would have never forgiven him. Will you tell me about her?"

He blinked, caught unaware at her rapid change of subject.

"She looks like you. Well, I guess it's more accurate to say that *you* look like *her*, but you know what I mean. Her smile can light up a whole room—I bet that's what your dad sees in her. How long after your diagnosis did she leave?"

"Twenty-four hours. Possibly less." He shook his head and stared at her as if unsure how she managed to get such an easy answer out of him. "Look, Sophie—this isn't some cute love story that's finally found its happy ending. You realize that, right?"

Sophie ignored him. "From a few things your dad mentioned the other day, it sounds like they're going to move in together—but not at your house. He said something, something about it having too many memories. I didn't know what he meant at the time, but that makes sense. She probably wants to go somewhere they can start fresh."

An expression of agony passed over Harrison's face, but the sound he made wasn't one of anguish. It was a laugh—empty and bitter, yes, but a laugh all the same.

"Of course she does. I'm sure it's killing her to see it like that. Her precious darling."

Now it was Sophie's turn to blink in confusion. Harrison saw it and laughed harder.

"Do you realize he hasn't let me put a single nail in that place until the day you and Bubbles waltzed in? Not one nail, not one coat of paint, definitely not a tablecloth. In a few short weeks, you managed to wreak nothing short of a miracle."

If Harrison's parents had reconciled over his coma, she had the suspicion it was Minerva, and not her, who had managed the miraculous, but she didn't say so. It was hardly a helpful observation under the circumstances.

"For twenty-two years, he forced us to live in the ashes of everything she left behind," Harrison said. The laughter stopped as suddenly as it had started. "I wanted to change it. I wanted to fix it. Believe me—I *tried*."

"But…" Sophie said, prompting him.

"He liked watching it go to ruin."

"Why?"

"Because it's *her* house, Sophie. Not his. Not mine. It's been in her family for generations, the place where all our happy Parks dreams were going to come true. Until, of course, I ruined it. One near-death experience, and Minerva realized that some dreams aren't worth the cost." He glanced away, his gaze fixed on the horizon. "It wasn't just her husband and son she left behind that day. She left everything she'd ever known—her home, her career, her friends. *That's* how little she wanted to do with me. That's how much she couldn't wait to get away."

Clarity was starting to take over her confusion—and, with it, some of that same bitterness that characterized everything Harrison said and did.

"Then why on earth do you and your dad still live there?"

This time, his laughter held a note of sincerity. "Sheer stubborn will, at least on his part. That man resented me every single day of his life, and he'd have gladly packed up and left if the opportunity had afforded itself. But a Parks doesn't abandon his duty. The house was left in his care, and so was I. He would never have considered leaving his post, however much he might have wanted to."

"And you?" she couldn't help asking. "Why didn't you leave?"

His eyes glittered. "I'm a Parks too, or hadn't you noticed?"

Oh, she'd noticed, all right. She knew it down to her bones. Unlike him, however, she didn't see it as a character flaw. Sure, Wallace's stubborn refusal to change so much as a board in that farmhouse was nothing short of perverse, and she couldn't imagine what it must have been like to be an eight-year-old Harrison, scared and hurt and abandoned by his mother, but Wallace had done an admirable job with what he'd been given.

Just look at the evidence—it was standing in front of her, glowering and grim and glorious. It was a six-foot bear of a man who'd fought incredibly hard for everything he had. Sure, the walls around his heart were so thick they were impenetrable by all but a tiny scrap of a puppy who'd managed to wriggle her way in, but he hadn't been wrong to put those walls up.

That heart had been worth protecting.

"Your dad *did* look happy," she said, extending a hand toward Harrison.

He didn't take it. Although Bubbles had found her foothold, Sophie's path was not as easy.

"I know it's hard to see it from where you're standing, but things change. People change. Maybe she's different. Maybe she came back to make amends."

"That's not how it works," Harrison said. He crossed his arms, making it impossible for her to break through. "She *shattered* that man, Sophie. Smashed him to pieces. And now she's just playing around with the shards."

"You don't know that. Maybe she—"

He shook his head. "She doesn't want the house. You said it yourself. Too many bad memories. And she doesn't want me either. If I hadn't walked through the door and found her there, how many days would have gone by before I found out? How many weeks?"

She opened her mouth to answer, but Harrison interrupted by pushing himself from the barn door until he loomed over her.

When he spoke, however, his voice was gentle. His gaze was even more so.

"I know what you want from me," he said. "I know what you want to hear. You want me to say that somewhere, deep inside, I still care about her. That I believe in forgiveness and second chances. That if my dad is capable of reversing twenty-two years of heartbreak and is willing to open his heart to the possibility of love, then I should be too."

Sophie nodded. For once, *she* was the one who couldn't find the words. That was exactly what she wanted. The Harrison Parks who'd showed her that attic space—who'd fallen to his knees in front of her and refused to get up until he'd tasted the deepest parts of her—that was a man she could love.

That was a man she *did* love.

But they couldn't spend the next sixty years hiding away from the world. Slipping past Harrison's walls and into his heart was everything she'd imagined it would be, but she couldn't *live* there.

"Well, I can't," Harrison said. "I *want* to—you have no idea how much—but I can't."

He sounded so beaten, so small, that her heart stopped.

"Don't look at me like that, Sophie," he said, his voice breaking. "You knew who I was going into this. I told you. I warned you."

That was true. He *had* warned her, listed his flaws like he was reading off the worst job application known to mankind. But what he'd forgotten to include, what he couldn't even see, was all that was great inside of him.

So she did it for him.

"You're brave," she said, ticking off one finger. "*Scary* brave, and in this weird kind of way where you won't even acknowledge it. Honestly, I don't know if you can. But most people don't just give up everything and spend months at a time fighting huge, dangerous forest fires. That's not a normal state of being."

"Sophie, *don't*—"

"You're kind." She ticked off another. "Oh, I know you try your best to hide it, but not even a magician could get the whole of your heart tucked away. You're kind to animals, to your friends, to me. Jessica upheld your original story, you know. She told me that you were so tough on her, you made her cry during training…but then she also told me that you made sure she was the one who got to keep fighting fires after her boyfriend left her. I'm sorry, Harrison, but that was a kind thing to do."

"It wasn't like that—"

"You're generous." She bit her lip and flushed at the memory of their lovemaking mere hours before. "And I don't just mean in bed, though that's definitely true. I mean as a person. As a human being. As someone who opened his home to me without a word of protest—and right when I needed it most."

"*You have to stop*." Harrison's hands came crashing down, clutching at her upper arms in desperation. "I know I gave you permission to push me, but I'm rescinding it now. No more. Not another word."

"Harrison, you can't—"

His hold on her didn't lessen, his eyes as hard as granite. "I can and I did. No more pushing, no more playing. The game is over."

"You're not thinking clearly right now," she said. "You're upset, and you're feeling hurt, and that's okay, but—"

"Goddammit, Sophie! Can't you understand?" He let go of her then, dropping her like a man who'd just been burned. "I've had *enough*. Enough of you sauntering around and acting like you know what I need, like you have all of life's answers stored up in the tip of your pinky."

She opened her mouth and closed it again. The hurtful things Harrison was saying were bad enough, but even worse was the way he was saying them. He was like a trapped animal, a puppy-mill puppy cowering in fear inside his tiny cage. He was howling and lashing out at his captor.

He was howling and lashing out *her*.

"Fearless little Sophie Vasquez, tackling the big, bad giant. Brave little Sophie Vasquez, taking on the case that no one else will touch." His voice mocked her even as his arms crossed in a protective and antagonistic move over his chest. "We both know you're not nearly as strong as you pretend to be. It's easy for you to tell me that I need to forgive my mother for what she's done, but you don't even have the nerve to tell your own mother that she's suffocating you."

Sophie stood motionless, feeling as though she'd been slapped.

He gave a short, bitter laugh. "It's not so fun being on the receiving end of all that pushing, is it? Do you want me to keep going?"

She shook her head against what she knew was coming, what she was powerless to stop.

"You push and you smile and you laugh and you *fuck*, but only because you know there are ten thousand people ready to catch you if you fall."

It couldn't be true. It couldn't be Harrison saying these things.

But it was. "Spend one day in my shoes, and I guarantee you won't be so bold," he said, his upper lip curling.

"There's no one here for me, Sophie. No sisters. No parents. No nice knitting ladies. When I fall, it's a long, dark descent that never ends. My mother abandoned me, my father gave up on me, and even *you* have finally realized that I'm not worth the effort."

"No," she said, but her throat was so thick with emotion she wasn't sure she made any sound at all.

"I can't spend another twenty-two years in that house waiting for a love that won't last," he said. "And even more to the point, I *won't*. Not even for you."

Every wall, every shutter, every barrier came crashing down over him at once, sealing him up tighter than a tomb. There would be no getting in there now, Sophie knew. Not if she pushed for the rest of her life. Not if she died trying.

Which was why she stood perfectly still and accepted the words she knew were coming next.

"I'm done, Sophie. We're done. It's over."

chapter
19

"I brought you some ice cream for breakfast—it's rocky road, your favorite."

"And coffee. Fresh coffee. With a little brandy in it. Okay, it's all brandy, but it's the good kind, so sip slowly."

"What about a hot pad? You always used to like a hot pad when you weren't feeling well."

Sophie kicked off the blankets that had been solicitously wrapped around her and took the mug of brandy from Dawn. Downing it in one quick gulp, she glared at the relatives hovering over the couch as though she'd rung death's doorbell and was merely waiting for someone to answer.

"Knock it off, you guys." The kick of the alcohol hit her in a fiery wave. She welcomed the burn both in her stomach and in her resolve—she could use it right about now. "I'm not going into a decline. I broke up with a guy. There's a big difference."

She didn't miss the look that passed between her two sisters.

"Is it really breaking up if you were never formally dating? I mean—"

"Lila, so help me, if you take it upon yourself to analyze my relationship with Harrison right now, I'm going to turn this bowl of chocolate ice cream over onto your pristine white couch. And I'm not going to clean it up afterward. In fact, I'm going to stand watch over it while it dries."

Dawn chuckled at this outburst. So did Lila, though she was careful to pick up the ice cream and put it well out of Sophie's reach.

Her mother, unfortunately, wasn't so easily put off. She placed a warm hand on Sophie's forehead and peered anxiously down into her eyes. "I still don't understand what happened. Did he yell at you?"

"No."

"Did he say all those terrible words like the ones Paulette heard?"

"I wish."

"Did you argue about something?"

"We argued about lots of things. That's the whole point of Harrison." She glanced at the clock sitting on the mantelpiece. "Oh, geez. Is it eight o'clock already? I still need to shower and change before I head over to the DNR office for the air force training."

All three women stared at her as though she'd spoken a foreign language.

"That clock isn't wrong, is it?" She cast a worried look at her watch, but it showed the same time. "Okay, phew. I should have just enough time if I hurry."

"Uh, Soph?"

"You're joking, right?"

"Darling, are you sure you don't want a few minutes with the heating pad first?"

"What's wrong?" Sophie asked. "Why is everyone looking at me like that?"

The women shared another one of those worrisome looks before Dawn stepped forward. "You're going to Deer Park? Now?"

"Um, yes? It's Monday, which means Oscar is bringing in a whole bunch of people for wildfire training today. I know I look terrible, but I doubt Harrison will notice." Sophie shrugged with a nonchalance she was far from feeling. She'd hoped that having a weekend apart would help ease the sting of his final words, but it hadn't worked. All the ice cream and brandy in the world wouldn't change the fact that Harrison had ripped her heart out of her chest, stomped it into the dirt, and then walked away.

I could have taken all of it—except for the walking away.

"Actually, he probably will notice, but I don't care. I hope he thinks I look like garbage. I feel like garbage. *He* made me feel like garbage. The least he can do now is face the steaming heap he created."

Lila opened her mouth to protest again, but Sophie forestalled her with a glare.

"Well, Dawn?" she asked, her tone falsely bright. "You're the expert when it comes to this sort of thing—is it cutoff jean shorts? A see-through tank top? Pasties with tassels on them? What does one wear to work with a man who destroyed all one's chances of happiness?"

"One could always ask one's sister to go to work in her stead," Dawn suggested gently.

Sophie set her face, remembering all the things Harrison had said about her—that her strength came from the safety net her family provided, that her bravery had never been *really* tested. "No, thank you."

"We wouldn't mind," Lila said. "If you're not up to the task of facing him, it's just as easy for one of us to finish up. In fact, I think it's in our employee handbook."

"It's true." Dawn cleared her throat with a false sense of authority. "*After sleeping with the client, dog trainers are allowed a two-week leave of absence, at which time one of her sisters solemnly promises to finish the job, no questions asked.*"

"No, thank you," Sophie said once again. She didn't know how to make them realize that their kindness, though to be expected, was only making her feel worse. It proved how right Harrison had been, how easy her life was compared to his. How could someone like her possibly understand what it cost him to open up? How could she know anything about real strength?

Everything she had, she owed to the people in this room. Everything she was, was built on the promise that their love for her would never falter.

"It's nice of you to offer, guys, but I was aware of the difficulties when I took this job. I made the decision to get involved with Harrison knowing the risks."

"Oscar will understand," Lila said.

"No one will think any less of you for staying home to nurse your broken heart," Dawn added.

"*You* might not think less of me for it," Sophie allowed, "but *I* will. It's going to be awful, and I'll probably cry before the day is over, but I have to do it. Not for Harrison or even for Oscar, but for me."

To her surprise, Dawn laughed—her familiar chuckle full of music, her dangling silver earrings shaking around her neck. "Well, crap. I can't argue with that. Lila?"

Her oldest sister offered a prim smile. "I *could* argue it, but I'm not going to. I know better than to go up against Sophie in battle. She wins every time. She always has."

Dawn heaved a mock sigh. "She does, doesn't she? The tenacious wretch. I'd hate her if I didn't love her so much."

"Wait—I do? I am? You really mean it?" Sophie looked back and forth between her sisters, waiting for the catch. "You aren't just calling me a tenacious wretch to be nice?"

She couldn't tell which of her sisters laughed the most at that, but she did know that the sound out it far outstripped their earlier sympathy. It always had. During her darkest moments and in the midst of her bleakest fears, Lila and Dawn had always managed to make her laugh.

Just thinking about it caused tears to spring to her eyes—not for *her* plight, but for Harrison's. When his world had taken the same path as hers, no one had made him laugh. No one had showed him love.

And now he won't even let me try.

"Sophie, you're a lot of things, but a quitter isn't one of them," Lila said. They all knew, without words, what Lila meant. Although all of their lives had been shaped by Sophie's childhood illness, it wasn't something they discussed in the general way of things—mostly because Sophie wouldn't let them. She was tired of living in the past, exhausted with trying to prove herself worthy of this life she'd been given. "I think every single person in this room can agree about that."

"Without a doubt," Dawn agreed.

As if by tacit consent, the three sisters looked to the one person in the room they weren't so sure of—their mother, who was watching them with an air of bewilderment and a frown pulling a line down her forehead.

"Don't you agree, Mom?" Dawn prodded.

"Girls, you're kidding, right?" That frown was pointed at each of them in succession, full of maternal solicitude and concern. Sophie felt her heart sink, sure she was about to be reduced to the barest minimum yet again—and just as sure that she was going to have to continue being a soft, overprotected piece of fluff for as long as her mother lived.

When her mom finally spoke, however, it wasn't to castigate Sophie alone. It was to criticize all three sisters as equals.

"Please tell me you don't actually have a clause in your employee handbook about what to do if you sleep with your clients. I raised you better than that." She paused, expectancy pursing her mouth into a tight bow.

When no one said anything, all of them mute with mingled surprise and guilt, she sighed and shook her head. "Oh dear. I always *meant* to raise you better than that. I guess I didn't do a very good job, did I?"

Dawn was the first to respond—a thing she did with her usual laugh on her lips. "You failed miserably, I'm afraid," she said as she took their mother into her arms. "But don't worry too much about it. The lesson on practicing safe sex went through just fine."

Sophie held back an inelegant snort.

"That one's not in our handbook though." Lila's expression was perfectly grave, but her eyes danced with mischief as she added, "The lawyers insisted we keep it out."

🐾🐾🐾

Sophie arrived at the Department of Natural Resources fully prepared for battle.

Her armor was the official Puppy Promise uniform, that bland and nondescript khaki outfit that proclaimed her status as an untouchable professional. Dawn had insisted that nothing would be more effective at showing Harrison that she didn't care than seeing Sophie appear for work unruffled and calm.

She brought weapons too. A clipboard, a dog clicker, and treats contained in a pouch on her belt might not have looked like much to an outsider, but they filled Sophie with a sense of purpose. She was Sophie the Dog Trainer, ready to report for duty. Forget heartbreak and pain. Screw the man who'd made her feel smaller than any man had ever made her feel before.

She wasn't going to apologize for having people who loved her.

"Oh dear. What's going on? Is there a fire?" Sophie barely made it through the front door before she realized something was amiss. The woman working at the reception desk didn't look ruffled as she directed people to and fro, but there was a calm efficiency to her that Sophie knew well. She'd spent enough time around medical professionals in emergency situations to recognize a 9-1-1 situation when she saw it.

"At the base of Mount Spokane—a house fire that's spread and is threatening a logging road," the woman said in a clipped but kind tone. "The local firefighters aren't able to contain it alone. We have a team prepping to head out now. Can I help you with something?"

Sophie didn't waste any time. "Harrison Parks. Is he here?"

"Yes."

"Is he trying to join the team?"

"Yes."

"Is Oscar letting him?"

The woman laughed. "Go right on through, hon. You seem to know what you're doing."

Sophie didn't bother correcting her. She had no idea what she was doing, especially where Harrison was concerned, but that hadn't stopped her before.

"Half the team is out of town right now, and the other half is working their regular jobs." Harrison's voice, loud and resolute, could be heard long before Sophie reached Oscar's office. "If you don't let me go, you'll only have Jessica and Derek and that weird, skinny kid who always puts his pants on backward."

"Jessica and Derek are perfectly capable of handling a fire of this size, and Benji almost always gets his pants the right way now."

"Dammit, Oscar. You know I'm fine."

"I don't know anything. I'm not a doctor."

"Look at me. Check my blood sugar. Take my goddamn temperature if it'll make you feel better. I'm ready. You heard Sophie—she gave me the all clear last week."

"She cleared you to train, not to fight fires."

Harrison grunted. "It's the same thing."

Sophie couldn't step into Oscar's tiny office without brushing her whole body against Harrison—a thing she was determined *not* to do, even with the protection of her khaki pants and blue polo shirt—so she cleared her throat instead.

Both men turned at the sound, one to shoot her a look of relief, the other to freeze as though the world had suddenly turned as icy as his heart.

The frozen one spoke first. "What the devil are you doing here?" Harrison demanded.

"I came to work, obviously." Sophie was pleased to find that her voice came out perfectly calm, although she did have to fight the anxious urge to check the state of her hair. It was all well and good to joke to her family that she didn't care how she looked, but a pixie cut with bedhead was no laughing matter.

"Yes, but…" He trailed off, unwilling to finish that sentence in front of Oscar.

The chicken. The coward. The puppy-wearing baby.

"I assume that the air force training is a no-go today?" she asked, directing her question to Oscar. "I don't want to get in anyone's way, so I just popped in to make sure I'm not wanted, and then I'll take myself off again."

Oscar's relief increased as he scrubbed a weary hand over his face. "Actually, you are wanted. I hate to admit it, but I could use Harrison today. Do you think he and that puppy are good to go, or is it too risky?"

One look at the flat, desolate line of Harrison's mouth, and Sophie knew she held all the cards. He'd never admit it, but he needed her. Maybe not to make his heart whole—he obviously didn't think her capable of that—but in a professional capacity.

It was something. Not much, but something.

"Well?" Oscar prompted. "I hate to rush the decision, but we need to get moving."

"It's up to him," Sophie said, choosing her words carefully. "I have my own opinions, of course, but it's not my call to make. If he thinks Bubbles can do it, if he feels she's ready for this, then he's free to do what he wants."

"Wait—what?"

"I'm not your puppy's keeper anymore, Harrison. You are. I even brought the paperwork to prove it."

For one long, suspended moment, Harrison didn't move or breathe. He held her stare for one second. For two. About halfway into the third, he crumbled.

"Goddammit, Sophie! Why are you so determined to destroy me?"

Sophie blinked, started by the violence of his reaction. "Um."

"A normal human being would have answered with a simple yes or no. Yes, they're ready. No, they're not. But no. Not you." He stared at her through those stony and oh-so-familiar eyes. "You'd never make anything that easy on me."

"Does this mean you…*don't* want the papers?"

He appeared not to hear her. "From the very start, you looked into my soul and took full measure of what's there, didn't you? You saw my weaknesses. You discovered how to hurt me. You learned where I bleed. And not for one fucking minute have you stopped stabbing me right there."

She almost laughed out loud at the villainous picture he was conjuring up, but her own emotions were too raw. Mostly because he knew her weaknesses too. He knew how much she valued her independence, how important it was for her to be seen as someone strong, someone confident, someone worth loving. He knew all that and still said those horrible things to her.

Harrison Parks claimed not to be great with words, but he'd managed to cut her down with them just fine.

"Excuse me for believing you capable of making rational, adult decisions about your life," she replied, her chest tight. "Go fight your fires, Harrison. Or don't. Alienate yourself from everything and everyone. Or don't. What you do with your life is no longer of any interest to me."

There were countless more things she could have said, all of which had to do with vulnerable puppies and the even more vulnerable men who carried them, but she turned to Oscar with a nod. "I'll stand by whatever he decides. Is there anything else you need before I go?"

It wasn't Oscar who replied.

"You're impossible," Harrison said, his voice heavy with meaning. "You have been since the day I met you, and I can't wait until I find a way to cut you out from under my skin."

"I take that to mean you won't be heading to the fire?" Oscar prodded.

Harrison threw up one hand, his other arm wrapped around the sling holding Bubbles. "Of course I'm not. It's what Sophie wanted from the very start, what she's been plotting since day one. She gave me this…this…" He trailed off and glanced at the puppy before heaving a reluctant sigh. "This beautiful little nugget, and now I'm trapped."

The beautiful little nugget licked his fingers obligingly.

"I won't put her in harm's way before she's ready,"

Harrison said. "Or myself. I'm sorry, Oscar. I'd like to spend a few more weeks here on the training field before we start tackling the real fires. You'll have to fight this one without me."

Oscar showed no signs of pleasure or distress at this, merely dismissing them both with a nod and a grab for his phone. Sophie decided to take a similar approach. Turning on her heel, she made it three steps into the hallway before she realized Harrison was right behind her.

"Sophie, wait," he called, his voice rough.

Although it would have been so much more badass to keep walking, her head held high and her pride intact, she slowed her steps to wait for him to catch up. After all, Harrison was technically still her client. At least, he was until she gave him the ownership papers.

She reached for them now, tucking her hand into her canvas bag to extract the puppy's vaccination records and the certificate of completion they gave all their clients. "Here," she said as she held them out. "This finalizes any and all business between us. She's your dog now, free and clear."

He didn't take them. He didn't speak either, just stood there glowering at her.

Shifting from one foot to the other, she searched for something to say. "I'm sorry you won't get to start your air force training today."

That got him to speak. "Bullshit."

"Excuse me?"

"You aren't sorry. In fact, you're the exact opposite of sorry. You're loving this, aren't you?"

"Um."

"You know what this damn puppy did all weekend?"

He didn't wait for an answer. "I'll give you a hint—it involves raisins."

"I hope you aren't going to tell me that she ate any, because grapes are highly toxic to dogs. You should take her to the vet before her kidneys shut down."

The muscle at the corner of his mouth twitched. "No, she didn't eat any raisins. It's her eyes. She kept *looking* at me."

"You're complaining because your service animal looked at you? I hate to break it to you, but she's going to be doing a lot of that over the years. If you'll note, she's doing it right now."

"You know very well what I mean!" He ran a hand through his hair, sending it into attractive disorder. "She *missed* you, Sophie. You did the training all wrong, spent too much time at the house helping me. Somewhere along the way, she got the idea that you're supposed to always be there. And now she blames me because you're gone."

His voice cracked at the end, but that was the only sign of any opening in his hard exterior. The rest of him was as unyielding and wall-like as ever, the harsh lines of his face unwelcoming, his stance squared and closed off.

Sophie knew, in an instant, that the moment was right for her to tear down the wall. Even though the argument from the other day was still fresh enough to hurt them both, her sisters had given her enough confidence to claw through those bricks and find her way back to him.

She knew how she could do it too. All she had to do was kiss that hard, stony wall of a man. Hug him. Hold him. Force him to understand that nothing he said or did would ever make her love him any less than she did right now. In other words, she could *push*.

And then she could keep doing it every day for the rest of her life.

But that wasn't love. That was a prison sentence. If Harrison wanted to escape from that locked hold inside his heart, if he wanted to wake up from the long, deep sleep that held him in its spell, he was going to have to do it himself.

"Because fairy tales aren't real," she muttered aloud, unconcerned with how strange she must sound. "Because there's no reason why the princess can't pick up a sword and meet the dragon halfway."

"What are you talking about?" Harrison asked. "What princess? I'm talking about my dog, Sophie. You broke her. I think it's only fair that you fix her."

Despite her better judgment, she gave him one last chance. Shifting her weight to one leg, she cocked her head and stared at him. "Are you sure it's the dog who needs my help?" she asked.

It didn't work. Harrison held her look, his gaze pulsating with intensity, but he didn't yield. "She likes you," he said. "She trusts you."

"And I like *her*," she retorted. "But that isn't reason enough for me to come back. Good luck with your new service dog, Harrison. And on behalf of Puppy Promise, thank you for your business."

chapter

20

Harrison didn't know what woke him up while the moon still hung heavily in the night sky, but he knew all the things it wasn't.

It wasn't Sophie waking up early to start the coffee-pot. It wasn't the sound of his father thumping around in irritable insomnia downstairs. It wasn't the snuffling, shuffling sounds of Bubbles alerting him to low blood sugar. And despite his puppy's small size, her bladder was like a camel's hump—it was rare that she needed to go out before his usual wake-up time around six.

In fact...

"Bubbles?" he called, extending his hand in an arc all around him. When he hit nothing but the twisted sheets, he sat up. "Bubbles, where are you?"

All around him, there was nothing but silence. *Empty* silence, the kind that could only exist inside an ancient farmhouse where he was literally the only remaining Parks in residence. His father had finished packing up and moved out yesterday while Harrison had been at the Department of Natural Resources. He'd returned home to find a set of keys sitting on the kitchen counter...and that was it.

No forwarding address. No parting gift. Not even a brief, *Thanks for sticking around for twenty-two years, Harrison, but I'm outta here. Enjoy what's left of your sad, solitary life.*

He swung his legs off the side of the bed and flicked on the bedside lamp, but the sudden illumination didn't make his puppy magically appear. Neither did calling her name a few times—increasingly anxious with each recitation.

"I don't smell smoke," he said, mostly to comfort himself. "And I don't see any flames. So where the devil did you go?"

Given that puppy's love of the underside of beds, his next move was to check each one: his own functional wood frame, the ruffled skirt of his parent's once-happy matrimonial bed, the cot-like twin that his father had moved to after his mom left. As much as it would have soothed his soul to find her quivering underneath one of them, he found nothing but the inevitable dust bunnies.

"This isn't funny," he called, his worry increasing with each dark corner and cupboard that turned up empty. "And if you're playing a game, I don't think I like it very much."

In fact, he kind of hated it. He'd once thought that waking up in a hospital bed with no memory of how he got there was the worst way to greet the day, but he'd been wrong. Having no control over his health was frustrating and difficult, yes, but at least he knew the cause—knew there was hope at the end of the IV bag.

To arise in an empty house, with Sophie off some-where enjoying her life without him in it and Bubbles God knows where, was worse. It was as though he had handed them both a half of his heart, and now the whole thing was out there walking around, vulnerable and exposed.

Which was the only explanation he could offer for why his chest felt so hollow as he reached the kitchen to find the back door swung wide open. The faulty latch had struck once again, making the cracked linoleum feel like ice under his bare feet.

"This stupid fucking house!" he said, running to the open doorway and scanning the dimming darkness for any sign of Bubbles. He couldn't see the puppy in the distance, but there were a few tiny footprints in the mud at the bottom of the steps that didn't bode well for this adventure's end. Given the size and scope of the land around the house, she could have gone anywhere. "My stupid fucking father!"

For twenty-two years, that man had frozen himself and his heart here. For twenty-two years, he refused to leave the only piece of his old life he had left. But he *had* left—and without so much as a backward glance at Harrison in the rearview mirror.

Just like his mom. Just like Sophie. And now, it seemed, just like Bubbles.

"No."

Harrison wasn't sure where the sudden resolution came from. Saying no had always come easy to him, but never like this. He normally said no to friendship and opportunity, to happiness and love. He said no to anything that threatened to shake him out of his comfortable misery.

This time, however, he was saying no to being left behind.

"I'm not letting you go without a fight," he said to the

empty kitchen. Which was just as well, because he wasn't sure *who* he was talking to. "You don't get to walk away without saying goodbye. You're a part of me now."

Despite the earliness—or lateness—of the hour, he grabbed his keys off the hook and shoved his feet into a pair of work boots by the back door. He had no idea where his puppy had gone or why, but he knew exactly who he could rely on to help find her.

She was determined and strong. She was resolute and insistent.

She was his whole fucking world, and it was about goddamn time he did something about it.

"She's gone."

Sophie awoke to find an unshaven, unkempt, and frantic man standing at the foot of her bed.

"I looked all over the house and the yard, but her footsteps stopped a few feet from the back door and I can't find any other trace of her."

She sat up, aware, as she did, that the flimsy camisole she'd worn to bed left little to the imagination. But her nipples peeking through the thin silk fabric seemed less important than the fact that Harrison Parks had somehow broken into her house.

"Harrison? What are you doing here? And how did you get in?"

"I don't know what the timeline for lost puppies is, but I know that for people, the first twenty-four hours are the most vital."

"Lost puppies?" she echoed, clarity beginning to wipe away some of her grogginess.

"Yes. I woke up about an hour ago to find Bubbles missing. She's not in any of the usual places, and she doesn't come when she's called. I need to set up a grid search—and I need to do it now—but I don't have enough bodies. Will you come?"

"Um."

"*Please*, Sophie." His voice had never sounded so bleak, his expression never been so harsh. He'd also never looked so good. Maybe it was the dim lights of dawn peeking in through the window, or maybe it was the fact that he looked as honestly, openly human as she'd ever seen him, but the worried lines of his face touched something deep within her. "I know you officially graduated us, and that you technically aren't responsible for her care anymore, but she needs you."

He paused. "*I* need you."

Those three words were all she needed to hear to click into awareness. She threw back her quilt and began tossing on whatever clothes were at hand. The result was a mismatch of knee-high socks, jeans that were two sizes too big, and a sweatshirt that proclaimed her the 2005 Northwest Volleyball Champion, but she didn't care.

Harrison needed her.

Okay, so he needed her help with Bubbles, and nothing short of an emergency would have forced those words out of his mouth in the first place, but she wasn't going to quibble over the details. Not when it came to one of her puppies.

Or when it came to one of her friends.

"Tell me exactly what happened," she said as she led him out her bedroom door to the kitchen. Her mother was already there, wrapped up in a fuzzy pink robe and starting the coffeepot, which answered the question of how Harrison got inside. "When did you last see her, and what did you do after you left the Department of Natural Resources yesterday? Hey, Mom. Make it extra strong, will you?"

"Triple strength," she promised. "Anything else I can do to help? That poor little puppy. She must be terrified out there on her own."

Sophie took one look at Harrison's expression—which had moved well beyond terrified to reveal a pale, tightly drawn frown—and laughed. It was difficult to get out in any sort of way that sounded natural, but she did it because he needed her to. "That *poor little puppy* is probably chasing a rabbit through the woods and having the time of her life. It's Harrison we should feel sorry for."

"You think that's what she's doing?" Harrison asked. He took a cup of coffee from her mom with a slight nod of thanks. It was a strange thing to see, her mother accepting a large, strange man in her precious daughter's kitchen at four o'clock in the morning, but Alice had always been good in a crisis.

"I do. We've probably been working her too hard, so she saw a chance at freedom and took it. She's still just a baby in so many ways."

It was the wrong thing to say. Mentioning how vulnerable Bubbles was only served to make Harrison vulnerable too.

"Hey." She reached out and placed a hand on his arm, feeling the tense strength of him through the worn flannel. "She'll be okay. Dogs run away from their owners and come home none the worse for their little adventures all the time. I promise."

"Maybe it works that way for most people," he said soberly. "But whenever anyone runs away from *me*, it has a tendency to stick."

She dug her fingers so firmly into his arm it caused him to wince. "We'll find her and bring her home where she belongs, Harrison. I promise."

He nodded once, accepting her vow as though she carried the authority of the world on her shoulders. Her mother watched the interaction with unblinking eyes peeping over the top of her coffee cup. Sophie knew she was paying attention because even though the mug was held to her lips, she hadn't taken a sip even once.

Sophie also knew that somewhere along the lines, her mom had begun to see what she saw—that Harrison wasn't some cold stranger bent on ruining her precious daughter's life. He was just a man. One who was scared and lonely and who had been that way for so long it had never occurred to him that he deserved more.

But he *did* deserve it, and for the first time since Sophie had entered his life, he was ready to push himself to get it.

"Harrison says he wants to start a—what was it?" She looked a question at him. "Grid search?"

He nodded, his firefighting training clicking into place. "Yes. It's standard whenever anyone goes missing in the wilderness. By putting up parameters and assigning everyone a region, we can cover the most ground without doubling up. Even if she moved as fast as her legs would take her, she can't have gone too far from the house."

"Okay, then that's what we'll do." Sophie released

her grip on Harrison and grabbed the pen and notepad Lila kept in a tidy pile next to the house phone. "You set up your parameters, and we'll recruit everyone we know to take them."

Her mom nodded. "I'll wake the girls and then give Paulette a call. She'll want to help."

"Paulette?" Harrison echoed.

"From Sophie's knitting circle. I'm sure she and Hilda can get most of the other women from the group to join in, not to mention their families."

"But—"

"And Oscar and as many DNR people as he can rustle up," Sophie added before Harrison could protest. She knew what he was thinking—that the women of the knitting circle were the ones who caused her mother to move into the house in the first place—but that hardly mattered now. When it came to protecting their own, those fierce, loyal women were a godsend. And Harrison, whether he knew it or not, was one of their own.

Because he's mine.

As Sophie was rapidly coming to learn, the people who loved her, who took such good care of her, didn't just throw the mantle over herself. It automatically extended to everyone she held dear, no questions asked.

If *that* was what it meant to be weak, to know that she and everyone she held dear was loved, then so be it. She was willing to accept the consequences—if not for her own sake, then for Harrison's. That man could use a safety net right about now.

"You should also include your parents," Sophie's mom added.

Harrison balked—as in *physically* balked, his entire

body rearing back like a horse stopping at a jump. "Parents? Mine?"

"Good idea. They'll have a better idea of all the hiding places out there, and Bubbles knows and trusts your father." Sophie took one look at Harrison's expression and added, "I'll give them a call right now. I'm sure they'll meet us out there."

"Perfect. That gives us a nice, big number." Her mom yanked open a cupboard and started pulling down all the to-go coffee cups she could find. "With a group this large, I'm sure we'll have that little puppy home by noon."

chapter
21

To no one's surprise, it turned out that noon was an optimistic estimate.

Harrison was no stranger to the weird ways time worked in an emergency situation. Some days, firefighting in the wilderness seemed to stretch into eternity, each second a minute, each minute an hour. Other days, he went from opening his eyes in the morning to closing them twelve hours later without so much as a memory of the events that occurred.

This was one of those former situations. True to their promise, the Vasquez women had marshalled a search party that was larger and more dedicated than he had any right to expect, but all the bodies in the world couldn't force a two-pound puppy to materialize out of thin air.

"Bubbles!"

"Oh, Bubbles!"

"Here, puppy, puppy. Come out, doggie, doggie."

The sounds of two dozen people scouring the woods outside his house provided a strangely soothing backdrop to his own part of the search, which was to turn over any large log and rip out any oversize brush that might have accidentally trapped her. He knew it was dangerous to undergo that kind of exertion without Bubbles there to make sure his blood sugar levels were stable, but that was sort of the whole point, wasn't it?

He couldn't do this without her. Not anymore. Somewhere in the past few weeks, he'd realized that the one-man approach to living wasn't the way he wanted to go about things.

He wasn't infallible. He wasn't an island. He was just a man, and he wanted his puppy back.

He wanted his puppy *and* Sophie back. He just had to find a way to get to them first.

"Oh. Um. Hello, Harry."

Harrison stepped out from behind a tree to find his mother sitting on a fallen log, her legs extended out in front of her and a bag of trail mix in her hand. To all appearances, she looked like a person without a care in the world.

Which, he guessed, was exactly what she was. She might have come at Sophie's mom's bidding—because, really, who could say no to that woman?—but she had no emotional investment in the outcome. She'd never had any emotional investment where her only son was concerned.

"Do you need to take a break?" he asked. As usual, his voice came out rougher than he intended, but he didn't know how to stop it. "If you're not feeling up to the search, you can head back to the house and we can reassign your section to someone else."

Minerva hopped to her feet and tucked her snack out of sight. "I'm fine. I was just catching my breath, that's all."

"It's okay if you need a rest," he said with a complete absence of irony. It may have taken a tiny puppy and a woman with a heart of steel to teach him that, but he'd learned his lesson. "The search isn't worth risking your own health."

"Thank you," she replied, equally unironically. "It's taken a lot more out of me than I expected, that's all. Being back here, seeing it again."

His sympathies stopped there.

"I've missed it—these woods, this place." His mom stopped. She must have seen the look on his face, because her voice quavered as she added, "You."

"The first twenty-four hours are the most important," he said, parroting his words from earlier that morning. He doubted that Bubbles was the real reason she'd come out here today, but he didn't care. She was the reason *he* was here, and that was all that mattered. "We need to keep searching while the daylight lasts."

His mom brushed her hands on the seat of her jeans and nodded, her eyes not quite meeting his. "She means a lot to you—this dog?"

He didn't know what it was about her tone that annoyed him, but it probably had something to do with how disbelieving it was, how unsure. He shouldn't have been surprised. Naturally this woman, who had seen a son in peril and walked away, couldn't fathom putting in this kind of work for a mere puppy.

"Yes, Minerva. *Mom*." He placed a heavy emphasis on her title. "Bubbles means a lot to me. I've only had her for a few weeks, but I love her."

She lifted a hand to him before dropping it well out of reach. "Of course you do, darling."

On the contrary, there was no *of course* about it. *Of course* was the last thing anyone would have expected when pairing a man like him and a puppy like Bubbles.

In fact, the only person in the world who would look at the two of them and think, *Huh, this seems like a great idea*, was Sophie.

Not because her world was one of comfort and coddling, but because she was the only person to believe he could change. She'd taken one look at him, seen straight through to his heart, and decided to single-handedly bring it to life again.

And that was exactly what she'd done—up until the moment he'd crushed her with a few callous words.

Yet she was still here, helping him.

She was still here, making sure that whatever was left of his heart had a chance to thrive.

"I don't believe in forgiveness and second chances," he said with an abrupt change of subject.

His mother's face fell. "I know I don't deserve either one, but—"

"Just because Dad is capable of reversing twenty-two years of conditioning and is willing to open his heart to you again, that doesn't mean I have to too."

"No, and I completely understand, only—"

"Don't hurt him," Harrison said.

She blinked, almost as confused as he was by the sudden change in his tone. But although *she* couldn't know what kinds of battles were being waged inside his chest, had no idea that Sophie had triumphed there so many times already, *he* did. Forgiveness and second chances sounded pretty good right about now. So did opening his heart to all those possibilities he'd shunned for years.

"That's all I ask of you," he said. "I don't know why you decided to come back now, of all times, or what you said to convince Dad that this time would be any different, but these past twenty years haven't been easy on him. *I* haven't been easy on him."

"Oh, Harrison."

This time, when she reached for him, she made contact. It wasn't much, just a press of her fingers before she dropped her hand away, but it was enough. This woman may not have had the strength to sit by his bedside and watch him in pain, but that was on her. *She* was the one who'd missed his childhood, his adolescence, his young adulthood. *She* was the one who'd run away rather than face the harsh realities of life.

She was the broken one. Not him.

"It must have been really difficult, seeing me like that," he offered.

His mom's lower lip quivered. "It was. You have no idea. I was—Oh, I don't know. Weak? Scared? A little of both, I think. I'm not as strong as your father. I never have been. I took one look at you, so tiny and unconscious in that bed, and had to get away."

It was a sentiment he didn't understand, since Bubbles was tiny and could very well be unconscious, and he had no intention of stopping until he had her in his arms again. But he softened anyway.

Especially when his mom muttered a curse and said, "You were better off with him anyway, believe me."

He had to chuckle. "I might not have agreed with you a few weeks ago, but I think I do now."

She looked a question at him.

"I always thought it was the worst thing about me, how much like Dad I am, but I'm starting to think it might be a good thing."

As if to prove it, his dad's voice sounded in the

distance. He called out for Bubbles in his usual cantan-
kerous tone, offering several reasons why tiny puppies
who took off in the middle of the night deserved their
inevitable fates.

"He won't stop until we find her," Harrison said. "He
won't leave when things get rough. In fact, he wouldn't
even leave me until a few days ago when he finally realized I'd be okay on my own."

"And will you?" his mom asked, watching him.

Harrison nodded. He had no way of knowing what
the future held for him, and there was a good chance
Sophie would never forgive him for hurting her, but he'd
wait. Twenty-two years if he had to, growing even more
irritable and set in his ways as the years progressed.

Parks men were built that way—for the kind of love
that lasted a lifetime. For the fairy-tale ending they
deserved. For the kind of life that refused to accept anything but a happily ever after.

"You should take a break."

Sophie approached the wooded copse Harrison was
searching with a bottle of water in her hand and a look
of determination on her face. "You're not going to do
anyone any good if you faint out here. It'll take at least
twelve of the men to drag you back to the house."

Even though it was the last thing he felt like, he
huffed out a laugh. It seemed like the least he could do.
They were nearing the eight-hour mark for their search.
Even though everyone else's optimism had flagged, she
remained determinedly positive, all smiles and encouragement and rah-rah promises.

"Thank you." He accepted the water and took a few deep gulps. "But I'd like to stay out here as long as possible."

"I'm sure you do, but my sisters want to talk to you, so you might as well take fifteen. Apparently, Lila has a theory she'd like to share with you."

"She has a theory?" He blinked. "Like…of relativity?"

"Something like that." Sophie's smile faltered. Clasping her hands in front of her, she became unnaturally focused on a hangnail on her thumb. "Lila's supersmart when it comes to animal behavior, so she's worth listening to. I told her what you said yesterday, about how Bubbles misses me, and she thinks you could be right. She says the puppy might be out looking for me."

He twisted his head to get a better look at Sophie. She was exhausted, obviously, with bags under her eyes and her hair an odd mixture of puffed-out spikes and sweat-dampened curls. She'd also shed her heavy sweatshirt for a faded AC/DC T-shirt of his that was tied in a knot at the waist.

To make matters worse, she was limping from a fall into a gopher hole. Of the two of them, she was the one who most needed a break.

Not that she'd take one. He'd never seen anyone so good at field morale, pushing when it was needed, pampering when it wasn't, indefatigable from start to finish. They could use a woman like her at the fire sites.

He could use a woman like her in his life.

"She thinks Bubbles went in search of you?" he asked.

"I mean, it's *possible*." She examined the hangnail with renewed interest. "Lila's in the kitchen making a few calls to animal control. She asked me to come get you so she can ask you a few questions."

The mention of animal control got him moving. In his experience, that was who you called to scrape up the roadkill from the side of the highway in winter, the people who put dangerous animals down and fought cougars that wandered a little too close to town. Not exactly the people he wanted to talk to about his lost puppy.

The walk back to the house was slow because of Sophie's limp, but neither one of them attempted to fill the minutes with small talk. Harrison appreciated it more than Sophie could possibly know. It was enough to have her beside him, to hear the soft sounds of her breathing and the steady crunch of her footsteps. He'd said terrible things to her, had blamed her for a situation that was well beyond her power to correct, but that hadn't stopped her from coming to his aid.

"Sophie, I—" he began, but she yanked open the back door and pushed him through it before he could finish.

"Not now," she said in a tone that was firm but kind. "You can tell me later. After we have her safe."

What if we never have her safe?

He couldn't voice the question aloud. It was caught, sharp and barbed, in his throat. Besides, he stepped into the kitchen to find himself facing not just Sophie's oldest sister, but Dawn too. Both of them were standing near the sink with their arms crossed, their conversation low pitched and ominous.

It became all the more ominous when they stopped the moment they saw him standing there.

"Ah, there you are," Lila said unhelpfully.

"Take a seat," Dawn added as she pulled out a chair

at the rough-scrubbed table covered with its nicks and scratches. For all that his house had been taken over lately, no one had managed to get a tablecloth over it. It sat there, ugly and stark, for everyone to see.

He might have run then, escaped with what was left of his energy, but Sophie stood by the back door, her hip resting against the kitchen counter. He was trapped on all sides by Vasquez women.

Strange that it should feel so comforting. Strange that he welcomed the cushioning, enveloping embrace of them.

"Why does this feel like you're about to give me bad news?" he asked, looking from one face to another. The sisters probably didn't realize it, but they were almost identical when they wore those serious expressions. They each had their own unique smile, but this earnest intensity was worn in the same flat press of their lips, the same dark eyes that appeared both troubled and concerned at the same time.

It was probably the shared tragedy of Sophie's youth that had done it. They'd learned to share their grief. They'd figured out how to tackle the harsh realities of the world together.

Oh, how he envied them that. To face another tragedy alone was more than he could bear.

"What did animal control say?" he asked, his voice sharp. "They found her? She's dead, isn't she? You just don't want to tell me."

"We haven't heard anything bad, Harrison, I promise." Lila's voice was kind but firm. "And you'll be the first to know if we do. Do you love my sister?"

"*What?*"

Harrison took a wide step back, eager to put as much distance between himself and that question as possible, but it didn't work. Sophie appeared just as startled as he was. She'd jumped away from the counter and was standing stock-still in the middle of the doorway. Instead of retreat, he only managed to ram his body into hers, which was *not* the place he wanted to go right now. Touching her, even by mistake, reminded him of how soft she was, how yielding, how warm.

In other words, of how much he loved her.

"Answer the question, please. It's important for finding Bubbles."

He swiveled toward Sophie. "Did you put her up to this?" he asked. He hadn't finished the question before he already knew the answer. That look of wide-eyed alarm couldn't belong to anyone else.

"Of course she didn't," Dawn said. She shook the back of the chair in a pointed effort to get him to sit. As it appeared he was trapped anyway, he sat. He might as well be comfortable. "If you haven't figured out by now that Sophie is the sweetest and most thoughtful person on the face of the planet, then you never will."

"Um, guys? Maybe now's not the best ti—"

Dawn waved her sister off. "The sweetest," she echoed firmly. "And the most thoughtful, and everyone who meets her falls instantly in love."

"Don't worry," he said, watching the woman in question. Memorizing her. "I know."

"That includes humans *and* canines," Lila added. "It's uncanny, to be honest."

"I know that too," he said, his voice gaining strength. A few months ago, this was the exact kind of conversation that would have had him shutting down and running away. These were his *feelings* they were talking about—he and these three women, he and the woman he loved. A Parks man didn't just loosen his tongue and say what he felt. He was supposed to hide these things, bury these things, pretend that he didn't need these things as much as he needed the air he breathed.

"Of course I love her," he said. "I'm *in* love with her. What kind of a fool would I have to be not to? She's beautiful and capable and strong. She sees good things growing in terrible places. She's the best person I know, and I've been hers since the moment she yelled at me for giving Bubbles table scraps."

"I didn't yell at you!" Sophie squeaked. Her cheeks were suffused with pink, her whole body motionless.

"You did, and you meant it," he replied, strangely relaxed now that he'd gotten over that first hurdle.

Dawn cast a wide smile over them all. "There now. That wasn't so hard, was it? Are you going to stand there glaring the whole time, Sophie, or are you going sit down too?"

She gulped. "I'll stand, thanks. I feel like I should be on my feet for this."

To be perfectly honest, Harrison would have preferred her in his *arms* for this, but he wasn't going to push Sophie into any kind of declaration she wasn't ready for. It was enough that she knew what was in his heart.

Lila cleared her throat. Of the three sisters, she was the most naturally authoritative—and it was a skill she obviously had no qualms pulling out whenever she felt the impulse. "Now, Harrison. Would you say that Sophie's presence in your life is integral to your happiness?"

"Yes, of course it is. She's everything to me."

An indistinguishable sound escaped from between Sophie's lips.

"Excellent." Despite her sister's growing discomfort, Lila continued her interrogation without so much as a blink. "Would you say that you've been particularly adept at hiding these emotions? Particularly from your puppy?"

"From Bubbles?" His chest squeezed at the thought of that tiny bit of fluff—the one creature in his life he thought he *hadn't* driven away. "Unfortunately, no. I've been miserable since the moment I said those awful things to Sophie, and the puppy knew it. I told you, Sophie, remember? I begged you to fix her."

"I remember," Sophie said, her voice low.

"Then, yesterday after we left the DNR, she kept licking my face and hands over and over again. She wouldn't leave my side even to go to the bathroom. I tested my blood sugar eight extra times yesterday, thinking she was trying to alert me, but it was always normal."

"And what were you doing last night that might have set her off?" Lila asked. "Anything out of the ordinary?"

He thought back to the evening before, trying to remember everything he'd said and done that Bubbles could have misconstrued as his determination to give up on life. He'd spent several hours digging his never-ending ditches, yes, and had eaten his sad, plain chicken breast for one while standing over the sink, but those were hardly signs of a man on the brink. A man who desperately wanted his woman back, yes, but that part went without saying.

"I don't think so. It was pretty routine, as far as life goes."

"His pillow," Sophie offered.

Lila cocked her head. "What's that?"

"Ask him about his pillow."

"*What?*" Harrison turned to the woman standing next to him—the light in his heart, the joy of his life, the missing piece of his soul. She looked the picture of innocence, but Harrison wasn't fooled for a second. Behind those wide, gorgeous eyes lurked the worst thing that had ever happened to him.

And the best.

"Don't you dare," he warned.

But of course she dared. She always had.

"He makes out with it sometimes when he's feeling lonely," she said, a gurgle of laughter at the back of her throat. "I don't know how hot and heavy those sessions get, but he might have taken things a touch too far. Maybe Bubbles was traumatized."

"Goddammit, Sophie!" He jolted out of his seat, pushing the wooden legs across the floor with a screech. "For the last time, I *don't* make out with my pillow—and even if I were in the habit of defiling inanimate objects, I wouldn't do it while my puppy was watching."

"Oh?" she asked, head tilted. "When would you do it? In the shower? That makes sense. That's where I like to—"

He took two long strides to stand before her, attempting to make his glare as menacing and outraged as it had ever been, but it was no use. He couldn't look at her and feel anything but love. He couldn't be near her and think of anything but joy.

"Since the day you entered my life, I haven't known a moment's peace," he grumbled, though his voice was soft. "You're the first thing I think of when I wake up in the morning and the last memory I have before I fall asleep at night. I picture you when I'm in bed and when I'm working out and when I'm driving my truck. I can't hear the wind without picking up the sound of your laughter in it. I can't look at Bubbles without seeing your face smiling up at mine. There's a good chance I'll never be able to shake you. Not for a single second. Not for as long as I live."

She hadn't blinked even once during his tirade. Perfectly still, she held his stare, matching it with an increasingly resolute one of her own.

"You're everywhere inside me, Sophie," he said, his voice cracking. "You're everywhere inside this house. I did everything I could to scrub you away, but even though I washed my sheets three times, I swear I can still smell you in them."

"That's it."

Harrison had forgotten that they weren't alone in the kitchen, that his audience included Sophie's sisters. To be perfectly honest, he didn't really care. He'd hid his emotions for so many years, buried any sentiment that might cause his father to decide that he too would rather live his life without Harrison in it.

He was done with that. He was angry at his parents, scared for Bubbles, annoyed with Oscar, and unsure about the future. Above all else, he loved Sophie Vasquez with everything he had.

And he didn't care who the fuck knew it.

"The sheets," Dawn said. "That's it. You say you washed them yesterday?"

He nodded. "I had to. They were killing me."

"No, they weren't." Lila's tone was matter-of-fact, but her gentle smile eased some of the sting of them. "But Bubbles wouldn't have known that. I was right."

He looked a question at her.

"Her job is to protect you, remember?" Lila asked. "And she's done nothing over the past six weeks but learn how to do that. She knows the way you smell. She knows the beat of your heart. She knows what you need long before you do."

He finished the rest for her. "She knew that if I wiped the last of Sophie away, I'd never be whole again. She knew she had to go get her for me."

If he'd thought having sheets that smelled like Sophie was painful, then it was obviously because he'd never felt anything like this before. That little dog was so much smarter—so much better—than him. Instead of accepting the way things were, instead of sitting around and steeping in her own misery, she'd gotten up off her tiny puppy ass and set out to change her fate. To change *his* fate.

She'd saved his life. Again.

"But where would she have gone?" he asked, transferring his gaze from one sister's face to the next. "Where would she expect to find Sophie?"

Lila snapped her fingers. "The kennel."

"It's a heck of a walk, but she could make it," Dawn said. "She'd do it for Harrison. That puppy of Sophie's is nothing if not determined."

"I know," Harrison said as he reached for his keys. He wasn't wasting another second. "It's the thing I love about both of them."

chapter
22

They found Bubbles straggling along the side of the highway a few miles outside of Spokane.

From the look of her, all matted fur and lolling tongue, the journey hadn't been an easy one. Those short, stubby legs required constant motion in order to gain any ground at all, and anxiety at being away from Harrison made her more frantic than usual.

Still, Sophie had never seen such a beautiful creature.

"Bubbles, you precious little monster!" she cried as she jumped out of Harrison's truck before it had come to a complete halt. The momentum of her leap threw her to the ground, but she brushed herself off and ran to the puppy's side. "Do you have any idea how worried we were? Do you know how many people are crawling over the fields right now in search of your tiny puppy remains?"

From the feeble wag of the animal's tail as she realized who was accosting her on the dirty side of a highway, Sophie was guessing she knew. She was also guessing she didn't care.

"Harrison, do you have the—?"

She didn't have to finish the question, as Harrison was already scooping up his puppy with a water bottle in one hand. He poured a cascade in front of the animal's mouth, allowing her to lap greedily until the initial pangs of her thirst wore away.

"You are never going to do that to me again, do you understand, young lady? I've been out of my mind since I woke up this morning." He glanced anxiously over at Sophie. "She's okay. Is she okay? She looks okay."

"Everything looks intact, anyway," she replied. When that answer won her nothing but a sharp look of rebuke, she added, "I'm not a vet, Harrison. I'm just a dog trainer. And a pretty good one, if I do say so myself."

"The devil you are." Harrison's oath carried zero malice—a thing that was obvious while he continued to allow Bubbles to wriggle and lick rapturously at his face. "You trained this animal to believe I can't live without you. I always knew there was something wrong with the way you conducted your business."

"I beg your pardon. Puppy Promise is a one-of-a-kind organization that you were lucky to find. You think we find last-minute placements and training programs for just anyone?"

He took a step closer. "Oscar made you do it."

She took a step closer too. "No way. Oscar might be the boss of you, but he isn't in charge of me. No one is."

"Well, obviously. I've known that since day one. The only thing I can't understand is why you let anyone tell you otherwise." He drew a long breath. "I'm really sorry, Sophie—for what I said the other day about you not being strong, about you not knowing what it's like to struggle. I was... Well, shit. I was hurting, and I was scared of losing you. I still am, to be honest. I can't think of anything worse."

A sob caught in her throat, preventing her from speech.

"I know why the people in your life are overprotective, and it's not because they think you're weak." He lifted a hand toward her, but when she still couldn't move to return the gesture, he dropped it. "It's because they can't imagine a world without you in it."

"Oh, Harrison," she said feebly. It was everything and nothing—and for some reason, her inability to put her feelings into words only caused Harrison to open up even more.

"You saved this dog today," he said. "You saved me. You called on the power of every godforsaken person under the sun and made them come to my aid. Believe me when I say that they wouldn't have bothered for anyone else."

That got Sophie to set her jaw. "Bullshit."

He almost dropped the puppy in his surprise. He also almost dropped the puppy when a logging truck whisked past, stirring up cold air and a whirl of dust.

But he didn't drop her. From the looks of it, he wasn't going to let that poor animal out of his sight for months.

"What did you just say?"

"Bullshit," she echoed, louder this time. "Every single person out there today would have come for your sake. Derek and Jessica and all the DNR crew. Oscar and that weird, skinny kid with his pants on backward. My sisters. My mother. *Your* mother."

He paused at the mention of his long-lost parent, but Sophie wasn't buying it. Not now. Not after he'd reluctantly, begrudgingly, oh-so-wholeheartedly professed his love for her in front of his sisters. He might like to pretend that he was a closed book and that no one was allowed to touch the pain he buried deep inside, but she knew better.

He was a marshmallow. He always had been.

"They like you," she said. "They respect you. The only problem is that you refuse to let any of them in long enough to do something about it. Yes, I know—people leave and people make mistakes and people let you down. So what? Open the door anyway. Step out from behind that wall and see what it feels like to have other people take care of you for a while. I think you might get used to it. In fact, I think you might actually like it."

Mentioning the wall had the effect of shutting him down. She could see it happening, was watching the transformation with her very own eyes. His eyes went stony. His mouth became a hard line. His shoulders came up.

And then, without a single word, it stopped.

"Okay."

She stopped as well, too startled by his sudden capitulation to do more than blink at him. "Okay?"

"Okay." A smile moved across his face. It was the real one—the devastating one. "I like the sound of that, but only if you promise to keep me company in there."

"Wait—what? That actually worked?"

Harrison tucked Bubbles under one arm and took the final step toward her. He was as exhausted as she was, drained both physically and emotionally, and it showed in every weathered line of his face. The shadow of his beard hinted of dark deeds, and his bull-like stance was as powerful as always, but none of that mattered. No matter how many times she searched his eyes, she didn't see any sign of the wall. Once again, she'd managed to get him to tear it down.

But this time, he'd taken it down it for good.

"I still think you're going to push me and poke me and make my life generally uncomfortable," he said.

"That's because I am."

He lifted a hand toward her cheek, holding it just above her skin until she turned into it.

"And I still think you're an evil dragon of a woman who trains sweet, innocent puppies to be her minions."

She choked on a laugh. "Why not? There have been worse crimes committed in the name of love."

His palm tensed on her cheek, his fingers pressing into her skin and pulling her close. It was impossible to wrap her arms around him and squeeze while he had Bubbles between them, so she did the next best thing and licked her lips. The edge of her tongue grazed the side of his thumb, drawing forth his deep groan.

"I do love you," he said, his breath growing ragged. "More than I thought possible, more than I knew people *could* love."

She smiled against the press of his thumb. "I always knew I could love you this much. I was just afraid you wouldn't want me to."

His deep chuckle was the only sound she needed for her heart to swell and her body to start throbbing with desire. Both of these sensations—of fullness and emptiness, of the entire world expanding within her—were nothing compared to the words that left his mouth next.

"Will you help me?" he asked, bringing his mouth down to hers. "When I stumble? If I fall?"

She accepted his kiss readily, prepared to stand on the

gusty side of the highway with a puppy wedged between them forever if it meant she could always feel like this.

"Of course I will," she said and laughed against his lips. "If I can train a broken, skittish puppy to love a grouch like you, how hard could it possibly be to train a man?"

Epilogue

This one's for you, and this one's for you, and this one's for you." Harrison tossed the paper-wrapped bundles at the people standing nearest him in the backyard. The billowing smoke that surrounded them came from a summer barbecue rather than the forest fires that had kept him from home for the past two weeks, which made for a nice change.

It was also nice to see so many friendly, relaxed faces. The backyard was still a pit of half-finished projects and Sophie's never-ending battle with the raccoon who refused to heed her eviction notice, but no one seemed to care. Sophie's sisters were there, which was a large part of the carefree ambiance, but his parents were in attendance too.

Dawn accepted her bundle greedily and started tearing in right away. Lila was a little more restrained, but she still shrugged and daintily began undoing the tape around the edges. His mom, however, just stared at hers.

"Go on," he said, his voice gruff. This time, at least, he had the excuse of two solid weeks of breathing smoke outside Chelan as the cause. Even though he'd been doing a lot better job of slowing down and putting his — and Bubbles's — health first, he had a tendency to sound like he'd gargled rocks for a few days afterward. "It's not a big deal."

His mom opened her mouth as if to argue, but she was forestalled by Dawn's shout of laughter.

"Is this supposed to be a shawl?" she asked as she held the deformed lump of red yarn to the sky. "Or a... dish towel?"

"It's a scarf," he retorted. "And it took me three weeks to make, so you'd better wear it every day."

Lila had managed to extract hers from the packaging and joined in her sister's laughter. "I think mine has an armhole. Or a breezeway. That'll come in handy, seeing as how it's ninety-five degrees outside right now."

"Four weeks. That one took me four weeks." He paused. "I sent one to your parents in Greece too. Your mom promised to take it to all the important sites. I think she's finally starting to like me."

"Oh, she hates you," Dawn said. "You took her precious darling."

"She loves you," Lila countered. "You took her precious darling."

Harrison just shook his head and gestured for them to put their garments on. He wasn't sure he'd *ever* understand the strange relationship that existed in a family as intimate and loving as this one, but he was getting closer.

The two sisters looked ridiculous, of course, and not just because it was the dead of summer and the need for handmade knitwear was slim. No matter how many times he tried to get the hang of knitting, or how well he thought he was doing at the time, he always ended up with a variation of the same awkward scarf.

Poor Bubbles would never get the full wardrobe he'd promised her—which was probably just as well, since the women in Sophie's knitting circle had taken it upon themselves to outfit her in every style and color under the sun. They loved that damn dog.

He was starting to think they loved him a little too. It was a nice feeling.

"Is mine a scarf too?" his mother asked. She still hadn't opened her package. She held it against her chest like something precious, a misty look in her eyes. "You made me a scarf?"

"It's not a very good one," he said. This time, his voice was gruff with emotion, but he didn't try to fight it. He and his mom weren't close yet, but he liked to think they were making progress. "But I like knitting. It's weirdly calming."

She nodded as if that made perfect sense. "You never were able to sit still for long periods at a time."

Which was another way of saying he was a lot of work. "Sorry about that," he said.

"Don't be." The mistiness in her eyes increased. "It's always been one of my favorite things about you."

"What is?" Sophie asked, coming up from behind him. She wrapped her arms around his waist and buried her face in his neck, drawing a deep breath as though inhaling his very essence. "His roguish good looks? That's what got me. Well, that and his puppy-like innocence. Isn't that right, Bubbles?"

The dog at his feet yapped her agreement.

His mom chuckled. "I was just telling him that he was always on the go, even as a baby. He was always awake, always alert, always looking for something to get into. Nothing ever seemed to slow him down."

"Chains did the trick occasionally." Harrison's dad

came up behind them, a beer in his hand and a smile on his face. Half of that sight was familiar to him, but he was still adjusting to the smile part. He'd been doing a lot of that ever since Minerva had come home.

"You didn't!" Sophie protested with a laugh.

"Sure I did. Plus ropes, zip ties, a pit in the backyard with chicken wire over the top…"

"Wallace, *no*," Minerva protested.

"Of course not," he said, agreeing. "But it would have served him right if I had. If you had any idea what I had to go through during his teen years…"

A few months ago, Harrison would have shut down at the reference to the past. A few months ago, he would have turned stiff and remote. But a few months ago, he hadn't been happy.

He was now. He defied anyone not to be with a woman like Sophie at his back and a dog like Bubbles at his feet. Literally.

"If it's any consolation, Sophie was a *much* worse teenager than I was," he offered. "You should hear some of the stories she has to tell about her wayward youth. The drugs. The needles."

"Don't you dare," she warned in his ear.

He dared. "The orgies."

His mom's eyes flew wide open, but his dad just laughed and wrapped an arm around her shoulders. "It's probably better if we don't ask," he said as he led her away. "If there's one thing I've learned about that girl, it's that she's capable of anything."

"He's right, you know," Harrison said as soon as they were out of earshot. "I knew it from the start—you're terrifying."

"Am I?" Sophie murmured, not the least bit put off by this confession.

"A veritable monster."

"Tell me more," she cooed, her lips brushing against his ear and sending a familiar jolt of electricity through him. "You know how much I love it when you get all romantic on me."

So he told her. From start to finish, using up the entire vocabulary he'd spend his wayward adolescence accumulating, he let the words fall gently over her head.

She was as tough as a dragon and soft as a puppy. As tempting as a devil and sweet as an angel. She was everything and anything she wanted to be.

She was finally his, and that was enough for them both.

About the Author

Lucy Gilmore is a contemporary romance author with a love of puppies, rainbows, and happily ever afters. She began her reading (and writing) career as an English literature major and ended as a die-hard fan of romance in all forms. When she's not rolling around with her two Akitas, she can be found hiking, biking, or with her nose buried in a book. Visit her online at lucygilmore.com.

*Don't miss the next book in Lucy Gilmore's
Service Puppies series, coming September 2019*

chapter
1

L ila was going to kill her sisters for this.

"Lila! Lila Vasquez!" A voice hailed her from across the crowded ballroom floor. It was followed by the bustling of a woman in a tasteful two-piece dress suit. A pang of envy flooded through her for that neat, pearly gray fabric, but it was a short-lived sentiment.

Mostly because it was immediately replaced by embarrassment. And despair. And the overwhelming urge to throw herself out the nearest window.

She changed her mind. Death was too good for her sisters. Nothing less than lifelong torment would do.

"Aren't you so brave," the woman cooed as she came to a halt. Her sweeping gaze took in the full glory of Lila's billowing bubblegum pink ball gown. If the color wasn't bad enough, then the fact that she was followed by a trail of sparkles everywhere she went *was*. She'd left the ladies restroom looking like a glitter bomb had gone off in one of the stalls. "I wish I could wear something like that, but at our age, you know…"

Yes. Lila did know. No one under the age of twenty-one should ever leave the house in this shade of pink. Unfortunately, Sophie and Dawn had interpreted the Once Upon a Time theme literally. Instead of the costume party she'd been *assured* awaited her inside these doors, she'd found herself inside a nonprofit event as upscale as it was elegant. She stuck out like a sore thumb.

A giant, pink, puffy thumb.

"It's so nice to see you, Kathy," she said, forcing a smile. It probably looked about as plastic as she felt, but she was determined to stay put. She'd been invited to this ball as an established and vital part of Spokane's hearing services community. Its purpose was to raise funds for the hearing impaired, largely for the purchase of medical equipment, implants, Hearing Assistive Tech…and service dogs.

Lila might look silly and feel just as ridiculous, but her dogs deserved a seat at the table, metaphorically speaking. She'd give them that even if it meant she had to stand here all night, shedding glitter into fifty-dollar glasses of champagne.

"I'm excited to hear who will be getting our puppy donation," she said in what she hoped was a casual tone. "So are my sisters. I'm supposed to text them the moment I find out. Do you know when they'll be making the announcements?"

Kathy waved an airy hand. She was one of the ball

organizers, but she had less to do with the details and more to do with squeezing large donations out of the city's finest. "You'll have to ask Anya. She has the full schedule. I only came by to ask where you got that gorgeous dress. My daughter's winter formal is coming up, and they're doing Candy Land this year. That's exactly what we've been looking for."

It was enough to send a lesser woman fleeing for the nearest hiding place. Lila had spotted several already, each one more appealing than the last. There was a huge banquet table she could crawl underneath to wait out the evening's events, or a swan ice sculpture dripping in the entryway that might provide an adequate shield. In a pinch, even that pair of waiters with giant silver platters could help her make a quick getaway.

But Lila stood her ground. Lila *always* stood her ground. Neither snow nor rain nor heat nor extreme social embarrassment—

"Oh, God." Catching sight of a familiar man by the entryway, she whirled around, her skirt ballooning around her legs. "This can't be happening."

"What can't be happening?" Kathy asked, her brows raised. She took a sip of her champagne, a wayward piece of glitter clinging to her upper lip. "Are you sure you're all right?"

No. She wasn't sure of anything except that no number of waiters with silver platters would be able to help her now. What she needed was for the ground to open up beneath her, for the world to swallow her whole. Risking a quick peek over her shoulder, she scanned the entryway again and—*Yep*. It was happening. It was happening, and there was nothing she could do to stop it.

She dashed a hand out and grabbed Kathy's forearm. "Quick—what's the easiest way out of here?"

"I think maybe you should sit down," Kathy said, frowning at where Lila was crushing the silk of her suit. "You look as though you've seen a ghost."

On the contrary, it was no ghost that had caught Lila's eye. That flash of white coming from the opposite side of the room was blinding enough to be supernatural, but Lila had never believed in that sort of thing. Ghosts weren't real and bogeymen were make-believe, but a smile as toothy and brilliant as *her ex-boyfriend's* had caused her plenty of sleepless nights.

"The kitchen?" Lila asked, mostly to herself. "No, I'll never make it that far. It'll have to be the emergency exit."

She knew she was babbling, but she could no more stop the words from coming out of her mouth than she could still the sudden thumping of her heart. *Patrick Yarmouth*. Of all the men to saunter through the door looking as though he'd dropped in straight out of a toothpaste ad, it had to be that one.

She could brazen this dress out for the sake of her company, Puppy Promise. She could smile and sparkle for as long as it took to woo the people who had the power to take that company to the next level.

But she could not, would not, *dared* not risk exposing herself to the man who'd accused her of perfection like it was a four-letter word. Especially since he hadn't spotted her yet. *There's still time to make my escape.*

"I'm sorry, Kathy," she said as she lifted her skirts and headed for the bright red exit sign. "I have to go."

"Does this mean you aren't going to tell me where

you got the dress?" Kathy called, watching her go. "My daughter will be so disappointed."

"I'll email you the details tomorrow," Lila promised as she pushed through the door to safety. *Better yet*, she thought as she navigated the steep flight of steps leading down, *I'll shove the dress in a box and mail it to you.*

After tonight, there was nothing on earth that could induce her to wear sparkles again.

🐾🐾🐾

It was only cowardice if she hid *behind* the potted plant.

"I'm standing next to it," Lila said to no one in particular, if only because there was no one in particular to say it to. She'd escaped the emergency stairwell to find herself on some kind of first-floor landing. There was a fountain and a ficus and a complete absence of other people—all three of which were serving to calm her rattled nerves. "I'm taking a break, that's all. Getting away from all those dark suits and demure gowns. I'll be back to my usual, capable self in a few minutes, and then I'll be able to face him."

Her attempt at boosting her own confidence failed. In truth, it was only her inability to pull her skirts in far enough that kept here where she was. There was no way she *could* fit behind that plant.

A soft sniffling sound stopped her before she could make the mistake of continuing her one-sided conversation. It wasn't like her to flee at the first sign of danger; even less to self-soothe with a running dialogue. She was supposed to be the unflappable Vasquez sister, the one everyone else turned to in times of emergency.

In other words, the *perfect* one.

The sniffle sounded again, this time accompanied by a hiccupping sob. Her own worries cast aside, Lila picked her way out from her hiding spot next to the plant and surveyed the room. As far as she could tell, it was still empty. There was a possibility that sound might carry through one of the vents, but—

A small voice sounded behind her. "Are you a princess?"

For the second time this evening, Lila found herself whirling about, startled. This time, however, her gaze landed on a small girl standing just a few feet away.

The first thing she noticed was that the girl appeared to be wearing a dress that was identical to her own. Bubblegum pink. Sparkles. Tulle. All things that made a grown woman look like she was one magic wand away from a starring role in the *Wizard of Oz*, but looked perfectly at home on a six year old.

The second thing she noticed was that the child had a pair of twin cochlear implants on either side of her elaborate updo. The small, purple-colored plastic pieces behind her ears attached to even smaller nodes via looped cords. They were, in Lila's line of work, a fairly common sight. They were also a clear sign that this girl's parents couldn't be too far away.

Upstairs in the ballroom, probably. *Where Patrick is*.

"Oh, hello," she said, somewhat taken aback. Surprise rendered her voice harsher than usual—a thing she regretted as soon as the words left her lips. The poor girl was obviously lost, staring up at her with wide, blue eyes that were swimming in tears. "I didn't know there was anyone in here with me."

The girl didn't respond, her breath once more catching on a sob. Lila's experience with children wasn't vast—she was much more of a dog person than a kid one—but even she could tell that a situation like this one called for tact.

She fell into an unladylike squat so they were level with one another. Not only was getting down the first thing a puppy trainer did when approaching a wary animal, but the girl was watching Lila's mouth with the intensity of long practice. Lila had enough experience with hearing service dogs and their owners to recognize that the girl most likely used a combination of her cochlear implants and lip reading to communicate.

"Are you lost?" she asked.

The girl nodded, her arms wrapped protectively around her midsection.

Lila held out a hand with her palm up to show she meant no harm and held it there. That was another good puppy-training trick. Maybe this wouldn't be as difficult as she'd feared. "Then you're in luck. I'm not lost at all."

"You aren't?" the girl asked, blinking at her.

"Nope. I have an excellent sense of direction." She held a finger straight up. "You go that-a-way."

The girl's gaze followed the direction she was pointing, but she had yet to take Lila's hand. "Through the ceiling?" she asked doubtfully.

"Well, no. You have to take the stairs, I'm afraid. There's an elevator around here somewhere, but I'm not sure where to find it."

That caused the doubt in the girl's voice to increase. "You mean this isn't your castle?"

The Davenport Hotel, where the event was being held, was about as fancy as Spokane architecture got, but it was hardly what she'd call a *castle*. "Oh, um. No. I think it's owned by local real estate developers, actually."

Apparently, that was the wrong answer. The girl's arms clenched tighter around her stomach, a fresh bout of tears starting to take shape in her eyes. "I thought it was your castle."

Lila had no idea how she was supposed to respond. It wasn't in her nature to lie to small children, but she didn't know what else to do. Her sister Sophie would have been able to comfort the girl with kind words and a smile, and Dawn would have had her laughing within minutes, but Lila had always been better with adults than children.

Then again, she'd also always been the kind of woman to dress sensibly and stand her ground when faced with an unexpected encounter with an ex-boyfriend. Clearly, today was an anomaly.

"My castle is much bigger than this one," she said, casting her scruples aside. "And it's located in, um, a faraway kingdom?"

It was the right thing to say. A look of relief swept over the girl, the beginnings of a smile taking shape in the perfect bow of her mouth. "You *are* a real princess," she said. "I knew it."

She finally slipped her hand into Lila's. For some strange reason, Lila expected the girl's hand to be sticky—children were usually sticky, weren't they?— but the palm pressed against hers was perfectly clean. And soft. It was a nice surprise.

"I'm not allowed to talk to strangers," the girl confided with a shy smile. "But a princess isn't a stranger."

"Oh, dear," Lila murmured. It wasn't her place to lecture children on stranger danger, but for all she knew, the girl would take this one successful venture and run off in the future with anyone claiming to be royalty.

"Actually, I *am* a stranger. It's important to be wary of grownups no matter what they're wearing. You know that, right? A fancy dress doesn't automatically make someone a princess. Just like a tuxedo doesn't automatically make someone a prince."

In fact, now that she thought about it, there were lots of warning signs that could be worn on the outside. Take, for example, a man's blinding smile across a crowded ballroom floor.

"It's all too easy for a person to hide their true nature behind clothes," she added. "Clothes and makeup and shoes and a smile you know better than to trust, if only because no man has teeth that white unless there's something wrong with him. I don't care what anyone says or how many times they say it. You shouldn't be able to see your reflection in someone else's molars."

The girl tugged on her hand, pulling Lila's attention down. She pointed first at her own ears and then at Lila's lips before blinking expectantly.

"Oh," she said, dismayed. "I went on a bit of a tirade there, didn't I?"

"Emily might not have had the privilege of catching all that, but I sure did," a male voice sounded from behind them, causing Lila to jump. *Again.* "And I, for one, am dying to meet this man. Does he gargle with bleach, do you think, or is it that new charcoal toothpaste everyone is going on about?"

"Daddy!" The girl—Emily—dropped Lila's hand and ran to the man, wrapping her arms around his knees. Her words were muffled by a sob. "I got lost."

He lifted the child into his arms and waited until her head was level with his before speaking. "Yes, I noticed that. But I see you found your time-traveling adult self and came to no harm. Strange that you never ended up buying a different dress. I thought for sure you'd outgrow pink sparkles."

Lila stiffened. He was making fun of her. This man, this stranger clad in a socially acceptable tuxedo, was making fun of her.

"Daddy, she's a *princess*."

"Is she?" He cast a scrutinizing look her way. "I didn't know princesses could time travel."

"She rescued me."

"Well, that is what princesses do."

"I know." Emily nodded as if that made perfect sense. "That's why I let her help me."

"A wise decision," the man said. And that, it seemed, was the final word on the subject. There were no lectures about wandering off on her own, no words of warning for what could happen to a little girl who trusted any crackpot in pink tulle. He merely shifted his daughter to his hip and continued his appraisal of Lila.

It wasn't an *unappreciative* appraisal, but she wasn't sure what she was supposed to do about it. There was something about the man's glinting blue eyes and slow, spreading grin that shot like an arrow straight through her. Okay, so she wasn't some six-foot underwear model in a well-cut tuxedo. Her jaw wasn't a chiseled shadow that had been timed to remain steadfast at five o'clock. She didn't have the sexy beginnings of gray starting to take over the winged sides of her well-sculpted brown hair...

"I'm sorry—did you say something?" She blinked as the man's grin deepened.

"Yes, I asked your name, but you weren't finished

yet." He cast a look down at himself and gave a rueful shake of his head. "Ridiculous, isn't it? I feel like a penguin. But the invitation said black tie, so black tie it is. Emily's a stickler for the rules. So, what is it?"

She blinked again. "The dress code?"

"Your name."

"Oh, um. It's Lila. Lila Vasquez." Aware that her usual demeanor—the careful, upright professional she was in all things—was slipping, she stuck out her hand. And then was forced to keep holding it out. She'd somehow forgotten that the man was using both arms to hold his daughter, which meant he had to shift and shuffle before he could return the gesture.

It didn't help that the hand he eventually extracted was his left one, which bore no signs of a wedding ring. His palm was cool and dry, his handshake firm. He might be holding a kindergartener and masquerading as a penguin, but he did it with a level of confidence Lila could only admire.

"Ford Ford."

"I'm sorry?"

"You're Lila Vasquez. This is Emily Ford. I'm Ford Ford."

"You're Ford…Ford?"

He bent in a slight bow. "The one and only. Or so I hope. If there's another poor b-a-s-t-a-r-d wandering around out there named Ford Ford, he has my deepest sympathies. And a heartfelt wish to give his parents a strong talking-to." His smile warmed as he continued. "I recognize your name. Are you one of the organizers?"

"Not an organizer, no."

"She's a princess," Emily interjected.

"Yes, moppet. We've already covered that. She's a princess and she rescues lost little girls and she doesn't like men who smile with their teeth."

"I never said—"

"She lives in a faraway kingdom," Emily interrupted with all the certainty of a six-year-old safely ensconced in her father's arms. They were strong arms, too, not wavering under their burden even once. "Were you at the ball, too?"

"As a matter of fact, I was." Lila glanced at the clock on the opposite wall and held back a sigh.

As much as she would have preferred to stay hiding down here for the rest of the night, she was eventually going to have to suck up her pride and face the ballroom. Patrick would still be there, of course, but some things couldn't be helped.

"I should probably get back there before anyone notices I'm gone, but…" She cast a look down at her attire and bit her lip.

"But you can't possibly go without an escort?" Ford offered. Even though his arms were already taken up with Emily, he managed to crook an elbow at her. "It's the least I can do after you rescued my daughter. She doesn't take to just anyone, you know. You must be something special."

"Oh, I'm really not—" she began, more flustered than she cared to admit. She couldn't tell whether it was the girl, her father, or the dress that was making her feel most out of her depth, but the room was definitely spinning around her.

"If it'll help, I promise not to smile any more than absolutely necessary," Ford said with a shake of his elbow. "It'll be nothing but frowns and glowers as far as the eye can see."

As he wore a particularly attractive smile as he said this, Lila wasn't fooled. She didn't have a chance to call him on it, however, since he winked and turned his face toward Emily. "I specially requested the Hokey Pokey from the orchestra. It'd be shame if we missed it."

"Daddy!" Emily protested with a giggle. "You did not."

"Of course I did. Why do you think it took me so long to come find you?" He gave up on the elbow and dropped a liberal kiss on Emily's cheek instead. "I also asked them to play the Macarena, YMCA, and, I'm sorry to say, Gangnam Style. Emily doesn't have the most sophisticated taste. I, on the other hand, am an arbiter of great music. I made sure to add the Chicken Dance to our lineup."

"The Chicken Dance?" Lila echoed. She thought of the string quartet that had been hired for the evening and suppressed a laugh. She'd known the violinist to throw his bow at anyone requesting a composition not written before the eighteenth century. "I don't believe you."

She should have known that playing into this man's nonsense was a mistake. The moment the challenge left her lips, he turned to her with a lift to his brow. That debonair arch was all that was needed to take his tuxedo from attractive to full-on devastating. "Are you sure about that? I can be very persuasive when I put my mind to it."

She didn't doubt it. She also had no plans to stick around and find out for herself. Even if she was in the habit of picking up strange men and their daughters—which she wasn't—there was the small matter of work to get back to.

"Well, I don't know the Chicken Dance, so it's no good asking me to join you," Lila said primly. "And before you ask, I don't know Gangnam Style or the Macarena, either."

Ford gave a gentle tsk and shook his head. "You seem sadly unprepared for a dance party like this one. What do you know?"

She thought quickly. "The waltz."

"How very princess-y of you," he murmured with an appreciative twinkle in his eyes. As if suddenly realizing he was still holding a child in his arms, he gave Emily a light shake and added, "Isn't that right, moppet? All royalty should waltz."

Emily's only response was a giggle and a request for her father to put her down. "I'm okay now, Daddy," she said as she began wriggling out of his grasp. "I promise."

He allowed Emily to slide down his side until she was planted on her own two feet. That, apparently, was yet another mistake, because she immediately bounced over to Lila and grabbed her by the hand. She gave a strong tug, which meant that unless Lila was willing to wrench a child's arm out of its socket, she had to take a liberal step in Ford's direction.

If Ford Ford looked good, he smelled even better. He wasn't, like so many of the other men upstairs, doused in expensive cologne. Instead, he carried the light scent of aftershave and what she could have sworn was peanut butter.

She was so distracted by this bizarre yet compelling combination that she missed it when Emily took her father by her other hand. Without waiting for either of them to guess what she was up to, she took herself out of the equation. That left only the pair of them, standing much closer than was appropriate, their fingers lightly touching. Every instinct Lila had warned her to jump back, but something about Emily's wistful expression gave her pause.

"Pretty please will you waltz with my daddy?" she asked. "I never saw a princess dance in real life a'fore."

There was something especially beguiling about the way Emily made the request. She didn't wheedle or plead, the way Lila always assumed children of her age did, and she didn't resort to a tantrum. She just blinked up at them with an expectant look in her big blue eyes. Her face was still puffy and red from her earlier tears, her careful hairstyle now falling around her ears.

Waltzing in a pink ball gown with a man she didn't know was the last thing Lila wanted to do right now—or, you know, ever—but at sight of those innocently tumbling curls, she felt herself faltering. She caught Ford's eye.

Had he turned to that easy flirtation again, said something dashing and ridiculous, she would have turned him down. She had places to go and people to avoid, and it wasn't in her nature to place herself in situations where she felt this far out of her depth.

But he looked almost as embarrassed as she felt, his grin turned rueful. "I'm not very good, but I'm game if you are." He gave a tiny shrug of one shoulder. "What can I say? She's never seen a princess dance in real life before."

Lila didn't bother demurring further. How could she? At this point, she had nothing else to lose. She was already wearing the dress. She'd already fled the ball in shame and disgrace. And she already knew what—or who—was waiting for her upstairs.

It's not as if this night can get any worse.

"Why not?" she said and gave what she hoped was a regal bow of her head. "I'd be delighted."

She was rewarded with a dazzling smile from Ford and a yank on her hand. She was propelled into his arms, which came up to provide a frame worthy of any dance teacher's beginning waltz instructions.

The music from upstairs was too quiet to trickle down, and Lila had never been very good at humming, so the only backdrop to their movements was the shuffle of their feet and the trickle of the fountain in the distance. There was something acutely disconcerting about doing a music-free waltz with a strange man, especially when his daughter stood a few feet away with a look of pure rapture on her face. Lila felt stiff and awkward, but at least her footwork was solid.

Well, it was solid until Ford started gaining confidence in his own steps. As they reached one side of the room, his hold on her waist tightened. That firmer touch, the press of his hand on the narrowest part of her, his body so long and lean against hers—it was impossible not to feel a little lightheaded.

Matters weren't helped any when Ford leaned close to her ear and murmured, "Thank you for doing this. I know you're probably itching to get back, but you're the only reason Emily's not sobbing into that ficus right now."

Her breath caught. "But I didn't do anything."

"Are you kidding?" he countered. His mouth was so close to her skin that she could feel the whisper of his words on her neck. There was an intimacy about it, a warmth she hadn't been expecting. "You made her night. H-e-l-l, you probably made her whole week. This sort of thing might be ordinary for you, but we don't run into beautiful princesses every day."

It went against all of her scruples and even more of her common sense to reward a heavy-handed compliment like that, but her eyes snapped up to meet Ford's. What she saw there wasn't flirtation or amusement or even laughter at her predicament. He looked, well, *sincere*.

"Oh." Her heart gave a flutter, her body gliding and moving with his. "Um. You're welcome?"

This time Ford did laugh, but it was a soft chuckle that was reflected in the light of his startlingly blue eyes. Lila thought that perhaps their steps slowed, that the music — was there music? — came to an end and the dance was over. But he still had his hand wrapped around her waist, his torso pressed lightly against her own.

As if drawn forward by some power outside herself, Lila leaned closer. Her head tilted up and her breath caught, and for one long, suspended moment, she could almost taste the touch of his lips against hers.

Until, of course, a loud cheer and a burst of applause pulled her feet back down to the ground.

"That was like magic!" Emily ran to her father and beamed up at him, her arms held up in supplication. "Like real princess magic."

Without a moment's hesitation, Ford let go of Lila and swooped his daughter into his arms. "It was, wasn't it?" he asked.

There was nothing flustered about him, none of the

awkwardness Lila felt at finding herself standing all alone in the middle of the tile floor. She still had her arms up as if he were holding her, her lips parted in anticipation of a kiss that was never coming.

"I enjoyed the dancing, but I'm not so sure I'm ready for the part where I turn into a pumpkin," he said. "Does it happen right away, do you think, or do I have a few hours before I begin my transformation?"

"Da-ddy!" Emily cried, clearly delighted at this piece of nonsense. "That's not how the story goes."

"I'd like to be a jack-o-lantern," he said, ignoring her. He rubbed his chin thoughtfully. "One of those scary ones with flashing eyes and sharp teeth. Then you can roll me out every Halloween to delight the neighborhood."

Emily giggled obligingly, but Lila was still rooted where she stood, unable to shake the feeling that she was standing on the outside of a joke never meant for her ears. As if to prove it, Ford turned to her and swept a bow.

"Thank you, Princess Lila, for saving my daughter—and for the dance." His eyes met hers, and he lifted his shoulder in another of those awkward half-shrugs. She assumed it was a prelude to more playful commentary, but all he did was frown slightly and add, "We won't take up any more of your time."

And that was it. Without waiting for her to say anything in reply—which was probably for the best, since she had no idea what she *could* say—he whisked his daughter toward the emergency stairwell and allowed the door to fall shut behind them.

The echoing silence they left in their wake had Lila

feeling even more unsettled than when she ran down
here in the first place. Ford and Emily might not have
been accustomed to running into beautiful princesses
every day, but Lila had even less experience with cracking jokes about the Chicken Dance and waltzing with
dashing strangers in tuxedos.

And by less experience, she meant none whatsoever.
Men didn't normally sweep her off her feet before running away like Cinderella hightailing after her footmen.
In fact, if it weren't for the floor dusted with glitter from
their waltz, she'd have thought she imagined the whole
thing.

But glitter was there in abundance, and another
glance at the clock on the wall reminded her that she'd
spent far too long down here already. They'd be making
the announcements soon, if they hadn't done so already,
and there were several people she needed to see before
the night was through.

In other words, it was back to business as usual. Now
that she was done with the mortification down here,
there was no use in delaying the mortification waiting
for her upstairs.

"It's not like you'll ever see the pair of them again,"
Lila told herself as she picked her way over to the stairwell. She was still feeling a little breathless, but that
could easily be blamed on the tight bodice of her dress.

Yes. It was definitely the dress. Not the touch of a
man's hand on her waist—not the whirling sensation
that had almost swept her into an indiscretion. Even if
everyone upstairs knew that she looked like a fool, at
least they'd never know that she *felt* like one.

She counted to sixty before she started up the stairs,

careful to give Ford and Emily plenty of time to clear
out before she followed. With any luck, it would be
nearing the girl's bedtime, and Lila could safely put the
interlude behind her where it belonged.

There was no sign of either Ford or Patrick as she
stepped through the door and re-entered the ballroom.
Her luck held while she chatted with a social worker
who very kindly made no reference to her dress whatsoever. It even lasted long enough for her to take a stuffed
mushroom from a passing waiter.

But just as she was about to pop the buttery morsel
in her mouth, the emcee stepped up to the stage to make
the announcement she'd been waiting for all night.

It's about time. Finally, her agonies could come to an
end. Finally, she could smile graciously and make one
more dash for the emergency exit—this time for good.

Or so she thought.

"Please give a warm round of applause for the recipi-
ent of a generous donation from Puppy Promise for a
service dog and six weeks of personalized training."
The emcee made a big show of looking around the ballroom. At first, Lila thought he was looking for her, but
he passed her over, not stopping until his gaze landed on
the only other female in the room wearing a sparkling
pink ball gown.

What? She reared back, her mushroom falling to the
floor with a *splat*.

It wasn't possible. She'd heard rumors that their
donation was going to a nice old man from Cheney. Not
him. Not her. Not…

"A big congratulations to Emily Ford!"